For California's Gold

Women's West Series

For California's Gold

A Novel by

JoAnn Levy

University Press of Colorado

Also by JoAnn Levy

They Saw the Elephant: Women in the California Gold Rush, 1990
Daughter of Joy: A Novel of Gold Rush San Francisco, 1998

Copyright © 2000 by JoAnn Levy
International Standard Book Number: 0-87081-566-0

Published by the University Press of Colorado
5589 Arapahoe Avenue, Suite 206C
Boulder, Colorado 80303

The University Press of Colorado is a cooperative publishing enterprise supported, in part, by Adams State College, Colorado State University, Fort Lewis College, Mesa State College, Metropolitan State College of Denver, University of Colorado, University of Northern Colorado, University of Southern Colorado, and Western State College of Colorado.

The paper used in this publication meets the minimum requirements of the American National Standard for Information Sciences—Permanence of Paper for Printed Library Materials. ANSI Z39.48-1984

Library of Congress Cataloging-in-Publication Data

Levy, JoAnn, 1941–
    For California's gold: a novel / JoAnn Levy
        p. cm.
    ISBN 0-87081-566-0 (alk. paper)
    1. Frontier and pioneer life—California—Fiction. 2. California—Gold
    discoveries—Fiction. 3. Women pioneers—California—Fiction. I. Title.
PS3562.E92718 F67 2000
813'.54—dc21   99-089207

09 08 07 06 05 04 03 02 01 00   10 9 8 7 6 5 4 3 2

For Dan
a praising kind of man

The story of thirty thousand souls accomplishing a journey of more than two thousand miles through a savage and but partially explored wilderness, crossing on their way two mountain chains equal to the Alps in height and asperity, besides broad tracts of burning desert, and plains of nearly equal desolation, where a few patches of stunted shrubs and springs of brackish water were their only stay, has in it so much of heroism, of daring and of sublime endurance, that we may vainly question the records of any age for its equal.

–*Bayard Taylor*
El Dorado, 1850

Preface

In the 1840s, the term *manifest destiny* arose to describe the belief that the United States possessed geographical predestination, that because of economic and political superiority and growing population, it was destined to rule from sea to sea.

No event more reinforced this presumption than James Marshall's discovery of gold in California in 1848, just one year after the United States wrested control of that country from Mexico. In 1849, more than twenty-five thousand people crossed the Missouri River and headed toward the setting sun as if it were the rainbow's end, all of them intent on gaining a share of the riches glittering in their imaginations. Of this historic migration young men constituted the greater number, but women and children participated to a much greater extent than generally supposed. Nearly every forty-niner trail diary mentions their presence. And a remarkable number of diaries, letters, and reminiscences written by women participants survive to the present.

It is that record, and those experiences, that form the bedrock of *For California's Gold*. For more than a decade, the experiences of women in the gold rush have been my passion. I have held not only typescripts in my hands, but actual diaries and letters, and felt I was touching these women's lives. Each was singular. Some women came west with no more loss than convenience. Others sacrificed everything — health, possessions, loved ones — on the memorable trek across half a continent. Some died. In California, although the struggle to survive and to acquire gold was universal, the means to that end varied as greatly as the fingerprints those women left on history.

For California's Gold is a patchwork quilt of women's experiences in the California gold rush. Sarah's fictional life is a composite of real lives. Select any event she experienced and know that it actually happened to someone who was there.

I am indebted to the men and women diarists who described the road west from St. Joseph to California in 1849 in such detail that I am confident of accurately recreating it. I am particularly grateful to Mary Ackley, Angeline Ashley, Mary Stuart Bailey, John Banks and the Buckeye Rovers, J. Goldsborough Bruff, Lucy Cooke, Mariett Cummings, Alonzo Delano, Lodisa Frizzell, Catherine McDaniel Furniss, Charles G. Gray, Catherine Haun, Mary Hite, William G. Johnston, Dr. Israel Lord, Eliza McAuley, Lucena Parsons, Bernard J. Reid and the Pioneer Line, Sarah Royce, William Swain, Joseph Ware, and the Wolverine Rangers. The character of Joshua Giddings was based, in part, on frontier evangelist Lorenzo Dow, even though he died before the California goldfields were discovered. Mr. Fogie and his argument against California's existence were inspired by George Payson. The story of Celia Giddings's horses belongs to Mary Powers. For descriptions of crossing the forty-mile desert, I have relied on Margaret Frink, Sallie Hester, and Luzena Wilson.

For accounts of early Sacramento City, I thank Stephen Massett, whose auctioneering is rendered verbatim in appreciation. Bayard Taylor contributed the description of the horse market and Round Tent; Howard C. Gardiner detailed additional Sacramento City sights of 1849. For portraits of early Nevada City, I thank Peter Decker, Charles Ferguson, Charles Mulford, and Niles Searles.

To all of them, I am deeply grateful for the joy of sharing, through time and the written word, the remarkable adventures of California's infancy. And for the legacy of their courage.

To all of the gold rushers I've come to know through diaries, letters, and reminiscences, I am immensely and profoundly thankful that in the midst of the tumultuous events of their lives, both joyful and sorrowful, they wrote.

For California's Gold

Illinois

I note the date by today's newspaper: April 3, 1856. Full seven years to the day since that fateful departure, yet the memory is as fresh as the wildflowers I gathered this morning while you slept. Now it is afternoon, and you sleep again. And I, being more accustomed to industry than idleness, take pen in hand to commence this heavy-hearted record of what must be told. I write this account, for I cannot speak it without tears, which I fear would frighten you.

The lupine on the table before me are lovely — blue, yellow, cream — and fragrant with California's magic springtime. I don't remember if we had lupine in Illinois. I took flowers for granted then. Except for Mother's roses. Little would have been in bloom when we left, in any event. Spring came later there.

I remember Mother, that last day at home in Illinois, watching me leaf though the book of fairy tales she read me as a girl. I think we still have that small volume somewhere. I'll have to look for it.

As a child, how those stories alarmed me. They so often began with decisions seemingly inconsequential. A young girl decides to visit her grandmother, or two children choose to explore the forest. But wolves and witches waited. In subsequent tellings I cried, "Go back, go back!" But we can never go back. That is the truth of the matter.

"Janey reads these stories to Hannah sometimes," I said to my mother that morning. She stood at the parlor window, lace curtain held back, watching Caleb and Douglas hitch the mules to the wagon.

"Take it, then," she said without turning.

"Are you sure?"

"Take it, take them all."

It was too late for argument, and I ignored the invitation to resume it that her tone implied. Had my father lived, he would have called her Rabbit, in the affectionate way he had. He called me Mouse just as fondly. We were women. We were expected to want our safe shelters, to fear what lay beyond. And we did.

I remember Hannah and George racing past me then, their excited squeals drowning the piano Janey played so disconsolately. They chased through the parlor, out the door, into the yard. They were never still.

"You better go after them, Sarah," Mother said. "They'll get those new coats dirty."

She had made them from my father's good navy overcoat, weeping as she sewed. For the loss of him? Or them? I didn't know. I should have asked.

"I'll go," Janey said from habit, not looking up. She wore the green merino cloak I'd made too large, thinking it should last her the two years until we returned. Only two years, just two.

"You keep playing, Little Miss Mouse," Mother said, her voice catching. "I want to remember the sound of you in this room." She stored memories like flowers pressed in a book, lamenting their inevitable fading.

Little Miss Mouse. Father had called Janey that, bestowing the diminutive of my timidity on my daughter. "Frightened by fairy tales," he'd say, and shake his head. But always with a smile.

Janey's pale blue eyes, so like my mother's, suddenly accused me. "Mama, please. I don't want to go."

Even at twelve, Janey, endowed with her grandmother's beauty, was pretty in a way that I, possessed of my father's plain features and ordinary brown eyes, never had been.

I ignored her. It was too late for this argument, too. "The twins are fine," I said to my mother, not thinking of dirty coats. They *were* fine, being too young to understand. And so was Douglas, who wanted to go. But not Janey. Nor I, truth be told. What we want and what we must . . . Lucky are those for whom circumstance reconciles the two.

The twins raced, laughing and squealing, back up the steps and into the parlor, excited by events beyond their four-year-old comprehension.

As Janey thumped the piano lid shut, I took from the bookshelf the old, gold-stamped, leather-bound volume of Byron.

"Take that one, too," mother said, watching me. "You always liked it."

"I thought I might take the Shakespeare."

"Take both of them, all of them, I don't care."

"Mother, please."

I did take the Byron and Shakespeare, although only the book of fairy tales survived the trip. I probably left the heavier volumes when we lightened at Fort Laramie, or maybe I lost them on the desert, I don't know. I do know that Mr. Shakespeare understood leave-taking not at all. Nothing sweetens the heartache of parting.

I can still taste my tears and hear my counterfeit promises as I embraced my mother and whispered, "You know I wish we weren't going." She pulled away and shook her head. "If wishes were horses, Sarah Jane, beggars would ride."

It was something she often said, and then I did, too. We mimic our mothers. I hear her in myself, repeating things she said. I never understood what she meant about horses and beggars. I say it anyway, and think of her.

At the last, she put her hands to my face, studied it as if to memorize it, a faint smile where none had registered in weeks. Her face was gray with grief, but her eyes were dry. In the months of watching our preparations, she must have shed every tear allotted her. Or perhaps she willed them away so as not to blur a vision of us she expected to be her last. I wept for us both. "Sarah Jane," she said softly, and brushed my tears away.

The twins giggled, clutched at my skirts, played hide-and-seek behind my cloak.

Mother knelt to them. "Shush, Hannah, let me look at you."

She put her hands to Hannah's face and stared as my younger daughter fell silent. There is a language of the heart, and I know Hannah heard it. She wrapped her little arms around my mother's neck, then turned and buried her face in my cloak.

Mother put her hands to George's cherub cheeks, her eyes absorbing his countenance. "George," she whispered, and kissed him. She stood then and turned to Janey. I thought my heart would break as my daughter burst into tears. Mother hugged her tight, then stepped back to hold Janey's face between her hands. "Janey." Tears coursed down my girl's cheeks. Mother kissed them away.

I hurried the twins toward the wagon, too pained to endure the parting a moment longer, and called to Douglas. He had grown so much of late, but still I was surprised to see Mother reach up to cup his face in her hands. He looked awkward, the way boys will in the presence of emotion. Mother just shook her head and said, "Douglas."

Caleb went to her then, his hat in his hand. Reality's hard edge framed his dream that morning, and he felt it. Mother silenced his assurances with a shake of her head and put her hands to his face. She stared at him longer than I expected, then said, "Caleb Daniels, I forgive you." I bless her for that.

I ran back up the steps, hugged her one last time, then fled to the wagon.

Mother watched us leave, Buck, my father's old dog, beside her on the porch, the two of them framed by trellising roses in bud, spring's promise. How she loved those roses. I helped plant them the year I was sixteen, when Mother refused to move one step farther west and Father reluctantly built the brick house. It was then the only two-story brick house in the county, as far as we knew, perhaps even the whole state of Illinois. I thought it looked as red and raw as meat. Mother loved it. On the day it was finished, she stood in the rutted track that promised to be the National Road, hands on hips, head cocked, smiling.

"We'll have beautiful pink roses all over the porch, Sarah Jane. I can just see it, can't you?"

It was Lacy Ridgeway's gift to visualize the future from the present, to imagine what would be from what was. I say it was a gift, because I never acquired the talent to any significant degree, hard as I tried.

"Sarah Jane," she had said, "someday you'll think this the prettiest house you ever saw. You'll never want to leave it. You'll see."

She was right.

How she found the strength to endure this farewell is beyond my imagining. I and my children and husband parted from her and still had each other. She parted from six of us and had no one.

Caleb slapped the reins against the mules' backs. The stiff, new wagon wheels creaked a slow rotation as we lumbered onto the rutted track that still awaited transformation into the National Road. I looked back, heart breaking for my mother, and myself.

The decision to accompany Caleb was my own, and to burden him with blame for that sorrowful leave-taking would have been cruel. Despite all our years together, he was, to my sentimental heart, still the boy I fell in love with. Which is why I tucked the volume of Byron into a corner of the wagon. I had been reading it when Caleb first came to us.

It had been a late August afternoon, the air hot and heavy. Mother lay napping upstairs, and I sat in the cool front parlor reading *Childe Harold*. I heard nothing, no horse's footfalls, no familiar "Hello, the house!" called by passing strangers seeking shelter or refreshment. But something caused me to get up and peer through the lace curtains.

He was just standing there, who knows how long, a profusion of curls framing a high forehead, eyes dark and soulful. He was holding his horse's bridle in one hand, his hat in the other, and staring at the house. Whether it was the unexpectedness of a brick house or the pink roses adorning it that captivated Caleb's attention, or whether he was too shy to approach without invitation, I never learned. I never asked.

To my adolescent heart he looked as wildly romantic as the poet Byron, whose likeness in a steel engraving decorated the frontispiece of my volume. If it is possible to fall instantly in love, I did.

I raced upstairs to Mother.

"Gracious sakes, Sarah Jane," she said, "don't leave him standing out in the sun like that. Tell him to go around back and you'll give him a glass of water. Where are your manners?"

I flew downstairs, heart beating more from excitement than exertion, and threw open the door. "Go around back!" I hollered. And then, in my nervousness, I slammed the door before he could acknowledge my blurted instructions with more than a nod of his curly, handsome head.

By the time Caleb had watered his horse and refreshed himself, Father had invited him to supper. We rarely saw travelers heading east. If Caleb had been west, Father wanted to hear about it. And Mother, seeing in Caleb's deportment a young man of good breeding, urged acceptance for her own reasons. "Sarah Jane has made an apple pie," she added by way of inducement.

Mother paraded my accomplishments, real and imaginary, whenever any young man visited. I was of an age to excite marital anticipations in her. Although I confess that even then my culinary talents merited exhibition (unlike many of my other "adornments," as Mother called them), I felt my color rise and busied myself setting the table.

Caleb's conversation, to my parents' combined frustration, consisted of little more than "No, sir" and "Yes, ma'am." I thought his reticence as mysterious and appealing as his appearance, to which I devoted surreptitious attention between passing plates and serving soup. I couldn't keep my eyes from his face. Whatever romantic inclinations Byron aroused in me, Caleb captured.

As his monosyllables began to tally up, Caleb revealed, to Father's disappointment, that he had traveled not from the west, but the north.

Mother passed a dish of sliced peaches. "How interesting. We hear of great numbers of Yankees settling entire townships there, whole colonies now that this unpleasantness with Black Hawk is behind us. And not just farmers, but professional people, too. Solicitors, bankers, physicians, clerics."

She paused through this list of gentlemanly pursuits as though inviting Caleb to claim one for his family, but he returned only a noncommittal "Yes, ma'am."

Mother offered her most engaging smile, unable to forestall the inevitable question longer. "Who are your people?"

Caleb hesitated, looked from Mother's smile to the dish of peaches, and then said so quietly I strained to hear, "I buried, just a week ago, both my mother and my father."

"Oh, I'm so sorry!" I cried. "How terrible for you!" Such losses were not uncommon, even then, even in Illinois, but this unexpected grief added poignancy to our visitor's spell over me.

Father put a hand on Caleb's shoulder.

"Oh, it's too dreadful!" Mother said. "Every summer we hear reports of so many perishing from these awful fevers, so much worse in the north than here. The high bluffs bordering the waterways there prevent the easy circulation of air, and leave all causes of disease to take their most concentrated forms among the unfortunate settlers of the bottomlands."

Mother prattled a confused terror harbored for years. Fever in Ohio had taken the life of my little brother, and Mother still feared I might suddenly succumb.

Only later, much later, did I recall that Caleb neither confirmed nor denied Mother's presumption.

When Mother finally rambled to a stop, Father asked, "Where you bound, son?"

"New York, sir. I have a married sister there."

I was taking dessert from the pie safe. I whirled just as Mother clattered her cup into its saucer and exclaimed, "New York!" She turned beseeching eyes on Father. "Harlan, this poor boy can't go to New York. Tell him."

"Surely you must have heard, son, about the epidemic. Everyone's fleeing the cholera there. Your sister and her family cannot have stayed had they any choice."

Caleb slumped as though staggered by a sudden burden.

"We have July papers, our most recent advice," I said, finding my tongue and immediately wishing I'd bitten it. Reports of dead bodies lying in gutters while coffin makers broke the Sabbath to meet the unwonted demand was no subject to broach with a young man who had just buried his parents.

For months the Boston newspapers sent by my grandmother, along with the *Godey's Lady's Books* she never failed to post, had devoted whole columns to the threatening specter of cholera, and then to its alarming arrival in New York. Grandmother's letters expressed the generally held apprehension that reckless and imprudent people invited this divine punishment by intemperate conduct. Reports of any person of substance dying of cholera excited her suspicions of some secret vice. No industrious workingman or regular household risked contracting the disease. Everyone knew this.

"A young man of your station, of course," Mother said, leading our guest into the parlor, "is not the least susceptible, but the city is quite unfit for habitation."

I followed with Father, who commendably forbore remarking Mother's uncommon agreement with his fondly held opinion of cities. Harlan Ridgeway was one of those men fidgeted by cities and hungry for whatever lay beyond them, which is why he had shifted his wife steadily west from Boston for nearly twenty years, until she would shift no farther.

In the parlor, Father riffled through newspapers, found what he was looking for, thrust the issue into Caleb's reluctant hand.

"See there," Father said, stabbing a forefinger into a column of type. "It's a general turnout for the countryside. Folks leaving by steamboat, stage, and cart."

Caleb winced and Mother saw it. "Harlan, let's not dwell further on this unpleasantness." She plucked the newspaper from Caleb. "The young man shall remain here until the pestilence passes."

Certain my emotions betrayed themselves, I hurried away to clear the supper things when Father said, "Be good you stay on here for a while, son. Could use some help, if you've a mind to learn the wagon trade."

I don't know whether weariness or grief or simply lack of heart for his journey prompted Caleb to accept. I was too timid to ask. And too enchanted.

At first we took Caleb's reticence for a grief too deep to intrude upon, and then, after a time, we grew accustomed to his quiet ways. Autumn came, then winter. In the East, reports of cholera vanished with the arrival of frigid temperatures. But Caleb stayed, at first forestalled by weather too inclement for travel, and then by me.

Over the months, we grew easy with one another, as people must who share constant association. For my part, I could no more imagine life without his quiet presence than life without sunshine. I orbited around him, basked in his shy smiles and little attentions. How quick he was to assist each of us, Mother in the house, Father in the wagon shed, me in the kitchen and garden. Did I imagine his hand brushing against my own as he helped me reach a bowl from the cupboard? Did I fancy him studying me as I swept the hearth? Did his smile betray a tenderness too much hoped for? I was never sure, so intense was my own attachment.

On a warm day in early May, I persuaded Caleb, at work repairing a farmer's wagon, to help me spade the garden. I remember still the rich earth smell as we turned the soil, the sun warm on my back. When a nearby meadowlark poured forth a song so joyous as if to burst with happiness, I put a hand on Caleb's arm and we ceased our labor to listen. Suddenly, and without thought, I turned, fitted my-self against his body, lifted my face to his, pushed back my sunbonnet, and kissed him. The impulse seemed as natural as birdsong, I had so often rehearsed it in imagination.

My girlish fantasies ill prepared me for Caleb's reaction. He dropped his spading fork, embraced me, and kissed me long and passionately.

When he finally released me, I gasped a half-mocking rebuke. "Why, Caleb Daniels! You shall have to marry me for that."

And, of course, he did. My one regret was that by commanding him, however playfully, I never knew if he desired the union or merely acqui-esced to it. And I never risked asking.

I doubt my so-called "adornments" turned his head. At the piano I was never more than acceptable, regardless of my diligent practice and Mother's patient encouragement. I wished I could play as well as she, and said so. "If wishes were horses," she'd say, "beggars would ride."

Still, I learned to sing a little, accompanying myself in my workman-like way. I read the works of authors respected by cultivated society, being inclined, as an only child, to private pursuits. As a sketch artist I succeeded admirably, with hazelwood copses at the edge of prairie views my best subjects. I loved the limitless landscape. Mother framed my best efforts and hung them in the parlor next to my em-broidery sampler, an achievement distinguished only by the fact of its completion.

In addition to fostering these modest accomplishments, Mother tirelessly embellished my appearance. I was plain as a brick, but thanks to her relentless efforts, uncommonly stylish. Copying the *Godey's Lady's Books* my grandmother sent from Boston, she tortured my hair into droopy curls I thought ridiculous and stitched precise likenesses of fashions from color plates. I was always amenable. More than profits character, I'd say now.

I often laughed at Mother's earnest efforts to turn me into a proper young lady, as though Boston society might suddenly arrive at the brick house in Illinois. Until Caleb, most of the young men paying the regulation parlor visits were farmers to whom music meant a fiddle at a barn dance, a book meant an almanac, and a wife meant a stout helpmeet for chores and children.

I don't think I ever knew Caleb's chief requirement in a wife. For myself, I wanted nothing more from life than what my mother had – a devoted husband, a comfortable house, a family. That's what women were expected to want.

Shortly after that precipitous kiss in the garden, Caleb spoke to Father. I can imagine him shyly mumbling his intentions while grappling a recalcitrant wheel from its axle. Then Father told Mother, who found me in the kitchen and whirled me around like a child. "Oh, Sarah Jane, you shall be the most beautiful bride! And the garden will be so lovely by then!"

The next thing I knew, great lengths of fancy silk and suiting arrived, as did the fashionable seamstress from nearby Vandalia, who took up residence with us. She called herself a mantua-maker, even though both mantua silk and the loose gowns called mantuas were no longer fashionable. I don't remember her name, but I remember that her spinsterhood excited my sympathy – until I overheard her whispered confession as she and Mother stitched one day.

"Oh, I had my chances, Mrs. Ridgeway, but having learned a trade at a young age, I determined to go my own way. My mother bore a dozen children and never set foot farther than her washtub. Struck me as a dull and lonely life."

"The sexton's wife tells me you've been to Boston," Mother said, snipping a thread. "I was born there. I miss the city."

"My sister's there. Her girls went up to Lowell, got jobs in the mills. I visited them, being interested."

"Such a shame, poor girls at work from dawn till dark."

"Oh, not so hard as all that, Mrs. Ridgeway. Not so hard as being a poor man's wife, or mothering a dozen children. No end to that work. No, my two nieces live in a nice boardinghouse, have their meals prepared, enjoy lectures at the lyceum and a circulating library. And you should see how they dress! Regular fashion plates they are, having their own money and all. Any evening of the week, the town's abustle with girls shopping and visiting, or just 'going upon the street,' as they say, to show off a new bonnet or pair of boots."

That I should recall so vividly a conversation more than twenty years gone is odd, but I'd never before met a woman who earned her own keep. True, I knew any number of farmers' wives who sold eggs or vegetables or put up jam. Even my mother earned a little each week from giving piano lessons, but that was just pin money.

What did I think then? Did life in Lowell draw me? Impossible, I would have said, being in love and about to marry. More likely, given the little I knew at the time, I pitied the spinster and the Lowell girls.

After the seamstress's arrival, time disappeared in a swirl of fittings and stitching, of walls and windows and floors scrubbed clean of winter soot, carpets beaten, lamps polished, the garden coaxed into flower.

And then there I was, wearing a gown with leg-o'-mutton sleeves so fashionably correct I could have strolled the Paris boulevards, grasping my bouquet of pink roses and skipping down the steps of our country church with my handsome Caleb into a throng of well-wishers.

And this I've come to know: it is from measurement against such perfect happiness that sorrow achieves anguish.

Upheaval

The next years passed in a state of grace.

Father ceased complaining about the rootedness of his life, gaining contentment in the pleasures of grandchildren and the companionship of Caleb.

"Your man has a hand for it, Sarah," he said one night, bestowing his highest wagon-making praise. "Caleb can already tell a hard ash from one that's gone biscuity."

I beamed as if I'd invented my handsome husband and all his talents. It cheered me so that Father had found in Caleb the son Ohio's soil had taken to itself, as well as a confidant. Many a time I'd find them in the wagon shed, tools idle, deep in discourse. My father's enthusiastic curiosity for the West remained boundless, and I think he achieved a measure of happiness previously unknown, just in imagining that distant land with an indulgent listener. I presumed indulgence, of course, not sympathy.

I don't remember many conversations with Caleb, we had so few of substance. With us it was weather and wagon-making, tasks, politeness, the surface of things. He kept his own counsel, that man. And I? I was the dutiful wife and daughter, then mother. My thinking and expectations lay on the pages of the domestic and family manuals my grandmother sent me from Boston after I married.

My mother's happiness exceeded reckoning when my firstborn, Douglas, entered the world with a surprised scowl on his serious little face. Then Janey followed two years later, a tiny bundle seemingly born with her grandmother's love of music. Almost from birth, Janey's baby countenance suffused with pleasure whenever Mother played the piano. At three, Janey would sit on my mother's lap before the instrument, her face contorted with concentration. At four, she pointed pudgy and surprisingly correct fingers at the keys, sounding out the musical nursery rhymes that so delighted her.

Mother, I suspected, found a special joy in these serious children, as if the little one lain to rest in Ohio had in some small part been returned to her. Of course, we never spoke of such things. It was not until I buried my own stillborn boy, two years after Janey's birth, that I learned my mother had lost another, a girl.

"Gone at birth to God," Mother said.

We women consoled ourselves with such sentiments and accepted the inevitable: children could die. That was the expectation, learned through experience. We were not strangers to death, even then.

Given my own vigorous health and the robustness of my surviving children, an absence of continued increase to our family puzzled me. After a time, I ceased my anticipations, and then suddenly they were fulfilled twofold. Douglas was ten, Janey eight, when the twins, beautiful little George and Hannah, blessed with their grandmother's delicate features and their father's curls, completed our family.

From my first sight of them, I believed them heaven-sent, as though I'd received an incomprehensible reward for some service rendered of which I remained ignorant. A year later, when we buried their grandfather, I remember gazing through my tears at those twin angelic faces, thinking that that was what it meant, "The Lord giveth and the Lord taketh away."

My father died facing west, a late February sun washing through his bedroom window, bathing his pained face in a cold yellow light. Buck, faithful companion to imagined adventures, lay whimpering at his slippered feet, the setting sun glinting copper from the dog's shaggy coat. On the floor beside my father's chair lay a book, a report of explorer John Fremont's expedition to Oregon and California, dropped from his one good hand. The other, swollen and bandaged, lay heavy in his lap. Savage crimson stripes laced the arm from the gash where the chisel had slipped as he shaped an iron tire to its wheel, an accident of stiffening joints clumsied by winter.

The loss of him slammed into the brick house like a tornado. The light went out of Mother's eyes, and for days afterward she wandered from room to room, picking up and stroking her husband's things — a pipe, a coat, a pillow. In that grief-crippled time, Caleb and Douglas silently saddled horses and rode out at dawn each morning, not returning until dark. Janey sat at the piano, staring at the keys, but didn't play. I wept regret into the curls of little George and Hannah, embracing them so tightly they squealed, and wished desperately I might have hugged my father more in the busy years disappeared behind us. If wishes were horses.

Caleb appropriated the copy of Fremont's book, paging silently through several long evenings by the light of an oil lamp. I took the scene as a gesture of respect for Father's failed ambition. Mother, as usual, saw more than met the eye. She said nothing, but I detected uneasiness in her expression and suspected she feared that my husband, like hers, harbored the westering urges then infecting the nation.

Hundreds of families were leaving Illinois, not counting the Mormons pouring out of Nauvoo. The state had filled up in a decade and now seemed to be emptying its excess west. Most were farmers, seeking the mild climates and fertile fields of Oregon. A good many passed our house, their wagons churning dust from the road.

Mother's fear that Caleb pined to follow them struck me then as preposterous. We were settled, a family. We had no cause to go anywhere. Douglas had joined his father in the wagon-making trade. Janey was my mother's constant companion. And the twins, my unexpected gift, filled my busy days with joy.

Both Hannah and George exhibited, almost from the time they started walking, intractably bold and curious natures. Yelping their fun, they crawled and climbed and then tumbled to the bottoms of stairs and chairs in surprised heaps of kicking legs and flailing arms. As soon as weather permitted, I herded them outside while I tended the garden, a task repeatedly abandoned to pry a handful of dirt or a beetle from their fingers, envoys for little mouths.

One day, when Caleb and Douglas had gone to the blacksmith for some ironwork and Janey helped Mother in the house, I was rescuing a luckless ladybug from Hannah's fatal regard when George tottered off to the wagon shed. I hoisted Hannah to my hip and gave pursuit, a game George delighted in.

For George, the place where his father worked was a tantalizing jumble of wheels and undercarriage parts, axle assemblies, wagon tongues, spokes and felloes, tools and wood and iron. Our chase ended in a corner filled with odds and ends, where he grabbed two fat little hand-fuls of nails from a bucket and with a squeal of excitement tossed them willy-nilly.

I placed my children under their grandmother's superintendence and returned to the shed to pick up the nails. That's when I found the newspaper tucked behind the nail bucket.

It was a copy of the *Sangamo Journal*, a Springfield paper we didn't often see, since travelers rarely passed from that direction. On the front page was a notice circled in pencil: "Westward, Ho! For Oregon and California!" The advertisement, by "G. Donner and others," was for young men who might want to "go to California without costing them any thing" with gentlemen who would leave Sangamon County the first of April.

On first reading the notice, I presumed my father had long ago hid-den the paper in the shed. It was the kind of thing he collected away from Mother's questioning eyes.

Then I saw the newspaper's date: March 26, 1846. A full month after we buried my father.

With the realization that Caleb, not Father, had secreted the paper, I felt suddenly lightheaded and without breath. Mother's imparted fear flowed through my veins as surely as her blood. She was Rabbit; I was Mouse. Her terror was now mine.

I didn't swoon then, for it's not my nature, but I nearly did the following year on hearing of the tragedy. For a time, almost every newspaper we saw filled its columns with reports of the unimaginably frightful and hideous conclusion to the Donner Party's westward trek.

"Dragged into the wilderness to starve, and worse!" Mother cried, hugging Hannah as if to rescue her from the grisly scene discovered in the Sierra.

Caleb said nothing. I forbore mentioning the circled advertisement I'd discovered crammed behind the nail bucket. Surely such ghastly peril as befell the Donner Party must extinguish westering fever in even the most foolhardy adventurer.

But I never figured on gold.

The first news we had of it was from a peddler whose route passed us twice a year. On a day late in autumn, we all clustered around his wagon draped with tinware and candle molds, examining his mantle clocks and combs, hearth brushes and ribbons, the little necessaries and luxuries it was such an event to see.

The peddler, a thin man radiating confidence sufficient to sell plows to Apaches, shoved a book at Caleb.

"This here's me last copy of Bryant's tour, guv'nor, all about what he saw in California in 'forty-six. Ever'body's scoopin' 'em up like ice in summer on account of the gold what's been discovered there, you know."

Seeing in our faces the blank look of raw recruits, the peddler grinned. He loved dispensing news and gossip as much as toasting forks. He slapped a loop of tin cups into a clanging rattle by way of celebrating our ignorance. "Well, you ain't heard on that? Papers from New York to New Orleans is all full of it." He leaned over the side of his wagon, groped behind a butter churn crammed with broom handles, extracted a bundle of newspapers, pawed through them until one caught his eye, and offered it to Mother. "Here it is, ma'am, in the *New York Journal of Commerce*."

Although Lacy Ridgeway's Boston breeding forbade impolite refusals, even to peddlers, she backed away, hands up, as if he'd offered her a snake.

The peddler mistook apprehension for ignorance. "I'll read it to you, missus."

He rustled the paper importantly and gave a preliminary cough. "Prospectors skirmishing through the diggings are picking up gold just as a thousand hogs, let loose in a forest, would root up ground-nuts," he read. "Some get eight or ten ounces a day, and the least active, one or two, while one man with sixty Indians working for him had been making a dollar a minute."

Douglas gasped. "A dollar a minute!"

Mother retreated up the path toward the brick house in a swish of skirts. "I shouldn't believe everything I read in the papers if I were you, young man!"

My eyes met Caleb's. He smiled, put an arm around me in unexpected affection, and nodded toward the peddler's goods. "You want something here?"

The peddler scrambled to exhibit his wares, extolling at length the virtues of a tin refractor oven especially designed, he insisted, to sit atop our Oberlin cookstove. Eager to put the anxious moment behind us, I examined the oven with pretended curiosity. Despite the convenience of our new cast-iron cookstove, so much safer than hearth cooking, I still held a preference for baking in the brick oven built against the chimney. I was used to judging its heat.

I did buy some lamp wicks and sperm oil, a pink ribbon for Hannah's curls, and a square of good linen for Janey to embroider a new sampler.

Janey had proved a talented needlewoman, diligently rendering under Mother's meticulous guidance all the plain and fancy stitches on an alphabet done in wool.

"There's a nice selection of silk thread, Janey," I said. "What colors do you like?"

She examined the choices as though her grandmother hadn't swooped into the house, her brother wasn't poring over the offending newspaper, or her father leaning against the wagon deep in conversation with the peddler.

"I like the green crinkled floss," she said, "and the white. And the plain red, too."

Douglas admired a hunting knife, which the peddler pronounced a genuine bowie. Caleb bought it for him, generous from the good business guaranteed by the steady progression of westbound, white-topped wagons passing our house in increasing numbers.

For himself, Caleb bought Bryant's book.

President Polk's address to Congress in December, reprinted in newspapers in every city and hamlet, sealed our fate. "The accounts of the abundance of gold," the president said, "are of such an extraordinary character as would scarcely command belief were they not corroborated by the authentic reports of officers in the public service, who have visited the mineral district, and derived the facts which they detail from personal observation."

Mother looked into Caleb's eyes when he glanced up from reading the account, and took to her bed.

Late that night, when all the house slept, Caleb, warm beside me in the featherbed we'd shared for fifteen years, turned to me and caressed my face with a work-roughened hand. "Sarah, I want to go," he whispered.

I didn't voice a terrified protest, nor indeed did I object by any word. Instead, I wept silently while Caleb brushed away my tears.

"Remember, Sarah, how your father talked of the adventure of it? Listening to him, I could almost taste it. Had he lived, he would have gone now, I know it."

I found my Mouse voice. "No, no, he wouldn't, Caleb. He loved my mother, and he loved me, and he wouldn't have done it, couldn't have."

"I love you, Sarah, and not the less for wanting this."

Caleb loved me! He'd never said it before. But then he was not a man to speak his thoughts, and I'd never expected him to. This was a gift. And I wept — for gratitude, for fear, for all the anxiety my mother had carried like a burden since the peddler's visit.

But in the thousand rememberings of that moment, I never imagined simply turning on my husband and defying him. I was a woman trained in the precepts of daughter and wife. The *Mother's Assistant* was my handbook on right thinking. I remembered the article entitled "The Father the King in His Family." Man was lawgiver and judge. I could not protest my husband's authority. All I could do was weep. Could I have changed our fate by refusing in whatever persuasive manner Lacy Ridgeway halted her husband's slow but determined progress westward? No. I was not force sufficient for gold.

His campaign begun, Caleb delivered arguments resolute as artillery fire. The next morning, as we sat at the kitchen table and a pitcher of milk passed from hand to hand, Caleb arrested its circuit.

"We'd be back in two years," he said, holding the pitcher and looking at me, intent as a preacher. "Two years, that's all. With enough gold to expand the wagon business like the Studebaker brothers are doing in Indiana — buying spokes, felloes, hubs, and other parts from shops that specialize in them, and then building wagons en masse, not just one at a time. Manufactories — that's the future, Sarah. And with just two years in California, we can assure Douglas his share in it."

I looked from Caleb to Douglas, who stared into his bowl as though it contained something more interesting than boiled oats.

"I wasn't aware Douglas had such an interest in . . . what was it you said? Manufactories?" From my restrained tone, one might have thought the subject of less account than the weather. My tears had dried. There was something of my mother's resistance in me yet.

Caleb plowed new ground. "After a visit to the California goldfields, the boy could do whatever he wanted. Why, he could go to Harvard's medical school if he wanted to."

Douglas and I gaped a unified astonishment at this suggestion as Mother smacked the platter to the table and exclaimed, "You say 'a visit to California' like it was a day trip to Vandalia!"

Douglas found his tongue. "Medical school?"

Mother crashed a pot lid on the porridge pan, startling Hannah into a whimper. Janey, frowning, shushed her sister and wiped a trickle of milk from her chin. George mimicked the fuss by banging a spoon on his bowl and crowing, "School!"

Caleb examined the slice of ham on his plate, sectioned a piece, and stabbed it with his fork. "All I'm saying is the boy could do whatever inclined him. He could have a choice about his life."

Was it bitterness I heard in Caleb's voice, or regret? Or did I just imagine it? But being a dutiful wife and mother, I put myself to worrying whether my reluctance limited my son.

For several days Caleb waylaid me at unexpected moments — trimming a lamp wick, peeling potatoes, collecting rose hips for tea — to assail my resistance with propositions for a new wing on the brick house, an excursion to Boston for Mother, Harvard educations for both Douglas and George. "Gold, Sarah, gold, all we want," he said. "Think of it."

I remained deaf and dumb to every argument. Except the last. It came late one evening in the parlor. I was sewing, I think, letting out a hem in George's winter coat, he was growing so fast. Caleb was reading. The children were in bed, Mother had retired. Caleb closed his book, and I could feel him staring at me as I sat across the room, concentrating on my stitching.

"Sarah, look at me."

I looked up from my sewing and smiled in the tentative way I had adopted, seeking peace while giving no ground.

Caleb ran a hand through his hair. "Sarah, you're right not to go to California if you don't want to. It was wrong of me to ask it."

Before the little leap in my heart registered happiness, he added, "Most men are going alone. That's probably the best way."

I dropped my sewing to my lap, felt my voice catch in my throat like a bone. "You'd go alone to California and leave us?"

"Sarah, it's two years. That's not such a long time."

"No!" I shot the word at him like a bullet.

He flinched. Then he stood, came to me, knelt by the side of my chair, and took my hand.

"Sarah, I'm going to California because I want to. Not for the gold, the wagon business, for you or anyone. It's just something I want to do."

"Why, Caleb? Tell me why."

"Because I'm thirty-five years old and I've never chosen or decided anything for myself. If I don't do it, my life will have been just a succession of drifting things that happened until the sexton buried me in the churchyard."

Seeing how his shoulders stooped, I wept. Gray had crept into his curls since the day he stood in the road and my girlish heart fancied Lord Byron himself had come to call. In the satisfying dailiness of our fifteen years together, I had long since forsaken doubt about my husband's feelings for me in return for the joy of adoring him. Now he all but declared our marriage something that happened, like a visit from his sister. Not something decided, like a journey to California.

Uncertainty crowded my thoughts. If he left, would he return? And how could I endure the torture of so dangerous an absence, not knowing where he was, how he fared?

Through my tears I saw the set of his jaw, unchanged from the day my heart sang at first sight of him. And I saw that his jaw had hardened into a determination I was helpless to oppose. Childe Harold would not be denied his adventure.

Caleb's decision coupled me to it like a plow to a mule. I had no choice but to follow. I say the decision was mine to go, but what decision was that? I could cut off my right hand or my left. That was the extent of my choice.

And now began the new torment, the tearing agony of abandoning my mother. For days she refused even to acknowledge the necessity I felt to go.·

"I'm not listening to you, Sarah Jane. I don't hear a word you're saying," she would say when I broached the subject, clapping hands over her ears or wiping them on her apron as though done with a disagreeable task. Then, when she deigned to listen, she refused to believe Caleb could not be swayed. But I knew he was going, with us or without us.

"Mother," I finally said, my voice crawling past the lump in my throat, "I couldn't face not knowing. Can't you understand that not knowing would be intolerable?"

She wept with me then, hugging me to her. "Oh, Sarah Jane, I fear for you, for all of us. I see only sorrow from such foolishness."

I rushed into the breach with a reassurance I didn't feel. "Caleb says we'll be perfectly safe. Families have been traveling the road now for years."

New tears crept down Mother's cheeks, lined now with time's passage. "But when I think of that poor Donner family — "

"Mother, please, things like that don't happen now. Everyone knows to keep to the trail, to hurry before the snows come. Caleb's read the books; he's not a man to take chances."

And he wasn't. He was as careful and deliberate a man as I ever met. How he came to take this one chance bewilders me still.

St. Louis

Following our rending departure, I determined to abide the adventure in good spirit. To be if not eager for the journey, at least cheerful. The twins were naturally so, as was Douglas. Caleb, anxious to ease my regret, adopted an exuberance even beyond the enthusiasm he legitimately felt, excitedly pointing out the sights and forecasting those to come.

Janey alone remained withdrawn. The poor child had less choice in this decision than I, was equally attached to the brick house and all it contained. Her reluctance so reflected my own, I couldn't reprove her. I allowed her the luxury of indulging her distress, confident that in due course she would regain her congenial disposition.

Our only mishap in the three-day journey to St. Louis was miring down in a muddy spot in the road. Our wagon was heavy, and the mules couldn't pull out. We stayed stuck most of the morning, until another wagon drew even with us. It belonged to a young man going on his own to California — Charles Cranson, his name was. He generously yoked his team of oxen to our wagon and hauled us out.

We all stood in the road after that, and he offered to trade us his oxen for our mules.

"You folks got a heavy load, probably be better off with oxen. I'm selling my stock in Independence anyway."

"We'll stick with the mules, I guess," Caleb said.

Cranson shrugged. "Mules or oxen, makes me no never mind. They're just to get me to Independence. Don't need them after that."

"No?"

"Nope." Cranson grinned, pulled a folded half sheet of newspaper from his back pocket, and showed it off to Caleb like a blue ribbon won at the fair. "I'm going to California with the Pioneer Line."

Caleb studied the circled announcement. "Sounds like a magnificent enterprise."

"You bet, mister. All specially built carriages for the passengers, like it says. Separate wagons for baggage, experienced drivers. Arranged as regular as a New York omnibus, sounds to me."

Cranson stuffed the paper back in his pocket. "Going to get us all there in sixty days, they say. I'll be picking up California gold in no time."

Caleb laughed and put a hand on Douglas's shoulder. "I expect you'll leave some for my boy here."

"Sure thing." Cranson winked at Douglas. "All I want is enough to get me home in style, marry my sweetheart, and help Pa pay off the farm. Shouldn't take me more'n a month, and then it's home sweet home for me."

He cracked his ox goad, prodded his team into their ponderous westward advance. "You should think about oxen some, mister. They're slow, but sure. And worse come to worst, there's more meat to a ox than a mule."

As we took up our journey again, the young man's warning tugged at my thoughts. Could it come to that, eating our animals?

It could, and worse. The specter of the Donners rose like a ghost, flitted through my mind dressed in regret. Perhaps I should have let Caleb come on his own, take the Pioneer Line's fast journey unencumbered by a family, reach California before the snows fell.

I confessed my thoughts to him.

"Thousands are heading across the plains this year, Sarah. It's history in the making. I want us to be part of it, all of us." He rummaged beneath the wagon seat, found a book, handed it to me. "Read this, you'll feel better."

It was a slim volume written by a man named Joseph Ware. The title was *Emigrants' Guide to the Trail.* I paged through it while we rumbled along the rutted road.

Regardless of whether any of us fully realized the extent of the journey's dangers, we were on our way. But the guidebook's listing of

provisions and all the necessaries of outfitting, and its table of distances
and campsites calmed me. The author cautioned that the journey was
long and not to be undertaken lightly, but, he added, it need not be
feared by careful travelers.

And Caleb was a careful man. I showed him where the book argued
for oxen. He agreed to seek advice in St. Louis.

Our arrival in that city filled me with the strangest emotions. As a
child, I'd heard my mother often speak against it as uncivilized frontier.
I think then that I pictured it an outpost of near biblical import, its
streets a Babel. This last was true enough. But the jumping-off place my
mother feared was no rough settlement. St. Louis in 1849 boasted a
population of nearly seventy thousand, not counting the daily augmen-
tation of hundreds of passing-through emigrants. It was as modern and
fine a city as I ever imagined Boston to be, with commendable houses of
brick and stone, and grand public buildings crowned with domes and
spires.

The most prominent of these, the courthouse, the children and I
toured. Douglas discovered on one of its walls a full-length portrait of
Clark, who, in the days of President Jefferson, had traveled the West in
company with Lewis. Gazing on the painting, I wondered how many
mothers, like mine, had wished these men had left the West unexplored.
But what was done could not be undone. There was no going back.

We took rooms at the Missouri Hotel. When Caleb left to purchase
our tickets for the steamboat to St. Joseph, I suggested to the children we
go out to see the city.

"I don't want to go anywhere," Janey said. "Can't I just stay in the
hotel?"

"No, missy, you can't," I replied. "Let's just be done with this. I know
you don't want to be here, but we don't always get what we want. We're
going to California, and then we'll come back, and it's going to take two
years. And you're not going to be sad for the next two years, Janey, you're
just not."

That said, we all ventured out into the chaos, my pretty daughter's
face still long.

What a bedlam. I had never before witnessed anything like it. There
was such an air of excitement, such a crush of drays, such shouting and
trading, throngs of people of all colors speaking all languages, so many
puffing steamboats on the Mississippi. After a stroll through the city's
main thoroughfare, we found some boxes to sit on near one of the liveli-
est wharves, with a view of the busy river up and down. The size of the
boats astonished me, but not as much as their numbers.

"Bet there's a hundred," Douglas said.

"Is not," Janey replied over her shoulder, catching George before he could scamper after a dog.

"Why don't you count them," I said, attempting to engage her interest.

She turned a grim face on me and looked away. Douglas counted the steamers. They totaled fifty-six, on the water and docked at the wharf.

We continued our excursion along the waterfront, reading on storefronts the exuberant claims of dozens of posted placards inviting the examination of every variety of gold-washing machine. Even I felt some contagion of gold fever. It was a disease easily contracted.

I also found my fears in part allayed by the sheer numbers participating in the dramatic enterprise. Surely the presence of so many thousands bound together for the same destination promised safety. Hadn't we already benefitted by the young man who kindly lent his oxen to our predicament? Weren't responsible businessmen, like the organizers of the Pioneer Line, taking part?

That evening, the children fast asleep despite the ceaseless noise from the streets, Caleb sitting nearby studying Mr. Ware's guide, I wrote my mother of these encouragements. As my pen scratched across the notepaper beneath the lamp, I sensed in myself a rising spirit. My determination to write only of our well-being and success, to recount nothing but that which would cheer her, cheered me.

Fortunately, I posted my letter before breakfast the next morning. Had I not seen it immediately into the canvas bag and out the door with the express driver, I wonder if I could have sent it, so unpracticed was I at deception.

We had the bad news from the morning papers at breakfast. I saw Caleb lower the paper, his face drained of color. My own countenance, though ignorant, must have mirrored his, my recent confidence was such a thin veneer.

Caleb collected himself, folded the paper, wiped oatmeal from George's chin. "Douglas, Janey," he said, "take the twins upstairs and get your things packed. We'll be leaving soon."

Douglas jumped up, so eager was he for the trip. Janey looked suspicious. "The steamboat don't go until this afternoon, Papa," she said.

"Doesn't," I said from habit. "Just because you're out of school for now doesn't mean you can forget what you know."

"All right, Mama, but the steamboat still *doesn't* go until this afternoon."

Caleb forced a smile. "By the time we get the wagon and our gear aboard, it'll be time. You go along now, get started."

I held my breath until they were gone. "What is it, Caleb?"

Caleb drummed nervous fingers on the newspaper lying on the table. "This is the Independence paper, so it's likely just propaganda. Talk says that city will do anything to prevent emigrants bypassing it in favor of St. Joseph."

"Caleb, what does it say?"

He hesitated, looked at the paper again.

"Caleb?"

"There's some sickness reported at St. Joseph."

"What sickness?"

I thought I saw some old, familiar expression in his eyes. When he spoke, I recognized it.

"Cholera."

Seventeen years, half my lifetime ago, I had seen in Caleb's eyes the same defeated look when my father forced on him the papers describing the epidemic then raging in New York. I remembered it as a terrible scourge. While the disease exempted those of temperate habits, one's sympathies must necessarily be excited for its victims. Is that what I read in Caleb's eyes? Or did he see us endangered?

"Oh, Caleb, let's take no chances! Must we leave from St. Joseph? Can we not go to Independence?"

"St. Joseph is seventy miles farther west. Saves us a week to start from there." He picked up his coffee cup. "I'm sorry, Sarah, it was just a surprise, that's all. I doubt it's more than rumor. In any event, you're not to worry. I'll go 'round to the druggist and get more medicines. I can take care of us."

He spoke with such conviction, I chose not to worry.

Douglas accompanied his father, reporting afterward with wide-eyed disbelief on a slave auction near the pharmacist's shop. "I saw a boy sold, Ma! Not as old as me! And his mother got sold, too, but to another buyer. And she just wailed something fierce when that boy went off from her. It was something terrible to see."

When his voice cracked in the telling, Caleb put a hand on his son's shoulder and apologized to me with his eyes. It couldn't be helped, his eyes said, I'm sorry.

Missouri was a slave state, of course, but the buying and selling of human beings like oxen or mules shocked us nonetheless. My son's distress, and thoughts of that poor mother, took my mind from imaginary fears. I was grateful for the occupation of packing up for the steamboat.

Caleb loaded into our wagon a box containing a reassuring assortment of calomel, quinine, sulphur pills, camphor balls, Dover's powders, castor oil, adhesive plasters, hartshorn for snakebite, and citric acid. A little of the acid mixed with sugar, water, and essence of lemon, he assured me, would make a fine substitute for lemonade, as well as an antidote for scurvy. I was surprised by how much he knew of medicines, and put it to his reading in preparation for the journey.

The wagon went onto the chuffing steamer, along with our terrified mules and what seemed like every other animal and wagon and box and bale in St. Louis. What a crush it was. The decks below filled with braying mules, stamping and snorting horses, lowing oxen. Passengers and stevedores crammed the upper decks with a remarkable assortment of wagons and baggage, innumerable sacks, barrels, crates, trunks, rolled-up tents and jumbled-up camp kettles, and a regular arsenal of rifles and hatchets. Every berth was occupied; even the cabin floor at night was covered by sleeping emigrants.

We were, as Lucena announced with her disarming smile, a company too compactly put together to remain strangers long.

We met Lucena and Will when Douglas dragged us all to the hurricane deck to watch a contingent of men drilling like an infantry company. They were impressively organized and wore complete military uniforms of gray cassimere pants and matching coats surmounted with rows of brass buttons, with white shoulder straps and belts.

"Do you suppose they're soldiers headed for one of the forts out west?" I asked Caleb. The idea cheered me.

"Not a bit of it," said a pretty, fair-haired young woman, overhearing me. "I had me a nice natter with the gent in command of these fellows, you see. He organized this company in the East, didn't Mr. Bruff say, Will?"

"Yep."

Will Semple wasn't as much for talk as Lucena, who charmed us with her engaging manner as we exchanged introductions. They were newlyweds going to make a home in California, she said, smiling up at the thin young man towering over her like a sapling cottonwood.

Will doffed his slouch hat, having adopted already the frontier attire favored by most young men traveling west, notwithstanding the company costumed as soldiers on parade before us. A trumpet announced the cessation of the miners' militaristic maneuvers.

Lucena laughed. "La, imagine miners all fancied up to dig gold, proper as India colonels."

Janey touched my arm. "She talks funny, don't she, Mama?"

"Doesn't, Janey, *doesn't*. And it's rude to say so."

Lucena tweaked Janey's chin. "Folks in London'd think you talk funny, you know, Mistress Jane."

"Did you travel all the way from London then, to go to California?" Janey asked, awed by the prospect.

"So it seems, though t'were not my intent when I started out, I assure you."

Lucena launched her travel tales that morning, enrapturing Janey and amusing us all with her adventures. Two years previous, Lucena had sailed across the Atlantic with her sister Liza. "Now happily married to an Iowa farmer, same as me, thank you very much," Lucena said, smiling up at her husband.

She related how she and Liza, sent for by an uncle in Illinois following the deaths of their parents, spent their first night in America at New York.

"Oh, la, what a fright we had at that hotel," Lucena said, laughing at the recollection. "Such a dreadful noise just after our arrival, we thought the hotel must be on fire, or Judgment Day come. We fled our room and, seeing a gentleman in the hall, implored him to save us. He quietly informed us the clamor was the boy beating the gong for dinner!"

What a wonderful storyteller Lucena was, and how she entertained us with tales of her travels. Janey adored her, hanging on every word of Lucena's adventures. I was grateful to see my daughter drawn from her melancholy, her eyes alight with interest.

From New York Lucena and Liza had taken a boat to Albany, from there a train to Utica, then a canal boat to Buffalo, and finally a lake steamer across Lakes Erie, Huron, and Michigan.

"My sister and I read from our tickets we were going to a place called 'Chick-a-go,' " Lucena said to Janey, laughing. "Have you ever been to 'Chick-a-go'?"

"I've never been anywhere."

"Oh, la, you're on your way now though, aren't you? And California's bound to be ever so much more interesting than 'Chick-a-go,' don't you think?"

"I never heard of 'Chick-a-go.' "

Douglas rapped his sister on the head. "Spell it out in your head, mouse brain."

"I'm not a mouse brain!"

Lucena laughed. "C-h-i-c-a-g-o."

"Oh, Chicago!"

"That's it, Mistress Jane! Imagine that, I've been to Chicago, and I didn't even know it."

At Chicago the sisters had hired a driver with a double team to take them to Rock Island, where they crossed the Mississippi River by ferry-boat to Davenport and hired a conveyance to take them upriver to LeClaire, their uncle's home.

"La, to think we'd been persuaded to leave a comfortable house in London," Lucena said, "to take that long and expensive journey, just to find our uncle and his family all crowded into a one-room cabin! Of course, we didn't realize at once that the dwelling had but one room. Just imagine our annoyance, to have been ushered into a room crowded with two double beds, a cookstove, and various accessories of domesticity! I felt vexed we had not been shown into the parlor. Seeing a door on the farther side of the room, I asked to inspect it. What a disappointment when my cousin opened the door and showed me the buttery. What I thought must be the parlor was a dish cupboard!"

For one like myself, who never until a few days ago had traveled farther than a day's ride to Vandalia, such a journey as Lucena had taken all but surpassed belief. That this diminutive female argonaut, barely a half dozen years older than Janey, had traveled half the world instantly engaged my admiration.

I took courage from Lucena's adventurous spirit and felt my fortitude for the long journey before us enlarged by her boldness. I think she knew she buoyed me, she so often cheerily announced in those early days that the journey to California would be "a perfect pleasure trip."

Our steamboat proceeded up the wide Missouri in slow fashion. Numerous river snags rendered navigation hazardous after nightfall, and we lay alongside the banks each evening.

We reached Jefferson City on the third day of travel, seeing in the distance the Missouri statehouse. Mr. Bruff, organizer of the Washington City Marching Company, as Lucena called it, was standing at the rail of the hurricane deck with Lucena and me when it came into view.

"One can't help but remark the statehouse's resemblance as a small edition of the nation's capitol," he said.

So many people had seen so many places I had only read about. I began to think then that travel was incumbent upon me, if only as an example to my children not to be as provincial as I had become.

Or so I thought until the steamer slowed and drew alongside the wharf. To my horror, two deckhands hauled a blanket-wrapped body onto it and left it there.

Lucena, seeing my alarm, took my hand and said, "It's a sorrow for the poor man's family, Mrs. Daniels, but from such a number as are collecting for this expedition, it must be expected that some will die."

She was right, of course, and I determined not to be provincial either by demeanor or speech. Others had traveled, knew the world. I would number myself among the argonauts, regardless of my trepidation. No one need know I was a coward, a mouse.

I presumed arrangements had been made for the body's burial, and notification to the man's family. Later I wondered, and wished I'd had the poor man's name for my journal.

We would learn at St. Joseph of steamers far less fortunate than ours. A deadly illness raged on one with such violence that crew and passengers abandoned the boat, leaving it tied to the shore. On another, eighteen young men died. We heard that the blanket-wrapped corpses accumulated on deck until the captain put by at a river island and deckhands buried them in hasty, shallow graves.

Until distressed by such reports, I had begun to enjoy my adventure. Lucena's company and the novelty of river travel lightened my heart. The Missouri's short bends and wooded banks prevented too distant a view ahead, and numerous little creeks and shaded coves provided scenic variety. Our journey thus far was indeed a perfect pleasure trip.

Caleb, gladdened by both Janey's and my increased cheerfulness in Lucena's companionship, asked the Semples to join us for dinner in the salon the last evening of our river journey.

After the steward poured coffee all around, Caleb leaned back in his chair and stared at Will, as though taking his measure. At last he said, "If you've made no arrangements, Will, and are, like ourselves, as yet independent of any joint-stock company or other arrangement, perhaps you'd like to join with us."

I had no idea he would propose we travel together, but it pleased me so. And great was my delight when Lucena and Will happily concurred in the plan. We agreed upon reaching St. Joseph to seek additional congenial company to form up a train.

Which is how, for the pleasure Francis Fogie gave us, we came to travel with the Germans.

St. Joseph

It was a backward spring that year, following a severe winter, which enforced a longer stay at St. Joseph than we anticipated. Across the river, the road we were to follow remained too muddy for fast travel, and the prairie grass insufficient to feed the thousands of animals preparing to advance upon it.

Caleb, after talking to several emigrants already arrived, reported most expected to wait two weeks more before crossing the river and getting on the road. Some had already crossed over on the two ferries operating on the river, and camped on the other side to avoid the crush.

The crowds of men, women, even children, stunned me. They filled to capacity every hotel and boardinghouse and place of entertainment in St. Joseph, a dirty little town of uninviting appearance. So great was the emigration that it filled the landscape as far as my eye could see. Thousands of waiting emigrants had set up housekeeping in tents intended for the prairie. They dotted the countryside like an encamped army.

Caleb fretted the need to move several miles from town to obtain accommodations of some willing householder, as we had on our journey to St. Louis. For me, that prospect conjured up Lucena's uncle and his one-room cabin. In that circumstance the sisters discovered hospitality consisted of beds shared with their host family.

I didn't often speak my mind, trusting to Caleb's decisions, but I wanted none of that. "I suggest we accustom ourselves to life on the plains," I said, "and set up camp forthwith."

Douglas and Caleb leapt at the proposal. Janey did not.

"Can't we please, please, find some nice house to sleep in, or a hotel?" she asked, directing her question to her father.

While Caleb assured her none was available, that camp life would be an adventure, I remember thinking how unfair it was that she held me responsible for her unhappiness. Her father was the lawgiver, of course, and being a dutiful daughter, she did not question his authority. Him she forgave for the family's upheaval; me she did not. But I understood her heartache. And if blaming me lessened it, then so be it. It was small enough recompense.

We found space for our camp, which did not lack for company. Lucena and Will set up their tent next by ours, and other visitors were equally frequent, the twins being a novelty to everyone. Little George and Hannah became quick favorites with the young men camped around us. Many of them already felt the first pangs of homesickness and came calling just to see the children.

They announced themselves less frequently by name than by their associations. We were surrounded by Hoosiers, Wolverines, Buckeyes, Yankees, and Yorkers. Occasionally, I saw a tent bearing the stamp of a woman's presence. Wherever bushes, trees, or logs formed a partial enclosure containing a more homelike disposition of goods, one might easily imagine a sitting room or kitchen.

Caleb procured us every comfort, St. Joseph offering supplies as varied and abundant as St. Louis's. We had India rubber blankets for the floor of our tent to keep out the damp, and a sheet-iron stove for cooking. Chickens and eggs were cheap and plentiful, and I put myself to cooking up supplies of them to carry with us.

Last-minute preparations consumed Caleb's time, and Douglas accompanied his father in the procurement of provisions and advice, becoming a young man before my eyes. Mules well broken to harness commanded good prices in St. Joseph. Ours were first-rate animals, and Caleb sold them for sixty-two dollars each, buying three yoke of oxen for substantially less.

Caleb invited the children to name these docile and gentle beasts with soulful eyes. The two black ones with white faces we put to lead and, at Douglas's suggestion, agreed to call them Lewis and Clark. Among the others was one that was solid russet.

"Buck," said George, who missed his grandpa's old dog.

Hannah took a fancy to a sweet-natured animal, petted its side, and announced importantly, "Cherry."

Douglas laughed and picked up his little sister so she could pat its head. "Cherry for this big old ox?"

Hannah nodded solemnly. "Cherry."

When Caleb bought a milch cow, that we might have milk and butter for the trail, I began to feel luxurious. Janey's affections attached to that patient creature from the first. "Papa, I'll have the care of her," she said, stroking its pink nose. "I'll call her Emma."

Caleb bought a web of muslin to make sacks for our provisions. Besides being easily handled, sacks dispensed with some unnecessary heavy boxes and reduced the weight of our load.

While transferring into a newly made sack some dried fruits I'd brought from home — prunes, raisins, and apples for stewing — I discovered a red tin cake box. The sight puzzled me. I recognized the box, but I knew I hadn't packed it.

How touched I was when I opened it and found a lovely plum cake, moist with rum for good keeping, and a note from Mother. "Think of me when you eat this," was all it said. I felt she had reached out and kissed us all again.

"We'll save it for California," I told the children, "to celebrate."

Janey helped me sew sacks, and she stitched on her sampler the beginnings of a nice likeness of the brick house. She liked camping, despite her initial opposition. There being so many more small female duties to perform than she had at home, I saw she began to feel important to the enterprise. With no complaint, she assisted with the continual packing and unpacking, the cooking, and the never ending task of watching the twins. When a gentleman in a nearby tent offered to teach her to play the banjo, she even smiled at me when I gave her permission.

It was during one of those banjo lessons that George disappeared. Which is how we met Francis Fogie.

I had gone to the wagon for something, I don't remember what. It was a constant trek back and forth to stow things and find others once our wagon was in line for the ferry. The line had formed early on, since several days, even weeks, would be required to get the dense mass of wagons, people, oxen, mules, and horses ferried over. Wagons filled St. Joseph, the line extending down the principal street to the riverbank. As soon as a wagon entered one of the scows, the next moved down to the water's edge, and those in the rear closed up to the front. Fighting for precedence was not uncommon. In one of these disputes, two teamsters killed each other with pistols, an incident I spared my mother in my daily letter home.

Our wagon was in line behind the Semples', and it was that morning I saw Lucena at the back of her wagon in tears.

"I wanted my blue dishes out, you see," she said, her pretty mouth in a pout. "But when I asked for them, Will said he was tired of carrying my things tent to wagon, wagon to tent, and I should make do with the tin."

She looked up at me, fresh tears starting. "Oh, Mrs. Daniels, I had so many nice things in London."

To me, it seemed she had brought them all. Rummaging around in the wagon with her, I was amazed at what Lucena had elected to bring to California. As we searched for the flour barrel in which she'd buried her blue dishes, I saw, besides the necessities of food and bedding, a box of music sheets, a complete set of Shakespeare's works, a looking glass and a Boston rocker Lucena said were wedding gifts she couldn't part with, silk shawls and velvet bonnets, and a trunk full of fancy dresses.

She pulled out a pretty black brocaded silk frock and held it up for me to see. "I shall wear this for my entrance to California," she said, brightening. "La, we must be presentable for the great occasion. I expect to astonish the natives."

For companion to the dress, Lucena exhibited a scuttle-shaped bonnet. It was a pretty thing, covered in lace and having a face wreath of tiny pink rosebuds, with a cluster of the same flowers to one side of the crown.

She beamed at it, fluffing the flowers. "Don't it just beat goose pie and applesauce?"

Just then Will stuck his head in through the back of the wagon and saw the spill our search had left. "Oh, Lucy, everything's all jumbled up. Now I've got to put it all to rights again."

Lucena glared at him, thrust the dress and bonnet back into her trunk, and slammed the top. "So you should have brought me the two plates and cups and saucers I asked for," she said, and burst into new tears.

The sight of his bride crying melted Will Semple like sun does butter. He climbed into the wagon, enfolded her in his arms, and kissed away her tears. "I promise never again to complain of your things. It will be my chief delight to tote them back and forth."

I was still smiling at the sweet scene of their making up, when I returned to our camp and found no one there. From the nearby tent of the Hoosier, though, I heard "O Susanna" awkwardly strummed on his banjo, signifying, as I supposed, the instrument's new recruit.

I peered through the tent flap and found Janey there, intent on her practice, her instructor singing along and keeping time as she played, slapping his hands on his knees. He stopped when he saw me, and Janey looked up, her face as full of concentration as when she sat on my mother's lap at the piano at three.

"Your playing's coming along nicely, dear," I said, grateful for the small happiness musical occupation brought her. "After your lesson's done, come help me make a skillet cake." I smiled at the Hoosier. "You'll have some, of course, with all of us. Little enough pay it is for your music lessons."

"It's nothin', ma'am," he said, "me bein' regular pleased to teach. But I don't pass up cake, nor visitin' with a regular family neither. My ma's got a passel a littl'uns, and I miss 'em."

He nodded at Hannah, who lay curled on a blanket at Janey's side, fast asleep.

I looked around for Hannah's twin. He was nowhere to be seen. I felt the first stab of anxiety. "Janey, where's your little brother? Where's George?"

She looked around, too, and jumped up. "Oh, Mama, he was right here a minute ago, napping with Hannah!"

"Where is he now? Where?"

Then all was panic and pandemonium. "My boy, my boy! Have you seen my boy?" I cried, racing from tent to tent, conjuring a rapid succession of disasters, imagining my cherub-cheeked George trampled beneath the hooves of horses, kidnapped into slavery, drowned in the river, every mishap and calamity a mother's mind invents on such occasions.

In my frenzied search I roused whole companies of Hoosiers, Yorkers, and Buckeyes. Half a dozen men remembered seeing the little fellow, but none knew where he was.

I had been raising an alarm for nearly half an hour when a tall old man with a magnificent white beard strode up with George riding on his shoulders.

"Heigh-ho and a how-dee-do! Francis Fogie, ma'am, last of the old Fogies. I reckon this here's the little character you been looking for." He nodded up at George, who was grasping handholds of white hair, his little face all delight.

Seeing my tears, Mr. Fogie apologized. "Sorry, ma'am," he said, his gnarled hands grasping the child's feet hanging over his shoulders. "I found the little fellow all tucked up in my buffalo robe, cozy as a bedbug. Wandered in sometime when no one was around and took himself a nice lay-down. Bold as Goldilocks, this one, eh?"

He loosened George's grip on his hair. "Down you go!" he said, stooping as I, babbling relief, reached for my little wanderer.

George squirmed from my grasp, faced his rescuer with a smile wide as the Missouri, and pointed at Mr. Fogie's beard. "Sandy Claus!"

The kind old man did seem to me, and Janey, too, St. Nicholas himself. In less time than it took to strike a match, we had him sitting by our new sheet-iron stove, drinking coffee, and picking skillet-cake crumbs from his beard.

When Caleb and Douglas returned from whatever errand claimed them that day, I was forcing a second helping on Mr. Fogie.

At their arrival, he rose and stuck out his hand to each in turn. "Heigh-ho and a how-dee-do! Francis Fogie, last of the old Fogies! Pleased to meet you!"

Douglas stared his amazement. Mr. Fogie was as old as anyone Douglas had ever seen. "You going to California, mister?"

Our new friend raised his tin cup of coffee in a salute. "You think there's a California, do you?"

"Why, sure," said Douglas, looking confused by the question. "That's where everybody's going."

Mr. Fogie set his coffee cup down on the stove and crossed his arms over his chest, capturing his beard beneath them. "Well, that's where they think they're going, but how do you know it's there? You ever seen California for yourself, boy?"

"No, sir."

"Then how do you know it exists?"

"Well, folks who've been there — "

"Heigh-ho!" Francis Fogie grinned and smacked his hands together like a boy catching a fly. "Folks who've been there, you say? Well, sure, any number of men and ships have set sail for California, but that's no sign they ever got there. They say so, of course, as no one likes to be humbugged. But for all anyone knows, they might just as well have gone to China!"

"You think California's a humbug?"

"I think the balance of probability is decidedly opposed to the existence of any such country." Mr. Fogie stroked his beard and winked a merry eye at Caleb and me.

Douglas caught the joke and grinned good-naturedly at the fun Mr. Fogie was having with him. "Well, we're going to California to get gold."

Mr. Fogie slapped his knees and laughed as though he'd just heard a fine joke. "Gold, you say! Even if there is a California," he said, shaking his head at Douglas, "there's no gold there, boy."

Douglas, to our amusement, got reeled in again. "Yes, sir, there is."

"No, sir, there isn't!"

"Well, if you don't even know if California exists, how can you know there's no gold there?"

Mr. Fogie laughed. "Oh, that's an easy one. It's mathematically impossible. A simple proposition will set the matter to rest at once."

Douglas saw that the old man was playing with him, and laughed too. "I'm pretty good with numbers, Mr. Fogie, so maybe you'll explain it to me."

Mr. Fogie, serious as a professor, placed a hand on Douglas's shoulder. "Happy to, boy. You see, the world has now existed, according to the strictest calculation, six thousand years, which being multiplied by three hundred and sixty-five, the number of days in a year, will give over two millions of days. On any one of them, the gold might have been discovered. The chances that it would not be discovered on the first day of the six-thousand-and-first year are two million to one. If we then take into account that during all this time the population of the globe has averaged about five hundred million, and that all this immense number has never made this discovery, the improbability that it should be made by a single individual is five hundred million to one. And these two chances multiplied together ought surely to satisfy any reasonable man that there is no gold there, and never has been!"

For the pleasure of Mr. Fogie's company, Caleb invited the two Germans he was traveling with to join the train he and Will Semple were making up. The Germans were brewers from St. Louis, where Mr. Fogie, a mule skinner seeking transportation to California for the adventure, had answered an advertisement for a driver. The Germans, who carried with them mash tuns, copper vessels, and the various other implements and ingredients necessary to their trade, knew nothing about mules or how to drive them. Their ignorance of animals Mr. Fogie tolerated more than their dispositions.

"Sour as green apples," he said. "Comes from drinking their own brew, is my guess, or maybe just from being Germans, poor fellows!"

Caleb and Will Semple enlisted a dozen or so wagons to make up our party, and each day the white-topped caravan advanced steadily toward the ferry. Craven Hester, a lawyer from Bloomington, with his wife, Martha, and their four children, joined us. Martha was nearly fifty and not well. Her boys, John and William, were strapping big fellows who helped her into and out of the wagon — good, dependable boys we were glad to have in the train. Fourteen-year-old Sallie Hester looked after her mother with the help of Lottie, her eleven-year-old sister. Sallie proved a

great steadiness for Janey when things got hard for us. I will always remember the girl with gratitude.

Among the others in that first train, which mostly dissolved before
we reached Fort Laramie, I knew best the childless couple, Phoebe and
Lewis Franklin.

The men of our initial company, concerned lest additional women
hamper the prompt morning starts necessary to fast travel, wished no
more families to join us. The Franklins had come from Canada, however, and passed muster for their experience, having traveled half a continent already. They drove a large express wagon with a tent strapped to
one side and bedding to the other. Lashed on behind were bundles,
pots, pans, and bags of feed for their animals. Emblazoned on their wagon
cover with axle grease were the words, "Have you saw the elephant?"

"What's that mean, Mama?" Janey asked.

We were standing in back of our own wagon, after handing in to
Douglas some new-sewn sacks for storing clothes.

"Everyone says it," Douglas answered, kneeling to talk to us out the
back of the wagon. He was getting so tall. "Means California mostly, Pa
says."

"It should be 'Have you *seen* the elephant,' shouldn't it, Mama?"
Janey didn't wait for my answer, knowing it. "But why does it mean
California?"

After the scare she caused in letting George wander, Janey talked to
me again as though I were forgiven for dragging her from home. We were
all beginning to enjoy the adventure, there being so many congenial
people to share it with.

"The expression means more than California," I said, "although that's
the point of it. We're all of us going to see California, and that's a wonder, isn't it? Remember when your father took us to Vandalia to see the
circus? Seeing the elephant was the most exciting part, because none of
us ever had. And there was just something so astounding and so wonderful about seeing something so extraordinary. That's how everyone feels
about California."

"Pa says that's where the saying comes from," Douglas added. "Seeing the circus."

"Your father and I heard a story at Vandalia, at the circus. It's one
everybody's heard, apparently. The way it was told us, a farmer who had
never seen an elephant heard the circus was coming to town. Probably
it's not a true story, but that doesn't matter. The farmer loaded his wagon
with vegetables to take to town and then go to the circus. But on the way,
he met the circus parade, led by the elephant. That strange animal so

scared the farmer's horses that they bolted, overturned the wagon, and spoilt all the vegetables. And the farmer is supposed to have said, 'I don't give a hang. I've seen the elephant.' "

"That's the way of it, yes," Phoebe Franklin said, joining us. "'Ceptin' seein' that elephant in a circus ain't no shadow on seein' California. Same principle though. Folks'll pay a mighty high price, more'n a wagonload of vegetables, to get a gander at California. Better'n the circus, gold is."

Phoebe Franklin, whose wagon cover caught the eye of many, was my age but stouter. And she was wild to get to California. Hers was as bad a case of gold fever as ever I saw.

"It'll be like gatherin' hen's eggs. I'll just be scoopin' those nuggets into my apron," she declared the day before we moved out.

"The reports of our President Taylor suggest the hope," I replied, "but there are a great many of us sharing it, don't you think?"

"Well, the numbers hereabouts worry me some. I'm fearful too many be ahead of us, gone by way of Independence or by ship, or whichever. And by the time we get to California, there won't be nothin' left worth pickin' up. But I'll tell you, Mrs. Daniels, there's more than one way to skin a cat. I've been figurin' how much I could earn me cookin' for these boys when they get to minin'. They won't be wantin' to stop for that chore. Or I could keep a boardinghouse for 'em. Or whatever else looks profitable. I figure I'll get my share of the rocks, one way or t'other."

Just hearing Phoebe talk induced the fever in me. None of us was really immune.

The evening before we crossed on the ferry, I wrote my mother the last letter I could reasonably expect her to receive until we reached California. I scratched away by the light of a lantern, long after my family slept, sharing descriptions of the families traveling in our train, the security and confidence we lent one another, Phoebe Franklin's great expectations. Hopeful these final assurances might lighten her fears for us, I repeated the particulars of Caleb's prudent arrangements. Our wagon was stoutly made. We carried with us all the provisions the guidebook advised, and more. We also had, as she knew, a thousand dollars stowed in a box Caleb constructed beneath the wagon bed, more than enough for any eventuality.

And then it was our last morning in St. Joseph and we were on our way, striking the tent, wrapping the canvas around its pole, loading all the last-minute things into the wagon, hanging the camp kettle on the side with the tar bucket and water bags. Janey tethered the milch cow to the rear, and I positioned the clever tin butter churn to hang in the bows to make butter by the motion of the wagon.

Mr. Fogie was behind us with the Germans' pack mules, each of which, as they approached the river, seemed possessed of a dozen legs, so constant was their excitement. Those mules kicked and turned and reversed again, exercising poor Mr. Fogie into considerable annoyance with the Germans for making a bad bargain in buying young, unbroken mules.

How very bad a bargain it was we would find out.

But at last our wagon was over and we were on the western bank of the Missouri, civilization at our back. I gave the letter for my mother over to the ferryman to send back to St. Joseph, having scribbled a final note on the bottom while on the river. I wanted to tell her about the colored man who told us he was going to California to get gold to redeem a wife and seven children. There was such a nobility about him and his cause that I blessed the discovery of California's gold that it could serve such good purpose.

I think I expended the remains of my courage, newfound or feigned, in writing that letter, for suddenly I was overcome by the enormity of our venture. I had been launched into the very wilderness my mother had spent her life fearing.

As if reading my thoughts, the ferryman, pushing off for the return, said, "You're in Nebraska Territory now. This is Indian country, folks. Good luck."

I felt myself go pale. Indians we had seen, of course, begging in the streets of St. Louis. We had even seen a whole caravan of Pottawatomi, a pitiful band, traversing St. Joseph with their overloaded, broken-down ponies. But the ferryman's warning conjured visions of murderous savages brandishing hatchets and strings of bloody scalps, and the image pierced me like an arrow.

Indian Territory

Calamity, I've learned, rarely arrives dressed in the garb we imagine for it. Our minds rehearse fearful inventions, but tragedy lurks elsewhere, preparing ambush.

How I squandered fear that first night on the prairie, certain as I was of Indian attack. My children were to me the most precious in the world, and to shield them from imaginary arrows, I crouched sleepless all night by the tent flap while they slept. Caleb, exhausted by the labor of the muddy road, slumbered unaware of my terror, while I fought the impulse to accost him with it.

Fortunately, my anxiety dissipated with the dawn, assisted in large part by the intimidating preparations of our men, and my fearful night remained my secret.

Everyone in our company was across the river. We had camped together about six miles up from the ferry and, as the guidebooks advised, formed our wagons into a corral to protect our stock. For the first day of travel, everyone wanted an early start, eager to see the path that would lead us to the elephant. Wearied by my long night of watchfulness, I was glad enough to dispense with baking fresh bread. I fixed a quick and tasty breakfast of pilot bread soaked in water and fried with bacon, then sweetened with molasses. Janey milked Emma and we had the sweet reward fresh with our coffee.

Afterward, while Janey dressed George and Hannah, and Douglas and Caleb packed the tent and mess things into the wagon, I looked for Lucena, to help me chase my ghosts. I found her leaning against her wagon, smiling at Will as he outfitted himself for defense. He wore a brace of holster pistols strapped around the waist of his pantaloons, a bowie knife stuck in his belt, and a rifle slung over his shoulder.

Seeing me, he slapped the gun's stock. "U.S. Army rifle. Caleb get one?"

"He bought a pair of Allen five-shooters, I think."

"Pepper boxes? He should have got himself one of these rifles from the war with Mexico." Will polished the barrel with his sleeve. "The government order to sell them to emigrants at cost was well publicized."

As her husband strode off to yoke up their team, Lucena shook her head and smiled. "A regular arsenal, ain't he? La, hope he don't hurt himself."

As it happened, Lucena's fears proved more legitimate than mine. The next evening one of our company set his gun against his wagon and while he was throwing out some bedding, the bundle struck the gun. It went off, and the charge hit his leg just below the knee, seriously injuring him.

As we traveled, we heard reports of several woundings by accidental gunshot, so heavily armed were the emigrants in their preparations for Indian encounters. A company of young men from Massachusetts even carried swivel guns in their wagons.

Indians there were, of course, a reduced people for the most part, sad-looking and starving. In the early days of travel they followed us like wary, whipped dogs. Whenever we stopped, they crept into camp to beg food and pilfer small things.

Some carried begging letters, written by white men, saying this was a good Indian and to give him something. These Indians were pitiful specimens and my heart went out to them. A few days of travel accustomed me to their presence, so I was not frightened when one evening, as I prepared supper, a pathetic-looking old man wrapped in a dirty blanket shuffled from the shadows. He handed me a grimy, folded piece of paper and nodded encouragement when I took it. Its scribbled message said, "This Injun is a lying thief. Shoot him."

I was heartsick that some emigrant should play so mean a trick. I gave the poor old Indian some hard bread and a tin cup of molasses, and put his begging letter in my apron pocket. I had hoped to keep it from him, but he refused to leave without it. I thought he might return my cup, but he didn't.

Near the Sac mission some better-looking Indians visited our camp and offered to ride and shoot on exhibition for ten cents. Several of the men keen to see them raised the ante forthwith. We all enjoyed the show, and the Indians proved more skillful than expected.

It was a Sunday, our first since leaving St. Joseph. After the exhibition, Caleb was arranging our departure when I realized his intent.

"Caleb, you don't propose to travel on the Sabbath?" My question surprised him.

"I do, if we're to put distance behind us."

"I object to it, Caleb. One day in seven can't make such a difference." I surprised myself, speaking up like that, being unaccustomed to it.

"Your objection being?"

"It's the Sabbath!"

"I never supposed you so religious, Sarah."

The truth was that at home I had always enjoyed church on Sunday, and a good sermon, but I was not particularly religious. That wasn't the point.

"I expect us to keep the Sabbath, Caleb, because that's what civilized people do. I'll talk to the other women. I expect they'll agree."

Although Phoebe Franklin wasn't eager to interrupt our daily advance, Lucena, Mrs. Hester, and myself were fixed on observing the Sabbath, and so Phoebe conceded. A few of the younger men grumbled at the delay when we announced it, but we women prevailed.

By way of showing our respect, several of us visited the Sac mission, it being nearby. The Presbyterians had built a handsome three-story stone-and-brick school for the Sac and Fox Indians. We had a good sermon there and the pleasure of hearing the Indian children sing.

From none of the Indians thus far encountered did we receive any threatening gesture. That our men should so have armed themselves against the people seemed absurd. The only occasion our company had for its weapons in our first days of travel came after crossing Wolf Creek.

River crossings were always difficult, especially where inclines went steep. At Mosquito Creek, the first river crossing on the road, our men had to cut brush and spread it over the inclines to keep the wagons from miring.

Where the road crossed Wolf Creek, however, some Sac and Fox Indians had either constructed a bridge or, more probably, as Craven Hester surmised, taken possession of it. In any event, what looked to be a hundred Indians had lined up along either side of the road leading to the bridge.

The sight of so many Indians should have sent ice water through my veins, but our visit to the mission had inclined me to the people. I believed they intended us no harm.

Ours was the first wagon in the train that day, the lead, by agreement, changing daily.

The Indians' spokesman pointed at our wagon and then at the bridge. "Two bits," he said.

The Indians, we had learned, knew all the words for money.

Craven Hester came up to see what the difficulty was, his wagon being next behind us.

The Indian pointed at the Hesters' wagon, and then at the bridge. "Two bits," he repeated, holding out his hand, palm up.

Caleb hollered back to the rest of the company, "The Indians are demanding toll! Two bits a wagon!"

The Indian nodded.

That was our company's first falling out, whether to pay the toll or not. It seemed a small thing. Unfortunately, some people nurse minor matters, then drag them out later, inflated to large resentments.

The older men, the married ones, were willing to pay, but some of the younger men argued against it and wanted to make a big show.

"Paying the toll for the convenience of the bridge," Caleb announced, "is no different than paying ferriage to the ferryman who brought you across the river."

"'Cept the ferryman weren't no Injun," growled a young man whose name I've forgotten.

Caleb and Craven Hester argued the fairness and won. We paid the toll, a few cents it was, and nothing worth arguing over. The problem came later that day when more Indians accosted us on the road and demanded toll for passing through their country.

"I'm not payin' again," said the young man who had spoken out earlier. "These look to me the same Indians, anyhow. Probably rode ahead on their ponies to get more dimes from us."

Will Semple, despite his armed preparedness for Indian troubles, argued peace. "Aw, let's not make no trouble here."

"I'm not makin' trouble. These redskins are askin' for it. This here's a free country, and no insolent red man has the right of it!"

And then suddenly the single men were brandishing pistols and rifles. "Out of the way, there!" they shouted at the Indians. "We intend to pass! If any among us should be molested, we intend to fire!"

Caleb had no choice, being first in line, than to go ahead. "Sarah, you and Janey and the twins get in the wagon till we're past this business," he said. "Douglas, you stay by me."

Seeing the Indians' disappointed faces, I said, "Caleb, can't you pay them a little something?"

He shook his head. "We have a necessity here to appear united."

All the women and children got in the wagons, even though we usually walked if the weather was good. Through the front of the canvas cover, I watched Douglas and Caleb goad the oxen into motion.

"They haven't much of anything, do they, Mama?" Janey said, peering out the back as our wagon rumbled between the double file of discouraged countenances. "It don't seem right."

"Doesn't," I said absently, searching for my reticule. I found the bag, opened the drawstring, and extracted a coin.

Janey, seeing my intent, said, "I have some coins saved up that Grandpa gave me for my birthdays. Can I give one?"

"This one will do," I said, handing it to her. "You just lift up the wagon cover a little, and drop it out the side."

"How do we know they'll find it?" she asked, doing as I instructed.

"We'll just hope so, Janey. That coin won't make any difference in those poor people's lives anyway, but at least we'll know we tried to be fair."

How innocent I was, to think fairness played a part in the scheme of things. Fate plays by no rules, as I learned at the Big Blue.

Ten days' travel brought us to that river, a beautiful, clear stream some forty yards wide, deep enough to touch the wagon beds but not swift. It was lined with the first trees we'd seen of any account. What a surprise the sight was, after more than a week of traveling over unbounded prairie.

Emigrants traveling ahead had stuck messages on nearly every tree, telling those of us behind of their passage. I was amused at one: "The Infantry Company F passed here; all well and in good spirits; plenty of game and good whiskey."

My amusement faded when I learned what "all well" meant. Lucena and I were wandering among the trees along the river when we found the graves. There must have been two dozen or more, all fresh.

"Only ten days out from civilization, and so many dead," I said, disbelieving my eyes. "How can it be?"

Lucena shook her head, speechless with the shock of our discovery.

Early the next morning, while Janey and Caleb packed the wagon and Douglas yoked up the oxen, I returned to the impromptu graveyard with my pencil and journal.

Caleb found me there, the wagon ready to go and I not returned. "What are you doing?"

I was crouched over a grave, recording a stranger's name from a scrap of board. "Someone should know the names of those left on the prairie, Caleb. I'm not sure what I think to do with them, perhaps give them to a newspaper in California, for families seeking news of a loved one. To know even the worst, is better than not knowing."

"Don't distress yourself with this, Sarah. Hundreds, thousands, are passing this way. It's inevitable some will die."

"I'm all right, Caleb, don't worry about me. I just want to do this."

Our company, excepting the man shot in the knee, were all well, but the next day we nooned near some emigrants decimated by illness. One of them, a distraught, hollow-looking man who said he had a sick wife and child, came into our camp looking for a doctor. The poor fellow had already buried his brother at Blue River. The name was in my journal.

Caleb made up a bag of our medicines and followed the man to his wagon. When he returned, he took me by the hand, saying nothing.

His look alarmed me. "Caleb, what is it? What is it?" I asked as he walked me away from the wagons.

When no one could hear us, he put his hands on my shoulders as though to keep me upright. "It's cholera."

I clutched his arms for support, feeling dizzy. As long ago as the epidemic in New York was, I remembered well the newspapers' horrifying description of the pestilence.

"Are you sure?"

He looked past me into the distance. "Yes."

"You can't be sure, you can't!"

"I can. I've seen the disease before."

I must have looked like I was about to cry out.

Caleb clapped his hand over my mouth. "Now, Sarah, listen to me. Cholera is not what you and your mother and your Boston grandmother think it is, some curse on the intemperate that infects anyone who associates with them. There is no shame in the disease."

I stared as he took his hand from my mouth. I didn't often feel anger, I had so little cause. But it rose then like a geyser. "Caleb Daniels, don't you lecture me! Here we are, out in the middle of nowhere, people sick and dying all around us. You don't know who these people are!"

"Listen to me, Sarah. Anyone can get cholera. Anyone. My father was a doctor. He and my mother died from it."

I felt as though I'd been shot, the jolt was that great. "But, the fever. In northern Illinois, you said — "

"No, your mother said. I never did."

"But, why — ?"

"I was too shamed to admit the truth, too shamed by my father."

"Shamed? I don't understand what you're saying, Caleb."

There was such a strange transformation of his expression then. I remember thinking I was gazing once again on the boy who stopped at our house that long ago August. I saw again the same soulful, melancholy eyes of that boy in the road. He looked so sad I thought for a moment he might weep, but he didn't. Men so seldom do. But his face suffused with grief, and it spilled into his voice.

"Oh, Sarah, it's so long ago." His eyes grew remote, as if he were seeing some faraway past, despite the firmness of his grip on my shoulders.

"Caleb?"

"My father was a doctor in New York when the cholera epidemic struck in 1832," he said, looking at me now. "He was convinced the disease was contagious, and for fear of it, he took my mother and me and fled the city."

"But — "

"Let me just say this out, Sarah, and be done with it. I was a student then, a medical student — "

I was stunned. "You never said — "

"Sarah, please, let me finish. I was idealistic, the way young medical students often are, with just one year completed at Harvard. I condemned my father's abandonment of the sick to save himself and his family."

Caleb put his hand to my back and slowly walked me with him into the tall grass off the road, where the animals hadn't foraged. That grass was so green, so tall. There was a springtime smell to it, like cut hay, from crushing it as we walked. And I remember, too, the sound of it swishing against Caleb's boots, and the insects flying up, and how the skirt of my dress looked against the green of that prairie grass. I was wearing pink — Portuguese pink, the color was called — in a rainbow print, stripe fading to stripe.

"My father took us north. We boarded a boat on the Erie Canal. But the disease followed, slaying the fleeing as impartially as the confined. Towns and cities along the canal invoked quarantine regulations. Families in flight of the pestilence leapt from halted canal boats and passed the locks on foot, despite contingents of armed militia to stop them. My father got us as far as Illinois before the disease overtook him, and then my mother."

Caleb stooped and plucked a long switch of grass. He tore it into little bits without looking at it. Neither of us said anything for a long time. I remember feeling dumbstruck by my husband's revelations. Married fifteen years, and I didn't know him at all.

Caleb tossed the bits of grass into the air. They swirled for a moment in the breeze, like insects. "I thought then that the failure of quarantines, and the unpredictable pattern of cases, argued against contagion. A couple of weeks ago, while we were in St. Joseph, I consulted with a physician who shared my suspicion that cholera possesses some specific cause and is not necessarily infectious."

"Cholera, yes, cholera," I said, remembering out loud why we were standing in this tall grass. I became aware of the sounds the insects made, the buzzing of bees and bottleflies. Back at camp, someone's mule set up a noisy braying.

"No one knows what causes the disease, Sarah, but I'm convinced it need not be fatal if its symptoms are arrested. I can take care of us. Trust me."

"Trust you? Caleb, I feel I hardly know you! Why didn't you ever tell me this before?"

"Sarah, you didn't ask and — "

"Ask? It wasn't my place to ask, it was yours to tell me! Why didn't you tell me?"

"I could say the same, Sarah. Why didn't you ask? It's the same coin."

That stopped me like a blow. He was right. It was the same coin.

And there it was. I hadn't asked anything of this man I'd married from propinquity and a melancholy resemblance to Byron because I was afraid. Afraid of what? Afraid he didn't love me? Hadn't really wanted to marry me? I don't know. I suppose I was just accustomed to being the mouse-coward.

I never looked at Caleb the same after that day. I didn't love him less, or even differently, although I wondered what else I might not know — or want to know — about him. But it seemed too late to ask.

And there was this: if Caleb wasn't who I thought he was, was I? I didn't have secrets from him, I thought, or did I? Every unasked question was a secret, and every unshared fear.

We were strangers to each other.

After that day, our years together in Illinois seemed to belong to people I once knew, like old friends who'd moved away. The life I'd left behind was all surface, mirror. And I stopped mourning for it.

Fort Kearny

Caleb's revelation overshadowed the fearful specter of cholera. For a few days I looked at him with new eyes, knowing him less and myself more. It was an odd perspective. My world felt bent. But I grew accustomed to the angle. Nothing remains a novelty long. We accommodate.

The St. Joseph road joined the main road from Independence about halfway to Fort Kearny. From this junction we would follow the Little Blue to the Platte. These rivers, and those lying ever westward, made the trip possible. Without this life-sustaining network of waterways, the nation's populace would have stayed east, stayed home, instead of moving west across half a continent. I rued geography as much as gold.

The nation didn't stay home, of course. The numbers of wagons on the road where ours joined the one from Independence astonished us. Douglas counted ninety ox teams in one string alone.

"Looks like the whole world is going to market, don't it?" Janey said.

"Doesn't it," I said, and meant it.

Along the road we saw bits of paper, cards, and broken boards stuck on trees, as we had at Blue River, notices of who had gone ahead, offers of rewards for lost animals, directions to a good spring or campsite. We called these roadside signposts the "prairie post office." The frequency of medical advertisements by one Dr. J. Noble, written in bright red ink, however, provoked annoyance after a time. Then Will Semple, satisfying our collective irritation, regularly began printing under the doctor's familiar red signature "Is a Jackass."

Graves continued to line the road, but I grew accustomed to them. We all did. Familiarity draws the potency from things, sucks away the awe of them.

I faithfully added names to my journal, names from scraps of wagon board, some carved, others painted with axle grease, and fastened to a cross of sticks or broken tent poles to mark the spot where some luckless emigrant ceased westering. Most markers reported only names and dates, age, sometimes the place of origin. Others offered explanations: "Shot Himself Accidentally," "Drowned," "Cholera."

In those early days we witnessed burials with ceremony. On one occasion, a fanfare of trumpets. Another time, we passed a company of young men laying a colleague to rest with such regard I remarked it in my journal. They all wore clean clothes and marched two by two to the odd accompaniment of a bugle, a flute, and a violin.

A decent interment required a coffin then, got up from tailgates or packing boxes, and, of course, a few appropriate remarks and a prayer. Later, haste replaced respect.

Despite almost daily reminders of our journey's dangers, we enjoyed its pleasures. How lovely was that springtime on the prairie! Perhaps death sharpened my sensibilities, but I came to believe I'd never before experienced sky so blue, clouds so white, flowers so beautiful, grass so fragrant and green, or breezes so gentle.

The valley of the Little Blue was a sight for angels, the stream fringed with oak, willow, and cottonwood, the uplands one vast rolling meadow alive with wild turkey, deer, antelope. And flowers! How I delighted in the flowers – wild roses, pink pea vines, morning glories, and a large yellow flower resembling a hollyhock. I felt a tug of homesickness for the garden left behind, the pink roses arching over the doorway, the scarlet runners on the fence, but their tameness paled in contrast with this vast and rampant Eden.

I felt an expansiveness just witnessing such unbounded beauty. How my father would have loved seeing it. I think I understood a little then the magnet drawing men west. Perhaps something of my father's dream had seeded itself in me after all, despite Mother's constant weeding. I understood a little, too, of Caleb's exhilaration in being part of this great migration. There was something heady in our thousands moving together across this magnificent landscape.

I was not alone in my enjoyments. Lucena, Phoebe, and I often walked together over the rolling prairie, admiring the scenery, sharing little hopes and confidences. Excepting river crossings, stormy days, or supposed threat from Indians, most emigrants, other than very young children and invalids, walked to spare the animals. This outdoor life, despite the omnipresent graves, was paradoxically healthful. Even Martha Hester, within two weeks of leaving St. Joseph, could walk two miles each day and get in and out of her wagon spry as a girl.

On one particularly fine day, the four of us walked most of the morning together. I remember gathering a bouquet of wildflowers I carried like a bride while Phoebe Franklin recited her California ambitions.

"A boardinghouse might should be the best way," she said, anticipating how to fill her flour barrel with gold dust fastest. "Lewis heard a woman in California can be makin' sixteen dollars a week cookin', and that from each man!"

She clasped her hands behind her and gazed up at the blue sky, the breeze fluttering the strings of her sunbonnet. I could see her calculating in her mind how many men she could cook for.

We were climbing a small rise. Martha Hester, pleased not to be winded, said, "I enjoy this journey more each day. And it is not so solitary as I feared."

"Solitary, Mrs. Hester? La, I should say not," Lucena said, glancing over her shoulder at the way we had come. "Just look at all these people."

We all turned to look. From the vantage of our rise, we could see, as far as the eye encompassed, people and animals and every manner of wagon, carriage, and cart, all hurrying forward.

"The multitude that is going is astonishing," said Martha. "I wonder that anyone has been left behind."

Phoebe Franklin shook her head and repeated her constant fear. "If half these people get ahead of us, there won't be nothin' left in California worth the pickin' up."

We continued over the rise, and there discovered a grave, a double one. It unsettled us all. The marker named a man and wife, buried together. We later learned they'd died of cholera and left two children their company sent back to St. Joseph with an Indian chief.

A feather mattress lay atop their final resting place. We stared at it, each, I suppose, imagining our own featherbeds.

Lucena broke the silence. "From such a number it must be expected some will die."

It was what she always said, had said ever since Jefferson City. But this time her voice trembled, and I saw she was no stronger than I, only more practiced at pretense.

I placed my gathered wildflowers on the double grave. "Yes, but it is hard to part with them here."

From the beautiful valley of the Little Blue, we traversed strange clay hills destitute of vegetation and from them had our first view of the Platte. It was like no river I'd ever seen, and I didn't like it. Perhaps I had a premonition.

The Platte River valley was six or seven miles wide, the river itself one or two. And the whole of it, the Platte included, was flat as a table-top. Excepting some wooded islands in the river, no timber lined its bank, not so much as a willow switch. In fact, the stream had almost no bank, it ran so near ground level. And its dominant shade was yellow. The Platte wasn't a normal river. We were right to despise it.

Fifteen miles up, at the head of Grand Island, lay Fort Kearny, in process of establishment by the government to subdue the warring Sioux and Pawnee. It had assumed, in my anticipation, a wonderful proportion. Never having seen a fort, I expected palisades and barricades.

"Why it's nothing more than a miserable little collection of tents and sod houses," I said to Caleb, my hopes for a sight of civilization dashed.

Our company camped about halfway between the river on our right and the fort to the left, among some five or six hundred wagons that had stopped. We learned there was a store of sorts, open to emigrants, and Caleb wanted to buy more medicines. Leaving the children to visit with Mr. Fogie, whom they adored, the Semples and I joined Caleb in a tour of discovery.

On exploring the fort, we found the place consisted of tents for the enlisted men, plus sod houses for the officers and a boarding-house kept by a Mormon family. There was, in addition to the store, a blacksmith's shop, a horse-drawn sawmill, and a frame hospital under construction.

"I think the place badly misnamed," I said. "It offers nothing in the shape of a fortification, not a wall or a picket."

Caleb agreed. "Had the government wished to awe the Indians, a moving company of dragoons would have been more serviceable."

Still, there was a novelty in these buildings, poor as they were. It was curious to see something stationary on a landscape that for the past three weeks had seemed constantly in motion, it being dominated by emigrants on the move.

We found the store easily enough. A hundred or more emigrants congregated in its vicinity. The prairie emporium did not impress us. Like much of the fort, it was constructed from blocks of sod laid up in the manner of bricks. The previous day having rained, the dirt floor sucked at our shoes and boots, and moisture seeped from the ceiling.

"La, another good rain might well wash the whole affair away," Lucena said, peering up at the water dripping down on us.

The store was, however, well stocked. Caleb bought medicines at fair prices and could have bought flour, bacon, and dried beef for half what he paid in St. Joseph.

"Most you folks overloaded," the sutler explained. "Come here lightenin' up, sellin' cheap. Bought what I could, more'n I can sell."

Will, hoping to lighten his own wagon load, tried to persuade Lucena to sell some of her things at Fort Kearny. "We could part with that rocker, I 'spect," he said, testing the waters.

Lucena's look closed the subject.

The fort's quartermaster visited the store while we were there, and the crowd took the opportunity to bombard him with their worries about Indians. We were in Pawnee country now, a tribe known to be troublesome.

"The Pawnee and Sioux," the quartermaster said, raising his hands to fend off questions, "are off fighting each other somewhere distant from the road. You should not expect to be annoyed."

"Do you have some idea of how many wagons have passed the fort?" Caleb asked.

Our participation in a grand enterprise disposed him to the journey as much as ever. We all wondered the emigrants' numbers, there being so many ahead on the road and as far behind as the eye could see. At night, campfires dotted the landscape multitudinous as stars.

"We here have counted, exclusive of government vehicles, nearly four thousand wagons thus far," the quartermaster said, confirming our suspicions. "Figuring four men to a wagon, that would be sixteen thousand, and perhaps as many behind as ahead. These figures represent only the road south of the river. The Mormons and others moving out of Council Bluffs travel the north side of the Platte, and we have no fair estimate of their numbers."

While Caleb further engaged the quartermaster in discussion, I inspected the sutler's provisions. It was a novelty, after three weeks on the road, to see shelves stocked with cigars and sardines and a dozen fine things. I was examining a tin of sardines when I overheard a chilling remark.

"This vast crowd cannot possibly get across the mountains in safety."

I turned to see a rough-looking man in dirty buckskins talking to some emigrants.

"These two roads flanking the Platte, the north and south, unite at the base of the mountains, and then the whole migration will roll along over the same road," he said, forming an arrow with his hands. "At a moderate calculation there will be some twenty-five thousand persons and sixty thousand animals upon it. The leading trains will doubtless succeed, but those behind will find the grass gone, and their teams must then fail."

As we returned to our wagon, I nervously repeated the conversation to Caleb. Fear still lurked behind my composure like a bandit, ready to steal it. Caleb carried a package of medicines wrapped in oilcloth and two tins of peaches. He stopped in the middle of a crowd heading for the store, handed me the package, and grasped my shoulders.

"Sarah, I wouldn't have let you and the children come if I didn't think we could get through safely. Trust me."

"But the man said — "

"You can't believe everything you hear. Most of it's rumor and half the rest supposition."

"But — "

"Sounds to me, from the description, you were taken in by some old mountain man hired for a guide. There's no guiding to be done, so he's trying to scare folks into turning around, to leave more gold for those paying him."

"The quartermaster said — "

"We know we're ahead of half those coming from St. Joe and must be well ahead of most companies out of Independence because Captain Van Vliet, the quartermaster, told me the Pioneer Line is not yet arrived here and they expected to make the journey fastest."

I remembered the young man who assisted us near Vandalia. If the Pioneer Line, promising a journey of sixty days, was behind us, we must be in front with those the mountain man said would succeed.

Mr. Fogie had picketed his still fractious mules in the luxuriant bottoms grass growing along the Platte. We found the children with him there.

"Heigh-ho!" he said. "I was about telling the tykes here on the great western peetrification, which I've every confidence you will confirm as scientific fact."

Caleb laughed. "And what 'peetrification' might that be, Mr. Fogie?"

"Why, the very peetrification reported by Bridger, old Gabe himself. And mountain men never lie, no sirree, they don't," Mr. Fogie said, boosting George onto his shoulders.

Holding George's feet while my son tangled his little hands in the old man's white hair, Mr. Fogie strolled solemnly back and forth before Douglas and Janey. Hannah came to me and I knelt to hug her. She was getting brown as a berry. All the children were. They looked wonderfully healthy.

"Yes, sir," Mr. Fogie said to Douglas, "Old Gabe told me personally about a land of peetrified trees way out west. Filled with peetrified birds on the branches, singing peetrified songs. Heigh-ho! Peetrification there is so far advanced that a mountain man who carelessly rode over the lip of a chasm was saved only because gravity itself had peetrified!"

Douglas laughed, and Janey looked dubious. Mr. Fogie did a little jig while George squealed his delight. "Heigh-ho! That's the truth, because mountain men never lie!"

Mr. Fogie lifted George from his shoulders and hugged him.

"Sandy Claus!" said George, and pulled the old man's beard.

Most of our company agreed to stay over at the fort an extra day. Mr. Fogie wanted to recruit his mules, hoping to forestall the galling he said was inevitable to young mules unaccustomed to hard use. Craven Hester needed some blacksmith work done. And we could all write letters. A Fort Kearny officer took mail twice a month to Independence.

I suspected the numbers of emigrants fallen to cholera must be filling newspapers throughout the States, and my mother no doubt worried we were among them. A letter would ease her mind. We were, after all, every one of us perfectly fine.

The women were happy for an extra day to wash clothes and cook up a pot of beans at one fire for the next day's travel. Usually we cooked our beans in installments.

Camp cooking taxed everyone's skills, our provisions being so limited and the fare accordingly monotonous. Our meals mostly consisted of saleratus bread started in the morning and baked at night in the Dutch oven, plus a steady diet of oatmeal or corn mush, stewed dried apples, skillet cakes, rice, beans, bacon. Our family had the advantage of milk and butter from our milch cow, and a larger variety of provisions, but some emigrants only varied their meals, as one young man complained, "by having bacon with bread instead of bread with bacon."

Along the Platte, having left timber behind us, we used the dried dung of buffalo for fuel. Janey and the twins collected the chips in muslin bags. If sufficiently dry, the chips kindled readily, producing an intense heat and little smoke. The smell was not so terrible.

Douglas found good water at a spring. Platte River water was nearly worthless. Being shallow and fast moving, the river carried a thick sediment.

"Too dirty to bathe in and too thick to drink," Will Semple said of it.

The prize presentation of our meal that evening was the peaches Caleb bought, which we served with a little cream, courtesy of our cow,

Emma. We carried no tinned foods because of the weight, so the peaches made an especial treat. Another was wild onions I found growing near the river. I cooked them up with bacon as accompaniment to a roasted sage hen.

Caleb had bought me a little "tin kitchen" in St. Joseph, a tin cylinder, open on one side, with a cupped bottom and a handle. With the open side exposed to a campfire, it cooked a sage hen or other small fowl while the reflecting tin roasted the other side.

We had the usual saleratus bread, with butter churned from the morning's travel, and for dessert I made a pie from dried pumpkin. My beans enjoyed a long, slow simmer and cooked thick enough that, when cold, I formed them into a loaf to eat next evening sliced on bread.

All of our company staying over luxuriated in a meal prepared at leisure, with delicacies, for those who could afford them, from the sutler's store. Lucena had bought a cheese there, but Will gave it to Mr. Fogie's mules.

"That cheese should have been mustered out of the fort long ago," Will complained. "It was too old to be in service."

Lucena prepared a syllabub for us all to try, a sweet drink popular in England. Interested, I watched her mix together in a large tin bowl a half pound of white sugar with a pint of sweet cider, to which she added some grated nutmeg and stirred in three pints of fresh milk bought from the Mormon family at the fort.

"La, drink up before the froth subsides," she said, handing me a cup.

I liked it, but her ginger cookies were better. She made them by first boiling a teacup of molasses with two spoonfuls of butter, plus one of ginger and one of saleratus. When hot, she added the mixture to flour to make a dough, rolled it thin, and cut it in rounds to bake in her Dutch oven.

Janey was nibbling one of those cookies like a mouse, to make it last, when a young man stumbled into our camp, nearly overturning the lantern balanced on the tailgate. It was late, the twins already asleep in the wagon, and the rest of us sitting around the dying buffalo-chip fire.

"You the doc?" he asked Caleb.

"What's the trouble?" Caleb said, standing.

"I shot my friend, some accidental like. Don't look too bad, but he could use him a doc, I reckon."

"Just happen, did it?" Caleb asked. "And not serious?"

We had heard a gun, but the discharge of firearms was so regular we paid no attention.

"Yessir. Both a' that."

Caleb, holding the lantern up to the back of the wagon, peered in, wanting his medicine box.

"I'll hold the lantern, Caleb," I said, and took it from him.

"You want to come, Douglas?" Caleb asked, finding the medicines. "Might interest you."

"Don't like seeing blood, Pa. I guess not."

"I'll go," I said. "You'll want the lantern."

I'd never before witnessed Caleb in such circumstance. I remember holding the lantern above the young man stretched out on a buffalo robe, his shoulder bleeding into it a dark, wet stain. And Caleb leaning over him, gently probing the wound. He spoke soft assurances, and I saw his patient's fright turn to trust.

Caleb exhibited such confidence, such earnestness. I was fascinated by his steady certainty, by how the task consumed his attention. He looked like he'd been doctoring all his life. Or like he should have been.

"That thick buffalo robe you had on slowed the ball some," Caleb said, stanching the bleeding. He treated the wound with sulphur from his medicine box and bandaged it with clean sheeting. "Count yourself lucky for it."

"Been luckier without it."

"That's right," his friend said. "Stupid trick, Lorenzo. Reckon you won't come creepin' up on the camp guard tomorrow night, pretendin' you're some dumb buffalo. He might shoot better'n me."

On the way back to our wagon, Caleb talked about blood and humors and medicines, as engrossed as a professor. And I remember thinking how life had cheated him, made him a wagon builder. So much unused promise. I hoped he didn't think of it that way, being cheated of himself. How many of us know our capability until called to it?

Caleb seemed to me more and more a stranger, he assumed such new dimensions. I would not before have called him tentative, but perhaps untested. All those years in Illinois he had been a steady, quiet man, building wagons. If he harbored discontent, he never betrayed it, and I was never one gifted at seeing more than presented itself. But he seemed to me now someone else, inhabiting Caleb's body but entirely different.

Seeing him doctoring enlarged my husband before my eyes, and I was struck anew by how quickly he had risen to the journey's responsibilities. I hadn't taken much note when he and Will Semple organized the company in St. Joseph, but as my husband formed up the train at Fort Kearny, I saw him with fresh eyes. He had the respect of everyone and by assumption was granted the position of wagon master. He shared the responsibilities, such as they were, with Craven Hester. The lawyer's age and position merited deference and consultation, which he dispensed affably but without expectation. Neither Mr. Hester nor Mr. Fogie, who knew more about this outdoor way of life than any of us, evinced interest in leading the train. Mr. Fogie's obligation to the quarrelsome Germans and their intractable mules consumed his energies, and he was happy to have Caleb select campsites and start times and make the mollifications necessary to keeping harmony among strangers.

A number of young men in our company had objected to staying an extra day at Fort Kearny. Those traveling with the man who had shot himself in the knee left their injured companion at the fort's hospital and announced their intention to move on. Others went, too: those who complained that women held up travel, those opposed to observing the Sabbath, those who grumbled still about "Indian lovers."

Fort Kearny saw a general reorganization of companies as differences, impatience, irritations, and just plain general annoyance divided companies and reformed others with fresh expectations.

It was at Fort Kearny that Big Mary joined us.

I remember Big Mary well. Anyone would. I should think of her as Captain Mary, I suppose. It has more respect in it. And we all respected her, especially after she got the company across the river and down the road into Ash Hollow.

At Fort Kearny when we first met her, she was traveling with only two other wagons — the people, like herself, originally from the Scandinavian countries — that she had gotten together in a small town in Missouri. One of these wagons belonged to a family with a lively little girl named Mary. It was to distinguish the child from the woman that the name Big Mary attached, but only in part.

Big Mary was the largest woman I had ever seen, nearly six feet tall and proportionately broad of shoulder. She was Danish, really quite fine-looking despite her size, with big, clear blue eyes and blonde hair she wore cut short. She traveled in a small wagon of her own and drove two big oxen so well trained they obeyed her every command.

Big Mary wore, as a matter of course, a man's wide-brimmed black hat, a coarse brown shirt, and baggy trousers she tucked into the top of heavy men's boots. When we met, I surveyed her costume with such poorly disguised surprise that she laughed her full, rich laugh and announced with heavy accent, "I got me no intention, Missus Daniels, to be hampered by skirts on such a trip."

Reflecting on it now, it seems odd to think I was taken aback by Big Mary. She wasn't the first independent woman I'd met. There had been the mantua-maker, with nieces who worked in the mills at Lowell. But

Big Mary wore pants, and she thought herself capable of doing anything a man could do. I thought her extraordinary.

Lucena looked at Big Mary sideways when they met. "La, she's all sixes and sevens, ain't she?" she said to me later.

I secretly admired her.

As we left Fort Kearny, Caleb's unwavering confidence bolstered mine. I jettisoned fear like excess baggage and let the tedium of travel absorb me. I held in my imagination only the next outpost of civilization, Fort Laramie, three hundred miles ahead.

Almost at once we began seeing barrels of bacon and sacks of flour abandoned along the road by overloaded emigrants. These discards, and graves marked by buffalo skulls, added variety to the treeless road and monotonous landscape. I recorded the names of the dead in my journal, trudged alongside the wagon, and took my turn at driving the oxen whenever Caleb, hearing of illness in a train ahead or behind, left to dispense his medicines. He reported to me symptoms and recoveries, his expression solemn but his interest constantly aroused. I listened with rapt adoration, admiring this remarkable man I'd married, and tried not to think of all the possibility buried in a wagon-making shed.

Each day resembled the next — up at four, on the road by six, noon for up to three hours midday to rest the animals, then move on again till evening.

The road along the Platte added to our monotony. Wide as a boulevard, it was in places as level and smooth as a plank floor, so beaten down was it by animals. In other places, grooves precise as a spade cut, fifteen inches wide and four deep, sliced across the road like plowed furrows. Mr. Fogie told us buffalo had formed them over the years, heading this way to the river to drink. The sight of those shaggy beasts at a distance enlivened us one day, and some men in our company rode out to hunt them, without success.

Eventually, even prairie dog towns failed to excite us from our stupefying boredom. We grew accustomed to their high-pitched barking as they scurried around their villages, and to seeing them perched upright and motionless at the edge of their holes, watching us pass by.

Only the novelty of mirage relieved the tedium of our travel. Fantastic apparitions lifted from the hazy distance. We all saw them. I often perceived the wagons ahead of us reflected in the air. They looked like moving specters. Sometimes we saw lakes, and sailing vessels on them manufactured from ox wagons or sand bluffs. The endless shimmering valley hypnotized us. We were all afflicted with drowsiness anyway, from too little sleep, but here the effect doubled and trebled.

In such a state of mind, even the real seems transmuted into something imaginary. Which is why I could not believe, as I walked behind
the wagon with Janey on a day that seemed like any gone before, that I
was actually seeing one of the Germans' mules dashing loose past our
wagon, kicking at its slipping pack. It was not real that the bucking mule
startled our oxen. It was not true that I saw the alarmed oxen wheel
about, jolt the wagon into a near upset.

And I could not believe, ambushed as I was by unrehearsed tragedy,
that I saw George fall from the wagon. And the great heavy wheels roll
slowly over his little body.

George

My George died where he fell, his head in my lap, incomprehension clouding his four-year-old eyes as he looked up at Mr. Fogie kneeling beside me. "Sandy Claus," he said, a bubble of blood gurgling from his mouth with his last words.

Mr. Fogie began to cry.

Hannah pulled at her brother's hand. "Up, get up, Geordie." Janey, face white with horror, walked her away.

I remember Douglas groaning, "Ma, oh, Ma," and Lucena and Mrs. Hester making consoling sounds, and Big Mary, with her accustomed practicality, saying "I'll dig the grave," and then Caleb running up and people making way for him and his face going white as I stared at him, our dead son in my lap, my skirt red with his blood.

I didn't blame anyone. Not Mr. Fogie, the mule, the oxen, not even Caleb for pressing our destinies into this dangerous drive west. At least not then, not at that moment, when I clung to my child. I had no feeling for blame, no thought for feeling. Sensation fled, left me vaporous, as though I and all this unreal scene were mirage.

Someone pried my fingers from George's tiny shoulders and wrapped him in a blanket. I think it was Caleb. And someone else made a coffin. It looked like a provision box. At the sight of it, I felt a rupturing in my throat and heard a terrible guttural, almost animal, noise escaping some dark place.

As the women hushed and petted me into silence, I became aware of a steady, scraping sound nearby.

It was Big Mary's spade.

"No!" I screamed. "No! Not here! Not here!"

Excepting the demented, insanity is not a maintainable state of mind. Insanity is, I think, a luxury. And ours was a journey without luxuries. I could not afford insanity.

We buried our child in a shallow grave, with little ceremony beyond a simple prayer. I stand witness to this: there is no greater sorrow. For a mother to watch her child buried is a grief beyond tears. And I shed none.

The sun glared overhead as I stared at the mounded sand, watching the wind lift it in puffs, and knew then my mother's fear for us had been born in Ohio. I had never understood before. How could I? Words, just words, the burying of her son, my brother. Words are as nothing to the experience, as removed from the thing described as shadow from substance. How had she survived it?

To turn one's back, to walk away, to leave in the earth the blood of one's blood, the flesh of one's flesh, alone in the wilderness. How was it possible?

I looked around, tried to memorize the landscape, how the road ran, the distance to the river, the furrow of buffalo tracks crossing the road. I feared memory would make of my child's grave just one more in the anonymous multitude lining the road, that I would not recall this place, this particular spot in the world where last I saw his sweet face, where he lay, wrapped in a blanket, buried in a provision box.

It was such a solitary place. How alone he would be. Would his spirit cry out for me from the grave when buffalo trampled above, or the river flooded, or wolves came digging? Would he cry for the family that had abandoned him to the sandy wastes of the Platte River valley, to an eternity alone beneath the soil of Nebraska Territory?

I couldn't leave the grave, that small mound at my feet. Lucena and Will and the Hester family remained last as the company dispersed, speaking softly their sympathy and kindness. Mr. Fogie had stood at a remove, stooped with grief, looking more ancient than his years. The Germans shouldered him into motion, and he slouched away.

Big Mary took charge, formed the company up, and eventually everyone but us moved out, the teams hooking a wide arc around our wagon, leaving in their wake dust settling into dust.

The creaking of the company's wagons and the plodding hooves of their animals faded into the distance beneath the cloudless blue of a June sky. Our wagon stood solitary in the road, the oxen and our milch cow patiently waiting. And by that wilderness grave our family remained gathered still, immobile from loss.

Confused, Hannah repeated in bewildered complaint, "Get up, Georgie, get up."

Caleb, firm throughout the burial, doing what had to be done, now, at Hannah's words, sobbed a grief unbearable to watch. The children retreated to the wagon so as not to see it.

And then, still dazed with disbelief, I took Caleb's hand and together we turned our backs on our buried child.

I remained in a stupor for days. Everything looked unreal to me, cast in a strange light. I have from my journal, and faint memory, but small recollection of the journey between George's grave and Fort Laramie, where poor Celia saved me from hating Caleb. A scrawl across those pages, looking not my own, tells me I noted little but Janey's crying, the Sioux village, crossing the Platte, Ash Hollow.

I remember mainly the Sioux village, or think I do. The memories may be Douglas's, borrowed by me. He refreshed them for me last week, when he brought us strawberries, the first of the season. He visits as often as he can, to make up for Janey's being gone.

The strawberries are lovely. They perfume the house. The fruit here in California is beautiful, perfectly formed and large, I suppose from the earth being all but virgin until recent times.

"Douglas, do you remember the Sioux camp on the Platte?" I asked, hulling the berries in the lap of my apron as he sat in my rocker watching you sleep.

"Never forget it, Ma."

"Were there a great many lodges?"

"Big encampment, conical lodges of dressed buffalo hides painted with red designs. I'd guess maybe two hundred men, women, and children wearing skins and blankets and traded-for emigrant clothing."

I don't know if I remember that or not. My memories may be his, collected from his talk and gathered into the place where mine should be. They seem too vivid, too colorful, to be my own from a time otherwise overwhelmingly gray. They have sharp edges.

For many weeks after George's death, everything appeared indistinct to me. If I were not so positive I never cried, I would say I saw the world through tears. Perhaps, in times of unbearable sorrow, the soul weeps, distorting perception with tears from the heart.

"I carry a vague picture in my mind of Indian babies in willow baskets," I said, "and the baskets being attached to long poles. And dogs. There were dogs, weren't there?"

Douglas nodded. "Harnessed to those long poles. The dogs pulled the babies in the baskets around the village."

"Yes. The dogs were large, black, and woolly-looking."

I think this is my own memory. The babies would have attracted my attention.

"Remember, Ma, the fellow who joined our train at Fort Kearny — "

"No, I don't remember any of them." Not by name or face. They had all begun to look alike, those young men disguised by their beards and dusty slouch hats.

" — the one that carried trinkets for trading. Had a sack of beads, mirrors, Jews' harps, tin horns, harmonicas."

"Maybe." But I didn't think so.

"He demonstrated the musical instruments, don't you remember? Amazed an old chief in a feathered headdress. The chief's face was streaked with smears of red, yellow, and black paint."

A ceremonial assistance, Douglas said, in support of braves gone to make war on the Pawnee. I believe it was a memory I had from Douglas, because of the color and edges to it, like the Indians prancing about, tooting tin horns.

Douglas laughed. "After tootling on the horn, our emigrant held the instrument to the old chief's lips and made blowing noises, which the chief understood to copy. The old Indian blew, his eyes growing wide with surprise. He danced a merry circle in the sand as he tooted. He was so delighted by his musical abilities on the horn, he insisted on extending his skill, and mastered next, to his own satisfaction at least, a harmonica."

I passed a bowl of strawberries to Douglas, my fingertips pink from the sweet juice spilled in hulling. "I think I remember painted-up old men, a few women in colorful shawls of cotton and wool, and a clutch of little brown children — "

Douglas took the bowl. "All clamoring to become musicians. A generous distribution by our trader mustered up an instant orchestra, instigating such a tootling and whistling and squealing and squeaking as we never heard."

And perhaps I didn't hear it. The recollection has too much curiosity in it to be mine.

Curiosity had fled me, along with feeling, when we buried George. It was then I began my steady descent into a sensation — if the absence of sensation can still be called that — I can describe only as hollow.

I walked and talked, did the cooking and washing, but as though I no longer inhabited my body. Which is why, I think, my memory of that time is so vague. I amassed recollections at a remove even though attending to daily necessities.

And still I scrawled in my journal the heart-numbing record of other families' deaths I insisted on keeping. I think it was on one of those days I knelt over a grave that I first noticed Janey crying.

"Mama," she said, leaning over me, "why do you do that?"

And she was crying so, her pretty blue eyes all puffed and red-rimmed.

"Don't cry, Janey, please don't cry. Please stop."

"Why do you do that?"

"Someone needs to," I said, copying the name. And then I looked at her hard. "Are you always crying, Janey? I think you are, aren't you? Don't do that. Please."

"I can't help it, Mama."

"You should try, dear."

"I wish we could go home is all."

"Oh, Janey, if wishes were horses, beggars would ride."

That must have been about the time we crossed the Platte. From Fort Kearny we had followed the river's south fork, but it was the north fork that led farther west, and we had to cross the south fork to get to it. Crossing the Platte was an unwelcome challenge most emigrants put off until there was no choice. It was a treacherous river, promising accidents and drownings. For most of its length the Platte flowed more than a mile wide, its course capricious and its murky bottom an unpredictable two to fifteen feet deep, the drops dangerous and invisible. There was no safe place to ford it. Even our guidebook abandoned us here.

The morning we readied for the crossing, I remember sitting on a box next to our empty wagon, unloaded in preparation for raising its bed. Douglas sat with me, the guidebook open on his lap, searching its advice, while I stared out at the wide expanse of the Platte. It shimmered a sunlit ribbon over the treeless prairie, its islands green as emeralds. It was a splendid sight, I suppose, to anyone not required to cross it. It filled me with dread.

Douglas had assumed most of the responsibility for driving our team. With Caleb off doctoring so much, or maybe just avoiding me, I leaned on my son, I realize now, from the habit of deferring to a man for advice. I'm shamed by it. I was the parent, and he but a fourteen-years boy.

"There's no fixed crossing place," Douglas said, closing the book. He stared at the river with me. "All it says is that crossing places change frequently during the season, and folks should get over where they can."

The wagons and teams of several companies lined the broad approach to the river, organizing, like us, for the crossing. Out in the water, a dozen white canvas-topped wagons bobbled like sailing ships in a wind, pulled by immense processions of oxen. Shouting men on horseback splashed alongside, urging them on.

In my imagination each wagon contained children about to fall out and drown. I looked around in sudden panic for Janey and Hannah, and with relief saw them with Mrs. Hester at her wagon. Bless the women, I thought.

I didn't know where Caleb was — probably tending someone's sickness, probably cholera. The disease still raged. Numerous graves gave it mute testimony, but I no longer paid the illness much attention. Like insanity, perpetual fear is not a maintainable state of mind.

I wondered, when I thought about it later, if he was trying to redress the life lost by doctoring others. But I didn't think about it much then. I was half glad for his absence. Since burying George, Caleb and I hadn't been comfortable together, couldn't look into each other's eyes. Our mutual avoidance plowed the field in which I was planting acrimony.

After George's death Caleb all but abandoned captaincy of the company. Not formally, more by neglect. He didn't offer it to anyone. It simply escaped his mind. And no man assumed it, not Craven Hester, or Mr. Fogie, or even any of those who joined us at Fort Kearny and hardly knew us.

Everyone seemed satisfied to let Big Mary continue. Capable as anyone, and more than most, she called halts, selected camps, roused the company each morning with a hearty "Good day, peoples!" I think we all were grateful to her. I know I was.

By default, getting the company across the river fell to her. She tested the waters with her own light, high-spring wagon first, her well-trained oxen starting across and returning at her command. Then she examined each wagon in the company.

"Better you block up your wagon bed," she told Douglas, "or your things, they wet for sure."

Douglas and I had done it. Caleb returned just before it was our turn to go over, eyes apologetic when he saw the labor we'd performed.

For the crossing, our wagon followed Mr. Fogie's with the Germans' brewing equipment hauled by the still-stubborn mules. I never told the old man I didn't want those mules behind us anymore, but he knew.

The mules balked at crossing the river, thrashing this way and that, splashing about in the muddy, yellow water. Mr. Fogie's voice had lost its timbre. "Heigh-ho, you fools," he croaked without persuasion, slapping

the reins against their backs to little effect. Big Mary finally commandeered a horseman to lead them. The mules took the example and, ac-
cepting the inevitable, crossed without further objection.

We crossed with Douglas and Caleb driving, following two men on
horseback. At Big Mary's direction, they rode side by side, surveying the
ford, marking it with sticks in the sand. Caleb hollered, urging our cattle
forward. Any hesitation and the wagon would mire in the river's sandy
bottom.

Cherry and Buck, Lewis and Clark, all those stalwart beasts pulled
harder across the Platte than anyplace on the road. The wheels of our
heavy wagon sank six inches into the sand, but we could not stop for fear
of getting stuck.

I sat inside, tight-lipped, with my daughters. Janey crouched in tears
at my side, despite her brother's shouted assurance that our milch cow
was fine.

"Emma's still swimming!" Douglas yelled to us again.

I held Hannah tight against me. The swift current rushing against
the many bars and islands made a terrible noise. You could not have
made a person hear you five yards distant.

Hannah, accustomed now to my excited surveillance of her every
move, nestled against me as the wagon jolted through the water. In her
baby voice, she murmured, "I don't fall out, Mama."

I don't know if it was a question or a reassurance, but in that long,
frightening trip across the river, I clung to my George's twin like life.

On the far side, having crossed without incident, we watched the
others come over. The struggling teams and splashing riders mesmerized
me. Men rode with their coats and hats and boots off, kerchiefs around
their heads, whip in hand. Downriver I saw a team, not in our company,
stumble and tangle. The wagon tilted, then slowly went over. There was
a great commotion, and we later learned a woman and four children
drowned. I registered the news without comment. There was nothing to
say. We were on a death trail, and everyone knew it.

Big Mary, to forestall such accident, teamed our oxen with others
and herded them back across the river for the heaviest wagons. Lucena
and Will crossed last, twenty oxen pulling. They hadn't raised their wagon
bed, and water washed from it as the oxen hauled up.

In camp that evening, I helped Lucena unpack a trunk of wet dresses.
We draped them on her wagon cover to dry in the wind.

She laughed as she wrung out the skirts of her good black brocade
gown. "La, not a dainty laundering, that river, is it? Rinse water ought to
be cleaner than the clothes, I always say, not t'other way 'round."

Will, dragging the empty trunk to their campfire to dry it, said, "Let's be thinking about lightening this load some, Lucy." He didn't look at her. It was an old bone they gnawed.

Lucena's eyes teared. Ignoring Will, she took my hand and walked me away from the wagon. "It's not what I thought it would be, Mrs. Daniels. It's not a perfect pleasure trip at all. Will and I scrap like dogs about my things, but I refuse to get to California and have nothing at all. Just look at my feet!"

She lifted her skirts to display Indian moccasins. "I'm trying to save my shoes," she said. "I traded some needles and thread to a Sioux woman for these. La, she wouldn't even look at money."

Without thought, I suddenly grabbed the silly girl by her shoulders and began to shake her.

"Shoes!" I shouted into her surprised face. "Dresses! Needles and thread! Money! Don't you realize what's at stake here? It isn't life as we have known it, it's life itself!"

Lucena's head bobbled like a rag doll's until I released her.

"I'm sorry, Lucena," I said then, staring at my hands as though they belonged to someone else. "Forgive me, I'm not myself."

Ash Hollow

I remember saying that. "I'm not myself." And I wasn't, although it's only in thinking back, of course, that I see the peculiar truth in my apology to Lucena. I wasn't then who I am now. Nor was I the woman who began that terrible journey. There are experiences so profound they alter us, or if not that, unfold us, leave us revealed.

It was at Ash Hollow that I realized Lucena sheltered herself from the journey's reality by a resolute focus on her things. It was a protection, like blinders on a horse. I envied her the ability.

None of us was blind to the descent into Ash Hollow, though. Fear makes indelible the experiences that rouse it.

After crossing the river, we traveled some eighteen miles over sand hills to the prairie's edge. The day had been rainy, and the weather cleared just then to reveal the Platte's north fork below us in a valley. The road into it descended so steeply that I thought, on seeing it, Providence alone must keep us all from tumbling downhill in a tangle of broken bones and splintered wagons.

Mr. Fogie looked vacantly at the labyrinth of ravines falling a third of a mile to the bottom. "Heigh-ho," he said and turned away.

Will shoved his hands in his pockets and shook his head. "The guidebooks might have mentioned that at this point the road hangs a little past the perpendicular."

Caleb took off his hat and ran a hand through his hair. I noticed how much more gray it had become.

"We could detach the wagons from their wheels and running gear," he said without enthusiasm, "and slide them down."

"Ropes," said Big Mary.

Ropes. No hesitation. I never saw a hint of uncertainty in Big Mary. I never met a woman with such assurance. I must have said something once to that effect, I don't remember what. But she laughed her big laugh and put a big hand on my shoulder and said, "Ya, Missus Daniels, you be surprised sometimes whats you can do when you gots no choice at it."

Ropes. Preparations consumed half the morning. Everything in the wagons had to be tied down to keep things from pitching out the front, the descent was that steep.

Phoebe and Lewis Franklin went first, their two wheel oxen leading and five yoke hitched behind. Those following, unaccustomed to the treatment, pulled back, which helped slow the wagon. Lewis also chained the rear wheels together to act as a brake. Then the men in the company eased his and every other wagon down the precipice with stout ropes.

In this way, our hearts in our mouths, we advanced into Ash Hollow.

"Oh, Mama, it looks like a flower garden!" Janey said.

And it did. The namesake grove of ash trees flourished within a wide hollow bracketed by high, chalky bluffs. The elements had scoured the bluffs into knobs and caves. Cedar and laurel crowned their summit. Birds chirped a welcome, and, oh, the sight of grass and flowers, the delicious scent of wild cherry! The wooded dell abounded with wild roses, peas, grapes, gooseberries. Midway into the hollow a spring of pure, cool water burbled forth. After the gritty Platte it tasted sweeter than nectar to our grateful throats.

Ash Hollow was an oasis where emigrants lingered as long as three days. Our company did, excepting Phoebe and Lewis Franklin.

"This place looks as crowded as a St. Louis hotel," Caleb said, finding us a camping place.

How distant and unreal a hotel was, a building of any kind, or civilization. We were well and truly in the wilderness, despite the thousands of people with whom we shared it.

I made no reply, and Caleb expected none, we had become so distant. "I'm going back to help the Germans down," he said.

"I'll help," Douglas said, following.

Mr. Fogie had held back until last. Ox teams had descended without much risk, but mules had to be eased down with ropes.

Janey and I had just set up camp for cooking when we heard a great crashing noise and shouted German curses, and then Douglas was back.

"One of the ropes frayed from the long day's service," he said, prowling through the provision box. "Halfway down with the Germans' wagon, it parted." He found a heel end of bread from breakfast and took a bite. "The wagon full of brewing equipment fell against two mules," he said, chewing. "Toppled them, hurt one bad. The wagon's bows are all smashed, and those kettles and things tumbled all over the ravine."

I was preparing portable soup over a campfire of wood, kindling being plentiful here, and listened without interest as Douglas told the story. It was a minor misfortune. I registered only death. Anything less was mere inconvenience.

"Where's your father?" I asked.

"I came for some tools. He's helping mend the Germans' wagon."

"Yes, of course."

If Caleb wasn't doctoring strangers, he was doctoring wagons. "Tell him dinner's about ready, will you?"

Even to me, my voice sounded distant, as though heard through water. Douglas found the tools and hurried off, leaving me stirring the soup and wondering if I always sounded that way, remote.

Remote as home, I thought, inhaling the soup's meaty smell. It took me there, that smell, and I nestled into homesickness like a kitten into warmth. I thought of the Oberlin stove, the tidy kitchen, the brick hearth, neat cupboards. And the parlor, the lovely parlor with lace curtains and Mother's beloved Hepplewhite sofa sent from Boston. And the garden. The roses would be in bloom now.

Boiled up with water, a chunk of portable soup makes a savory broth. I stirred the liquid, recalling how — was it just months ago? it seemed years — I'd boiled up a big pot of meat and bones, stirring and cooking, adding wood to the stove, stirring and cooking all day, until the meat and bones reduced to soup thick as jelly and yielded up this rich, dense aroma. "Soup-in-his-pocket" my mother's old cookbook called it. Following the directions, I'd turned the gelatinous substance out in pans to dry and then broken it into chunks and packed them in our provision box. No, not the provision box, a sack, most certainly a sack.

"Soup smells good, Ma."

Douglas back already? Had my mind wandered so long? I watched him unpack dishes from the wagon while Janey sliced bread and Hannah set out tin cups for milk and water. Had my daughters been at my side all this time?

I stared at them, and Douglas. Was he still only fourteen? How assured he was, how capable. He looked more man than boy to my eye, but I may have seen him that way as much from need as anything.

"Set up the table, will you, please," I said.

A board balanced on boxes made do as a table, and for stools we used logs or rocks or whatever served. Some people just took their meals leaning against a wagon or standing over the fire or hunkered down on the ground. I still insisted then, whenever possible, that we sit to a table. It was like keeping the Sabbath, even though we had no church or preacher. These small imitations preserved civilization for me.

"Pa said we should go ahead and eat without him," Douglas said, picking up a spoon Hannah dropped. "There's a sick lady camped over by the spring," he added, without looking at me. "Her husband asked Pa to look at her."

"Yes, of course."

Caleb never did come to supper that evening. I kept the fire going until Douglas put up the tent, leaving soup in the kettle.

Hannah was uneasy. She often was when any of us stayed too long from sight. I suppose her young mind connected absence with George and worried that we'd disappear, too.

Janey read out loud by lantern light some fairy tales from the little book until Hannah fell asleep. Hansel and Gretel. Go back. But there was no going back. And for us, there was no back to go to, not as it once had been.

I escaped into sleep with Hannah cuddled up to me on the feather bedding where, since George's death, I had turned from Caleb and he from me.

I awoke early, before the children, and found the soup congealed in the pot and no sign of Caleb. I didn't know what to think. I threw on my clothes, wrapped a shawl over my shoulders against the morning chill, and hurried through the camps of waking emigrants to the spring. I found a gaunt-looking woman bending over a skillet balanced on a grate, frying bacon over a morning campfire. I asked if she knew of a doctor visiting a sick lady.

The woman looked up. "Sick lady? Oh, poor thing, she's just a bit of a girl."

She pointed at a tent. "She be there. Doc been with her all night, but she about be dead. I seen her. Nasty business, the cholera is."

Cholera! I ran to the tent and threw back the flap, half expecting to find Caleb lying sick inside.

The stench staggered me. Clutching the tent flap with one hand, I clapped the other over my mouth and nose. A pile of clothing, damp with cholera's chief symptoms, diarrhea and vomit, lay at my feet. A calico dress in a tiny pattern of blue and red flowers, and a heap of petticoats, once white, now a dull grayish brown.

Caleb, his back to me, bent over a woman wrapped in blankets. I could see her face, pinched-looking and a ghastly blue. Opposite, a young man with an old man's eyes stared at me as though I were the angel of death. He held the woman's hand, the skin puckered and dark.

My husband, oblivious to my entrance, dipped a cloth in a pan of water. Holding it over the woman's open blue lips, he wrung water into her mouth. It dribbled from her lips and trickled down her neck.

She died within the hour.

Her name was Rachel Pattison, eighteen years old, married just three months. Her distraught husband buried his bride in Ash Hollow in the hurried manner of cholera deaths, with Caleb and me and a few of their company in attendance. Afterward, he spent hours painstakingly carving her name and age and date of death into a headstone.

I took that young man some soup, but he wouldn't see it, so intent was he on his task. On the stone, he had no room for the year of death when he got to the space where it should go, and so he carved it at the top, all on its own: 1849. I remember he had the four backward. Watching that poor, sorrowing young man laboring over his bride's gravestone was beyond heart-wrenching. Some cried at the sight. I didn't. I was suddenly and overwhelmingly angry, fired with rage.

Soup in hand, I returned to our camp to find Caleb inspecting the wagon. I threw the tin pot to the ground. It banged against the stones of the campfire, soup drenching the gathered kindling.

Caleb turned and stared.

"Caleb Daniels, you've dragged us into a trail of horror! For what have you done it? For gold? For adventure? To do something 'big'? That's what you said, wasn't it, you wanted to do something big? To make a decision for yourself?"

"Sarah — "

"Here's your big decision, Caleb — death, and more death. Every day I count another name gone, witness another senseless loss. And it's you who have done this to us! You who dragged us from our home and into the wilderness to witness horror!"

He came to me, tried to comfort me, but I would have none of it. I pulled away. I was unraveling like loosened knitting, yanking my fears into one long string.

"An eighteen-year-old bride, Caleb! A bride! Hardly had a life at all before she went into her grave in a makeshift coffin fashioned from a wagon side. One more death on a trail needing no guide. Follow the grave markers, the guidebooks should have advised, and you'll find California."

"Stop it, Sarah."

And fortunately I did stop, stopped short of naming the unnameable, of saying what I was thinking, that our son lay beneath one of those grave markers and it was his, Caleb Daniels', doing.

I was bitter as old coffee, but the expression on Caleb's tired face, his shoulders stooped with defeat and exhaustion, ought to have stung me. It didn't. I'd lost my resolve not to sorrow Caleb with my reluctance for this journey. Perhaps I thought it didn't matter anymore; he surely knew how I felt about this death march. Still, I'd never put it to his face before that day.

Janey crept out of the tent then, crying, "Mama, please."

I hadn't known she was there, thought she was with Douglas and Hannah, who had gone to the Hesters while Caleb and I attended the funeral.

Caleb dried her tears with his kerchief. "Don't cry, Janey girl, it's going to be all right."

"You're always crying, Janey," I said, accusing and just as quickly not. "Why are you always crying?"

The better question was, Why wasn't I?

I hugged her, calming myself with the warmth of my child against my body. "I'm sorry, dear, I'm sorry."

But my rage had not dissipated with my outburst. I kept it still, nursed it like a secret child. It gave me solace in a strange way, transmuting fear into resentment I carried willingly in its stead.

That afternoon I even confronted Lucena with the fact of Rachel Pattison. "She was eighteen," I said, "like you. And just married, too."

Lucena looked at me, then through me, put a finger to her chin. As if she'd just thought of it, she said, "Big Mary says we're staying another day to repair wagons and recruit the stock. I think I'll ask Will to dig my blue dishes out of the flour barrel."

She smiled. It wasn't her smile. It looked like something she'd found that didn't fit but that she'd decided to wear anyway. "We'll have tea this afternoon, a proper tea, and use the cups. La, won't that be nice? They're quite pretty, you know. Did I show them to you?"

That was the day Phoebe and Lewis Franklin, the couple from Canada with the big wagon, left the company.

"We just can't afford no more delay," Phoebe said, taking my hand. "Our outfit's in good repair, cattle fine. If we hang back every time someone needs a rest or a new wheel, there won't be nothin' worth pickin' up by the time we get to California."

They were for getting on with it. I didn't blame them.

I felt terrible about Janey's having witnessed my outburst at Caleb and so took her with me as I walked with Phoebe to the mouth of the hollow. I held Phoebe's hand as we followed her big express wagon with the tent and bedding strapped to the sides, a clatter of pots and pans lashed on behind. Women formed bonds on that journey. We became sisters, and it was as hard to part from one another as from family.

Lewis, driving the wagon, hollered for Phoebe to hurry along so they could join up with another company raising dust on the road ahead.

She and I said a last goodbye, hugged one another, kissed each other's cheeks. And then she ran to catch up.

I put my arm around Janey's shoulder as Phoebe looked back a final time and waved from beside the wagon, its weathered canvas still bearing its faded but legible axle-grease message: "Have you saw the elephant?"

I read it now with educated eyes. Behind me, a distraught young husband had just carved his wife's death date into a slab of stone. Behind me, my child lay beneath the blowing sand of the Platte River valley. What worse could lay ahead? Yes, I thought, I have seen the elephant.

If I had known then that I had only seen its tail, I would have turned around that very moment, deaf to argument, and dragged my family back to Illinois.

We would have had company. Emigrants, even this far into the journey, occasionally went back. They passed us on the road, discouraged-looking people, offering their provisions for sale, saying they had seen the elephant's tail and that view was enough. For a time Hannah feared some terrifying animal lay in wait for us.

"It's just another word for California," I assured her.

Even as Janey and I watched the Franklins departing, a man in a small, neat wagon with a trim team of mules passed them, returning.

He lifted his hat to us. "Afternoon, ma'am. You, too, miss," he said, nodding at Janey.

Then, as if by rote, probably having repeated his explanation for every curious emigrant he passed, he said, "No problems. Got as far as Independence Rock. Decided I loved my wife more than gold."

I repeated the encounter to Caleb, word for word. The man's sentiment hung in the air between us like wet laundry. It dripped insinuation.

Then Caleb said, "I promised Will I'd look at his running gear. Their wagon is taking the road hard."

"Yes, of course. You have your responsibilities."

The next morning, tidying things in the wagon for our departure, I found Janey's sampler tucked up between some sacks. Perhaps she hadn't been hiding it from me, or perhaps she had, to spare me the sorrow of it.

Centered into her square of linen was a neatly stitched likeness of the red brick house, two stories, a tidy fence on each side. In front of the fence on the right side of the house, where at home a garden gate had stood, she had worked, in careful padded satin stitches, a tiny gravestone. On it, with a single strand of crinkled silk thread, she had fashioned the letters 'G.D.' and the numbers '1845–49.'

I held the cloth to my breast, eyes closed, imagining my tearful daughter stitching this reminder of her little brother's too-brief life into a square of linen, and into her memory.

If I had been capable of tears, I would have shed them then.

Between Ash Hollow and Fort Laramie I recall nothing of the journey but landscape. Beyond Ash Hollow the road followed high bluffs washed by rain and carved by the wind into all manner of curious shapes. The spectacular scenery awed the emigrants. It enveloped me. My awareness, surfeited with death and grief, fled to it, was enfolded by it the way Lucena's bonnets and dishes encompassed hers.

One can so focus the mind that a single thing utterly absorbs it, suspending all else. It is something like a Colt's revolver, the mind. The chamber accommodates but one bullet at a time. I aimed mine at the landscape.

There are in my journal two sketches from this stretch of road. The first looks like a courthouse. It is mine, done by my hand, although I don't remember drawing it.

Twenty miles after starting up the Platte's north fork, we first saw what everyone called Courthouse Rock. Its resemblance to a Missouri courthouse amazed us.

"Court must be in session," Douglas said on seeing it, "there's that many horses drawn up to the front."

Like so many, we must have stopped to admire the rocky edifice, although I don't recall doing so. My sketch suggests an imposing and symmetrical architectural shape, with a low dome in the center and two wings, standing isolated on the plain. Its appearance must have struck me, that I took the time to draw it. I suppose I was hungry for something, anything, reminiscent of civilization.

So must everyone have been. Within a few miles of Courthouse Rock was a ledge carved with water-worn fissures. Across the top someone had etched in capital letters "Post-Office," and inside one cavity we saw a number of letters deposited.

The second sketch in my journal is Chimney Rock, which was visible on the horizon long before we reached it. Because of the dust raised by the wind and the army of emigrants tramping past it, Chimney Rock looked at first like a pillar of smoke in the distance. It was yellowish gray in color, and arose solitary from the landscape. We camped by the river opposite.

The atmosphere of the region produced a remarkable clarity, so much so that distance could not be judged, as Douglas and the Hester boys discovered. Their legs paid the penalty for their deceived senses. Eager to climb the rock and view the plain from its vantage, they started out for it after supper, thinking it stood but a mile or so from camp. They didn't return until past nine o'clock, having found the distance to be four miles.

The rock towered two hundred feet above the surrounding plains, Douglas told us. He described the shaft of it, which he climbed, as springing from an isolated mass of ill-shaped sand rocks around which cactus grew with flowers large as hollyhocks. The boys carved their names on Chimney Rock, like hundreds of others.

My sketch of that landmark suggests a resemblance to one of the tall chimneys of the steam-propelled manufactories we had seen in St. Louis. Or perhaps it is more like an Egyptian obelisk. I remember a similar drawing in a book bound in fine calf with gold stamping on the spine. It had sat on the shelf next to Byron's *Childe Harold.*

My pencil could not do the scenery justice, could give but the faintest idea of it. Beyond Chimney Rock, the gigantic form of Scott's Bluff rose from the plains toward the heavens in marble whiteness, presenting the outline of two contiguous cities, miles in extent. Despite reason, from the distance one saw long ranges of buildings of vast height and uniform architecture, dome and spire, tower and wall and battlement. The elements had worn down the whole range of river hills, from Courthouse Rock to Scott's Bluff, into every shape that clay and sand can assume.

On the shelf in the parlor at home was a book of travels in the Yucatan, with descriptions and plates of drawings of ancient ruins. Their likeness to what lay before our disbelieving eyes was striking. The form and size and variety of Scott's Bluff, viewed from a distance, seemed a perfection of ancient architecture.

It was near Scott's Bluff that Douglas discovered the buffalo skeletons. We had seen for miles the skulls of the beasts scattered in profusion over the country, white as chalk. But at the foot of a perpendicular bluff, Douglas found six buffalo skeletons entire, bleached white, all in a heap, as though they had tumbled off together. I went to see it. It spoke of death. I turned away. My aim was on the landscape, the distance, California, safety.

The nearer view evidenced a growing fear among the emigrants. We had grown accustomed to seeing wagon tires, hubs, boxes, any quantity of iron scattered by the road as emigrants continued to lighten their loads. But here we discovered a new earnestness, the road lined now with scattered trunks, valises, clothing and boots, piles of bacon and flour.

And man's nature revealed. The journey exposed everyone's most basic fiber. In the clutch of survival, man is selfish or he is generous.

Along the road, man's most selfish nature lay clearly visible where property abandoned was rendered useless. We found sugar on which turpentine had been poured so no one else might have the use of it, flour in which salt and dirt were mixed, clothes torn to bits, a waste of valuable property simply because the owners could not themselves use it.

Honorable exceptions were notable. We found some bacon, flour, and sugar nicely heaped up, with a card directing anyone who stood in need to use freely and be welcome.

It was here, along the North Platte, we first saw whole wagons abandoned, large and heavy ones broken up and sold for firewood, in exchange for small, light ones bought from those deciding to pack ahead on mules instead, to hurry, hurry.

The sight of those abandoned wagons echoed a forbidding reminder. I heard again the voice of the mountain man at Fort Kearny: "This vast crowd cannot possibly get across the mountains in safety."

Fort Laramie

Fort Laramie encouraged no hope that imagination had inflated my reborn fear.

I didn't expect much here, having seen Fort Kearny, and so was not disappointed. Fort Laramie was a rough and primitive-looking place, not much more than a dilapidated adobe trading post located a mile above the fork of the North Platte and Laramie rivers.

The grass having been destroyed in the fort's immediate vicinity, we camped at the edge of the Laramie River with hundreds of other emigrants. One of them was Celia, but our acquaintance was to be delayed by my visit to the fort with Lucena. Novelty netted us like fish.

It was a hot walk up, there being no trees to shade us from the sun. En route Lucena and I passed at least fifty abandoned wagons, many of them burned, and an immense wreckage of freight: picks, spades, guns, clothes, cooking utensils, barrels, boxes, piles of bacon and hard bread. Every discarded spade and shoe testified to the emigrants' collective fear: lighten the load, lighten the load, too slow, too slow, hurry, hurry.

We had been, all of us, nearly two months on the road, had not yet come half the way, and the forage that meant life for our animals was disappearing. Along with courage. Without our animals to transport us, we were all lost.

I felt regret for the emigrants who, hoping to sell here to advantage, had hauled goods all this long way only to discard them. Everyone realized now it was foolhardy to slow their animals' advance by any unnecessary weight. Animals in the rear would find nothing to eat, and so must perish. Mountain men don't lie, not about such as this.

Lucena, oblivious to the dumping ground, said, "The emigrants, with all their wagons, stock, and trappings, give this place a pleasant appearance of animation, don't you think, Mrs. Daniels?"

I was thinking, enlivened by fear, my stupor departed, that if worse came to worst, this miserable shelter must prove our refuge. The fort had that week passed into the hands of a half dozen army officers and some sixty enlisted men charged with establishing a military post to protect emigrants from the ravages of wild Indians. Since no one in our company, nor in any we knew, had suffered any loss beyond a few pilfered items, we concluded the gain was all on the side of the American Fur Company, to whom the U.S. government had paid the astonishing sum of four thousand dollars.

The money would have been better spent protecting the Indians from the ravages of the emigrants.

Some emigrants perpetrated dreadful deeds against the native people through whose lands we passed. There were unprovoked murders by stupid men vowing to kill the first Indian they saw. Just as bad, any number of Indians contracted the cholera. And I personally saw, on the road approaching Fort Laramie, a burial desecrated. Some senseless young men destroyed an elaborate ceremonial funeral platform suspended in a tree on one of the islands in the Platte. It held the desiccated body of an Indian. They stole the burial goods intended to accompany him into the afterlife. It was a shameful act.

Outside the fort, Indians squatted in miserable camps against the walls, many of them squaws with children born from acquaintance with traders and trappers. Their matted hair and the filth of their persons shocked us.

Lucena, wrinkling her nose, waved off an Indian woman urging her wares. "La, soap and water must be scarce among these people, or greatly neglected."

I was more sorrowed than affronted by the reduced state of the fort Indians. The abandonment of their traditional homes had not been an improving choice.

I could not escape the comparison to my own decision.

The fort's one pretension to distinction was a large front gate surmounted by two brass swivels, the guns atop them bearing the inscription of their manufacture in Pittsburgh. I remember the date, 1829, because I thought how insubstantial the fort's construction that it should so decline in twenty years. The front wall of adobe bricks appeared about to topple, even with the supporting timbers propping it up.

Inside, the enclosed quadrangle measured, by my estimation, some four hundred feet square, with stores and workshops shedded against three walls.

Lucena and I toured the fort, seeing little of interest beyond the fur presses. In the store, two trappers traded for jerked buffalo meat, the only commodity the French clerk offered.

"They're a rough, outlandish, whiskey-drinking set from the looks of them, aren't they?" Lucena said of the trappers.

Her voice had the aroused interest of someone on tour viewing curiosities. She seemed not to see at all the discouraged, bereft, affrighted faces of emigrants whose countenances spoke volumes of the difficulties ahead.

Celia Giddings, on the other hand, possessed no more protection from the realities of our circumstances than did I. I first saw her on my return from the fort. She was sitting on a box behind our wagon, her bowed head hidden by a faded blue sunbonnet. She wore a calico dress to match, and one large boot, old and scuffed. Her other foot was bare, bruised, and swollen. Hannah sat on her lap, examining a stocking, and Janey stood by her side, watching Caleb tear a length of sheeting. As he knelt with it to bind the injured foot, I saw the mate to the oversized boot on the ground at his knee. It looked like a man's.

It was a perturbing tableau. I felt as though I were intruding, the scene looked so homely and intimate.

Janey, seeing me, said by way of explanation, "I seen her down by the river, limping bad, and told her that Pa could doctor her."

So taken aback was I by the scene, I don't think I would have corrected my daughter's decaying grammar even if Hannah and Celia had not both glanced up. But they did, and their resemblance disconcerted. A tangle of curls tumbled from beneath Celia's sunbonnet, the face and hair a perfect enlargement of my youngest daughter's.

Then Celia, from beneath the brim of her sunbonnet, smiled so radiantly I blinked. She had the luminous face of an artist's painted saint, eyes blue as summer sky, hair the color of ripe wheat.

"Hello. I'm Celia," she said. "Celia Giddings. This good, good man is binding my ankle. I was so careless, you see. I always am, Joshua declares, but I seem not to help it, however much I try."

"Sarah Daniels. Pleased to meet you, I'm sure."

And I was, although why I couldn't say. She looked as though she had stepped into my own family portrait and replaced me, yet I felt no consternation. She radiated too much goodness.

Caleb gave me a wan smile. "Mrs. Giddings has hurt her foot. I don't know how she's managed to walk on it."

"Always trust in the Lord," Celia said. "He'll help us manage, that's what Joshua says. And it's true." She pointed at the oversized boot on the grass. "I found these big, comfortable old boots right after my foot swelled up like to burst my shoe. But the accident was all my own fault. Our poor horse couldn't pull our wagon up the riverbank, and he slipped, and the wagon rolled back and then right over my foot. I tell you it was a fright, seeing that wagon coming back on me. My clothes will be a world too large for me for a week to come, I shrunk so at the prospect!" She dismissed her plight with a laugh.

The remark struck me as more literal than figurative. Celia Giddings looked slight as a fence slat inside her calico dress. It hung on her as though she were no more than a closet hook.

After Caleb bound her ankle, Celia lowered Hannah to the ground, put on the worn stocking my daughter delivered with a serious assistance, then tugged the large boot over her bandaged foot. She stood, took a tentative step. She was a tiny woman, and in the oversized boots and loose calico, she looked like a doll dressed in children's clothes.

Staring at her feet, she walked around the box she had sat on, limping slightly but looking much relieved. "Oh, this is ever so much improved, Dr. Daniels. I don't know how I can ever thank you. How much do I owe?"

"I'm not a doctor, Mrs. Giddings, and you owe me nothing," Caleb said, folding the remnant of sheeting. "Happy to help."

"But I surely must repay your kindness."

Celia Giddings looked from one of us to the other, from me to Janey to Caleb, her face flushing.

She appeared so distressed at the prospect of an unpaid debt, I said, "Perhaps if you have a little tea to share?"

Emigrants, in return for assistance, traded these small commodities constantly. And although we had as much tea as we expected to require, I saw the suggestion relieved her.

"Oh, but of course. I shall fetch it at once." She beamed at Hannah and Janey. "Such lovely daughters you have, Mrs. Daniels. Might I borrow them to see me to my wagon? I'm not so very far." Smiling, she held out slender hands to my daughters. "And I should be ever so pleased if you might join us," she said to me. "I left the kettle over the fire, and we can take tea together, if you would do me the honor. I should be most grateful for the company of another woman. I do so miss feminine associations on this long journey."

She smiled so winningly I couldn't refuse had I a mind to. Which I didn't. Something about Celia Giddings calmed me.

Caleb and I nodded to one another, and he said to me, in the distanced way we'd adopted since George's death and my outburst at Ash Hollow, "Douglas and I'll finish setting up camp. You and the girls go visit."

Celia's smile faded as she caught the undertone, then returned behind forced cheer. "It's settled then. You're most kind, Mr. Daniels, to lend me all your lovely ladies." She knelt to Hannah and took her hand. "Shall we take our tea then, Miss Daniels?"

Hannah giggled. I had not heard her laugh in a long time. Poor little thing, confused and infected by her family's grief. Hearing Hannah laugh, I came back a bit from my self-made grave. It was Celia's doing, a gift, and not her last.

At Celia's camp, I repaid her hospitality poorly by undisguised shock at the sight of the Giddings' two pitiable horses, heads drooping, so thin their hides looked glued to their bones like wallpaper.

"Are those your horses!"

"Yes, poor creatures," Celia said, looking at them. Her eyes filled. "It cleaves my heart to see them like this. They were so large and strong when we left Iowa. I fear for their lives, Mrs. Daniels, I do."

Sorry to have distressed her, I made myself useful in stirring up the fire under the kettle while she set out cups. She poured us tea and we spoke of inconveniences, the kind of talk emigrants typically exchanged. Janey soon became bored, and Hannah drowsy. I said I thought I should go.

"Oh, please stay, Mrs. Daniels," Celia said, taking my hand. Her blue eyes pleaded. "Mr. Giddings is gone so much, and I so rarely have the chance to visit with a woman. We can put your darling Hannah to nap in my wagon, and you'll stay? Please say you will."

She so wanted me to that I agreed. Janey left to find Sallie Hester, and Celia and I settled Hannah into the wagon.

"We travel lightly, for the poor horses," Celia said, seeing my surprise at how little they carried.

We stood at the back of her wagon, watching Hannah's eyes close in sleep. "I'm frightened, Mrs. Daniels. I try to be brave, but I'm not. I fear we shall die out here. Our horses cannot get us through. They struggle and reel like drunken men, they are so weak. We have lost one already, and he the largest. Poor beast, he endured all he could. A few miles back, I saw he could pull no more, and persuaded Mr. Giddings to let the poor animal rest. I took him some water, but he could not swallow. His throat was all closed up, swollen hard as stone. I bathed his throat and did all I could for him, but to no purpose. Mr. Giddings wanted to tie him to some brush and leave him. But then the suffering beast just dropped, all huge and black. And he lay there beating the ground with his head, Mrs. Daniels, and died in a great and terrible agony."

I saw in her eyes that she revisited the scene, and the pain of it tore at her. We had each of us seen too much suffering, and it had collected on our hearts like winter's ice. She felt my sympathy, for Celia sobbed then, and I put my arms around her and held her while she wept. I wanted to weep, too, for the great dying horse, for all the dead this terrible trek had taken in toll, but no tears came. In my mind's eye I saw my child die again and felt my own throat swell hard as stone.

We sat then, Celia and I, and talked. She told how when the horses had begun to fail, her husband, a Methodist preacher, stared at them without seeing and said the Lord would get them through.

Celia wrung her hands and looked from me to the feeble animals grazing nearby. "I fear my faith is insufficient, Mrs. Daniels, and I dare not say so. I do what I can, Mr. Giddings is so often away visiting the various companies to preach, and the animals' care is left to me. The last miles to this camp, so exhausted were these two I feared they would drop. At the last I unhitched one and let him follow while I coaxed the other forward with a bit of bread. In this way, unhitching one and hitching the other every hundred yards or so, coaxing each poor animal in turn, we arrived here."

"How awful! Your husband allowed this?"

Celia forced a smile. "His is the greater responsibility, Mrs. Daniels. He feels it keenly. Great numbers of young men heading west succumb now to evil ways, drinking and gambling and forgetting the Sabbath."

"But what about your company? Surely someone might have assisted you, lent a yoke of oxen for a time?"

"We have no company, Mrs. Daniels. We're alone, all alone."

"Alone!"

"We traveled with one company, and then another, then none. There were disagreements," she said, and didn't elaborate.

The sky had turned pink and orange behind Laramie Peak, looming forty miles west.

"Supper will be late," I said. "I must go."

Celia jumped up, winced at the pain, apologized for keeping me, thanked me for my kindness in visiting. While I collected my sleepy-eyed Hannah, she folded a packet of tea from her small stores into a square of paper.

She looked so forlorn as she handed it to me that I said on impulse, "We're staying through tomorrow. Please join us, you and Mr. Giddings, for dinner at noon, will you?"

The next day they came. I don't know what I expected, but it wasn't the narrow, ferret-faced man with suspicious eyes who arrived. Lank, unkempt hair fell over the shoulders of a black broadcloth coat tinged green by age. His hands fluttered when he spoke, yet there was something perfectly still about him, like a cat watching a rodent's hiding place. He said little.

Celia seemed anxious throughout the meal to redeem her husband's sullen presence. She chattered brightly of how charming my children were, how delicious was the meal, praising especially my strawberry dumplings.

As a treat, I had stewed the last of my dried strawberries and prepared a sweet dough. It was a simple dessert, the strawberries spread over the dough, the whole rolled up in a cloth and boiled. With the juice of the strawberries, a little sugar, a bit of nutmeg, I had made a sauce to serve over the dumplings.

"Your dumplings are light as a cork, Mrs. Daniels," Celia said, licking sauce from her spoon.

"My wife's a wonderful cook, Mr. Giddings," Caleb said, offering the plate a second time. "Have another?"

Giddings sprang to his feet then, eyes bright, hands twitching. He stared at Caleb, who, taken by surprise as were we all, still held the plate out.

"Feed me with ambrosia! Wash it down with nectar! What will it avail if men love darkness more than light?"

Then he sat, scooped up a dumpling, and devoured it in two bites.

I thought Celia might cry, but she caught her falling expression and fastened a smile on it. It was too neat an interception to be unfamiliar.

"This has been such a pleasure, Mrs. Daniels," she said with sunny pretense. "You were so kind to invite us."

Her eyes beseeched mine, and I, in turn, caught Caleb's. The three of us resolutely launched the politely meaningless conversation that camouflages awkwardness.

Despite appearances, Joshua Giddings wasn't crazy. Some people lost their minds on this journey. Celia did, ultimately, but her husband did not. He possessed too much outward purpose to qualify as a madman. His odd behavior, I concluded as I came to know him, he initially adopted for effect, to promote his preaching. And it had become a habit.

The couple, Celia particularly, was eager to unite with us. Caleb took their petition to Big Mary, explaining the Giddings' horses required another day to recruit. Our company's plan had been to stay but two nights at Fort Laramie. Adding the Giddings wagon to our party would require a third. Most of the younger men without families protested the additional delay. In the end, those opposed moved on. The Germans with the brewing equipment left, and Mr. Fogie with them.

He and Douglas had a long goodbye, and then he came to me, his hat in one hand, the other pulling his beard.

"So," he said, eyes dimmer than I remembered, "I told your boy I reckoned there was a California after all, and full of elephants at that. Should we meet up again, I told him, the last of the old Fogies would count it proud to hunt gold with him if I don't get stomped."

It saddened me that the merry man who had walked into our lives in St. Joseph, eyes twinkling, little George on his shoulders, had disappeared to leave this ghost behind. We said goodbye and wished each other luck. We didn't say the things we couldn't speak of, but we heard each other's sorrow. He didn't ask my forgiveness, but insofar as he needed it, I gave it and he knew I had. Despite everything, I expected to always think fondly of him. And I have.

While we were at the fort, Lucena wrote her sister and paid twenty-five cents to a man taking up mail for return to the States. Whether the letter ever reached its intended recipient I do not know. As we later learned, unscrupulous men commonly gulled emigrants in this way. As for me, writing my mother was too dreadful a task to consider. I counted it a sin to burden her with our anguish sooner than necessary. I determined to write her of our arrival in California, and at least give her that comfort to counter the heartache of our shocking loss.

I used our three days at the fort to wash and mend clothes, cook up provisions in advance, and repack our stores. Caleb kept busy with his doctoring, there being more than enough call for it. Near the fort's entrance he discovered a sick man lying in a wagon, deserted by his company. They had left him two barrels of liquor and the wagon to lie in, and he told Caleb he didn't think he'd been done hard by.

To our great surprise, the Pioneer Line came in while we were at the fort. By our calculations the promised speedy passage of sixty days should have put them nearly to California. Two of the passengers toured our camps with goods they hoped to sell. Among the things offered was a mold for making gold bars.

Caleb, on seeing it, asked, half laughing, "What do you think that iron weighs, boys?"

I looked up from the pot of beans I was stirring and saw the two were not much older than Douglas, hidden behind wispy beards and slouch hats. The one holding the mold handed it to Caleb.

"Comes with a booklet on smelting, mister."

Caleb balanced the iron in one hand, calculating. He shook his head as he handed it back. "Give it up, boys. If you don't want to haul four extra pounds of iron, you can be sure no one else does either. No one's going to give you a dime for your gold mold."

"It's not rightly mine, mister," said the young man, reluctantly taking it back. "Belonged to a chap on the train what died. Me and Jim here are just trying to sell Cranson's stuff to get up some money to send back to his pa."

I stood. "Cranson? Caleb, wasn't that the name of the young man we met near Vandalia who pulled our wagon out with his oxen?"

"That'd be him, missus, right enough," the young man said. "He come to St. Louis with oxen and joined up with the train there. Bought this mold in St. Louis, he did."

I bent to my beans, not wanting to ask, but I did. "What happened?"

"The cholera got him. We all had a regular bad time with that illness."

"Had us a bad time most all the way," added the young man named Jim. "Fact be known, been unfortunate 'bout every mile."

"Buried ten so far," the other said. "Bad food, bad management — all around bad for everyone joining up with this bad-luck outfit."

Caleb gave the boys two dollars for the mold and, after they left, tossed it out. The booklet on smelting he gave to Douglas. I think we used the paper for kindling during the terrible time out on the desert, but I'm not sure.

At Fort Laramie, we still had sufficient money to feel easy about dispensing it freely. Caleb's gesture pleased me. He was a good, good man, as Celia had said. The image of her sitting contentedly in the midst of my family stayed with me, especially after the awkward encounter with Joshua Giddings. Celia's choice in a husband perplexed me. She was sweet-natured, pretty, hard-working, and would be a credit to any man fortunate enough to win her heart. I wondered how Joshua Giddings had prevailed.

The only commodity worth buying at Fort Laramie was stock. From here there was no inhabited place nearer than Fort Hall, a good distance ahead, and everyone had to depend on the animals they had to see them through. We bought an extra yoke of oxen for safe measure from a man who abandoned his wagon at the fort to pack the rest of the way on mules.

I don't know if Caleb was thinking of Celia's plight when he bought those animals or not.

Devil's Gate

We left the fort in a light rain, beginning the ascent into the Black Hills by an easy road. The barren country soon was cut by ravines and the route grew rough, rocky, and crooked. Advance became more difficult, with all of us intent on negotiating the descents, ascents, and spurs of ridges. Grass grew thin and poor in the red and brown sandstone dominating the landscape. The higher we climbed, the scarcer the grass already reduced by the animals ahead. We scouted farther and farther from the road in search of it, often as much as a mile.

We traveled then as the mountain man at Fort Kearny had predicted. I feared for our animals' lives, for ours depended on theirs. But constant fear exhausts one, and cannot be sustained. By the time we reached Independence Rock, I had become inured to my own anxiety.

We were two weeks traversing the one hundred and eighty miles from Fort Laramie to the landmark the guidebooks described as a singular curiosity standing isolated and alone on the landscape. It had been named some years earlier by a party of explorers who had camped by it on the Fourth of July. We had hoped to reach it by that date, but missed the anniversary by a week. My journal shows our arrival there as July 11.

We nooned near the gigantic stone, and I think I sketched it, or perhaps the drawing I have is Janey's. I remember we all walked around it, Douglas estimating its height at one hundred and fifty feet, its length at six hundred yards, its width one hundred and twenty. Thousands of emigrants had inscribed their names on it with tar, paint, and chisel. Caleb took the tar bucket from our wagon and clambered up on the stone with Douglas to add theirs to the roll.

Our company camped that night five miles farther west, near where the Sweetwater River pours through the cleft called Devil's Gate. Celia's horses, although much recovered when we left Fort Laramie, were declining again. She worried constantly for their well-being. Our spare oxen being as yet unnecessary, Caleb determined to offer their use to Joshua Giddings.

For the opportunity of visiting with Celia, I accompanied Caleb to their camp. We found the preacher sitting on a stump, stabbing at a plate of beans. Celia leapt up from tending her campfire, begged us to eat with them, urged coffee. We declined, knowing their supplies low, and Caleb directly made his suggestion about the oxen.

Giddings, eyes suddenly and glitteringly bright, rose so abruptly he seemed propelled from the stump he sat upon. He leaned into Caleb, glaring and jabbing the air with his fork. "Those horses be not slowin' this company no more than your doctorin' and wagon fixin'! Those horses be doin' the Lord's work, sir!"

Celia covered her mouth, smothering a tiny "Oh!"

I didn't know what to do or say and mumbled something inane about their horses being no slower than oxen, and the company respecting him. The truth was, the company respected the work, but not the worker. "Jitters us, that Giddings," Lucena had said, capturing the consensus. "Looks always about to mount a box and sing us up a hymn, he does."

Caleb rescued our awkward moment. "My apologies, Giddings," he said, sincere as a suitor. He put a hand on the man's arm, stayed the stabbing fork. "I assure you my intent is not to do a favor, but ask one. Those new oxen of mine I've had trailing, you know, they being as yet unnecessary. Should be put to pulling, to keep fit. I hoped you might trade me for a time, take my oxen on your wagon, lend your horses so my boy could scout grass. I'd count it a service, Giddings, a kindness. Grateful if you'd oblige."

And that was how it was done.

The company agreed to lay over a day on the Sweetwater, grass being good there, and the next morning some of the women and children walked out to see Devil's Gate at closer vantage. The cleft stones rose some four hundred feet above the river gushing through the narrow space between them.

"La, it's a sublime sight," said Lucena. "Worth the whole distance to see, it is!"

Celia and I looked at each other, sharing the thought, I suspected, that no scenery or curiosity, nothing, not even gold, justified this terrible journey. But the sight was magnificent.

"In some distant past these colossal stones must once have been joined," I said, admiring their lofty grandeur. Their opposing outlines endorsed a united conformation, but the cataclysmic event necessary to their severing confounded our imaginations.

At the river's edge, I bathed Hannah's feet and legs in the water, and I recall Mrs. Hester saying to her, "You most likely won't remember this place, Hannah, but your ma will tell you someday you were here in 'forty-nine with the great emigration, and it'll make you proud."

I suppose it would have, if all had gone as Caleb hoped. Was it Burns who wrote, "The schemes of mice and men gang aft a-gley"?

Janey and Sallie Hester had wandered off to explore, leaving me, Celia, Lucena, and Martha Hester sitting on the riverbank in the morning sun, watching the Sweetwater pound through Devil's Gate. I had Hannah in my lap. Celia sat down on my right and asked to hold her. My daughter settled into Celia's lap like a pet.

Celia combed Hannah's hair with her fingers. "My Rachel would have been Hannah's age."

She spoke so softly I wasn't sure I'd heard. I watched her twirl curls in Hannah's hair. "Rachel?"

"My little girl."

"Ah, you lose some," said Martha Hester, staring at the river, "that's the way of it. But you never forget them. Fever, was it?" she asked, looking past me to Celia. "I lost two that way."

"The Lord just took her," Celia said. Sorrow clouded her eyes. "To punish me. She went in her sleep, mercifully. I buried her myself, Mr. Giddings being on the circuit at the time. I was alone, all alone."

There was such terrible isolation in her words, I felt the unbearable grief of her loss. We all did.

"Alone, all alone," she said again in a faraway voice, staring up at the cleft stones of Devil's Gate. "No neighbors for miles, no woman to comfort me."

She looked at me over Hannah's curls, eyes brimming with the remembrance. "Not thinking, I laid her out in a bureau drawer, she was so small, used my shawl for a shroud. The ground was near frozen. I dug at it with my spade most all day to put her in the cold, cold ground. Afterward, that bureau with its missing drawer was like seeing my heart pulled out. I couldn't bear the empty space of it. I burned the bureau. It was a stupid thing to do, we had so little. Joshua was furious when he returned, things being so dear and we so poor."

Mrs. Hester stood, brushed dirt from her skirt. "Poor thing. Fever, probably."

Celia looked up at her through tears. "Mr. Giddings said the Lord took her. To punish me, he said, because I loved the gift more than the Giver."

"Oh, that's too cruel," I said, "blaming the parent for the child's death. Why, it but doubles the agony of the loss."

Mrs. Hester, behind me, bent to my ear, put a hand on my shoulder, and whispered, "Yes, Mrs. Daniels, it does."

There was something in her tone and I looked up at her. She squeezed my shoulder, shook her head, then walked away. Lucena got up, too, and nodded at me, as though confirming the gentle rebuke I'd heard in Mrs. Hester's voice.

I needed no more than that. Realization opened in me, and just as suddenly all the resentment and anger I'd directed at poor Caleb poured away like the Sweetwater through Devil's Gate. Sorrow I kept, will always keep, but not the poison of blame. I put my arm around Celia's slender shoulders and kissed her cheek.

When Hannah and I returned, Caleb was at the wagon, sorting through his dwindling medicines. He looked worn, worried, older than his years. Even without the tragedy of our son's loss, this journey was not what he anticipated. I wanted to put my arms around him, take his around me, but he glanced up and quickly away and I lost the moment.

"The Pioneer Line's having an auction this afternoon," he said. "I might pick up something useful."

"I'd like to come, if you wouldn't mind the company."

My request surprised him. "I'd like that, Sarah."

And so it was, without words, we surrendered the mutual injuries inflicted or imagined. I loved my Caleb again wholeheartedly.

And he loved me. I believed it then, and believe it now. I will always believe it, despite Joshua Giddings' vicious accusations.

The Pioneer Line had been just behind us ever since Fort Laramie. For the past week, since the Fourth of July, Joshua Giddings had frequented their encampments, preaching against drinking and gambling.

My heart went out to the passengers of the Pioneer Line, so beset by difficulties and disappointments. They had paid handsomely for a list of promises that had not been kept in any part. They cooked their own food, harnessed and drove their own teams. Generally, they went on foot, the too few mules provided being so unequal to the task and now so used up they had fallen behind the ox teams.

The passengers had been promised they would celebrate the Fourth of July in California. Instead, they spent it with us, and the Knoxville Company, some forty wagons and more than a hundred men, barely half the distance there. The occasion received its due from a quantity of speeches and expressions of appropriate sentiment, which satisfied most of those assembled on that date. But a number of Pioneer Line passengers imbibed more enthusiastically than necessary. We women did not approve, of course, and retired with our children when celebratory gunfire exceeded what observance required. After a drunken man shot his thumb off, Joshua Giddings mounted the speaker's box and closed the ceremonies by denouncing the Pioneer passengers as sinners and backsliders.

In the week since, he had haunted their evening camps, condemning and censuring.

I was not surprised to see Giddings at the Pioneers' auction, he so dogged their footsteps. I could, however, hardly bear to look at him, his pitiless indifference to Celia's loss — his own daughter! — so amplified my aversion.

The Pioneers' auction was precipitated by the critical need to lighten loads to keep their mules from failing entirely. All passengers, it had been agreed at a stormy meeting, must reduce their baggage weight to seventy-five pounds. The Pioneer Line's captain, a Mr. Turner, employed a large scale he carried for the purpose of weighing his passengers' traps. We witnessed a general war of reduction as men weighed and sorted all manner of goods: pins, needles, books, crowbars, shirts and shovels, boots and shoes, buffalo robes bought on the road, gold washers, carpenter's tools and writing paper, hatchets and rifles, brandy and tobacco. A few things sold, and some were burned. Most of the discharged property, which Caleb estimated at worth no less than five thousand dollars, was abandoned. A few of our company scavenged trunks, exchanging heavy ones for lighter.

Caleb was disappointed at acquiring no medicines, expecting, since three or four doctors traveled with the Pioneer Line, the possibility. But Captain Turner granted the doctors a collective dispensation for an additional seventy-five pounds of baggage weight.

I had not before so closely observed the Pioneer Line's passengers as I did this day. Half, perhaps more, looked to be a hard set, their faces ravaged by drinking, their reckless demeanor suggesting men without character. To a man like Joshua Giddings, appointed to fight the Devil, they must have looked like his adversary's minions.

The numbers gathered together that day may have prompted Giddings' sudden outburst. Most of the Pioneers' two hundred passengers were present, lined up at Captain Turner's scale set on a convenient rock in camp. There must also have been twenty people from our train, and perhaps another fifty or so from the Knoxville Company, behind which we had traveled since the Fourth.

Whether inspired by the size of the crowd or the insensible waste of property, Giddings suddenly leapt upon an abandoned trunk, arms windmilling, eyes wild. "Repent! Repent!" he shouted. "Repent! All ye who be as messengers of Satan, possessing the latest authentic news from Hell, and hear this!"

Giddings loved his own voice. He often preached an hour, haranguing listeners with exhortations to abandon the Devil and embrace the Lord. But this day he was brief as an explosion. And I will never forget the unforgivable words he hissed at his surprised audience.

"Yea, ye be as messengers of Satan! And I beseech the Lord for something fearful, something purposely awful, to alarm you to your careless state! Yea, I beseech the Lord to smite ye in your evil!"

Was I the only listener dismayed by Joshua Giddings' reckless petition? Perhaps. Most had turned back to whatever engaged them before he began shouting. Giddings was an old story now, heard before, ignored. Even as Giddings called out for the Lord to smite us, Caleb resumed some medical discussion with a doctor traveling with the Pioneers.

But I was outraged. Perhaps it was Celia's story, so fresh in my mind. Perhaps it was the image of her dead baby in a drawer, so near to mine of little George buried in a provision box. Perhaps it was the imprecation itself that propelled me to my improbable action. But before I knew what I was doing, I had marched to the foot of Giddings' platform and called him a scoundrel to his face.

"How dare you, Mr. Giddings! On such a journey as this to publicly pray for calamity! Surely opportunity suffices without pleading increase from the Almighty. I do not see you to be a man of God, sir. I see you to be a fool!"

My denunciation slid Giddings into a brief, surprised silence. He stared at me with blazing black eyes for a moment, then leaned over, hands fluttering from his sleeves like captured birds.

"And I see you," he whispered, his eyes nailing me. "I see you for what you are, Mrs. Daniels. And you are without courage in the Lord's work. You are a coward, Mrs. Daniels, a coward."

There was more, a rambling insinuation of portentous retribution. I stood there insensible to all but the one word: *coward.* Mouse. It was Burns, I believe, who wrote, "Oh, would some Power the giftie give us, to see ourselves as others see us."

I saw myself in Giddings' accusation, regardless the sanctimonious association. The badge was mine. I was a coward. Fear formed me. I was a coward on instinct, having acquired the trait, I suppose, from my own mother's milk. But a new realization smote me that day like a prophet's malediction: my cowardice had not been in fearing this journey, but in not fearing it enough. I had agreed to come. I had insisted. And had I not been so affrighted by the prospect of Caleb's absence, I would have stayed in Illinois. And my children with me. And kept them safe. And George would have lived. The realization that I was partner to his death sunk me like a stone.

While my mind reeled, Giddings preached at me. I must have looked bested, for he trapped his flying hands on his knees and bent to me further, as if to share a secret. "It is easy to despise human nature," he said in his glib preacher's voice, "from such a showing of it as our fellow travelers display, Mrs. Daniels. Three quarters of them are, at the least, peevish, capricious, profane, vulgar, idle, quarrelsome, contrary, and stubborn."

He did not add "cowardly" to his disgracing list, but I heard it. Giddings' false smile slipped into a smirk. "Surely you do not disagree, Mrs. Daniels?"

"Mr. Giddings," I said, collecting myself, "I doubt you and I should concur on whether or not it is raining."

It was a poor rejoinder.

Pacific Springs

I absorbed my new awareness like the landscape. I became accustomed to it despite its unfamiliarity. And there was no use dwelling on what might have been. We can't go back.

Celia never mentioned my confrontation with her husband. Though she wasn't witness, I thought the incident must find her ears. But perhaps it didn't. In the company, a delicacy about Celia induced a general solicitude for her. She caused kindness in people as unconsciously as her husband intentioned irritation.

I wondered how such opposites had united. At Pacific Springs, I asked.

Pacific Springs, where we encountered the first waters flowing west, lay atop South Pass, our avenue across the Rocky Mountains, and the most exalted milestone of the journey. From our guidebook and Fremont's account of his travels west, we knew no mountain peak announced the summit. Still, we were surprised to find the ascent so broad, gradual, and regular. Without Fremont's description, Caleb and I, walking together ahead of the wagon, would not have discerned the summit at all. He carried Fremont's book, referring to it for descriptions of prominent landmarks.

"There they are!" he said, pointing the book at a hill rising fifty or sixty feet high on one side of the broad plain, and then at another of equal elevation on the other. He signaled Douglas to halt the oxen and called back, "Bring your sisters and come ahead here!"

Caleb put his arm around my shoulders, kissed my forehead. "It still excites me, Sarah, forgive me."

Pretending pleasure for the occasion, I discovered genuine enjoyment. It gladdened me to see Caleb's boyish enthusiasm resurrected from our unspoken absolution. More than that, he had recovered the assuredness that marked him before George's death. At the Sweetwater camp he had regained himself, and with no word spoken, he assumed again captaincy of the company as though he hadn't noticed he'd relinquished it. Big Mary grinned to see it and said nothing. She and I exchanged a look of unspoken understanding.

On the summit of South Pass, my returned husband gathered his family into the circle of his excitement. "Take a farewell look," he said, solemn as a deacon. Together we gazed back at the way we had come. As we peered past the line of wagons and rocky landscape and into the eastern horizon, Caleb said, "We stand at the meridian between the rising and setting sun, midway between our far-off home and California."

Then he turned us west and said, "From here on we follow waters that flow into the Pacific."

It was then, I remember, that Mr. Vasquez rode up. Ours was the lead wagon that day, with Lucena and Will following. They joined us as Vasquez's black horse pranced a circle in the dust.

Mr. Vasquez, a portly gentleman of medium height and middling years, introduced himself as a proprietor of the Fort Bridger trading post, in partnership with Jim Bridger, the celebrated mountain man.

"Got a temporary trading post nearby," he said, getting down from his horse and shaking hands first with Caleb, then Will. "For the emigrants' convenience," he added, nodding to Lucena and me. "And I've advice on the road ahead for anyone as cares to hear it."

Since we expected no opportunities for trading before Fort Hall, the company agreed to the unexpected halt.

The makeshift trading post lay snugged against a rise half a mile off the road. It consisted of little more than Mr. Vasquez's tent and a dozen or so Indian lodges occupied by French-Canadian trappers with their Indian wives and children. Emigrants traveling ahead of us had largely depleted the goods for sale, leaving mostly buffalo robes, deerskins, and buckskin goods in the process of becoming coats, leggings, and moccasins by means of the Indian women's industry. One of our company traded some bacon, and another purchased a mule for packing, being

furnished with an order from Vasquez to select from the stock at Fort
Bridger.

The Fort Bridger road lay off our route, but to those of us gathered
in front of Vasquez's tent to learn what lay ahead, he touted it as prefer-
able. While the rest of the company tended to their animals or examined
the Indian women's work, Big Mary, Caleb and I, Craven Hester, and
some men who had joined us at Fort Laramie watched Vasquez lick the
end of a pencil and draw the route on a scrap of paper.

Caleb examined the drawing and said, "Our intentions were to
follow the road from South Pass via Sublette's Cutoff."

Vasquez shook his head. "A mistake, my friend. Big desert, no water,
no wood. You want my road. Past Fort Bridger it comes to the Salt Lake.
Mormons there got vegetables up. Sell some, they do. And beds to rent,
for those care to stay a time."

Vegetables? Beds? Such things seemed improbable to us, accustomed
as we were to wilderness, and tempting as a mirage.

"Caleb — " I started to say, but he didn't hear.

"That not being our destination," he said to Vasquez, shaking his
head, "the company won't likely want to take the time for a detour."

Vasquez shrugged. "Salt Lake road meets up the regular road coming
from Fort Hall."

Debate consumed the company. Big Mary and the Scandinavians
were for the Fort Bridger/Salt Lake road. Descriptions of the Mormon
community's hospitality, of vegetables and beds, tempted all the women.
Caleb claimed the regular road and Sublette's Cutoff saved five days.
Craven Hester suggested Vasquez's recommendation arose from self-
interest, since emigrants taking the Salt Lake road must necessarily
pass his trading post.

A general argument ensued for and against the proposed roads, with
nearly everyone finding fault with those opposed to their own preference. Some men, it seemed to me, were faultfinders by nature; others
acquired it from proximity, like disease.

My daughters were engrossed in a children's game with Sallie Hester,
and my husband and son in a discussion promising no swift conclusion.
I wandered away and found Celia watching an Indian woman beading
moccasins.

"There's a spring ahead," I said, "the first waters flowing toward the
Pacific. I'm going to walk over to see it, Celia. Come with me."

I had, despite myself, absorbed some of Caleb's fascination with our
endeavor. This immense movement of people across the landscape was
indeed dramatic, something big to be part of. If one were not a coward,

I thought, my mind drifting into dark territory. And if I had not broken my mother's heart, if the journey promised less of death and disaster, if my son had not been sacrificed to it. If, if, if. A coward's word.

"I should be delighted for the pleasure of your company, Mrs. Daniels," Celia said.

She was always pliant as grass. Women often are, I've decided. It's unwise. Blowing with the wind unmoors us. But I wonder, do we trail others' convictions for lack of our own? Or do we fail our own for lack of courage? And if so, how came we to be deprived of a characteristic so essential to happiness? I've thought much on the matter. It may be that courage is not so much acquired by women as extinguished in them by fathers and brothers and husbands. Women with courage and convictions seem not to suit a great many men. But perhaps that's only because they are unfamiliar with such women. I suppose it's a chicken-and-egg situation, it being impossible to settle which came first.

In the three hundred miles since Fort Laramie, Celia had gained a robustness it pleased me to see. Her familiar calico dress fit her better now, even if her adopted oversized boots didn't. She kept them, she said, for their good understanding, winking at her little joke.

Celia's horses, too, under our care, had filled out, a great comfort to her. She still remained as alert for good grass as Douglas, who often took them a mile or more off the road to find it.

As we strolled toward the patch of green we took for the springs, Celia scrutinized the distance. "This is a desolate, barren-looking landscape. I fear I miss the woods of Kentucky more than I expected."

"Is that your home? Kentucky?" She had not spoken of it before, that I recalled. I pressed the opportunity to satisfy my curiosity. "And Mr. Giddings, too?"

Celia's stride slowed, and she glanced up at me from beneath the brim of her faded blue sunbonnet. "My home was Kentucky, yes, but Joshua is a New Englander. Can you not tell? He has such certitude."

Celia rarely called her husband by his given name. I detected no affection in it.

"I wonder, then, how came you to meet," I said, "if it's no trespass to inquire."

Celia stopped, her skirt catching on a sage twig, and she bent to free it. When she stood, she looked distracted, as though she had lost something but couldn't remember what. The place was unusually quiet, I recall, no creaking wagons or shouting teamsters within earshot, no fractious company discussions, no braying mules, nothing, really, except the emptiness into which a distant train of white-topped wagons crawled.

The overriding sense was emptiness, with the warm scent of sage on the wind.

"Have you ever been alone, all alone, Mrs. Daniels? It's as frightening as that," she said, pointing a slender finger at the infinity of sage and sand and gravel stretched before us beneath an immense and cloudless sky. It was a benign scene to the uninitiated, but I, like Celia, sensed its menacing possibilities.

"My brother and I had a little farm, just a few acres our parents scratched from the woods before the consumption took them." Celia looked at me and smiled sadly as we resumed our walk. "I was nearly eighteen, and Gideon two years younger, when we buried them beneath the magnolia next to the house. For ceremony, my brother and I read from the family Bible and sang the hymns our mother taught us. It was the best we could do, having no preacher. We lived miles and miles from the nearest settlement, and we had no church of any denomination. I suppose that such absence later leaned me toward Mr. Giddings."

Celia stooped, plucked a bit of sage, sniffed it. "This is a harsh land, isn't it, Mrs. Daniels? Even its smells. Turpentine, this reminds me of," she said, tossing the twig away. "Magnolia is the sweetest smell, but I can barely recall it."

"Roses. I miss roses," I said, slowing my pace, remembering the fragrant abundance surrounding the door at home. How far away it seemed.

Celia stopped and looked into the distance. "My brother lies beneath that magnolia tree, too," she said softly, "and baby Rachel."

"Oh, Celia, forgive me. I'm so sorry to have reminded you."

She turned to me, smiled sadly. "Please don't be. I need no reminding. No day passes without my remembering as though it were yesterday. I'm grateful for your understanding, and for the friendship of your family and all the company. I've never known such companionship before. It's a great comfort, not to be alone."

And she described then such a desperate loneliness it tore my heart. Celia's brother had contracted the illness that took their parents. Frantic for help, she sought the nearest neighbor and found at his house a visiting circuit preacher firing up attendance for a camp meeting.

"He spoke to me of faith," Celia said as we resumed our walk, "and I believe I felt it spring up in my soul. I begged him to raise it in my brother, and Joshua came to our little cabin and knelt on his knees next to my brother's cot and prayed over him. I remember Gideon, his face all fevered, asking him, 'Cannot God raise me to health as in olden days?' and Joshua said, 'He can.' 'Then why don't he?' Gideon asked, and Joshua said, 'Because you lack faith.' "

Celia kicked at a little stone with her boot and sent it rolling down the road. "Mr. Giddings called on me the following year, his circuit being an annual one. I was alone, Mrs. Daniels, all alone, managing as best I could, taking in sewing, raising a few vegetables and chickens. He came to my house and said straight off that he would call again the following year. He said that if in that time I found no one I liked better, and if I would be willing to give him up to his calling and never stand in the way of his going, and if he should find no one he liked better, then perhaps something further might be said on the subject."

Pacific Springs was a boggy, mosquito-infested place. Celia and I stared at the waters trickling westward. I only half listened as she spoke of the lonely time on her little farm after her marriage to Giddings, the long empty months of his absences, the brief joy of her baby's companionship, the devastating loneliness following her loss. I was thinking about propinquity, remembering my mother's story of how she, Boston-bred Lacy, wed Harlan Ridgeway, the stable boy. It was as unavoidable as Celia marrying the circuit preacher, and I my handsome passerby. I remembered Caleb decrying his fear that life would just happen to him if he didn't decide something big on his own. It seemed to me that a woman's life always just happened, and the happiness of it lay inexorably tied to whatever good, bad, or indifferent man stumbled into it. A woman did nothing much of her own, I concluded.

Whether I felt regretful or angry over the revelation, I don't recall, but a revelation it was. And I thought cowardice not an unnatural consequence of such unopposed eventuality. Fear follows dependency like a gosling its mother.

From South Pass to the Big Sandy River, the road was, except for one rocky ravine, excellent as a turnpike. Grass near the road was all fed out, and Douglas caught two sage hens while looking for it. I roasted them in my little tin cooker over some sagebrush. It burned my eyes, but the aromatic shrub made a good fire. It smelled to me of camphor.

At the Big Sandy, the road forked left for Salt Lake and right for Sublette's Cutoff. Big Mary and perhaps a third of the company had decided for Salt Lake. Mrs. Hester and I waved wistfully after them as they departed. She and I had talked of the Mormon community at Salt Lake, of seeing houses, stores, farms. But our men were for the other road, and we went where they went.

I'm not so tractable now. I have my say. I may not prevail, not being deaf to argument, but I have my say.

While we nooned at the Big Sandy in the thin shade our wagons afforded, a light wagon coming up the Salt Lake road halted with us. It was driven by three Mormon men carrying mail from Salt Lake for the States, and the Mormon Constitution to submit to Congress. It was beautifully written and very neatly put up. I remember it because I wondered about the women's lives affected by such a document. Were they worse off than Celia? We talked, Mrs. Hester and I, of how the Mormons lived. In the States, their beliefs and practices provoked hostility, but here, I think, in the wilderness they had selected for themselves, we emigrants found them mostly curious.

I later learned, I can't recall from whom, that Big Mary elected to stay with the Mormons. The knowledge inclined me toward the people, from my admiration for Big Mary, but her adoption of beliefs so against a woman's independence puzzled me. I concluded a man had chanced into her life. I hope he was a good man.

At the Big Sandy, despite Mr. Vasquez's warning for the desert ahead, I neglected fear. Perhaps it was knowing the Mormon community lay not far distant, or that our animals were in good condition, or perhaps it was confidence in Caleb.

He had resumed the captaincy with no word against him, and it was he who fired the gun at midnight, rousing us from our slumbers to commence the crossing of Sublette's Cutoff in the cool of night so the animals might suffer less from thirst.

We later traveled by night on worse deserts, but this was the first. It was very cold, and it seemed strange, getting ready in the dark, the noise of preparations hushed by habits of night.

Sublette's Cutoff was hard going through one dry ravine after another. Dead cattle lined the road, the stench becoming very offensive to our olfactories. One of the Hester boys remarked that the road resembled a long, beastly charnel yard indicating the house lay ahead. Yet I still remember daybreak, and the beautiful pink sunrise from over the scenic mountains that lay on our right.

We guessed some seven out of ten companies took the cutoff, the saving of five days' travel too attractive to decline. Men, animals, and wagons had spread out over the desolate landscape, most too intent on their own progress to acknowledge strangers. We did, however, make the acquaintance here of Colonel Hamilton.

We came upon him sometime after our nooning. He was engaged in animated conversation with a band of three or four traders, nondescript-looking men with oxen, mules, and ponies for sale. But then, Colonel Hamilton was nothing if not animated.

He drove a carriage, shockingly dilapidated, but he had a fine-looking four-horse team. The colonel himself more resembled his conveyance, being small and his exterior not of the smoothest. He was about fifty and may once have been a handsome man. A new hat would have greatly benefited his appearance. The one he wore, a rusty-looking vestige of straw, had in the majority of both crown and brim departed. From where he sat on the driver's seat of his carriage, he doffed the remnant at our approach without slacking his censure of the traders.

"Gentlemen," he said to them, leaning an elbow on his knee and shaking his head, "I myself witnessed your acquisition of this pony for which you ask 'a mere two hundred and fifty dollars,' as you say. You bought him from an Indian near Fort Laramie for six shirts. You ought to be horsewhipped for thievery on both ends!"

One of the men shrugged and said, "You want him or don't you, mister?"

"Colonel!" Hamilton slammed the straw hat back on his head. "I'm Colonel William Hamilton, youngest son of Alexander Hamilton, of Revolutionary memory. Perhaps you've heard of him?"

The traders looked at one another, and blankly back at Hamilton, who erupted into merry baritone laughter. It was so exuberant and so unexpected from such slightness of person, it made one smile to hear it.

"Go on, off with you!" he shouted. "Thieves you are, and ignorant to boot!"

The colonel had lost his entire company to the Salt Lake road. At Caleb's invitation he joined ours, with no objection from the company, his addition being no hindrance. He fed his horses oats he paid a dollar a bushel for from Salt Lake traders. We encountered several bands of them in this area, enterprising Mormons making money off the emigrants. Who could fault them? This great unexpected emigration past their isolated community offered valuable commerce. But we resented their greed.

We traversed Sublette's Cutoff without loss of animals, but many of them suffered. It distressed Janey to see our milch cow and the oxen becoming so footsore from the rocky terrain. She brushed and petted Emma, and Buck and Cherry, and wept new tears. The guidebook specified the cutoff as thirty-five miles, but we didn't reach Green River until late that night, and we knew it was more.

At the river we found two primitive ferries carrying emigrants across the swift, deep stream. Mormon men operated one, charging ten dollars a wagon. Some French-Canadians competed with them at eight dollars a wagon. Although they were a rough-looking set, luring the gullible into drinking and gambling with them, Caleb engaged them, their services being equal.

To Giddings, the mountain men embodied the very curse of Satan. "You have no claim to humanity but form!" he shouted in preclusion to the lengthy inventory of their supposed sins he then flung at them.

I concluded Giddings' perturbation derived as much from the unanticipated expense of the ferry as the mountain men's offensiveness. He was not comforted by their laughter.

"Do you propose acting captain here, Daniels?" Giddings challenged, turning on my husband.

Caleb was unloading our wagon, a separate ferrying of contents necessitated by our wagon's weight. "Have you an opposition, Mr. Giddings?"

Giddings did, launching a harangue of objection to both the ferrymen and the ferriage fees while Caleb, Douglas, and I emptied the wagon.

Weary of the tirade, Caleb said, "I'll take it as my personal contribution to your good works to pay the cost myself, Mr. Giddings. Thank you for the opportunity to assist your cause."

The preacher said nothing, but I saw resentment, and something more, as he watched Caleb count the money into his hand.

The ferrying over of the company took all day and exhausted Caleb. In addition to supervising the loading and unloading of the wagons and their contents, there were the animals to be swum across. Caleb got our team over, plus Celia's horses, and then went back for the oxen loaned to Giddings, the preacher disavowing responsibility for their care.

In repacking our wagon after his return, I noticed the red tin cake box. "Oh, Caleb," I said, "let's taste my mother's plum cake. It would be such a treat!"

"If you want to, Sarah," he said, weariness shadowing his eyes. "None for me. I'm too tired to eat anything."

"We'll wait, then," I said, "until we can enjoy it together."

Janey got teary when I handed the cake box to her to put back. "Oh, sweetie," I said, "go ahead and have some." But I think she was remembering the cake maker more than the cake.

She shook her head and tucked the tin beneath her unfinished sampler, untouched since Ash Hollow. "Let's save it for California, Mama. That'll be a real celebration."

I wish we'd at least tasted that cake at Green River.

Bear River

I suppose Joshua Giddings had an opinion, as religionists must, on whether places like Ash Hollow and the Bear River valley represented God's mercy or Satan's temptations. I never asked, nor did I arrive at any conclusion of my own. These Eden-like oases lifted our spirits with their lush beauty. And they deceived us, or at least me, into believing all was well.

It was not.

The long road west passed through both Eden and the Devil's playground. The cruelty of the map was that the easy part came first, when we and our animals were fresh. The prairie, green with grass and adorned with wildflowers, greeted us first, not the mirage-ridden barrenness of the dangerous Platte. Ash Hollow, with its bubbling springs and chirping birds, came first, not the difficult climb into the Black Hills. And now the beauteous Bear River valley preceded — what?

From the Green River we had a good road into the valley of the Bear, steep but not so formidable as the descent at Ash Hollow. The road slanted down, winding around the mountain, from which we enjoyed a heartening view of the green valley below. Its actuality exceeded our anticipations. Dense and tasseling grass rose high as our knees. We waded through wild oats, barley, rye, flax flowering with tiny blue blossoms, fragrant as a garden. The Bear flowed gentle and generous, offering trout from its depths and ducks and geese from its surface. Hunters found herds of elk and antelope, shared their bounty. We women made stews with fat meat and wild onions. How we all feasted. Savory aromas wafted from every campfire, and after, late into the night, there drifted on the clear night air the sounds of singing and violins and jews' harps.

Along the Bear River we encountered several bands of Snake Indians. A half dozen or so visited our camp one evening. Some had guns, including a squaw on horseback, who carried a rifle in a buckskin case, complete with horn and pouch. She had two young children with her. One, about three years old, clung to her shoulders. Another, no more than a year, wearing a handsome little buckskin shirt, was curiously fastened to a board hung from the pommel of his mother's Spanish saddle. I held Hannah tightly in my arms, unsure of the Indians' intentions. The Indian woman and I exchanged long and inquisitive looks. I offered a tentative smile. When she nodded in return, I felt a kinship that transcended the vast chasm of our differences. We were mothers.

The Indian woman was handsomely outfitted in a buffalo skin fashioned something like a mantua. Finely dressed antelope, with the hair on, she wore like a mantilla. But it was the chief who took the candle for fashion.

On seeing him, Colonel Hamilton, who had joined our family for supper, jumped to his feet. "Oh, out of the way, Broadway dandies!" he exclaimed, banging a fork against his tin plate. "This fellow does beat all!"

The Indian on his pony was a striking sight, enveloped in a fine gray blanket right down to his moccasins. His handsome face glistened with vermilion. His long black hair, beautifully dressed and parted in the middle, exhibited surprising decorations of bits of brass and scraps of red flannel.

He, too, carried a gun.

Seeing it, the colonel shook his head. "These people acquire guns from the emigrants, who trade an old rifle not worth three dollars in the States, with a little powder and lead, for a pony worth a hundred dollars. Some future emigration may have trouble from these guns yet."

The Indians had come to trade. Like most Indians we had thus far encountered, however, theirs was also a begging expedition. They inquired after every little article they knew the use of, until, to be done with the visit, someone gave them a bit of gunpowder, despite Colonel Hamilton's advisement.

The valley of the Bear was a week's easy travel, and it lulled us. Even I, wary by old prejudice, hardly demurred at Caleb's enthusiasm for another cutoff when it came.

Dozens of emigrants' notes impaled on sticks at Soda Springs announced the Emigrants' Cutoff, as we called it. None decried it. No one had returned to say it nay.

It was the natural place to try. It was here that we left the Bear River behind, saw it loop around Sheep Rock and head south again, leaving us to the dry valley through which the road continued north to Fort Hall. That tried and true route to Oregon had served emigrants well, but gold seekers had little patience for a road heading north. They wanted west.

The old route went north to the Snake River, followed it to the Raft River, then dropped south again. With such geography, a cutoff directly west was an inevitable venture. Thus the cards and notes stuck on sticks at Soda Springs.

The thicket of notes announced the various companies ahead of us taking the new shortcut. One said it saved seventy-five miles over the Fort Hall road, another said sixty. One claimed this route intersected the headwaters of the Humboldt in a hundred miles.

The cutoff being newly opened, there was nothing in our guidebook about it. We saw wagon tracks branching west, nothing more. We had only emigrants' notes to recommend it, the fact that no one had returned to warn against it, and the hope for better grazing on a road less traveled.

Perhaps it was our sojourn in the lush Bear River valley that primed us for a gamble, or perhaps it was the success of Sublette's Cutoff. The promised savings of miles and days tempted every traveler. As much as anything, though, I think we took the cutoff because those ahead had.

It proved a mistake.

The area of the springs was a strange landscape, strewn with volcanic rock and pocked in profusion by deep basins and chasms from which hundreds of gaseous springs gushed from cone-shaped deposits. Some of these cones rose ten feet, with water bubbling out of the top or seeping through crevices and down the sides.

Soda Springs, Beer Springs, Steamboat, they all astonished us, far surpassing our guidebook's note as "a place of very great interest."

At Beer Springs, Colonel Hamilton laughed his good laugh as some men rushed with their cups at a dozen foaming and roiling springs. "Busy as a brewhouse, ain't it?" he said.

I tasted the water, too. It looked like lager beer, and tasted like it, only flat. I added lemon syrup and sugar to it, which made a delicious and refreshing soda drink for the children.

All the springs were cold except Steamboat. Taking its name from the noise of its waters, it boiled up furiously in a fitful pulse three feet high through an aperture in the rock a foot in diameter.

Lucena walked round and round it, shaking her pretty head in disbelief. "La, ain't this just the most interesting spot on earth you ever beheld," she said to Janey on one of her circuits.

Janey looked over at me, where I stood watching the exhibition with Hannah. She caught my eye, smiled, and said, "Yes, it is, Mrs. Semple, it is."

I hadn't seen Janey smile in such a long time. Poor thing, she seemed always in tears or on the verge of them. And who could blame her? But it was like seeing the sun come out after a month's rain, that day at the springs when she smiled at me. I took it for forgiveness. Even so, I don't think I remember Janey smiling again until the saloon keeper at Nevada City invited her to play his piano.

From the springs, westward travel on the new cutoff was a daily toil up and down mountains and ravines running north-south. Wrecked wagons and dead cattle littered the landscape. There was no road to follow. Our company spread out across the ravines and rises, shouted to one another the discovery of likely tracks or water.

Lacking landmark and guide, we could not say where we were or how we progressed. We were simply "there," and heading west.

There was much suffering on this road. Water was difficult to find, grass scarce. Our animals stumbled in the rough declines. Wagon accidents slowed progress. I remain amazed that we ever found a passage through those rugged piles of rocks. Douglas, Janey, and I had the responsibility of our wagon and stock, while Caleb assisted Celia with her wagon and our spare oxen. Giddings doubtless noticed, despite his raving through this country like a madman, decrying sin and Satan to the unfortunate passengers of the Pioneer Line.

We came upon them here, scattered over the countryside, mostly afoot, mules nearly used up, and provisions, too. Douglas and I, driving our oxen, overtook one of the Pioneer passengers. He was plodding wearily ahead on his own, a young man named Reid. He said men in his mess had quarreled over some sugar, and he feared their desperation. The Pioneer Line's subscribers, he reported, were on rations now, and his only food that day had been a drink made from flour and water. I gave him some milk and bread and invited him to share our supper.

I remember the young man's visit because we heard a violin that night, and singing, from a company camped nearby. It surprised us both.

"Oh," he said, "listen to that! It seems almost unimaginable to me that anyone's heart should be light enough for singing."

A tear crept down Janey's cheek at the sound of the instrument. I knew she was thinking of Illinois, the parlor and piano and her grandmother. I was, too.

For Giddings, the Pioneer Line's debacle bespoke God's punishment. He rebuked them day and night for a week until we intersected the road from Fort Hall. That's when we discovered we'd saved nothing. A comparison of roadometer readings from emigrants taking the Fort Hall road showed our nine days of hard travel on the cutoff saved but twenty-five miles.

I went to school on that lesson. It served me when the time came.

We met the Jenkins family shortly after. I suspect Mrs. Jenkins' transgressions diverted Giddings' attention from the poor passengers of the Pioneer Line.

Colonel Hamilton knew the family. They had gone the Salt Lake road. On seeing their wagon, the colonel waved the remains of his straw hat and hailed them with his good laugh. "You make a poor advertisement for the speediness of that route, Jenkins," he said.

No less than we did ours, I thought, but didn't say it.

We nooned with them. Mrs. Jenkins was a nervous, well-formed woman who spoke little. I tried engaging her in conversation, eager to hear what she had seen in Salt Lake, what the Mormons were like, how they lived. But she averted her eyes when addressed, fussed distractedly with her hair. Gleaning little from her inconsequential responses, I abandoned the effort.

They traveled with three inconsolable-looking children, the eldest, a girl named Alice, about eighteen, comely in the manner of her mother. Mr. Jenkins, a thin and miserable man, bore the pain of a month-old buckshot wound in his back that Caleb dressed for him. It was suppurating badly.

We invited them to join our company, but Jenkins declined, made uncomfortable, perhaps, by Colonel Hamilton's knowledge of their scandalous story, told that night in camp amidst much laughter. I was in our wagon, writing in my journal, but snatches of the story found my disbelieving ears.

Mrs. Jenkins, according to Colonel Hamilton, had formed an attachment to another in their company, a man named Lancaster that Hamilton described as a watery-eyed old scoundrel with a wife and daughter in Illinois. Lancaster traveled with a grown son, a young man named Henry. Mrs. Jenkins and the elder Lancaster, anxious to rid themselves of Mr. Jenkins, persuaded Henry and a friend of his named Chase to assist them in the endeavor, their reward to be the hand of Alice Jenkins to Henry Lancaster, and Lancaster's daughter to Chase.

As I discerned the story, young Lancaster, carrying a rifle, and Chase, with a shotgun, lured Jenkins from the road, pretending to have seen gold. They fired simultaneously and Jenkins fell, to his death as they supposed. They ran back to the company yelling, "Indians! Indians!" and reported Jenkins dead or kidnapped, I don't recall.

Jenkins, however, unbeknownst to his assailants, survived the assault, the rifle shots not proving fatal, and that night he crawled to the camp of a passing company. The two Lancasters, later arrested, were tried at Fort Laramie and sentenced to return to the States. Chase escaped. And Mr. and Mrs. Jenkins and family resumed their journey, the husband abiding his wife for the sake of the children.

The tale staggered me. That such an alliance as that formed between Mrs. Jenkins and Mr. Lancaster should thrive in this great open space, I thought astonishing in itself. And in the midst of the misery no company evaded. Staring sleepless at the stars that night, I pondered the implications. I concluded that human nature, regardless of circumstances, will not be denied.

I was not alone in the presumption. Later, furtive glances and whispers dogged me and my family from the Humboldt until the company dispersed at the Sink.

Indians

The Emigrants' Cutoff, the Fort Hall route, and the Salt Lake road all converged near the City of Rocks, a valley some two miles long and perhaps half a mile wide. It was strewn with queer rocks and sandstone formations worn by the elements and time into all manner of strange and romantic shapes.

Our imaginations readily identified resemblances to wigwams and haystacks, riders astride, thatched cottages complete to eaves and chimney, turrets and canopies, huge likenesses of petrified fungi, sphinxes and statues. Travelers ahead of us had inscribed the more elaborate forms with tar, naming them as their fancies dictated; Napoleon's Castle and City Hotel are two I recall.

In number and diversity, these hundreds of domes and masses and spurs were beyond description, and none of us was immune to the scenery's curiosities. Lucena, still the cheerful sightseer, said she thought an hour's look at it worth the whole journey.

But after the City of Rocks, even Lucena lost spirit.

Travel got hard, then harder. From the City of Rocks the road descended abruptly into a broad valley, then climbed steeply to the top of Granite Mountain over terrain so stony it threatened constant overturn of the wagons. From the summit of Granite Mountain it was four miles down to Goose Creek, the whole descent rugged and difficult for wagons, the road dropping more precipitously than on any part of the journey thus far.

Ours was the first wagon down, with the team behind, the rear wheels locked, men holding it back with ropes. Janey and Sallie Hester walked our milch cow behind, while I carried Hannah in my arms and followed with my heart in my mouth. A dozen times the poor cow slipped and Janey cried, "Emma!" I feared any moment I might see us all lose our footing and roll to the bottom in a shower of stones and pebbles, but fortune preserved us.

Colonel Hamilton's carriage and horses followed our wagon, and after a heart-stopping descent he joined us in safety. "This beats all the going downhill I ever heard of," the colonel said to me, mopping his face with his shirttail. "This would not appear a practicable road to any but a California emigrant."

Together we watched the remaining wagons in their perilous descent. It seemed all but impossible they could be held back from tumbling straight down. One stretch of the road pitched down a hundred yards at an angle of nearly forty-five degrees. We saw an axle break on one wagon, another completely overturn, animals fall and tear their knees.

That night Caleb, still ashen from the terrifying and wearying effort of getting the company down, collapsed into a fitful slumber without eating.

We rose early the next morning, commenced a hard drive through a landscape gray and barren, our animals exhausted by hard pulling without adequate feed or water. That was the day we encountered an ox slumped in the road. We could not get around, or advance, and so were forced to watch a man whip him while another yanked the poor beast's tail.

Hannah, drowsy from the heat, had been sleeping. She woke when the wagon stopped, and climbed from the back to sit between me and Douglas. I don't know where Caleb was. She pointed at the poor downed beast and began to cry, "Cherry! Cherry!"

"It's not Cherry," I said, turning her curly head from the scene and kissing her tears away. "Cherry's fine, we won't let anything bad happen to Cherry," I promised.

I sent Janey and Hannah back to the Hesters' wagon to prevent their witnessing more cruelty. The men lashed the fallen ox until blood came, but without effect. Poor beast, he had given his all. In a united effort, several men dragged the suffering brute from the road and left it to die. Like so many others.

I remember that poor animal's suffering, its eyes full of defeat and agony, because I date the downward spiral of our journey from that moment. Every day from then on it seemed some new and terrible burden befell us.

It was next day, on Goose Creek, near Thousand Springs, that Indians attacked.

Indians attacked. As I write them, the words seem wrong, both inadequate and too stirring for the Paiutes and their insidious depredations. In the beginning, back when Will Semple and so many others outfitted themselves for defense, when we envisioned savages on horseback screaming war cries and swinging tomahawks, we thought we knew what that meant, Indians attacked.

Our expectations so often fail reality. On this journey that lesson repeated like Colt's revolver.

Sioux, Pawnee, Cheyenne, Arapaho, even the Snakes' fancy chief with the vermilion face and brassed hair, met our expectations of "Indians" — the savages of myth and legend. But the Paiute, never.

Four of them, the first we had seen — and we saw them rarely afterward despite their persistent presence — came into our camp at Thousand Springs, a valley pocked with hot springs, lying between Goose Creek and the Humboldt River. Colonel Hamilton was visiting with me while I prepared supper over a campfire of sagebrush.

"Well, well, what have we here?" he said, jumping up from the volcanic rock he'd been sitting on.

Startled, I looked up from stirring my kettle of beans to see four pathetic-looking humans — a status some emigrants later argued. The men were, in form, short, squat, and stout, with heads nearly perfectly round and complexions dark as Negroes. Coarse black hair, filthy and matted, hung down to their massive shoulders. Whatever philosophy ruled these primitive people, cleanliness was clearly not one of its tenets.

Each carried a bow and quiver of arrows and wore only a breechcloth for cover. Around their waists, suspended from a kind of woven belt, hung what appeared to be a dozen or so roasted rats.

They laughed excessively and appeared eager to obtain our friendship. They greeted Colonel Hamilton with a cheery "How-de-do!"

At that he laughed his good laugh and returned the greeting. They seemed quite excited by the success of their conversation thus far and advanced it by exclaiming "Whoa!," "Haw!," and "Gaw-dam-you!"

This exhausted their mastery of English learned from passing teamsters, because they after repeated these expressions regardless what Colonel Hamilton said to them. This so delighted the colonel that

he engaged them in conversation for an hour, to the general amusement of the company. He discoursed at length on whatever came into
his head — his family, federalist government, Aaron Burr's politics —
while the Indians grinned and chattered back in their own language,
punctuated by merry expressions of "How-de-do!," "Whoa!," "Haw!,"
and "Gaw-dam-you!"

After this optimistic exchange impervious to understanding, our visitors indicated by signs a desire to trade their belts of dead rodents, roasted
complete with tails and entrails, for tobacco. Their wearers apparently
considered them a great delicacy and a generous trade, but found no
takers. Some young men offered to give the Indians tobacco, against
Craven Hester's advice.

"Don't encourage them, boys," he said. "These Diggers are all thieves."

At the word *Diggers,* I saw merriment erased from our visitors' countenances. They knew the word and disliked it.

Like the Mormons whose territory we passed through as an economic
boon, the Indians took advantage. It was hard to blame them, living as
they did in this desolate land, on a diet of rats and roots, for helping
themselves to the passing parade of meat.

They stole two mules and one ox from our company that night,
in the first of several diligent assaults. On the road the next morning we met a distraught man whose entire team had disappeared. He
was stranded, hopeful only that the men in his company searching
nearby ravines would find the animals before the Indians slaughtered
them.

Reports of Indian depredations continually reached us as we jour-
neyed deeper into a country terrible beyond anything yet seen. High,
barren mountains bordered the narrow valley of sand and hot springs
through which we now traveled. It was a dry, dusty, bleak, and colorless
landscape of hills whited by lime and blacked by volcanic rock. While we
followed this valley, Indians stole, killed, or wounded more than ten
animals belonging to our company. Including our milch cow.

Poor Janey, she looked like a ghost, her face was that white the morning she raced up to me as I was preparing breakfast. "Mama, Mama!" she
cried, taking my arm as though to pull me after her. "I went to milk
Emma, and I can't find her!"

Douglas, putting up our table, said, "I tethered her with the rest of
the stock."

"She's gone! She's gone!"

"Douglas," I said, "you go and see. And find your father."

"She's gone!" Janey cried as Douglas took off on the run.

"Janey, I want you to set the table," I said, walking her to the box of dishes at the back of the wagon. Hannah was inside, dressing herself, I remember that. She had learned how, and took particular satisfaction in the achievement, practicing each morning by repeatedly putting on and removing a sacque or pair of pantalettes.

"We've got things to do here," I said, "and we'll just keep busy at them until your father and brother get back."

Tears streamed down Janey's face. "Oh, Mama — "

Seeing her sister's distress, Hannah began to cry, and I collected her into my arms. "We'll all just wait here, and we'll let the men handle this."

Even then I had already turned my son, still a boy, into a man. And placed my expectations on him. And on Janey and Hannah, too. "We'll just wait," I had said. It's what women were expected to do, and I was teaching what I had been taught. I catch myself now, knowing more.

We never found Emma, but Janey never stopped looking for her, hoping against hope, all the rest of that hard way to California, that our cow had wandered off and might just as suddenly reappear. I was glad not to have found her, certain as Caleb was that she'd been slaughtered by the Indians. I wanted Janey to remember Emma as whole.

The constant threat of Indian attack, and the desolate landscape all but devoid of grass for the hard-used stock, made us all uneasy and stirred disputes. A mute witness to growing contentiousness was a fresh-made grave we passed in this valley. I wrote in my journal that a proper restraint on tempers might have averted the unfortunate incident, then copied the marker's notice of another senseless death: "Samuel A. Fitzsimmons, died of a wound inflicted by a bowie knife in the hands of James Remington, August 25, 1849."

From Thousand Springs we debouched through a rocky pass into the valley of the Humboldt River, a rough, broken, sterile country. Like emigrants ahead and behind, we would follow the Humboldt's sluggish, serpentine path three hundred tortuous miles, dogged by Indians, illness, hunger, and more.

Our particular trouble, if so benign a word suffices for the ensuing calamity, erupted at our first camp on the Humboldt. We didn't expect it here, our guard was down. There was grass near the water's edge, and some stunted willows useful for fuel.

I remember Will Semple joking about the campsite's attractiveness for our stock. "Looks good for the 'Whoa Haws,' " he said. "And not too bad for the 'Gaw-dam-yous' either." And Lucena saying, "Oh, Will," in the affectionate, chastising way she had with him.

The river here, near its headwaters, though without current, was wide and deep and pure, with ducks and some small fish to vary our monotonous diet of hard bread, bacon, and beans.

Since the first loss of stock, the company had hauled in close together during the day in defense against the Indians, and at night we camped close and kept watch. Here, on the banks of the Humboldt, perhaps the guarding grew lax. The watch changed every two hours, so as not to work a hardship on anyone. Consequently, no one knew for sure who, during that night, missed hearing the Indians approach.

In the morning we discovered three oxen with iron-tipped arrows jutting from their sides like giant quills. The Paiutes dipped their arrows in a slow poison and followed wounded animals for hours, even days, waiting for them to drop. Now we had three more we knew would die. One was of the pair Caleb had loaned Giddings.

Until now the company had at least been fortunate in that none of the animals killed by Indians disabled any wagon. But a single ox could not pull a wagon, especially through the ankle-deep sand and dust of this region. Nor could the Giddings' horses answer; in this grass-barren country they had grown gaunt again.

The morning was icy cold. I was frying bacon for my family's breakfast over a smoky campfire of green willow, Hannah hanging on to my skirt and wearing a shawl of Janey's she fancied matched her sacque. Celia sat nearby on my provision box, her face wan with this new difficulty. Janey and Douglas were packing up our tent in preparation for the day's journey. Their breath puffed from the cold as they loaded our frost-whitened wagon.

The men of the company, warming their hands with tin cups of hot coffee or slapping their arms against the chill, conferred nearby, attempting to solve the problem of Giddings' injured ox.

"I don't see any other way, Giddings, except to stow your stuff among the company and leave your wagon," Caleb said.

I saw Celia bury her head in her hands as the men grumbled about the added weight.

"Reckon it's the only thing we can do," one of the Hester boys said.

A general nodding of heads confirmed the plan, and Giddings, eyes black as jet, looked around at the men. I felt my breath catch as he suddenly turned and shook his fist at Caleb.

"You're the captain, hey, Daniels? You can just make the decisions here, you think? Here's my decision, Daniels. You owe me an ox! You have my horses, which you say cannot be spared, so you owe me another ox!"

I jabbed the bacon from the frying pan, forked it onto a tin dish, saw Celia stand, grow pale, clutch her shawl, stare at her husband.

In all my years with Caleb I had never seen him lose his temper. But a man would have to be a saint to endure what he had without complaint. The death of our son, the nearly four months of hard travel, the responsibility, the doctoring, repairing wagons, coddling Giddings — it was too much. Caleb's restraint burst like a frayed rope.

"Giddings, I'm out of patience, it's used up, man! I will not, I cannot, let you have another ox without crippling my own wagon. So, get your stuff and stow it around."

"You owe me an ox!"

"I don't owe you anything!"

"I'm a man of God!"

"You're a ranting zealot!"

I stood, my heart in my throat, fearful they would come to blows. Celia had covered her mouth with her hands, but a high-pitched cry escaped them, and both Caleb and Giddings turned toward us.

There was silence for a moment, broken only by one of the men tossing his coffee into the sand and spitting. "Damn stuff tastes like alkali," he said, and sauntered off.

And then Giddings, his voice a smirky growl, said, "Well, it's my mistake to be asking, isn't it? I'm sure you'd be only too happy to accommodate the request, *Captain* Daniels, if my wife asked. You'd not deny her anything, would you?"

Caleb advanced on the man. "What in hell does that mean?"

Giddings smiled, if the expression could be called that, and shrugged. "We know what we know, don't we, Daniels?"

"You insulting, sniveling snake, I ought to — "

I thought, to the extent I was able to think, registering the accusation like a death, that Caleb would strike the man. Giddings thought so, too, for he backed away, hands raised.

"I am a man of God! I need only God, not the likes of you, Daniels! I don't need your ox. I have two good horses. I don't need you. I have God!"

I turned away, stirred the fire, wiped my hands, sloshed coffee into a cup, I don't know what I did. I know I didn't want to see or hear. I wanted all of it gone. I turned my back to it, trying to make it go away, but I heard their voices. I heard the men arguing, and Giddings shouting his leave-taking from the company, and Caleb calling him a fool. I heard Celia moan, "No, not alone! Alone, all alone! No!," and was aware she ran off. But I heard it all at a remove, something like a terrible, frightening play, like seeing little George falling from the wagon again.

I recollect little of the next hour. I know the men dispersed, with Giddings shouting his trust in God, and after a time Caleb sat down to breakfast, taking deep breaths and slamming his cup down and spilling coffee. He started to apologize. Whether for the spilled coffee, the terrible scene played out in front of the children and me, the humiliation of Giddings' accusation, or what, I don't know. I stopped him.

"It doesn't matter, Caleb," I said. "Let's just eat breakfast."

I wanted it all not to have happened, and I couldn't pretend it hadn't if we talked about it. I suppose that's what I was thinking. But I could not have been thinking clearly. I was too stunned by the accusation. Had Caleb denied it? Yes, of course, he had. Or had he? And if so, to what avail? Such an accusation, true or not, once cast, fastened like a leech.

Long silences occupied the space between "Is there any sugar?" and "How's the bacon holding out?" and other empty affectations of normalcy. The children had overheard the exchange, with only little Hannah unaware of its implications. I knew Douglas and Janey understood. They remembered the Jenkins family.

Janey disguised the awkwardness with pretense, saying, "Bacon's still good, Mama," a false note betrayed by a voice pitched higher than usual.

And Douglas said to no one in particular, "Looks like a good morning for travel, maybe not too hot."

No one knew what to say, and so, for the most part, said nothing. For Caleb, silence was familiar as day. He was a quiet man. And for me, silence was an old habit. But that day I recognized it for what it was. It was a coward's habit.

We were just packing up our breakfast things when we heard Giddings shouting for Celia. Shortly after, he came into our camp, glowering at Caleb. "Where's my wife?"

Caleb rose, fists clenching. He started for the man. "Get out of here!"

I stepped between them, heart racing, mouth dry. I stared into Giddings' ferrety face. "Celia's not here! She's not here!"

"Then she's gone," he said.

There was a general turnout of the company then, with everyone shouting Celia's name and men fanning out in a search over the rocky countryside. Mrs. Hester, near hysterics, hid Sallie in their wagon, convinced Indians had abducted Celia.

It was Lucena and I who found her. I will never forget the sight of those boots.

Celia had set her adopted boots neatly side by side on the riverbank, as if by a doorway. Her folded shawl and faded blue sunbonnet lay next to them.

Lucena and I stared at the boots for I don't know how long, and then at one another. Horror deprived us of speech.

Silently, we continued downstream. Eventually, through a thicket of slender willows, we saw the blue skirt of Celia's dress ballooned in a marsh of reeds at the river's edge, and blonde hair floating on green water. Lucena turned me from the sight.

"I'll stay," she said. "You go tell the men."

Celia

I remember the rest of that dreadful morning as a succession of pictures, like a book of daguerreotypes, everyone quiet and stiff, as if posing to have a likeness made. I see in memory still the young men silently watching Giddings build a coffin from the sides of his wagon, Mrs. Hester and I fashioning a shroud from sheeting, two men digging by the river. And then the company gathered around a mounded grave while Giddings, dry-eyed, droned a passage from his Bible. I recall Janey's head bowed to hide her tears, Caleb wooden, Douglas staring at nothing, Lucena's face buried against Will's chest. Afterward, the company packed up for the day's journey, and Giddings, on horseback, stopped at our wagon and growled at Caleb, "I hold you responsible, Daniels. God will avenge me." I buried my face in Hannah's hair as he sauntered away, and Caleb muttered, "God forgive you, man."

We never saw Giddings again.

The page in my journal for that date in August of 1849 remains blank, but every detail of it is recorded in memory, forever. I wish I could forget it, have it unwritten like that page of white paper.

Of all the graves I paused beside in that long, terrible trek overland, only Celia's is without record in my journal. I had begun that sad habit back on the Big Blue, thinking the practice might someday prove a grateful one for unknowing and worried friends and family. But for Celia, there was no one to notify, not one living soul. Poor thing, in all the world she had no family but those who lay in graves, and no friends but us. And on that desolate desert of the Humboldt Valley, that cruelly barren country, she would have not even that. She would be alone, all alone.

I think I was the only who understood why she drowned herself. It was terror, a maddening, suffocating fear of loneliness. And how I cursed her madness! As much as her death tormented me, it doomed me. From her, I would have known, as a woman can from another woman, the truth or falsity of her husband's accusation. Now I could never know, not for certain.

And Celia's death doomed Caleb, too. I date his decline from that blank page in my journal.

We were two terrible weeks slogging from Celia's grave to the sink of the Humboldt. It seemed like two years. I squared my broad shoulders, held my head high against the company's stares and whispers. Real or imagined, they pierced me and my family like iron-tipped, poisoned arrows.

In that long, desperate march along the Humboldt, I replayed a thousand times in my mind the scenes of previous weeks, imagining my husband with Celia. When? When he said he'd gone to doctor someone? Or repair a wagon? It seemed impossible to have been so betrayed by someone I loved so completely. But did he love me? Had he ever? Celia was so hauntingly beautiful, and I, I was plain as a sunbaked brick.

At night, folded into myself against the cold, listening to Caleb sleep his exhausted sleep, I imagined him taking me in his arms, professing his love, decrying the insanity of my thinking he could ever love anyone else.

But he never said a word. It was as if the whole terrible scene with Giddings had never happened. Sometimes I took that silence for love, believing Caleb intentionally said nothing so that I might pretend the awfulness never happened. It may have been. I've decided to think so.

Other times I tortured myself, imagining in his silence a terrible grief. There must have been some of that, too.

And while we trudged those desperate miles westward, for every torment in my mind, this awful region leveled an equal and real torment to the body. Nights of bitter cold led into days of fiery, stultifying heat. The sun's blinding rays staggered us, glaring silver off the barren peaks and rocks and domes and bluffs, and imparting a monstrous and treacherous vacancy to the horizon. A tin plate or a frying pan left an hour in the sun could not be touched without a holder. The backs of our hands blistered, our lips cracked from heat and dryness, our tongues turned swollen and tender.

For a few days, to avoid the worst heat and spare our animals, we traveled at night, resting the stock from the nooning until sunset and resuming our journey then. I remember the eeriness of night in this godforsaken land, mountains silhouetted by moonlight, the brilliance of countless stars. Fires lit the dark like a hundred torches, consuming wrecked or abandoned wagons at which emigrants warmed themselves.

These night marches exhausted us. During the day, we lay in the shade of wagons and tents, sleep made impossible by the noise of passing emigrants anxious to get ahead.

We soon abandoned traveling after sundown. We now commenced our daily march at half past two in the morning. We were never alone. All the emigrants, the many thousands of us, had funneled into this one road. There were no shortcuts here, no wide expanses inviting wagons to fan out over the countryside. We were forced to keep to the road here. Away from it, the country was too thick with sagebrush and rock for progress.

And so we plowed the road with our thousands of turning wheels, pulverized its sand and lime into a fine dust that rose in suffocating clouds with our thousand footsteps.

It was parched, scorched, this land, dried to dust by a relentless sun, raked by hot winds. The soda-whitened earth lifted with the wind into columns of ashy alkaline dust two hundred feet high. It covered everyone.

We traveled in dust, clouds and curtains of it, raised by the wind, our plodding animals, our groaning wagon wheels, our own trudging footsteps. Our ankles stung from wading through it, six inches deep and more. There was no escaping it. Away from the road this alkali formed a crust. It crunched beneath our feet like snow. It got into our cracked skin and cuts, and burned. It got into our eyes, our noses, our mouths. We wore goggles, covered our faces with handkerchiefs. I remember a woman tramping past and saying to me, "We're a strange-looking army, aren't we?"

So dense was the dust that from a rise the long stretch of wagon tops ahead appeared to float on it like sailing ships, the heads of men and beasts like ducks on water.

Our poor, footsore animals, laboring through the heavy sand, suffered with us, surviving on practically no grass at all. Caleb shortened our wagon's running gear to eight feet to make it run easier. Janey and I fashioned boots from sacking for the cracked hoofs of our oxen. Their patient, soulful eyes tore my heart.

Our guidebook had promised grass here, described the Humboldt Valley as richly clothed with blue grass and clover. It was gone now, if the claim had ever been true. But I think it was not true. This was a land of greasewood and sage, not clover. Later, in Sacramento I think it was, I learned our guidebook's author, Joseph Ware, wrote his book with sights unseen, cobbled together from Fremont's writings and various accounts by earlier emigrants. I suppose he assumed all rivers nurture grasses. He never saw a river like the Humboldt. There is none.

I think it was Zeb I had the story from, who told me Mr. Ware had been one of us, an emigrant of 'forty-nine. He died on the road. Another grave marking the way west. Our guide to the desolate Humboldt region never saw it.

No, the Humboldt could have grown no grass. The river was, below its headwaters, chokingly bitter, too alkaline to stomach. But we drank it anyway. We disguised it with coffee, and drank it, and so did our suffering animals. We had no choice.

Along the Humboldt, Indians continued to plague us. Gunfire punctuated the nights as men on watch fired randomly into the willows to drive off the unseen scourge. Notices along the road, stuck on sticks and shoved in the sand, the emigrants' post office, offered rewards for stolen horses and larcenous Indians. One note commanded us to shoot all Indians, called them thieves destitute of gratitude, satisfied by no amount less than all. The man who signed it wrote he'd been wounded and all but one of his mules stolen.

We soon saw more and more people packing through with their belongings on their backs, wagons abandoned. It was the first hint of panic.

We overtook several Pioneer Line passengers here. When we had last seen them on the Emigrant's Cutoff, they had been on short rations. Now they were starving. And worse. Ugly skin sores, bleeding gums, joints swollen and discolored marked them with severe symptoms of scurvy.

They were a pitiable spectacle, ragged and sick. Caleb stared at them vacantly, oddly unmoved by their awful state. I think he was feverish then, or maybe he just felt helpless. His strength had ebbed steadily after Celia's death, but he had driven himself harder to keep the company moving, to find forage, repair wagons, curb tempers and fears. The heat sapped him; he ate little, slept poorly, his strength and spirit daily eroding.

Douglas cared for our oxen now, set up camp, took to himself the burdens his father had borne. But he said little, perhaps from being his father's son. Janey, too, spoke seldom. So did I. There was too much discomfort in it, talking. Too much pain, from heat, from dust, from thinking. Only Hannah was herself, but her little lips were cracked and dry like ours and she prattled less than she should have.

The Pioneers were considering a new cutoff. Reports had reached us about it some days earlier, along with rumors of hard traveling ahead, no grass at the sink, a waterless desert of forty miles to traverse. The new cutoff, rumor had it, bypassed the dreaded desert, offered an easier crossing over the mountains.

I remember standing in the shade of the wagon, leaning against a wheel with Janey silent at my side, Hannah playing in the sand at my feet, while I listened to desultory speculations among the Pioneers, Caleb and the men in our company, and other halted emigrants. I saw ahead the wagon tracks bending away from the old road, making a new one. I could see the diminishing dusty covers of wagons on it, lurching into the desert's distance.

"There'll be better grass and water off the main road," Caleb said.

His conviction surprised me. How could he know that? No one had returned to attest to the road's resources. The guidebook said nothing about this region.

Arguments ranged from diffident and laconic to spirited and confident.

"I heard the mountains cross easier to the north, but Indians be troublesome."

"Hard going to Rabbit Springs, about thirty-five miles, then an easy road."

Colonel Hamilton wiped his brow beneath the felt hat he'd found and adopted when his straw one finally refused further duty. "Anyone taking a vote has an 'aye' from me," he said. "Let's just get on with it."

No one announced a vote, but a scatter of subdued 'ayes' followed the colonel's.

"Not me, I'm against," said Craven Hester.

Caleb appeared confused, his face flushed and eyes vacant. When he said nothing, Craven Hester added, "Let's noon here, then decide."

"Caleb," I said, as the men dispersed, "you should rest a while."

He looked at me blank as new paper, then hauled himself into the wagon and fell into a feverish sleep from which I refused to wake him when it was time to move on.

And that's when I made the decision against the cutoff. I watched with Douglas as most of the company moved onto the new road. I was not convinced by their willingness to follow the example of the wagon ahead. I remembered the wagon tracks veering from the Fort Hall route and into the unknown on a cutoff with nothing to confirm it but men's hopes. That cutoff availed nothing but bad road and then no road at all.

Without a guide, even such an aspiring one as Mr. Ware's book, I was for the tried and true. "We'll keep to the road," I told Douglas. "Let's head for the sink."

I was no captain, no Big Mary. With no one I trusted to say nay, I suppose I decided from cowardice: I was afraid of the unknown. Whatever the reasoning, I decided. Decision was new to me, as unfamiliar as someone else's coat. But I put it on and never again took it off. No one, not mother, father, or husband, was taking care of me. For better or worse, I was my own captain.

My decision was a good one, despite all that befell us. I later learned from Zeb that the shortcut saved nothing. His company took that road, the Lassen Cutoff, he called it. The Black Rock Desert, he said, was as terrible as the forty miles we faced, the mountain crossing worse, the journey longer.

And people died on that route, too.

Desert

We followed the Humboldt as it dwindled to a muddy ditch that announced the sink. Mr. Ware's guidebook described this place as where the river lost itself in the sand. Before seeing this terrible desert, we'd imagined a huge hole in an ominous landscape, through which the river poured. Now we understood. The desert drank its river. The last swallow, the place where the Humboldt oozed into a marshy residue, was the sink.

I suppose the wonder of this sweltering wasteland was not that its river disappeared, but that it ran at all.

The Hesters and Semples stayed this road, too. That we were but three wagons mattered little. Companies fragmented here. Either we would catch up to the train ahead, or the one behind would catch up to us. Human companionship did not number among the emigrants' insufficiencies.

The sink, where the Humboldt withered from a muddy ditch into a large and malodorous slough, sustained, to our grateful surprise, a vast grassland. That bounteous green, dotted with men scything, reminded me of haying days back home, despite my anxiety for Caleb's health and the perils before us. Our oxen waded in with the rest, and Douglas and I, the Hester boys, and Will Semple, we all started cutting and drying grass for the crossing. I tried not to think of the desert ahead, the guidebook's warning it was the worst part of the journey. I concentrated on the grass. It smelled so sweet, that cut grass.

Grass and water, water and grass. Needing it, finding it, that was an emigrant's preoccupation. Here was grass, tall and lush. But, oh, the water!

There was none obtainable except from the slough. Following the example of other emigrants, Douglas and I dug a well four feet wide and just as deep, obtaining from it a brackish, foul-smelling, briny water, bitter with salt and sulphur. But there was no other, and drink it we must. Douglas and I filled all our waterbags and canteens for the desert.

At the sink, we learned two roads crossed the desert, both forty miles, both devoid of forage. One, opened the previous year by Mormons heading east from California to Salt Lake, ran southwest to the Carson River. Word spread that it offered a slightly easier crossing of the Sierra, but I found nothing in Mr. Ware's guidebook about it.

The other route, which ran nearly due west to the Truckee River, offered some boiling springs for water halfway across. It was the way the Donners had gone. Ignoring its horrific associations, I decided for the tried and true.

Caleb was too ill to decide anything.

He had drifted in and out of fever for two days. That we were at the sink and cutting grass for the animals seemed to cheer him. I doubt he remembered the cutoff or missed the company gone that way.

He rose once at the sink, instructed Douglas to soak the wagon wheels. The dryness of the region had shrunk the wood to a rattle against the iron. After seeing the wheels snug, Caleb lapsed into a feverish sleep again. All I could do was cool him with rags dipped in marsh water. We had no more medicines. I boiled up some portable soup, fed him by the spoonful, and tried to quell the anxiety I felt enlarging to dread.

Lucena, seeing my distress, insisted Caleb looked much improved. "La, he'll soon be 'fit as a fiddle,' as Will says. Whatever that means."

"Another day," I said. "He'll be better with another day's rest."

And so the Hesters and the Semples moved out from the sink a day ahead of us. We all knew no one could assist another anyway, that everyone must get ahead as fast as possible.

They had decided for the Truckee route, too, and promised to wait for us at the river. But behind our falsely cheerful farewells lurked the unspoken knowledge shared by all: necessity now must dictate every decision.

The next day, Caleb was still sick. Getting us safely across the desert to water had fallen to me. Words cannot describe my terror at the prospect. I imagined the desert lying in wait like a predator, a monster indifferent to suffering, indifferent to necessity, merciless.

Perhaps my fear is retrospect, resurrected from knowledge. I had thought the terrible trek down the Humboldt was hell on earth. It wasn't. It was merely the road in, a preamble.

I commenced the crossing at three o'clock in the afternoon. I intended we should rest for supper at sundown and then move on until midnight. With luck, I thought two days' hard travel would get us across. Caleb was asleep in the wagon when we started, Janey bathing his flushed face with wet cloths. Douglas drove the oxen. I walked, carrying Hannah on my back, to save the animals any unnecessary burden.

Within two or three miles we were on the desert. The sand, soft beneath a white crust of ancient salt, made hard pulling for our three yoke of oxen. How low hung the heads of our faithful Buck and Cherry, Lewis and Clark, poor brutes, as they labored through it.

The desert was beyond imagining. Never before or since have I witnessed a scene more desolate, more barren of life. Except for hillocks drifted and heaped by the winds and tufted with stunted greasewood, sand stretched white and flat to the horizon. Wagons ahead moved slowly in the distance. Men, countenances desperate, packed past on foot. Yet it was eerily silent, as if the relentless sun extracted not just moisture from the earth, but sound from the atmosphere.

We had become accustomed to seeing dead and dying oxen and mules lining the road, but here their numbers doubled and trebled. These fallen animals, eyeless from pecking birds, bloated beneath the fierce and blinding sun, emitted an indescribable stench. Huge birds of prey, disturbed from their loathsome feasting by our advance, flapped their great wings to hover watchfully until we passed. As they resumed their banquet, they buried their heads in the putrid corpses, then raised them to stare at us with suspicious eyes. Shreds of flesh hung from their ferocious beaks like bloody rags. No page from Dante's *Inferno* depicted a more hideous view.

Hannah hid her face against my neck and began to whimper, "Bad bird, Mama, bad bird."

Fearing she should suffer nightmares from the frightful spectacle, I signaled Douglas to stop. I made a place for her next to Caleb, who slept soundly.

"How's Papa doing, Janey?" I asked, settling Hannah into a nest she'd made of favorite clothes.

"Mostly he sleeps, but sometimes he opens his eyes like he's surprised, Mama, and it scares me," she said, laying a newly dampened cloth across his brow.

"I think he looks improved," I said, anxiously wanting to think so. "You're a good nurse."

To subtract Hannah's weight from the wagon's load, Douglas and I ladled out a half bucket of the terrible-tasting water for each of the oxen. It was early in the crossing. We didn't realize the folly of so generous a ration.

That was my last clear memory of the desert. After that it seems a nightmare, a confusion of shapes and forms and figures out of Dante's book, a disordered recollection of sights and scenes from hell.

I remember the glaring sun, squinting my eyes at mirages, seeing the endless desert through a wavy heat. After the first day, we traveled but little during the worst heat, moved slowly at night, two hours pulling, two hours resting, doling out the grass that must last and the water I soon realized would not.

Perhaps the sun, so terribly pitiless, unbalanced my mind a little, but I don't think so. I think the mind protects itself from madness if it can. And a mother's mind must. In all that long journey, I recollect no woman but Celia succumbing to madness, and she had no children to save. But men lost their minds on that desert. I saw them.

I can't say just when it was, as we were, in all, three days and two nights on that arid, burning waste. Probably it was toward the end of the crossing, when, for many emigrants, all water, strength, food, and hope had given out. But I remember two men lying in the frail shade beneath a halted wagon and refusing to rise when their companions said they must. When the wagon moved on, leaving the men exposed to the burning sun, they started to cry. One, with a desperate moan, called for his mother. But despite the pleading of their companions, they still refused to move. In the end they were tied with ropes and secured in the wagon. I remember them sobbing.

Or perhaps it was the sobbing of the animals. What a terrible sound that was, the poor beasts crying for water, eyes frantic. Time cannot erase those awful cries from my memory.

Nor the feeble weeping of the old couple who had given up. They were probably no more than fifty. They looked a hundred. I remember a pale light and the silhouette of their team collapsed in the road. It may have been dusk. Perhaps it was dawn. The oxen lay dying, still yoked, forcing wagons around them. The couple, weak and starving, lay together on a quilt by the side of the road, awaiting death to take them, too.

I remember the woman's beseeching eyes and twig-thin fingers reaching up when I opened the red tin box and silently gave her my mother's plum cake.

And on we slogged, our animals nearly to their knees from the effort. Poor brutes, I hope the carcasses of mules and oxen swelled to bursting beneath the burning sun did not suggest to them the fearful futility it did to me. The sight of those gruesome corpses and the pitiable animals still afoot, wandering aimlessly, waiting to die, filled me with a terrible despair. I knew then we were at risk for our very lives.

Everyone crossing that fearful desert knew it from the evidence strewn in reckless abandon across the blistering sands. Emigrants, forsaking everything not necessary to life itself, left on that desert treasures of the heart hauled half a continent. Through the daze in which I forced each weary step, I remember seeing Lucena's overturned rocking chair by the side of the road, and her looking glass, a collapse of brilliant shards blasting a bright reflection of sun. I knew the chair and mirror were hers. Next to them lay a spilled flour barrel and familiar blue dishes dusted white.

Abandoned wagons stood everywhere, some burned, others intact, loaded with goods. I saw carriages in perfect condition for moving on standing ghostly silent and empty, and open trunks, goods tumbled out. Everything that constituted a California outfit littered the road — tents by the hundreds, harness, water casks, tools, chains, yokes, shovels, clothing — everything except food. The ruin suggested an army in retreat, desperation, a rout.

Just after nightfall of the second day, we reached the boiling springs, chalk-white cavities emitting a great noise and a nauseating sulphur smell. The water was so hot some starving emigrants reduced to eating their mules cooked the meat in it. Caleb was awake but still ill, so Douglas and I hauled up buckets of the steaming, stinking water.

While setting some to cool for the cattle, Douglas took my arm. "Ma, look."

In the moon's silvery light I saw silhouetted dozens of gaunt and desperate people. And then I saw what Douglas saw, a man so thin he looked like clothing draped for drying on the limestone rock he leaned against. But the pale light illuminated a long white beard.

"Heigh-ho," he croaked, as we knelt by his side.

"Oh, Mr. Fogie," Douglas said, "where are the Germans?"

"Germans?" Mr. Fogie looked around, as if Douglas had asked him to find someone. Then he closed his eyes, exhausted by the effort.

"You remember, the Germans with the beer-making stuff," Douglas said, insistent.

I put my hand on Mr. Fogie's arm and felt bone beneath the sleeve of his ragged shirt. "It doesn't matter, Douglas, what happened to the Germans."

Mr. Fogie opened his eyes, found mine. "Left me by the road," he said slowly, the words inching out. "Way back, wagon, too. Mules done up. Walked till I was — "

"Douglas," I said, "see if you can find some cooled water."

He ran off, grateful for the task.

"Water," Mr. Fogie said after me, eyes open but unseeing. "Water, that's how I'm going to get me to California. Sailing ship, 'round the Horn."

"You rest, Mr. Fogie — "

"Yes, that's how we'll do it, sailing ship, sea breezes, and white sails, I see 'em."

He stared at a cloud drifting past the moon. "I see 'em, heigh-ho."

I watched it with him, his head against my shoulder as I held to his lips the cup of water Douglas brought. The poor old man hadn't the strength to hold the cup himself, or did not seem in want of it. He turned his head from the cup to stare at the moon. "Sailing ship, sailing ship," he said, voice cracking like the desert's salt crust.

"Ma," Douglas said.

I shook my head. "There's nothing we can do, Douglas, nothing. You go on back, give the animals some water, if it's cooled."

It was from necessity the emigrants grew hardhearted. On that desperate desert, it was all most could do to help themselves. I had my sick husband and children. I could not risk their lives trying to save another's. God forgive me, frail as Mr. Fogie was, I could not add even that slender weight to our wagon. Two of our oxen had totally given out, and I had left them by the wayside to die. The others were failing. And we were but halfway to the river.

I had no choice. I had no choice.

I sat with the old man a long while. "Forgive me, Mr. Fogie," I whispered, staring at the moon with him. "I promise I'll come back when I get my family to safety."

I folded his frail fingers around the cup of water, but he seemed unaware I had done so. And if he heard me, he gave no sign. His gaze was fastened on the moon, and he murmured to it of distant seas and sailing ships.

A terrible shriek frightened me from his side, and I rushed back to my family to find Janey weeping. The scream had not been human. Someone's dog, poor thing, falling into one of the boiling springs, had scalded to death.

We moved on, slogging slowly west amid pitiable sights. People on foot, bereft of supplies, begged for food and water. One man, destitute beyond endurance, demanded another sell him provisions, shouted, "By God, I won't starve!" and threatened to take what would not be sold. Mules, crazed by hunger, attacked wagons, eyes desperate, gnawing wood, canvas, anything. Horses, some saddled, others in harness, lay dead by the roadside.

Weary and gaunt, our surviving oxen dragged our wagon slowly through the desert's heavy sands. Its bitter dust coated their tongues hanging swollen with heat and thirst from their mouths.

It tore my heart, but I baited those suffering animals. Keeping ahead a few feet, I waved a paltry handful of grass I dared not give because it was the last. I had no choice. Our animals must get us across the desert or doom us to it.

Then the water gave out, and it was clear so must the animals. We were still seven or eight miles from the river, nothing less than eight hours, even without stopping to rest. Pulling, in their jaded condition, the oxen didn't have eight hours of life left in them.

I didn't panic only because I didn't have the strength for it. I knew only that the waterbags were empty, the canteens nearly so, that the wagon could not be got to the river without the oxen, and the oxen could not pull without water.

I had no choice but to get them to water.

Did I discuss with Douglas which of us should go? I don't recall. Did I tell my fourteen-year-old son, who had become a young man on this journey, that I thought him better able to protect our provisions from desperate men than I? Did I tell Caleb, lying prostrate in the wagon, heat or fever or both flushing his face, that pure, sweet water must certainly put him right and that I was going for it? Perhaps.

I cannot with certainty recall anything of that urgent leave-taking except unyoking the poor oxen and roping our empty canvas waterbags to their sides. And then I was alone with them on the desert, not daring to look back, only forward, driving them through the hot sand to the life-saving river.

Everywhere on those final awful miles of desert, emigrants slogged silently, each desperate to save himself. I remember no sound but the moaning of animals — perhaps some of those cries were human.

I do remember when Buck and Cherry raised their heads, quickened their pace. What sense told them water lay ahead? Did they smell it, as some people say? We were then nearly three miles from the river. At half a mile they began to run, dredging energy from I know not where in their half-dead bodies.

What a welcome sight was that cool river, crowded with grateful men and beasts. My oxen plunged into it on a run, tossing their great heads, splashing and reveling in its life-giving waters. On my knees at the river's edge, I cupped my hands into that welcome water and drank, a prayer of thanks to God for it, sweet as nectar to my parched and swollen throat.

The animals drank and drank, and I filled the waterbags, and some men helped me secure them to the animals' sides, and I hurried the oxen back as fast as they could travel, and I don't see how if Douglas had gone instead of me, it would have made any difference.

Except that I would have been by Caleb's side when he died.

Caleb

Improbable as it seems now, looking back, I cannot recall thinking Caleb might die. Death surrounded us, traveled with us, marked our road with its conquests. But it belonged, with the nearly unendurable exception of little George, to strangers. To have conceived the possibility of Caleb's death, to have expected and anticipated and awaited it, would have, like Celia's unbearable fear, deprived me of my senses. And I could not afford the luxury.

Some numbing mechanism protects the mind from horror it cannot encompass. I believe this must be so, else we should all go mad. I have thought much on death and dying, from the too frequent witnessing of it. Sudden death puts terror in the eyes, like the man I later saw hanged in California, his mind extinguished mid-horror. In a slow dying, where death softly inscribes itself on a life rather than dashing it out, the eyes reflect a peaceful acceptance. Perhaps it is resignation, or perhaps just a last, gentle insanity.

Death took Caleb like that, bedded beneath the wagon's sunbaked canvas, Hannah asleep at his side, Janey and Douglas in woeful witness. At the last, Douglas said, Caleb seemed to see his mother in Janey, called her "Mama" and wept with joy at the sight of her.

My poor children, the terrible ordeals they endured. On my

return with the oxen and water, I found them huddled in the narrow shade beneath the wagon, the awful news written on their faces.

Douglas unfolded himself, crawled out, stood to meet me. "Ma," he said, voice cracking. That was all.

Janey remained where she was, buried her head in her arms, and started to sob.

My throat clutched sound to itself, stifled breath into my chest, where it battled my pounding heart.

I don't recall climbing into that death wagon, but I did. Etched on memory is the image of Caleb lying there, his handsome face almost young again, worries and burdens and illness erased.

Too blasted by loss to weep, I simply stared, saw the boy in the man, my melancholy Byron again beneath the crown of curls that stole my heart. Mindless with grief too monumental for tears, I sat by him, stroked his ashen face, felt happiness vacate the place where my life had been.

But we endure what must be endured. I collected my shattered self into something that would walk and moved on. I had no choice.

Lucena and Will waited for us at the Truckee River, having missed my frantic arrival earlier. They saw me when I came in with the wagon. Lucena, her dress ragged as my own, ran to us, then stopped. How doleful we must have looked. Our expressions confirming her suspicion, she scooped my daughters into a tearful embrace, wept condolences while Will scuffed sand with his boot and looked away.

The desert and my loss chastened Lucena. She said nothing, then or later, of her abandoned treasures — the blue dishes, the Boston rocker, the gilt-framed looking glass shattered to a thousand shards, like my life.

"The Hesters," Will said at last, "gone on. Lost one ox, got anxious to be over those mountains." He gestured a shoulder at the Sierra Nevada towering behind him.

"They were right to do it," I said, helping Douglas unyoke the oxen, now raising their heads, sniffing water.

There was nothing that good family could do had they stayed. I never saw any of them again. I heard recently they settled in San Jose, that Craven Hester is a judge there.

We took our cattle to water. And then we buried Caleb.

We were a forlorn little group gathered there on the desert's edge where the emigrants buried their dead. There were so many we named the place Pioneer Cemetery. It lay not far from the river with its bordering shade of cottonwoods. I remember how green those trees seemed, we had been so long without sight of any, and how the warm desert gusts set their dusty leaves to dancing against the heat-bleached sky.

Janey and Hannah clung to me, and I to them. I remember so
vividly Hannah's curly head pressed against me, her little hands clutching fistfuls of my skirt, its grimy cotton shredded by a thousand
snaggings, hem and sleeves frayed to rags. We all of us looked pitiful
and dirty and doomed.

Poor Hannah understood now, tragic little thing, that once beneath
the sands, our loved ones do not rise, and she sobbed inconsolably from
the terrible new knowledge. Janey, old to death, wept silently.

I dislike recalling the feeling that hurricaned through me then, it
seemed so fierce and wrong. Poor Caleb, it was not his fault strength
ebbed and he slipped away into eternal night like a thief. But it felt to
me like a theft, his death, a robbery of happiness.

Or did anger slam me like a hammer to deter further unforgivable abandonment of those innocent children? I don't know. But rage
enveloped me and kept me upright while Douglas, weeping from
the responsibility, hammered closed Caleb's coffin of scavenged wagon
boards.

I remember looking back, dry-eyed still, at the way we had come,
across that burning desert, haunt of the elephant, from which emigrants
still straggled in half dead, half mad. And then I stared west, into those
towering mountains, a taunting elephant fortress of rocky, mocking preci-
pices as seemingly unassailable as Jericho. The banging of Douglas's hammer on the scrapwood box abruptly turned my attention from what lay
ahead to what lay behind. It marshaled anger in me like an army band,
and the desert sun fired it white and hot.

Suddenly, I wanted to smash that box, tear it open with my bare
hands, pound on Caleb, scream at him for dragging us into this intolerable wilderness of heat and sand and mountains and death and heartache, for dragging us from our comfortable home to the gates of hell and
abandoning us. Inside my head I screamed, *Caleb, your children are father-
less! I am widowed! For what? So you could see the West? Dig a lump of gold? For
this you died? For this you destroyed us?*

For a time beneath that awful desert sun, hearing Douglas's hammer, Will's grating shovel, Hannah's sobs, seeing sand cascade over that
makeshift coffin, I hated Caleb, simply and furiously hated him.

And then, while Douglas pounded into the sand a broken board on
which he'd cut his father's name, and Will solemnly recited a simple
prayer, I felt hatred seep away like the Humboldt into its sink. *What's
done is done,* I thought. *Let's go home.*

From that moment, I turned my focus as wholly and intently on
home as an archer on his target.

I knew we could not, of course, go back the way we had come, even had we sufficient provisions and fresh oxen. To turn back, to retrace every step slogged across the desert, along the desperate Humboldt plagued by Indians, over the Rockies, back to Fort Laramie, the Platte, Fort Kearny, St. Joseph, that awful distance to be traveled in despair, was as unthinkable as it was impossible.

And so our mournful little family must go on, up and over those fearful mountains, to whatever lay beyond them, and from there I would get us home. That night, while my children slept, I sat by my campfire studying the tattered guidebook. And then, on a page torn from my journal, I calculated with my stub of a pencil the cost of getting us back to the States.

Besides the overland road, Mr. Ware's little book described two sea routes to California, Cape Horn and the Isthmus of Panama. The latter was fastest, he wrote, the whole distance from the States to San Francisco requiring but thirty days.

Purpose swelled me like a woman with child. I sped through the pages, glossed past warnings of disease and wretched accommodations. I remembered how my father would laugh at my mother whenever she decried his westering. "I was not born in the woods to be scared by an owl," he'd say. And now I said it, too. I'd come two thousand miles by wagon, crossed death's desert, seen the worst. Two weeks on the Isthmus of Panama? Ha! I was not born in the woods to be scared by an owl.

Mr. Ware's book estimated steamer fare from New Orleans to Chagres at eighty dollars, another twenty dollars for each person to hire a mule to cross the Isthmus, and cabin fare between Panama City and San Francisco at two hundred dollars. The return trip could cost no less. What riverboat accommodations from New Orleans to St. Louis might cost was unknown to me. As was the amount of money now remaining in the box Caleb had stowed beneath the wagon bed.

The next morning I stood by the wagon, my shivering children at my side, and stared into that nearly empty box, my bright plan in ruins. Of the thousand dollars we had started with, less than a hundred remained. Where had the money gone? But, of course, there had been expenses, many expenses — accommodations in St. Louis, provisioning, steamer fares from St. Louis to St. Joseph, ferry fees, the oxen purchased at Fort Laramie, and medicines, always the medicines. Caleb had been forever buying medicines, caring for everyone. Everyone but us. Anger rose again, flapping up like a feral thing.

Douglas, sensing it, put his hand on my arm. Only fourteen, already old.

"Don't worry, Ma," he said. "There's gold in California. I'll dig us what we need."

If ever I came near to tears, it was then.

And so we prepared to go on. I moved through the necessary chores like a dead person, washed ragged clothes in the river, cooked beans, baked bread. Preparations, preparations, how those small tasks salvaged dead hours.

The Semples, dear friends, waited with us another day while our cattle strengthened. Will joined an emigrants' relief effort organized at the Truckee to take water back to those still struggling over the desert. He returned with the sad burden of Mr. Fogie's lifeless body.

We buried the old man next to Caleb. Douglas, face long, carved a twin to the board identifying his father. Above this newly mounded sand, Will recited a short prayer while I watched a solitary tear streak my son's cheek. "Heigh-ho, Mr. Fogie," he whispered, "heigh-ho."

And so we left another casualty of the elephant, a funny old man who had once laughingly announced California probably didn't even exist. For him, and Caleb, and hundreds of others, it never would.

The following morning I rose early, wrapped myself in Caleb's worn, brown wool coat, comforting myself with the smell of him lingering in it, and went again to that raw cemetery of mounded sand. While the blue-purple, still-starry sky faded to pink, I knelt by the grave I would never see again and said goodbye to my husband and all I had known of happiness. And to whatever he had known of it, too, this curly-headed, melancholy man to whom life had just happened, this man who had only one dream and sacrificed his son, and then himself, to it. In the distance, camps were rousing, mules braying. "I'm going home, Caleb," I whispered. "I'm going home."

And then my children and I resumed the sorrowful journey Caleb had set us on. They must have consoled each other, poor things, for I was small comfort to them. Except for my beacon vision of the brick house, I was as empty as Celia's boots.

My journal, from which I write this account, displays me to myself. The long habit of keeping it stayed with me. I bent over it every night. And wrote nothing. The pages for the days on the desert and a week after are, like I was then, all but vacant.

I recorded miles. The numbers are there, penciled small and faithfully in a journal otherwise silent. In the ten days of that brutal and difficult ascent into the mountains, my journal reveals only these faintly penciled words: John Banks, onions, cabins, summit, gold.

Ah, that gold. How it cheered me, urged me on, promised home.

Mountains

From the desert's edge the California road led into the mountains along the winding Truckee, a river as sinuous and fast as a snake. Were it not for its constant bends and turns, it would have made a perfect millrace, the current was that swift. It was delicious water, though, so sweet. And it was beautiful, too, the river bottom clear as crystal, a jumble of rocks and boulders in colors of greenish-blue and black and gray, some coppery and shiny as new coins. How we came to abominate it. As the guidebook warned we must, we probably crossed it thirty times before we reached the summit.

Along that river, up and up into those fearsome mountains I and my children and the Semples trudged, following the three wagons of a good-hearted company of young men from Ohio, as attached to them as a tail to its dog.

On the desert's edge, while grazing our cattle, Douglas had met John Banks. I remember him as such a homesick young fellow, thin and sandy-haired. He'd left behind, and missed terribly, a brother Douglas's age. Never before separated from brothers and sisters and parents, he fastened to us in substitution.

He was one of a dozen young men in a company formed in Athens County, Ohio. They called themselves the Buckeye Rovers. They had stayed together all that long way from Ohio, of one mind, traveling slowly to conserve their oxen, even keeping the Sabbath. None of their number had died and no disagreement or dispute had risen sufficient to separate them. I thought them a "good luck" company and was grateful when they invited us to travel with them.

It was eighty miles to the summit, a daily fatigue of urging our weary oxen up the rough, stony road into the gradually timbering mountains, and the constant crossing and recrossing of the Truckee. Along it, emigrants encamped and traveled with us in crowds as thick as on the Platte. Here, as there, we had no trouble finding the road; it was "plain as Broadway," I remember young John Banks remarking.

What staggered us as much as its boulders was the difficulty faced by those who first forged the way. I knew who they were and put the thought from my mind.

Each evening after supper John Banks announced the miles traveled that day, reading from the roadometer strapped to a wagon wheel. I hoarded the numbers, counted them over in my journal like a miser his coins. I see in those pages a little penciled *six* for the first day. Only six miles, that's how rough the road was. We managed ten the second, fifteen the third, twelve the fourth, only nine the fifth. That's the date in my journal with the word *onions* penciled in.

One of the Rovers found them growing by the road. No green tops were visible, and how the onions were discovered I do not know. Everyone not otherwise employed set himself to digging the first edible greens seen in weeks. I offered to cook them up, flavored with bacon and the last of my nutmeg. That evening, all the Rovers gathered around my cookfire, sniffing those fragrant onions. Everyone enjoyed a share, exclaiming how delicious they were, and that pleased me.

On we went, eight miles the next day, a day to rest and recruit the cattle, and then . . .

Lucena spied them before I did. We were well into the mountains, and in memory I hear the soft sighing breeze through the towering trees, see again the pine needles fallen among the huge rocks the oxen labored over, the boulders the iron wheels of our wagons scraped against. She suddenly stopped and pointed.

"La, Mrs. Daniels, look!" Lucena said, lively and chirk as a bird. "We must be in California!"

When I saw where she pointed, my throat went dry as desert dust.

Lucena clapped her hands in excitement. "It must be a little settlement we're coming to!" And then she brushed at her skirts and said, "Oh, and me in this raggedy old thing."

I put a hand on her arm and shook my head. I knew at once who had built those cabins. They were surrounded by axe-scarred stumps towering ten feet and more, which defined in striking measure the depth of snow that trapped the poor travelers who had sought refuge there. It was the most desolate and gloomy place I ever saw.

"Perhaps," I said, finding my voice, "being from England, you did not read of the unfortunates — "

"Oh," Lucena cried, eyes widening. "They're the cannibal cabins?" She stared at the foreboding scene, then put a hand to her mouth and squealed. "La, just look! There's bones!" she said, pointing again. "See them all piled up there, kind of charred-looking?"

Later that evening, John Banks, who had read Bryant's account of the Donner Party's rescued survivors, confirmed to the curious Semples that a relief group sent from California had burned human skeletons found at those cabins.

"Some of those bones had been sawed to get the marrow out," he added, telling the terrible story the way boys will, hoping to scare each other with night tales of ghosts and goblins.

I barely noted the frightful remark, so filled was I with thoughts of the brick house and how many miles we had come. I remember thinking only that I was grateful my sleeping children were spared the overhearing. Like most emigrants, I grew insensitive to tragedy not my own.

The next day we reached the head of the Truckee. It flowed from a lake some four or five miles long, perhaps two wide, a beautiful sapphire blue surrounded by an emerald forest of lofty pine and fir and cedar. Truckee Lake was our last camp below the summit. Despite the absence of telling in my journal, in those days that I ticked off in miles, memory preserves a vivid recollection of that dreadful final ascent.

Our course lay through a slight declivity in the mountains, perhaps fifteen hundred or two thousand feet lower than the surrounding crests. The road from lake to summit rose about five miles, initially a gradual climb, although exceedingly difficult due to the rocks. About three hundred feet below the summit, the mountain offered a broad shelf of meadow, but from there the road climbed desperately steep, at an angle near forty-five degrees.

It looked like a wall, so nearly vertical it was, erected where our route must take us. At its base, emigrants grimly prepared to scale it. Someone clever had constructed a roller on the summit by coating with axle grease two forked tree-trunks supporting a round log wrapped with chain. A number of us used it to assist our oxen in their torturous climb.

It took eight yoke to a wagon, the road was that steep, to get each wagon to the summit, even employing the windlass. Every step of that terrible final ascent, I thought it a wonder that those patiently heroic oxen proceeded another yard. Teamsters yelled and cursed, urging those mute beasts up, up, up over rocks they fell against, again and again, tearing their knees and staining boulders red. Both Hannah and Janey wept as we struggled up the mountain alongside our wagon, seeing poor Cherry and Buck straining with the Rovers' borrowed teams, eyes wide with effort. Faithful beasts, they displayed no sign of distress, even as they stumbled and bloodied themselves, but we knew they suffered.

From below the summit, we could see those who had gained the crest, hear their shouts of joy like schoolboys let out to play. They and their wagons and cattle looked like miniatures, almost suspended, so far above us did they seem.

And then, slowly and painfully, we too attained the mountaintop. The scene is forever engraved on my memory. Despite shouting teamsters, clattering chains, blowing mules, and puffing oxen, a strange tranquility shrouded the summit. I remember seeing my children sitting on a boulder together, gazing silently into the vastness spread west before them. I stood behind them and stared, too, at peak rising beyond peak in endless succession as far as the eye could see. The singular and unexpected grandeur surprised everyone. The scene was unearthly in its beauty, unlike anything I had read in books or imagined from poets. Nothing but the spiraling flight of hawks disturbed the magnificence of limitless forest and granite-crowned peaks.

A man came up and stood with me as I stared, not one of the Rovers. He was older than any of their number, and even more ruined. I knew him for one of those who traveled now on charity, having lost all on the desert, begging from train to train for food. He had no shoes and his clothing hung from him in rags.

"Purtiest sight I ever did see," he said. "Pays me for all my hardship."

I stared at him, dumbstruck.

Is there no cost too great for men infected with westering? How could anything, even all the scenic wonders of the world, all the gold in California, redeem that ghastly passage across half a continent, hounded by loss and destruction, starvation and thirst, and death?

I remain bewildered by the secret hunger that draws men west like iron to a magnet. My father died still yearning for it, this West of his imagination. Caleb Daniels and countless others perished for it.

On that mountaintop, gazing into that endless west, I wondered at the mystery of things. How was it that I, all but born, as my mother's true daughter, with a dread of this West, came in my father's stead? I, who flailed against my husband's quest of it, how came I to fulfill, however reluctantly, his dream?

Bowing before my awful destiny, I sent each a silent prayer. Then I lifted my head and drank in that beauty like the desert takes water.

Getting off that mountain frightened us fully as much as climbing it. In places the wagons moved over rocks the wheels would fall two feet off of. In others the road dropped so steeply we let the wagons down with ropes. I remain grateful to those good-luck Buckeye Rovers who got us down that first perilous mountainside without mishap, and would get us down the rest, too, despite the scattered remains of crashed wagons testifying to the dangerous descents.

At the bottom of the first descent lay the Yuba River. Reaching it, we felt well and truly in California. According to our guidebook, we were fast approaching the gold region. Douglas began to itch with the fever of it.

"Don't worry, Ma," he kept saying, "I'll dig us the gold to go home."

He fully thought he could, and so green were we all, so did I.

The road continued bad. One of the first sights along it, where the road met the river, was a tent set up against a large boulder. No wagon or other sign indicated that its owner was a traveler. My wagon was fourth behind the Rovers, but I could see, from where I walked with Janey, that John Banks peered into the tent. The train halted, and young John came back to me.

"There's a sick man in the tent, ma'am," he said. "His companions have gone on with the wagons and teams, except two who are staying to see him die."

I stared at our sandy-haired young friend. Did he think that because I was a woman I should instinctively tend the sick? Perhaps his mother would have, and he took all women for her, I don't know.

"My children need me," I said.

I was growing hardhearted, from seeing too much of death. My children had seen too much of it, too. I didn't want to watch another stranger die in a tattered tent in the middle of nowhere. I wanted to be safe in the brick house, with curtains on the windows and books on the shelves and sheets on the beds, my family tucked safely within.

The next day was Sunday, and we laid by the river to recruit our stock and observe the Sabbath. Forage was poor here, although it had been lush before the thousands of animals passing ahead of us devoured it like locusts. Someone discovered a wild pea vine growing luxuriantly on the mountainside. We all of us, the children and I, the Semples, and most of the Rovers, spent the day pulling pea vines for our animals.

Sometime during the afternoon, the sick man died and his friends buried him.

That night a traveler heading east to Salt Lake placed a ten-dollar California gold piece in my hand. He had been with the Mormon Battalion, conscripted on the plains three years previously for the war with Mexico. Mustered out in California, he had found work as a carpenter with John Sutter, been present at the sawmill when Marshall discovered gold. It was later that night that we learned this, when he conceded to tell his story to the Rovers. He seemed wearied by it, I suppose from being prevailed upon so often.

I have only the penciled word *gold* in my journal, but memory captured the scene like a daguerreotype. I see myself sitting on a log by my campfire, flames leaping as I feed it small sticks, tending my old, blackened Dutch oven. It was doing duty on a loaf of bread, and the warm smell of it mingled with the pine of the forest. I suppose it was the fragrance that drew the traveler to my fire and the Rovers' camp.

I remember hearing someone walk up, becoming aware he stood there. I saw his shoes first. They were worn, but not ravaged like mine and those of most emigrants, the soles barely adhering to their uppers. Then I looked up. And saw a white shirt, an honest-to-goodness boiled shirt.

"Evenin', ma'am."

I couldn't take my eyes from the man's shirt. Whether that Mormon man had a mustache, a beard, red hair or black, or even any at all, I cannot say, but I remember that shirt. I hadn't seen a white shirt on a man in months. We emigrants were all in rags, being too engrossed with survival to be particular about dress. How quickly vanity returns. Embarrassment flooded over me for my tattered dress and shabby appearance.

"If you'd be kind enough to sell me that bread, ma'am," he said, "I'll pay you five dollars for it."

Five dollars! That was a congressman's wages back home. I stared at that man in the boiled white shirt and simply could not speak. From mute embarrassment I slid into stunned disbelief. My visitor took my silence not for astonishment but hesitation.

"Well, then, let's make it ten dollars," he said, pulling a buckskin bag from his coat pocket. "Bread baked by the hand of a woman is surely worth ten dollars."

And he opened that little bag, withdrew a golden rectangle, knelt down, and pressed it into my hand.

My disbelieving eyes fastened on a thick ticket of gold, wide-ridged and stamped "Moffat & Co. 14 1/4 carat, $9.43." The man folded my fingers over the tiny ingot.

"Same as an eagle in the States, ma'am," he said, "but it's California gold, true enough, got up by one of the private mints."

That night, eating hardtack with our bacon, my children and I passed back and forth that shiny oblong of gold, admiring its weight and gloss. Lucena and Will, and each of the Rovers, too, all had a turn marveling over it, the first California gold any of us had seen. And late that night, just before I dropped it into my money box with a satisfying thunk, I stroked its shiny surface and whispered, "Here it is, Caleb, California gold. And it's going to take us home."

But it was fool's gold. No, not the metal, that was true enough, but it was fool's gold all the same.

I started keeping my journal again after that, expecting to tally up gold pieces like miles. I recorded small incidents mostly, filling the pages with bits of this and that.

I have in that little leather book, as example, the Indian scare that occurred the next night. We had camped on a tributary of the Bear River, and in the early hours of the morning, I heard an uproar in the Rovers' camp. Someone swore, there was shouting, the sound of a horse thundering past in the dark, then gunshots. Sleep was lost to me. Fearfully, I sheltered my children, whose slumber, to my amazement, continued undisturbed. Through the remaining hours, I imagined the worst, our oxen killed and men dead or dying outside my tent.

As dawn broke, I heard laughter. I crept out of the tent and saw John Banks laughing and slapping his knees. Next to him stood a sheepish young man whom I knew only as Graham.

"Morning, Mrs. Daniels," Graham said, lowering his eyes, kicking at pine needles.

Banks turned and grinned. "Hope the excitement didn't disturb you, ma'am. You can thank Graham here for keeping us all safe last night."

Graham stared over my head at nothing in particular. "Thought I heard Indians."

Banks laughed and slapped him on the back. "You're a brave man, Graham, to run them off single-handed like that." To me, he said, "We all watched till daylight, when we discovered the awful scene." He pointed to a freshly scored gash on the trunk of a pine. "Two or three trees were badly wounded, but I think they will recover. They were unable to stir, except their tops. They are now certainly cripples as far as moving is concerned."

I was relieved, of course, but in later months I couldn't help thinking back to that scare. What seemed an innocent event was steeped with a sentiment that doomed the Indians of California. Most emigrants too readily suspected, too quickly blamed. Whenever I heard those frequent early reports of Indian slaughters, my heart hurt in a kinship of grief. Of all the calamity attending the discovery of California's gold, none surpassed that suffered by those poor people.

Two days later we were down from the mountains, the difficulty of descent vying in my mind with the wrenching departure of the Semples.

The march that final day was of great fatigue, without interest or incident, beyond the constant climbing and descending of mountains. Canyons and chasms and ravines fell away on either side of the road, while above our heads loomed immense ledges of granite. Late that afternoon we began the final descent, so steep the Rovers felled trees, which they fastened to the rear of the wagons to hinder their running too fast. We and our animals may be said to have slid more than walked that last distance.

At the bottom we entered a ravine the Rovers called Steep Hollow, first named by Bryant. Our wagon was last down, behind the Semples. At the side of the road, Lucena stood with her hands on her hips, surveying a pile of logs apparently employed by emigrants before us to retard their own descent. Will added to it the one that had slowed their wagon.

"Place looks a regular wood yard, it does," Lucena said as I joined her with Janey and Hannah, the three of us still catching our breath.

Nearby, a little brook gurgled over its rocky bed. Several of the Rovers knelt at its edge, drinking deep from cupped hands. Downstream, a dense tangle of wild berries choked either side of the brook. In the distance, sheltered by spreading oaks, tents of permanent residence dotted the landscape, thick as a settlement.

Lucena saw them first and squealed. "My goodness gracious, we're in California at last, sure as rain!" Her eyes went from the tents straight to her ragged dress. "La, just look at me!"

Dear Lucena, my familiar companion of that long and arduous and sorrowful journey. The association had begun to feel permanent, like family, so constant was it. Those friendships of the plains must be something like soldiers form in war, I think — never forgotten, shared forever in memory however lost they might become to circumstance.

We parted there, in the vale called Steep Hollow, Lucena all trotted out in her best black silk and lace bonnet. I always think of her not as I saw her last, but there, at Steep Hollow, up on the wagon seat in a cloud of brocade, smiling a tearful farewell from the midst of the little pink rosebuds wreathing her bonnet. And Will, good and faithful, beaming on his bride like the sun itself and doffing his hat a last time to me and mine, saying, "Well, guess we're full chisel for Sacramento City."

Then they were gone from us.

And next, most of the Rovers, too.

Those Ohio boys, their journey done, hardly knew what to do with themselves, they had been so long at going forward to California. Now they were here, their goal attained.

Purpose had cemented them, but its achievement collapsed them. I think a great many emigrants experienced a kind of bewilderment at arrival. After so many days, weeks, and months bent upon the task of getting to California, journey's end produced a kind of confusion, with the need to decide, what now? Now they could follow the road to Johnson's Rancho or Sutter's Fort, or no road at all. Now there was no need to stand guard, no need to pull and carry and haul wagons. For miners, wagons were a hindrance. They had need of mules now, and not much for oxen. Or each other.

At Steep Hollow these dozen Rovers determined to divide the possessions and provisions remaining to them and strike out for their waiting fortunes in numbers less collective. But the habit of connection broke hard. They dodged around each other like ants disturbed from a trail, forming and reforming finally in twos and threes. Most stayed on at Steep Hollow for a few days, as did we.

For Douglas, when he took a bucket to that little burbling brook, came back waving his arms and whooping with excitement.

"Look, Ma! Look what I found! Gold!"

The Diggings

In all, my children and I continued six weeks in the "diggings." That's what the miners called the Sierra's western flank of hills and canyons and creeks they assiduously spaded up and washed for gold. It suited me, that life, that place, then. My emptiness was at home there. No one laughed in the diggings. Every face not ill with scurvy or dysentery was grave with earnest endeavor and heavy with disappointment. The getting of gold proved a far more formidable enterprise than anticipated.

Douglas's chance find of that piece of coarse gold the size of Hannah's littlest fingernail did not repeat. There was gold at Steep Hollow, yes, but not much and not certain. There was no gathering up nuggets like chicken's eggs, as the greenest emigrant imagined. Most gold was found in the form of flakes and dust, dispersed through the dirt nearly as fine as flour and as difficult to rescue. Retrieval required backbreaking digging and washing, labor with substantially less assurance of gain than a laundress at her board. I cannot think but few gold-hunting emigrants found the prize worthy the pursuit.

I once saw a man toil all day to extract from nature's bank but twenty-five cents. Most averaged an ounce, sixteen dollars — good pay in the States, barely a day's keep in the diggings. In California towns, I later learned, a washerwoman earned as much.

But for those men with the fever, there always loomed the promise of a strike, or "pound" diggings. They chased possibility like a
dog does a cat. They were more gamblers, those men, than miners.
For many of them, the quest was the thing. The prize gained, they
staked it on three-card monte, drank it in eight-dollar ale, ate it in
dollar oysters and eggs or five-dollar cantaloupes, then returned to the
hunt.

For me, the hunt meant home, an Isthmus passage to the brick house
in Illinois. And so, adding our tent to the cluster beneath the towering
pines and cedars of Steep Hollow, we took our first lessons in luck.

Eager, then, as any fever-stricken greenhorn, I joined Douglas and
the Rovers in studying the technique of a veteran miner at work on Bear
River.

"Takes a little practice is all," he said, squatting at the river's edge
with a panful of dirt.

I watched him dip the pan's edge into the stream, adding water.
Then, holding one side of his pan a little higher than the other, by a
rotating motion he induced a revolving current. Water sloshing out carried with it the lighter portions of soil.

"Gold's heavier than dirt, that's the principle," the miner said, stirring with roughened fingers the mass remaining in his pan. There, to
our wondering eyes, lay exposed a few shining grains of gold.

"Anybody can do it," he said, nodding at me.

"I believe I can."

"Sure you can. You just keep washing till all that's left is this black
sand. You let that dry, then blow it off just like coolin' soup."

"About how much you think you got in that pan, mister?" Douglas
asked.

The miner shrugged. "Without weighin' it out, I'd guess mebbe a
dime."

With my ten-dollar Moffat & Co. ingot, the easiest gold I ever got in
California, I bought two goldpans from a nearby tent store purveying
goods to miners. Traders were ubiquitous in the diggings. Every little
camp, even Steep Hollow, had someone selling necessaries at luxurious
prices, and luxuries at costs no one who wasn't witness would believe.
"California prices," we called them.

While I was making my purchase, one of the Rovers came into the
tent store looking for a newspaper, any newspaper from the States, he
said.

"Sure thing," the storekeeper said. "I know I got one here
somewhere." He rummaged around in his piled up goods, soon finding

the object of his search. "Here she is," he said, handing over a rumpled paper. "That'd be three dollars."

"Three dollars! I don't want a subscription, mister, just a copy!"

"That's the price, boy. That paper been six months gettin' here. Took passage in New York, crossed the Isthmus by canoe and mule, steamed from Panama City to San Francisco, boarded a boat for Sacramento City, and been some days in a wagon from there to here. Can't sell it to you for no nickel, no sir. That'll be three dollars, and no cheaper, if'n you can find one, anywheres in the diggins."

The Rover spurned the California-priced newspaper, but I parted with my gold piece without reluctance, the investment in the pans, I confidently believed, a sound one.

Hopes high, Douglas and I went to panning along Bear River, equal prospectors with the rest. No mining district having been organized at Steep Hollow, nor claims made, everyone was apt as the next to discover an auriferous concentration.

No one did.

Douglas and I spaded and washed dirt while Janey and Hannah pulled pea vines to feed our hungry oxen. After two days as a prospector, I remember staring at my hands as I prepared bread for our supper. Could these be the hands my mother thought so gracefully suited to the piano? Rough and work-worn they had become in the journey west, but now I saw dirt ground into skin cracked and sore from two days' steady wet labor. The embedded vestiges refused to yield to soap. And how long would the soap last? How long our dwindling provisions? How long would I? My arms and legs and back ached from stooping by the river, rotating the heavy pan. What if I became ill? What would happen to us then?

I dizzied myself with questions while I stirred a stick through ashes left from the morning's fire. I added a handful of pine needles, rekindling the fire as Douglas scuffed into camp. Poor boy, he was exhausted, too.

He handed me our two days' shiny earnings neatly cleaned and deposited in an empty brandy flask he'd found. A miner in a tent near ours had a small brass balance scale and had offered to weigh it for us.

"How much?" I asked.

"Less than an ounce. About twelve dollars."

I said nothing. There was nothing to say. We both knew that at this rate, we'd never unearth enough gold for the Isthmus passage.

"Ma, some fellows are leaving for Sacramento City. They got a cradle they'll sell for ten dollars."

The cradle's price was cheap. Later, downriver, we saw one sell for seventy dollars to three anxious miners possessed of a good claim. By then, we had sold ours for twenty and thought the bargain good.

A cradle is to a pan like a stove is to a campfire, a substantial and scientific improvement. Fashioned like the child's furniture for which it was named, the gold cradle was an oblong box, top and foot open, mounted on rockers. At its head a sieve or hopper was attached and, along the bottom of the box, cleats were nailed at intervals. Its operation was simple enough. Dirt was poured into the sieve, which allowed the finer, and, it was hoped, auriferous, particles to fall through to the box below. The vigorous bailing in of water moved the dirt along, and the cleats captured the gold, if any there should be. To expedite the action, the whole machine was constantly rolled back and forth on its rockers.

With the cradle, we moved slowly down the Bear River valley with John Banks and those Rovers still remaining, prospecting as we went. It was mid-September, and the intense heat of the season added lassitude to our labor. Temperatures rose daily to a hundred degrees, sometimes more. On one particularly sweltering day as we trudged along the Bear, I saw several men up to their necks in the river, cooling themselves. Their hatted heads reminded me of pond lilies.

Although our cradle washed more dirt, and faster, our work did not diminish, and the machine's efficiency demanded three of us. Douglas shoveled the dirt into buckets, which I hauled to the river, where Janey washed it. Despite a week's steady labor, we had deposited less than sixty dollars' worth of gold in our brandy-flask bank when we and the remaining Rovers settled at a place later emigrants eventually called Dutch Flat.

To add to our troubles, the oxen were starving. Little grass survived from the emigrants and animals passing ahead, and few pea vines outlasted the scorching temperatures. There was nothing for the poor animals to eat closer, we learned, than grass eighteen miles north on Deer Creek. One of the Rovers, deciding to drive their oxen up and recruit them for two weeks, offered to take ours.

"Your cattle aren't branded, Mrs. Daniels," he said. "Want me to mark them?"

"I'd know those animals in the dark. You take them and bring them back, my children and I'll know them."

The absent oxen enforced our stay at Dutch Flat. Like Steep Hollow, it was a spontaneous settlement of tents and crude cabins and greenbrush shelters. It differed from Steep Hollow only in the fact of a rich strike made earlier that year, and its fortunate discoverers' staking claims. In those days, all that making a claim required was four corner stakes, the size of the square being equal and agreed upon by all the miners involved. A shovel or pick within those bounds announced ownership. So respected was this agreement that miners commonly left washed gold visible and unprotected on their claims. A lawless element eventually destroyed the trust of those early days, but I remember it.

Douglas and I prospected for a week beyond those staked boundaries, but our labor yielded only discouragement. How hopeless I felt, especially at night while my children slept, and snores drifted from neighboring tents. Fearful thoughts skittered through my mind like mice as I sat late by my fire. Wrapped in Caleb's coat, I watched the flames disappear into embers. I stared up at the stars twinkling above the silhouetted treetops, wondering if the stars at home looked the same, and if I would ever see them again. I have never felt so lonely.

Janey and Douglas felt the loneliness there, too. Perhaps I infected them with it, I don't know. But that's where I first discovered their private pastime.

"Janey does it all the time," Douglas said. "She misses everything."

"I do not," Janey said, rinsing a dinner dish in the bucket of water Douglas had hauled from the river.

I dried the dish and handed it to Douglas, who placed it back on our makeshift table for breakfast. "What does your sister miss?"

"She's got a list, starts with Gran, the piano, music sheets — "

"You said you missed the whole state of Illinois!"

"Not now I don't."

"You did at St. Louis, you said so!"

"That was a long time back," Douglas said. "Now I mostly just miss Gran — "

"And Buck, you said Buck!"

We finished the dishes amid the recitations of Janey's "miss list," as Douglas called it. I wanted to hear more.

"Let's sit together by the fire for a while," I invited, "and watch the stars come out."

Hannah nestled into my lap and Janey continued her list. It included almost everything in the brick house. She had so memorized the rooms, she could recall exactly where any item sat. Douglas amused himself by drilling her.

"Grandpa's pipe," he said. "You miss that?"

"Gran keeps it on the side table in the parlor, next to the chair he always sat in. I remember the smell of it. And I miss that."

"I miss the roses," I said, half to myself, remembering the parlor, the brick house, my life.

"Rugs," Janey said, "especially the hooked one with the flowers on it at the top of the stairs."

I cradled my sleepy Hannah against me and said to Janey, "Can you remember it all? The whole house?"

"Most of it, Mama. It's like the music, I keep it in my head and play it there. I go through the house over and over, the same way. I don't want to forget. I learned it from you."

"Me?"

"You used to read favorite parts of books over and over, memorizing poems and things, don't you remember? And you said that way they were yours forever, even if someday you lost the book."

Douglas said, "She doesn't forget anything. She knows where every pickle dish is, even misses the windows, she says."

"You said you missed your bed, Douglas," Janey reminded, "and sheets, you said sheets."

"Nothing more?" I asked Douglas, trying to get at something, I'm not sure what. Something like Janey's revelations, perhaps, which surprised and pleased and distressed me all at once. Why didn't we talk more, my children and I? Why hadn't Caleb and I?

The truth was, Douglas possessed more than his share of the family reticence. He was his father's son. But I had sanctioned Caleb's reclusive manner, permitted the silence that kept him a stranger in so many ways. I didn't want that to happen with my son.

"Tell me, Douglas, what else do you miss?"

He hesitated, looked away. "Well, I guess I miss going off with my friends, riding and fishing."

I bit my tongue to keep from embarrassing him with my impulsive regret. I realized instantly that Caleb and I both had stolen boyhood from our son on that long trek west, had piled responsibility on young shoulders. Worse, I leaned on him more than ever, I knew, a stance bad for both of us.

Suddenly, Hannah squirmed in my lap, sat up, and looked at me. I thought she'd been sleeping.

"I miss Geordie."

Only the crickets and the soughing of the wind through the trees broke the long silence that followed. I saw tears start in Janey's eyes, and Douglas pick up a pine needle and examine it like it mattered.

I collected myself, swallowed the lump in my throat, brushed the curls from Hannah's forehead. "We all do, sweetie, and we should talk about missing him, to keep him with us always."

Hannah wriggled in my lap and looked up at me. "Like Grampa's pipe and roses and Buck."

She had heard every word.

"Yes, we can do that. We'll go over and over everything we remember about George, like Janey does her music, and then we'll never forget. Tell us what you remember, Hannah."

"He ate ladybugs."

Douglas laughed. "That was you, silly!"

Hannah turned to him and shook her head. "He did it first!"

"I remember how he banged his spoon at the dinner table and repeated what people said if he liked the word," Janey said.

And Douglas remembered how George squealed with delight when caught at some mischief.

And I remembered, and didn't tell it, and probably should have, how utterly entranced I was by the miracle of him.

We talked long into the night then, my children and I, remembering George, buried out on the prairie. And then I told them about my little brother buried in the wilderness, too. They didn't even know I'd had one.

"His name was Jeffy," I said, "but I don't remember him. He was just three when he died, younger than George, and I was five."

"I'm five," Hannah said.

"Almost, sweetie, almost."

"Mama," Janey said, "don't you remember anything about your brother?"

"Nothing at all."

"Oh, Mama, that's so sad," she said, brushing away her tears.

"Well, we won't let Hannah or any of us forget George. If we talk about him, and keep telling his stories, he'll live forever in our hearts."

Hannah snuggled against me, warm and sleepy. "Like a pome, Mama, we can mem'ry Geordie, and Papa, too, like a pome."

Dutch Flat

While at Dutch Flat, John Banks and two other Rovers decided on a prospecting tour to the north fork of the American River. I suggested to Douglas he go with them. It was hard for me, that decision, but right. And I needed him to go as much as he did. I'd had the habit of leaning my whole life, and I determined to break it. Later, I did the same with Janey, let her go. Australia being so far, though, that was as hard a thing as ever I've done.

"You could make a big strike there," I told Douglas, giving him reason as well as permission to have a boy's adventure.

They thought they would, of course. Every miner, I think, imagined himself James Marshall at Sutter's sawmill, and the fame of the American River was such that it drew gold hunters like bees to honey.

Douglas sold the cradle for twenty dollars and with the money bought dried beef for his expedition. That and the last of our hard bread made up my boy's provisions. He intended to travel light, taking only a blanket, a pan, and his bowie knife.

Seeing that knife, bought by Caleb from the Illinois peddler just the year before, stirred such memories. Only a year. It seemed a lifetime ago, that day, all of us crowding around the peddler's wagon in that rutted road in front of the brick house, where roses spilled pink and fragrant above the door.

Only a year, and how different our circumstances now. Caleb and George buried in the wilderness, my daughters in ragged dresses and worn shoes and living in a wagon, my poor mother waiting confirmation of her worst fears, Douglas and I scratching in the dirt like chickens for our survival. I felt a hundred years older than thirty-four.

"Good for crevicing, Ma," Douglas said, fastening the knife to his belt.

Gold did bed down in those deep and undisturbed places between boulders. We'd had some luck finding it. The miner who showed us how to scrape and dig with a knife or stout iron spoon had grinned and said, "Old mother earth's been hoarding up in her pockets a great many years. She's a savin' sort of body. You try it. It's easy to get gold in California. Difficult to keep it, though."

He was right.

I had no worry at my son's departure beyond a mother's care. Nor, as I assured him, had he for me. Despite being the only woman in camp, I had not the least concern for myself or my daughters. Never have I felt more protected or respected than I did in the diggings. Even had I not been widowed, that sad estate bestowing sympathy enough, I was safe as money in a bank. Any woman was.

We were a novelty, a woman and children in the mines. Those passing our camp stared, of course, to which we soon enough became accustomed. But not one untoward word or sign of disrespect reached my ears. My tented neighbors seemed to cherish our presence as reminders of loved ones left behind. They were great comfort, all those bearded, nameless men of the mines in their slouch hats and flannel shirts. I believe they would have starved themselves sooner than see me and mine want.

At Dutch Flat, I feared it might come to that, our provisions had become so reduced. I used the last of the flour the day Douglas left for the American River. All my provision box held then was a little bacon, a few pounds of beans and rice, some sugar and coffee. This diet my daughters and I varied with wild berries we gathered from dense brambles crowding a nearby dried-up streambed. The berries, black and sweet, were free for the picking, but their vicious thorns exacted a painful price from our hands and arms.

There was, of course, a store at Dutch Flat, if the tent with its plank-on-a-barrel counter merits the title. The storekeeper, a jaunty little man with an eager cast to his one eye, cheerfully dispensed dollar-a-cup whiskey to celebration-minded miners, along with shirts and shovels and what few provisions remained so late in the year.

"Sorry, ma'am, I got no flour, not at any price," he said, leaning on his makeshift counter and giving me the entire attention of his one eye.

"When might you expect to have?" I asked, anxious for that dearest of commodities.

"Don't rightly know, if'n at all. Mebbe a mule train'll get up here again, mebbe not. Season's gettin' late."

His most plentiful commodity being whiskey, I found little among the storekeeper's provisions useful to my purpose. A can of sardines caught my eye, and I inquired its price.

"An ounce, ma'am," he said, handing me the dusty tin.

I looked at it in my hand, and from it to the storekeeper's one keen eye. "Might you be referring to the weight?"

He laughed, and slapped his countertop. "Oh, glory, that be a good'un! Weight!" He crossed his arms across his chest and beamed at me. "Think on it a bit, I s'pose I do. Weight of gold, that is!" He laughed again.

"You are asking, then, sixteen dollars for this tin of sardines?"

"Yes'm."

I handed it back. "Have you anything else in the way of groceries?"

"Got a bit of cheese and butter," he said, taking the tin from my hand and returning it to its former position among the whiskey bottles. He searched the arrangement for the advertised cheese and butter, and finding same offered them for appraisal.

"The cheese is moldy," I said, examining the box. "How much do you want for it?"

"Six dollars the pound, same for the butter."

I sniffed the butter, and shook my head. "Rancid."

He shrugged. "I'll be lookin' for whatever I can find. You stay put, ma'am." He turned to his commodities and made a great noise of banging bottles but found nothing. He was reluctant to let me go, keen, I suppose, to see a woman.

I remember standing in that tent with my brandy flask of gold, staring at whiskey and wondering what to do for bread while the storekeeper rattled through his bottles and told me how he lost his eye in the war with Mexico.

His vanity rose with his story, and at its conclusion he fussed with his patch fashioned from a rag of scarlet sash. "A Mexican general's," he boasted, twisting its bright folds and tugging the whole into a rakish angle on his forehead. He reminded me of Lucena and her coal-scuttle bonnet.

Two days later, praise be to heaven, the mules and Angelita arrived, truly a delivering angel.

Hannah was the first to hear the cheerful tinkling of the horse's bell. "Mama!" she cried, pulling at my sleeve as Janey and I rubbed the last of the soap into some never clean clothes we scrubbed on rocks at the river's edge. "Come on! Chri-mas! I hear Sandy Claus!"

For a brief and terrible moment the image of little George tugging at Mr. Fogie's beard dazed me. Then I, too, heard the bell.

I hurried after Hannah, drying my hands on my apron, reaching camp just as the bell horse clopped into view with Angelita at its side. She held in one small, black-gloved hand its silver bridle, and by the other a little boy. How I stared. And how vanity assaulted me, standing there hiding roughened hands in the wet and ragged muslin apron I wore over an old linsey-woolsey dress, aware of what a sight I must be in my faded sunbonnet and broken-toed shoes.

Angelita was a vision. I had never seen a woman looking so splendid, and in my ignorance then assumed all Mexican women wore fitted black pantaloons and white linen leggings, with embroidered short jackets and wide-brimmed hats. The little boy, about Hannah's age, was his mother's miniature in complexion and costume, except for his helmet of cropped blue-black hair. Angelita's hair fell in two long, thick braids down her back.

Behind the bell horse thudded a string of pack mules. There must have been forty of them, stirring a cloud of fine red dust from the road with their dainty hooves. Roped to the mules' sides was a bulky cargo of canvas bags and small barrels.

Everyone in camp gathered around the storekeeper's tent to watch while Angelita's four mule skinners transferred harness and burdens into piles by the trail, a process the mules endured with the patience of statues.

The miners greeted Angelita's good supplies of ale and porter and brandy by enthusiastically betting the bottles on next Sunday's footrace.

I saw conveyed into the store a good supply of flour, beans, sugar, and bacon, plus luxuries for those with the price: eggs and potatoes, boxed herring and onions, salt and soap.

Nothing was cheap. Freight charges of seventy-five cents a pound added substantially to the cost of goods already dear. One good-luck miner paid two dollars on the spot for a single onion, then stood there in front of everyone and ate it raw, declaring as he crunched and tears ran from his eyes, that he never before tasted anything so delicious.

After concluding her business, Angelita sought me out, that her little boy, Roberto, might visit with Hannah. What beautiful children they were together, his hair straight and black, hers fair and curling. They played some invented game with pebbles, needing no language but childhood, while their mothers watched proud as peacocks.

Angelita said they didn't often see children, and Roberto was a lonely little boy. She didn't speak English. I had the translation from the miner everyone called "California Hat."

I never knew his real name. In the diggings, we were anonymous. Most miners knew me as the widow woman. And I knew few of their names. It was the miners' code, like respect for a claim, and arose, I suspect, by unprompted agreement. One's neighbors might stay a week or a day, or they might die. A name conferred more attachment than that wandering population wanted. And so a short man was "Stumpy," a thin one "Slim," and any number answered to their state of origin, like "Tennessee" or "Tex."

I never knew California Hat's real name, only that he had once sailed on a whaling ship, which he abandoned at Monterey years before the gold discovery. He spoke Angelita's language fluently, from constant association with the native Californians. Among the miners at Dutch Flat, he disdained the regulation slouch hat for the Californio style. With that exception, he looked like any other bearded miner in dirty clothes and scuffed boots.

California Hat, holding his name in his hands, stared first at me and then at my visitor. A man didn't often enjoy the company of even one woman. Much rarer were two. He was accordingly stiff with privilege and politeness. Angelita simply smiled.

I hadn't talked to a woman, even seen one, since Lucena's departure, and was hungry for it. I wanted to know all about Angelita. Excepting the mantua-maker at Vandalia, I'd never known a woman who worked for her own living.

California Hat nodded at me and then at Angelita as he translated, solemn as a judge with the importance of his task. Spanish sounded clumsy on his tongue, like poetry on Angelita's.

"Angelita says to tell you in California, women all work, *es verdad,* is true. She says some more stuff, but that's the heart of it. Says women in Sonora — that's the camp in the southern mines where her husband digs — make as much or more than the miners, from washin' shirts and sewin' buttons and bakin' bread."

Angelita said something else in the pretty way she had. California Hat pondered it, then translated with a shrug, "Says she likes mules better'n washtubs."

There was more. California Hat listened, then added, eyes cast down, "Says to tell you she's sorry for your loss." He awkwardly examined his hat. "So be we all, ma'am."

I don't know how Angelita knew I was alone in California, that, unlike her, I didn't have a husband in the mines somewhere else. Perhaps a Dutch Flat miner told her, or perhaps it was just that women know certain things without the necessity of language. Or perhaps I just looked ravaged by the grief that had emptied me.

I learned my first few Spanish words there at Dutch Flat, standing in the dust with the handsome young Mexican woman. "*Gracias, señora,*" I said awkwardly, getting the words from California Hat. Angelita hugged me when she left.

In memory, Angelita remains a wonder to me. The novelty of a woman working for money, though, has long worn off. The novelty soon enough was any woman who didn't. In California, especially in those earliest years of gold, everyone worked. Or starved. Even in San Francisco, I heard, women arriving by sea found themselves faced with necessity. Some returned home, from California's failure to provide them servants as they were accustomed. Since everyone able-bodied preferred to take their chances in the goldfields, there were no servants.

For women less particular, California was a study. Later, after leaving Sacramento City, I met a woman who chopped her own wood and hauled it off the mountain to bake pies for miners. And another, a little woman one wouldn't think capable of wringing suds from a doll's dress, laundered shirts and pants all day for more money than her husband dug up.

I remember Big Mary saying, "You be surprised sometimes at what you can do when you gots no choice at it."

I've come to agree, and more. We not only can do what we have to do, we can do what we decide to do.

Angelita's delivery of goods to Dutch Flat was celebrated that night by the miners with their onions and ale, and by me. Having traded most of my gold to the storekeeper for flour, I baked in my Dutch oven three little berry pies for a treat. But while Hannah and Janey enjoyed theirs, I watched Lord York eat mine.

That wasn't his name, I don't suppose. That's just what the miners called the pale Englishman with the watery blue eyes whose tent was nearest mine and whose poor health prevented mining. While my pies were baking, my neighbor dragged himself to my fire to inquire after the "delectable bouquet," as he called it, then asked if he might buy my pie.

I had had my lesson on top of the mountain, and I spoke right up. "Indeed you may, but I don't know what to ask for it," I said. "Do you think fifty cents — "

"Madam," he said, slipping a slender hand into his pocket and taking from it a leather pouch, "there being little silver in circulation, the nobler metal performs its menial service. A pinch 'twixt finger and thumb we take here for the equal of a dollar, there being no call in California for value less than that, and small demand, I might add, for so trifling a sum as one dollar."

So saying, he offered a generous pinch of gold dust, and I held out my nearly empty brandy flask to take it. In exchange, I offered up my fresh berry pie, which my customer ate on the spot.

"Delicious, madam, the first water," he said, wiping his fingers on a kerchief he took from his back pocket. "Should you bake more, you may count on me for regular custom."

And so my business was launched. Every miner at Dutch Flat was glad for a pie baked by a woman. My customers bought them as fast as I picked berries and baked them, lining up at my tent-kitchen morning, noon, and night.

By the time Douglas returned, I had filled the brandy flask with gold, and half a pickle jar besides, pinch by pinch, pie by pie. I figured my profits at nearly a hundred dollars, and in my imagination calculated the Isthmus costs in pies. I determined if I could bake and sell a thousand, providing the flour held out and I could get more fruit, home was but weeks away. How the prospect lifted my spirits, especially as Douglas's search netted nothing more than the adventure.

I urged a full report. "Tell me everything, Douglas," I said, sitting him down by my fire and handing him a pie. "I want you to talk more, you're too quiet. Now, tell me what you saw."

He wolfed the pie, and I could see him thinking as he chewed. "First," he said, wiping berry juice from his chin with the back of his hand, "there's the river, the American River. Oh, Ma," he said, grinning at me, warming to his recitation, "you should see it, that river. It's way down at the bottom of a canyon, bad stony and a rough descent. From above, it looks like a mercury ribbon, all silver-like in the sunshine. We had to hang on to the bushes just to get down, the road's that steep."

He licked his fingers. "Good pie, Ma, really good. Fellows on the American eat mostly hard biscuit and jerked beef. You could make a thousand dollars, I bet, if we could get there. But there's no wagon road down yet. Will be someday, though; all those men, they can make anything happen if they want to, if there's gold."

I handed over another pie, still warm. "You didn't find any?"

"Panned some, no luck. Heard there's good diggings at Yankee Jim's, way up top of the mountain. An Australian outlaw built a corral for stolen horses, and some men tracked him there and dug around and found gold. We all started for the place but had to help bury someone and didn't go after all."

"Who died?" I asked, questioning more from habit than curiosity.

"Just some poor miner whose friends were too weak from sickness to get his body up the mountain. We were climbing to Yankee Jim's when we came to their tent with the body in front, wrapped in a blanket. Two men lay in the tent, exhausted from roping their dead companion to a bier they'd fashioned from two boards and some pine branches. They were waiting, they said, for anyone strong enough to come by to help carry the body up the mountain to a miners' burial place. We were going that way and offered our services."

Douglas reached over and patted my hand. "Your pies are really good, Ma."

I looked at my son, talking and talking so bright in the light from our campfire, and saw reflected in his eyes the suspicions I had of my own heart. We had seen too much of death to be shocked by it, or even much moved. Death seemed out of place in California, somehow strange and unaccountable. People had come to California for such different purpose and for so short a period of time. For whatever reason, we had grown callous toward death and dying. It bothered me and I said so.

"We buried the fella best we could, Ma. And no easy task at that. The path was steep and slippery, and we had to cling to the bushes and slide the bier along the ground to get it up the mountainside to the burying place. There wasn't much we could do for him, you know, in the way of ceremony, but dig a grave and put him in it. We threw a few handfuls of ferns on top of his body and added the two boards from the bier to form a roof. Then we shoveled in some dirt, and it was over."

And the next day, so, too, was our stay at Dutch Flat. My wild berries were all but depleted, and the few remaining looked shriveled and dry. Like me, I thought. Both of our seasons are past. While Douglas did some last-minute panning, Janey and I packed up my kitchen tent and loaded the wagon. Lord York, offering help he was too weak to give, sat on a barrel with Hannah on his knee, telling puppet stories with a doll he'd made for her from a red kerchief stuffed with moss.

Our cattle had returned to us looking not much better than at their departure, poor beasts. We yoked them to the wagon once more, and I bade farewell to Lord York and California Hat and my other customers, and regretfully to the last of the Rovers. John Banks and his friends, setting their sights on Yankee Jim's, sold their cattle and wagon to the one-eyed storekeeper, who was off to Deer Creek with the remainder of his whiskey and goods. It was mid-October and the rains would come soon, he said. Time to move on.

And so I and my children did, too, heading in our wagon, alone, down the parched Bear River valley, where even the trees looked thirsty in the late October sun. We had entered the lower elevations, and oaks now grew among the pines. Their leaves had yellow in them. The sere hillsides and changing leaves, the deserted places where ashes announced a miner's fire had been, the whispering wind in the treetops, all heightened my sense of how utterly alone we were. Now I had not even the Rovers' coattails to hold on to. We were well and truly in California, we had well and truly seen the elephant, and we were alone, all alone.

You Bet

We were heading for a place the Dutch Flat storekeeper called You Bet. "Can't miss it," he'd said. "Got a hotel and everything."

I pushed that promise into the space where loneliness and fear had set up camp, loaded the chamber of my mind with the idea of a hotel. We had a little gold, perhaps we could afford a room and a bath. Better, I imagined myself obtaining a position – cook or housekeeper, I didn't care, whatever paid the most. I recalled Phoebe Franklin totting up how many men she could cook for as we strolled across the springtime prairie. I wondered what fortune had been theirs, those cheerful Canadians off to California in such a hurry to find gold. Wherever they were, I wished them better luck than fortune had allotted me.

It was a measure of my naivete that I even imagined the hotel as civilization knew the concept. I assumed something on a scale more modest than the accommodations we enjoyed in St. Louis, but a hotel nonetheless, a place with rooms and beds.

We were only a day's travel, the Dutch Flat storekeeper had said, so when we arrived at a settlement of rude cabins and tents the following afternoon, I inquired at a wooden building that stood near the road, roofed with blue canvas and flanked by two large oaks.

It being substantially larger than a miner's tent, I peered through the open flap of canvas that served as door to a dim, blue interior about twenty feet square. At the rear, facing the doorway, I saw a makeshift bar of planks on barrels swagged with red calico. Behind this unexpected drapery a rotund barkeep in a dirty apron poured drinks for two miners.

"Excuse me," I said, stepping inside and discovering, to my surprise, a rough wooden floor, "I'm told there's a hotel in this area. Could you direct me, please?"

The customers, startled by a woman's voice, turned, and the barkeep grinned.

"You bet," he said, putting his twirled and waxed mustache into motion. "This here's my place — bar, store, hotel, all on one stick. Onliest hotel around. Been here long as me, near onto a year, you bet."

Ignoring the stares that greeted me like an apparition, I looked around again, lest my initial appraisal had overlooked a doorway or stairs. I saw little more than the rude bar lined with bottles of spirits, behind which the proprietor preened, stroking his mustache like a pet. To the left I noticed some piled-up goods — shirts, shovels, boxes, and small barrels — which my Dutch Flat experience recognized as a store. On the right, two crude three-legged stools sided a small stove, its pipe punched through the blue canvas roof. Nothing save its proprietor's assertion suggested a hotel.

"This is a hotel?" I asked.

"You bet," the barkeep said, uncorking a second bottle.

" 'Course, no proper place for a lady, not being private, as you see."

His nod at the floor took my gaze with his. On it I now noticed chalked squares.

My obvious puzzlement amused the miners. One leaned an elbow on the counter and hooked a thumb at the barkeep. "The proprietor," he said, "more than his guests do, I assure you, madam, esteems this establishment the equal of a hotel and thus claims the distinction in title. He doubtless presumes the appellation appropriate to any shelter. The absence of beds we do not take amiss, as no traveler in the diggings enjoys such comforts except in memory. The neglect of blankets, however, is taken exception to." He turned to the proprietor and laughed.

"I told you the blankets was stole." The barkeep poured a drink for himself. "Got no apartments, ma'am, if that's what you be looking for," he said, raising his glass. "Sell you a drink, if you've a mind."

I shook my head, too perplexed by the roomless, bedless hotel to be insulted by the offer.

"Them blankets was stole, alright," said the other miner, turning on the barkeep, "and was you what stole 'em, Mr. You Bet Charlie. Stole 'em right off our backs while we was sleepin'."

His companion drank off his liquor, enlarging his amusement. "That's right. Give it up, Charlie. You can acknowledge the corn with us." He turned to me. "The suspicion is rife, madam, that our ill-esteemed proprietor, who exacts two dollars for two blankets and the privilege of lying upon his floor within the confines of the accommodations outlined, collects the blankets back once his guests sleep. The plan is an elegantly frugal one, two blankets doing the duty of forty. As each guest falls into the arms of Orpheus, our proprietor purloins the blankets for the next arrival. And when all the house sleeps — a noisy employment, to be sure — Charlie here appropriates them to his own use."

"Ever' man jack has stole my blankets," the barkeep complained, "and this lawyer here putting the theft on me!"

Later, after determining to bake pies for the miners of You Bet, I was inclined to agree with the lawyer's appraisal of his host when I bought from him some dried peaches. It was nearly November by then, and the berry season over. The peaches were an excellent fruit, having come dried from Chile pressed into a round, like a cheese. But their California price appalled me.

"Twenty dollars!" I saw my profits, in proportion to the cost of my supplies, dissolving like salt in water.

"You bet, ma'am," he said, taking the pickle jar of gold dust from my reluctant hand and pouring from it onto the little brass dish of his scale. "And cheap at that. Late in the year, you see, and won't be more when them's gone."

Disconsolately, I set up my tent kitchen next to a large nearby oak. For almost a week Janey and I baked peach pies for small profit while Douglas prospected and Hannah made friends with the miners. As at Dutch Flat, the men of You Bet readily bought my pies, so grateful were they for food not prepared by their own hands.

Few men in the mines had the least understanding of cooking, most surviving on bacon and half-cooked flapjacks. For variety, I once saw a miner make bread by pouring water directly into a small sack of flour, then knead the mass through the bag. The resultant dough he molded to a stick which he then held over a fire. The consequence could not have been a great success. I did not see the method repeated.

I had custom enough at You Bet, but my plan to go home on the gold earned from pie-making deteriorated with the cost of supplies and the weather. On the first day of November the rains came.

The storm arose unexpectedly from a cloudy sky, a sudden gust of wind extinguishing my fire. Ashes scattered everywhere, dirtying my flour and fruit, getting in our eyes. Then the tent blew over. It was everything Janey and I could do, there was such a howling and blowing, to secure it against flying away. Douglas returned to find us huddled in the wagon, its worn canvas cover leaking the pelting rains, the whole in imminent danger of being toppled by winds. Finally, with thunder rumbling and lightning flashing from the darkened sky, I grabbed Hannah, hollered at Douglas and Janey to grab our blankets, and we all ran for the hotel.

We stayed two days, courtesy of the proprietor's unexpected generosity. With gratitude, we took for ourselves a corner and curtained it off with the remainder of his web of turkey-red calico, lent for the purpose. Having our own blankets, we enjoyed a snug comfort in the hotel, protected by its flanking oaks from the worst of the screeching wind and lashing rain.

Thinking back, it was there, in the blue-tented, red-calicoed confines of the You Bet Hotel, watching men's muddy boots tramp erasure through the floor's chalked purpose, that my life veered. It was a moment as decisive as Caleb's halt before the brick house. Except I didn't mark the traveler then.

I noticed little, consumed as I was by fears for our future, for my pie business was surely over. Miners were leaving the mountain in droves, heading to the towns for winter. Some had less to show for their season in the mines than we did. One man dragged wet and miserable into the blue tent hotel that first rainy day, desperate for food and lacking gold sufficient to buy it.

"Give me five dollars for this gun?" he said to the proprietor, placing a double-barreled shotgun on the plank counter. "It's worth fifty."

"Don't need your gun, mister," Charlie said, pulling on his mustache with one hand and jerking a thumb toward his stock of goods in the corner. "Got stacks of old guns, and no customers for any such article."

Desperate, the traveler looked around at the dozen or so men taking shelter beneath the blue canvas. "Who'll give me five dollars for this gun?" He held it out to anyone who wanted to look.

One or two smiled, others shook their heads. No one wanted it.

Finally, Charlie, seeing the man's need, reached for it. "Let me look at it." He examined the gun. "Tell you what," he said, handing it back, "I'll play you five dollars' worth of pork against the gun."

"Agreed!"

Everyone gathered around, and although from my corner I could not see the cards dealt, I heard the miner win. "Hooray!" he hollered, "I'm going to eat!"

The onlookers cheered. Miners delighted in seeing an underdog, one of their own, come victorious. And they gambled incessantly, on anything.

Perhaps the spectators' glee spurred the proprietor of the You Bet Hotel, or perhaps it was the same soft spot that lent me a corner and a length of red calico. In any event, I heard him say, "Now I'll play you five dollars' worth of flour against that gun."

The traveler agreed, played again, and won.

The nature of men in the mines was such that a run of luck, as displayed by the man with the shotgun, provoked their speculative bent. Someone offered to bet five dollars in money against the gun. The traveler consented and promptly won.

"Now, boys," he said, his spirits uplifted by good fortune, "any of you can have the gun that wants it, the bet's five dollars."

Men respected a run of luck at cards. No one bet, and the traveler left, taking the pork, the flour, the five dollars, and the gun he couldn't sell but that had served him well.

I took the incident for a lesson, and in bad times later, I tried to think on the traveler and the shotgun that wouldn't sell. Mostly, I could do that, and keep hope alive.

Except for the time of the flood.

What deceptions California is capable of. So much sunshine and fair weather, who would imagine what rains can do here? Those two days of pounding rain at You Bet should have warned me how many forms the California elephant could assume, but they didn't. Had I seen what our future was to be in Sacramento City, I never would have sold the wagon to the freighter who walked into the You Bet Hotel and agreed to take us there.

Given wishes, of course, I would have wished us all back in Illinois, and California just a name out west, and no such thing as gold. But, as Mother so often said, "If wishes were horses, beggars would ride."

He stomped through the canvas doorway of the hotel on the afternoon of the second day of rain, smelling of wet wool and tobacco, face hidden behind an overgrown mustache and beard. Later, at Nevada City, a Chinese man who worked for me there confided that white men all looked alike to him. So, too, did men in the diggings to me. I couldn't have said what this one, strolling across Charlie's chalk-smeared floor, looked like then.

A measure of how small an impression he made is that later, when he visited my restaurant in Sacramento City, I didn't recognize him until he spoke. He had a gravelly, kind of prayerful voice, like he was tasting his words and didn't want to give them up until he had their whole flavor.

The voice I remembered, and the eyes.

It was the eyes I noticed first at You Bet. He stared at me and my children as he passed through the room to the bar, like the others, to which I paid no mind. But there was more to his looking at us than surprise. Or maybe I just thought so later.

From my calico corner, I glanced up and then returned to the old book of fairy tales I was reading to Hannah. Douglas had dashed to the wagon for it that afternoon. It was probably the story of Hansel and Gretel. That was one of her favorites. Nothing ever scared Hannah, and certainly not the story that had so distressed me at her age.

"Excuse me, missus," the gravelly voice said. "Charlie tells me that's your wagon. The big, well-made one?"

I looked up from my book into deep gray eyes beneath a thatch of hair escaping a black felt hat. He took off the hat, dripping rainwater from its brim onto my half-curtain of red calico. The drops left wine-colored spots.

"That's my wagon, yes," I said, standing.

"If you're of a mind to sell, I'll give you two hundred and fifty dollars for it."

Douglas, playing checkers with Janey in front of the stove ten feet away, overheard. "My pa built that wagon, mister. Best wagon maker in Illinois after my grandpa."

The man turned. "I believe it, son. Fine wagon. That's why I want to buy it."

"I can't sell my wagon," I said. "I need it to get to San Francisco."

"San Francisco?"

"To get the steamer to Panama City."

"Oh, the Isthmus, yes, I see."

He spoke so slowly I could almost see him testing the words, chewing their edges to determine they'd serve.

He glanced at the hat he held, brushed raindrops from it, adding more wine-colored spots to our calico wall. Then he studied me, as if gauging my readiness for instruction. His eyes had the color of rain clouds.

"Well, missus," he said, "most folks wanting to get to San Francisco generally go by water. From Sacramento City. It's faster, you see. Folks here — in California, I mean, as you'll discover in San Francisco, and

Sacramento City the same — are all on the go. Hurry, hurry. Must think the gold is going somewhere else, want to catch it before it does."

"Sacramento City?"

"Yes, ma'am. You want to get to San Francisco, you take the river. There's a neat little iron-sided steamer, the *McKim*, regular on it from Sacramento City to San Francisco. You sell me that wagon, I'll be going to Sacramento City for supplies and I can take you there. You want the steamer, right enough. That's the best way."

Hannah tugged at my skirt. "Mama, read."

The gray eyes found her. A smile formed behind the brown beard and mustache. "Well, hello there, pumpkin."

Hannah, clutching her red-kerchief doll in one hand, hanging on to my skirt with the other, peered up at him from beneath her cap of curls. "Who you?"

He bent down to Hannah's level, and they contemplated one another across the red calico divider.

"Zeb," he said, with a smile radiating like sun through breaking clouds. "My name's Zeb."

Sacramento City

Zeb. Zebulon Walker Tillman. Zeb. A man rock-steady as his name, as warm and reliable as the rising sun. And just as uncomplicated. What I came to prize most in Zeb was, for want of a better word, a kind of evidentness. He held no harbored secrets or regrets. He was as open to view as the crystal water of the Truckee River, every stone and boulder and grain of sand on exhibit and available for inspection.

When I think of Caleb, and I do, I think of the Platte, its mysterious opacity concealing sudden and hidden depths, secret places, confusions.

The Platte and the Truckee. So different, yet both beautiful. I'm a fortunate woman. Caleb answered a girl's romantic fancy, fulfilled the dreams of first love praised by poets. And Zeb? Yes, Zeb. I'm a fortunate woman.

I would not have said so then, of course, being possessed of a grieving heart. And that was the heart I carried with me when we left the blue-tented hotel in company with Zeb that first week of November 1849.

The long months heading west had left their rhythm behind, like sea legs. And so the wagon trip from You Bet felt familiar — the sound of creaking wheels, the oxen's plodding hooves, the sway of the wagon, Janey quietly reading to Hannah.

I shouldn't have worn Caleb's old coat. It still held the smell of him. When Zeb unexpectedly hollered "Whoa!," I resented his gravelly voice. It was not the one I knew, and I felt immeasurably saddened at the repeated realization that Caleb was gone from me, truly gone.

"Missus, you should take a look here," Zeb said, coming around to the back of the halted wagon. "This California, she's something to see."

I had no interest in the deadly magnet of golden promises, but to be polite, I climbed out the back of the wagon with Janey.

"Come on, pumpkin," Zeb said, leaning into the wagon, "you, too."

Hannah liked Zeb as much as she had Lord York. She held her little red-kerchief doll up to him. "Punkin," she said, and giggled as he lifted her out.

Zeb laughed. "Bring your dolly. We'll show her something she's never seen before." He took Hannah's hand and led her past the wagon.

Janey and I followed. The oxen stood patiently on the crest of a hill.

Zeb knelt by Hannah and put an arm around her. "Take a look, pumpkin."

Below, summer-browned hillsides, already hinting green from the recent rain, fell away from the Sierra, indented by ancient creeks and rills that joined, by crooked, wet fingers, the rivers wending through the valley beneath us.

Hannah held her doll up. "See, punkin."

Zeb stood, turned to me. "You won't see a sight finer, missus. *This* is California."

After three days' steady rain, the cleared atmosphere unveiled a crystalline quality. A gentle breeze touched our faces, soft as kitten fur. The air smelled fresh-washed, like laundry hung out to dry.

Sometimes in California, after a cleansing storm like that one, the sky is so blue it looks like paint. On such days, nature's artist, inspired by the canvas, adorns the sky with the whitest, puffiest, most perfect of clouds, high and drifting. This was one of those days, so pure and translucent the eye could see a hundred miles.

"That's the Feather River there, joining up with the Bear." Zeb pointed north at a thin ribbon twisting south to join the river we followed. "And there, beyond where the Feather and Bear come together, that's the Sacramento River."

I saw a distant cord of green warping south. "Trees?" I said, to be polite.

"Willows, cottonwoods, and oaks so big you could build a house out of one." Zeb paused, gazing. "And all that river bottom. Richest land on the continent. Imagine the wheat it could grow, just imagine."

His words came slow as an old rope from a well, the voice verging on reverence. He sounded like my father had when he talked of the West, like a thousand emigrants dazed by golden visions. Here was another one fevered, I thought.

Douglas scooped up a handful of red earth, examined it, dropped it, brushed his hands off. "Any gold down there?"

"Nope, and that's all right by me. Dug gold three months, along the Yuba, and the Bear." Zeb glanced at the mountains behind us, then west to the vast plain below. "A rational man won't do it."

I had a sudden sense of having been here before. Then I remembered. South Pass, where the first waters flowed west. Caleb standing with us, looking back at the way we had come, then west at the way we would go. I shoved the painful memory away.

Beyond where the Feather and Bear joined the Sacramento, the valley, scattered with dark dots, lay flat as a platter to a rim of distant mountains.

Zeb boosted Hannah to his shoulders. "See down there, pumpkin? Looks like little bitty ants from here. It's all cattle and horses, elk, deer." He turned to Douglas. "Grass year-round. Dry now, but nutritious. Good haying, too." He put Hannah down, touched Douglas's shoulder to turn his attention. "That's Captain Sutter's fort," he said, pointing.

My gaze followed Zeb's over a thin scar of wagon road, red as dried blood, crossing the plain to the broad junction of the American and Sacramento rivers. The clarity of the atmosphere was such that we could see a white dot in the far distance below. It looked like a child's tiny toy block.

It was from this innocent-looking white dot that James Marshall had gone east into the mountains to build Sutter a sawmill. And discovered gold. And wrecked my happiness.

Zeb looked at me. "Just this side of the fort, that's Sacramento City, right there on the river."

That's what I wanted to see — a city, hotels, a steamer. As we climbed back into the wagon, I hugged the thought of home.

We descended to the mountain's hem, where the Bear River fed a rich bottomland. Our route now lay across thirty miles of waterless plain, Zeb told us, so we filled the water bags and cut grass for the oxen.

They looked better, Buck and Cherry especially. Douglas, while prospecting at You Bet, had found a spring. A week's grazing on the grass it fed recruited our oxen admirably. They remained lean, but not so thin their bones showed.

Parting from them would pain the children, and me. They had been faithful friends. Should a poet one day apply his pen to the awful trek of bravery and misery that was the California emigration, I trust he'll devote a verse to the suffering beasts who brought us west.

In crossing the plain to Sacramento City, we passed some ranches neighbored by the humble dwellings of worker Indians, who observed our progress without curiosity. Rancherias, Zeb called the villages. These Indians looked even more pathetic, degraded, and impoverished than those huddled outside Fort Laramie. Gold wrecked the California Indians' happiness, too.

We forded the famous American River about three miles from where it joins the Sacramento, their juncture being the site of Sacramento City. The road then took us along the edge of a swampy forest. In boggy places we saw where cattle, roaming free, had mired and died, their bloated bodies caught in a wet stench of marsh grass and log jams. I tugged Hannah away from the back of the wagon when I saw her staring out wide-eyed at the frightful sight. She looked at me and whimpered, "Cherry?"

"Cherry's fine, sweetheart," I said, hugging her. "Buck, too. And Lewis and Clark. They're all fine. You crawl up and look out the front. You'll see. They brought us all the way to Sacramento City. We're almost there."

We came into Sacramento City along Front street. It borders the east side of the namesake river, which flows wide and green, beautifully fringed with trees on both sides, some of immense growth. To the trunks and exposed roots of these trees were cabled, for a mile along the river, vessels of every description: barques, brigs, schooners, sloops, and smaller craft.

This collected forest of masts mingled a curious contrast of boughs and spars, but the foremost sight was a large sidewheeler adorned with banners and pennants. It lay downriver a couple of hundred feet, moored to a landing at the head of what I later discovered to be J street, Sacramento City's principal thoroughfare. I could see the ship's name, *Senator*, emblazoned on a sign fastened to the railing opposite her paddle wheel, and a pennant bearing that name flapped from a towering mast. From the stern, a large flag of stars and stripes lifted in the breeze. Later that evening, while inquiring about passage aboard her, I learned that the *Senator* had arrived just the day before from San Francisco on her maiden voyage of less than twelve hours. A booming cannon and a welcoming reception of hundreds of cheering men greeted her arrival. So I was told. I have it in my diary of November 7, 1849, a Wednesday. Along with the cost of passage.

With the exception of this floating palace, most of the vessels along the levee looked more permanent than transient. Signboards and figure-heads, set up on shore, indicated the majority doing duty as stores. One handsome brig reduced to merchandising bore the courtly name *Lady Adams*. Several vessels, as their homey appearance testified, served now as habitations.

I was not then so green a newcomer that my expectations of Sacramento City much exceeded the sight. It passed for a city in the same fashion as the blue tent at You Bet passed for a hotel. Had I then sufficient spirit for amusement, I would have laughed at how the California emigrants subverted Mr. Shakespeare's observation. What's in a name, they must have asked, then answered, "Everything."

The aspect of Sacramento City was a novel one in every direction. Trees along the levee dividing the river from Front street sheltered a lively open market. Deck cabins, excised from their vessels and set up onshore, served as shops. A din of shouting, enterprising merchants conducted a brisk, if improvised, business from open boxes, barrels, and crates. They hawked with equal and urgent enthusiasm boots and blankets, cheese and oysters, lumber and nails, pressing upon the throng of booted, slouch-hatted passersby every conceivable provision as absolutely indispensable.

Along Front street, which bordered this busy, noisy bazaar, men by the dozens hurried on foot and on horseback. They clattered past in wagons. They hauled carts. They shouted urgent encouragement to laden mules. The lively tableau suggested an entire population tardy for critical appointments.

We traversed Front street at a crawl, slowed by this industrious traffic. With Hannah at my side, I peered from beneath the canvas, rolled up for a better view. Janey leaned her chin on two hands, staring out the back of the wagon.

"Something like St. Joseph, ain't it?"

"Isn't," I said from habit. We hadn't seen a city since then, and here, for all I knew, thronged the same population, activated now by arrival rather than departure.

I was not impressed, except by the huge, spreading oaks and towering sycamores thus far surviving the newborn city's impromptu erection. So huge were they that despite their distance one from another, many interlocked ancient branches in a graceful canopy of green above the raw, crude, and fragmentary foundations of Sacramento City.

With few notable exceptions, the city was all improvisation, make-shift, and stopgap. It covered the east side of Front street in acres of canvas doing duty with equal impermanence for roof and door on houses, stores, and hostelries. Most of these rudely framed places advertised themselves in large black letters painted on their canvas fronts: Fremont House, General Jackson House, The Elephant House.

Canvas covered the rough-hewn, unpainted, and poorly carpentered facades of saloons, too, and provisioners and gaming halls. Most of these establishments, with an apparent eye to invitation, repudiated doors. We could see, between patrons surging in and out, their dim interiors.

"Listen, Mama!" Janey said, enlivened by the scene.

Concentrating, I heard the sound of a piano in energetic performance drifting from an open door. Possibly it was the Hotel de France, a neat but narrow two-story wooden structure. Or, more likely, the music emanated from next door, where the City Hotel rose a lofty, whitewashed three stories, with broad balconies and, even more notable, a wooden roof. It was the largest building on the street. From its size, I presumed a superiority of accommodation. Should we fail to gain a steamer cabin for the night, I concluded we could stop there.

Just south of the City Hotel, past a provisioner's, a signboard fronting a plain frame-and-canvas structure announced the Eagle Theatre. On the boardwalk in front, a three-piece string band, more noisy than musical, added an inharmonious contribution to the piano up the street.

The wagon inched to an intersecting thoroughfare wide enough to turn wagons and teams. Looking up it, I could see several substantial buildings, including one that glinted in the late-day sun. Zinc, it turned out to be. More remarkable was the round tent of mammoth proportions commanding the north side of the street a block up. Its canvas top, from which multicolored pennants waved, proclaimed in large letters, rather unnecessarily I thought, "Round Tent."

A scrap of wood nailed to a sycamore on Front street announced the intersection as J street. We had arrived at the very center of this spontaneous city, such as it was, and drawn opposite the steamboat landing and the magnificent *Senator*.

I made my way past Hannah, asleep now, to the front of the wagon and called above the hubbub to Zeb. "If you'll help us unload our things, you can leave us here."

He turned, looked puzzled. "Missus?"

"I'll find a ticket office for the steamer," I said. "If need be, we can put up in a convenient hotel for the night."

"I can't rightly stop here, missus. I need your oxen to get to the livery, bottom of K street at Sixth. That's where my mules are."

"Mules?"

"Yes, and I figure you'll want to sell your oxen. They're pretty used up, but you can probably get something for them at the horse market, next to the livery."

"I sold you my oxen!"

Zeb shook his head. "I bought your wagon, not your stock. My wagon's used up, but my team is good, and mules are what's wanted in California. Oxen are too slow for freighting. I don't need oxen."

"Need? Need!" I shouted. Or think I did. I'm not sure.

From long ago, when books and poets filled lazy days, I remember a line from John Donne: "'Tis all in pieces, all coherence gone." It defined me that Wednesday afternoon in Sacramento City.

For months I had silenced fear with illusion. For weeks I had willed my every step, ordered sanity from insanity. I suppose I could no more maintain that commanded equanimity than one can hold shards in the shape of a bowl.

My composure shattered. I don't recall if I shouted out loud, or only in my head, that those oxen had saved our lives. I would not abide their sacrifice, I cried. Or think I did. Did I pound my fists against the wagon sides, or only imagine it? Did I scream that my children and I had torn our hearts from hearing those faithful beasts sob for water on the desert, from seeing them bleed on the mountain? Parted from the wagon that made them useful, I knew what would happen to them. They would be butchered. I refused the possibility, would not abide it.

"I will not allow them to be slaughtered!" I yelled. Or think I did. Images rose before me, bloating bodies beneath a blazing desert sun, eyes pecked, buzzards feasting. And others, swamp-rotted carcasses jamming river fords. "A cruel reward that!" I shouted. Or think I did.

The oxen, of course, were but the spark behind the blaze. They were the shadow of the thing. The substance was fear, death, Celia, Caleb, George, all of what had gone before and all that lay ahead: how to keep us from starving, how to get us home. I had thought us all but aboard the little *McKim*, or the palatial *Senator*, steaming west to San Francisco, on the way. And now we weren't. The disappointment and the frustration and the anxiety was suddenly more than I could bear. I suppose it was the coward in me.

I remember glimpsing the Round Tent on J street. My next recollection of Sacramento City was a sign with a "6" on it nailed to a sycamore tree. Between the one and the other, the distance between the corner of Front street and J street, and the corner of K street and Sixth street, I was "all in pieces, all coherence gone."

I had climbed down from the wagon, although I don't recall doing it, and stood, holding Hannah in my arms, staring at that "6" on a piece of scrap board nailed to a tree trunk. And as I did so, having no alternative, I put the pieces of myself back together.

"This is the horse market, missus," Zeb said, touching my elbow as I stood staring at the tree, Hannah's arms around my neck.

"Yes, of course," I said, turning to look. How could anyone miss it? "Sacramento City is picturesque, isn't it? This must be one of the principal sights of the place."

I heard a metallic edge to my voice, like tin snips. I sounded rude. I didn't care.

The only thing picturesque about the scene was the immense evergreen oak rising from the middle of K street. The horse market surrounding it extended irregularly into a grove of trees, among which tents clumped like mushrooms. They belonged to emigrants without homes. Like me and my family.

On the far side of the horse market, an open frame of poles roofed with reeds sheltered huddled mules and rawboned horses. This was the livery stable. Beyond it lay stacks of hay and wheat straw, feed for the animals.

These sights were but the sawdust to the circus. The market, then in full flourish, commanded center ring beneath the huge oak. Men and animals pushed, prodded, paraded in equal confusion. There was no order, no pattern, no arrangement, no progression to the business at hand. There were no regulations except those fancied by the sellers, and every seller was his own auctioneer. Several occupied the center ground simultaneously, each shouting the fine points of some poor starved-looking pack mule or swaybacked horse.

How the sellers recognized the buyers in the discord and disorder, I could not tell. Nor how the buyer figured, in the chaos, how the bidding was running. It might be slow as well as frantic. One long-bearded emigrant stood his ground without progress, unwilling to let his spavined animal go for the offer. He was apparently determined on advance, however long it might take. How any of it reached conclusion, I did not know. And didn't much care. What had to be done, had to be done. The oxen, regardless my misgivings, must be sold.

"So," I said, addressing Zeb as though he were the master of ceremonies, "what do we do now? Parade our cattle around like dancing bears?"

My mother would have been appalled to hear me speak so rudely. I should have been. I wasn't.

Douglas stepped between us. "I can do it, Ma. Why don't you and the girls go to a hotel and let me do this."

I was grateful for the suggestion, especially since Hannah suddenly comprehended the significance of the proceedings.

"Cherry! Cherry!" she cried, wrenching from me and struggling to the ground.

Zeb reached for her.

"Let her go," I said. "She needs to say goodbye."

The oxen, their expressions ever patient, remained yoked to the wagon beneath a tree at the edge of the horse market. Hannah ran to them, put her head against Cherry's huge bulk, and weeping, petted the dusty coat. Janey, watching, bit her lip, then walked across the street and leaned against the sycamore with the K street sign.

"Do the best you can with the oxen," I told Douglas. "We'll be at the City Hotel."

I turned to Zeb. "Douglas will remove our things from our, excuse me, *your*, wagon. I presume he can hire a dray? There will be *something* from the oxen, as you said."

"Missus — "

I held up my hand. "We had our agreement, as you said, and I thank you for your honesty. You could have sold them yourself and pocketed the proceeds. Some men would." My attempt at cordiality I undermined by a voice stiff as my back. I hadn't regained enough pieces of myself to care whether I should be embarrassed by my possibly public derangement, however temporary. I only wanted this business with the wagon and the oxen concluded so I could get on with getting on.

I went to the wagon for my reticule, took a handkerchief from it to wipe away Hannah's tears, and continued my polite speech of departure, reminding Douglas to collect the clothes, bedding, and provision box. "Bring the tools, too," I added. We could sell those, and the tent, for something.

I turned to Zeb again, thanked him for his trouble. He wanted to speak, I could see that. He started to say something. I interrupted.

"We shall have something for the animals, as you so rightly pointed out. I apologize for the misunderstanding. I regret, you see, that their future appears as perilous as our own. But that, of course, is not your concern."

"Missus — "

"Good luck to you, sir. You have purchased an excellent wagon."

I turned to Douglas. "The City Hotel. On Front street."

Mr. Massett

The founders of Sacramento City shared my mother's talent for envisioning something from nothing. Despite being laid out at right angles, with streets running east-west being identified by the alphabet and those running north-south by numbers, it was a city of tents.

The City Hotel, equally more ambitious than substantial, was the showplace of the town. Its size alone, some thirty-five feet wide and nearly sixty deep, heralded pretensions to importance. But it was its architectural peculiarities that caught the eye. On the hotel's porch, ignoring the gawking men passing through its double doors, Janey, Hannah, and I stared up at the medley of columns supporting the verandah. I could identify them neither as Corinthian, Ionic, or Doric — nothing save a flattering fusion of classical intentions.

"She's a showy edifice, isn't she?"

At my shoulder, and no taller, grinned a dapper young man. "Stephen Massett," he said, removing his hat. "Allow me to pay my respects, madam. Not fifty women in this city. A rare pleasure."

Poor representative I was in my unadorned bonnet, Caleb's old coat thrown over my plain brown merino traveling dress, my down-at-heels Alberts peeping beneath a mud-stained hem. I looked the little end of the horn compared to the sartorial splendor greeting me.

The young man was a dandy. A striped brocade vest and knee-length coat trimmed in velvet hugged his round little body, and a cloud of red pongee cravat plumed at his throat. He held his black silk hat in two hands, like a gift.

Despite my worries, I couldn't help returning the smile widening the pink beardless face with its squattish nose and squinchy eyes. The natty Mr. Massett reminded me of a trick pig trotted up for a circus show.

"Mrs. Daniels," I said. "Pleased, I'm sure, and these are my daughters, Jane and Hannah."

"A treat, a treat," he said, bowing to each and dancing a little jig in his patent leather boots.

Janey just stared, but Hannah held up her red-kerchief doll for introduction. "Punkin," she said.

Stephen Massett solemnly shook between thumb and forefinger the protuberance of red kerchief stuffed with moss that passed for the doll's arm. "Pleased to meet you," he said. "Touring our fair city, are you, Miss Punkin? This hotel ranks among our foremost curiosities. I regret I cannot recommend the accommodations."

"Why is that, Mr. Massett?" I asked.

"Oh, dear, were you intending to stay, Mrs. Daniels? Dear me, I hope not. Looks a wonder, this hotel, with all its cutting and carving and scratching of decorations. They're as pretending a character as green wood will permit, but there's less here than meets the eye, I can tell you. Or more, as I think on it. The myriad of fleas and bedbugs will greet you and congratulate your arrival." He hopped from foot to foot as though to trounce them all. "And the noise! I stayed here my first night in town, and what with the swearing and snoring of occupants, the barking of dogs, the departures of numberless trains of mules and donkeys outside, it was a perfect pandemonium, what with the clamorous applicants for the daily stage to Sutter's mill at Coloma. And to cap the climax, just when sheer exhaustion dropped me into a doze, I felt a heavy bump come up against the slender board that screened me from the street. To my astonishment, the head of a big ox presented itself, and with its cold and moist snout commenced rubbing against my knee!"

I puzzled Mr. Massett, I suppose, smiling as I did through his escalating catalog of woes, but I enjoyed his exuberant storytelling. It took me from my worries. Besides, I had crossed the plains. I was not born in the woods to be scared by an owl. No such discomforts as recounted by this dandy intimidated me.

"Thank you for your concern," I said, "but my son is meeting us here. We'll only be staying until the next steamer."

"Alas, so soon arrived, so soon departed." Mr. Massett plunked his hat on his head. "Then the best of it. You'll allow me, Mrs. Daniels, the honor of conducting your tour of the interior."

With that, he bowed me over the threshold and into the hotel's main room like a footman announcing a queen, my daughters trailing in attendance.

Through the haze of cigar smoke, I saw a spacious bar along the right-hand wall. Patrons crowded its length, downing the contents of cut-glass goblets or heaping plates of meat collected from a cloth-draped table at one end. A barkeep popped a champagne cork and filled half a dozen proffered goblets. Another dispensed potables from a shelf burdened by bottles of every shape and hue. An elongated counter of decorated kegs with polished brass cocks fronted a huge mirror in a gilt frame.

"Not a propitious day for inspection, madam," said my guide, ushering my daughters inside. "The election of California's first governor is in full sway, and the hotel's lessees, in support of their candidate, Peter H. Burnett, have spread a persuasive and gratuitous board of hams, joints of beef, mutton, and venison, plus quantities of champagne for potential voters. Not of the best preparation, but abundance has its appeal."

Janey coughed and Hannah wrinkled her nose. Our months in the outdoors ill prepared us for this confined smell of cigars, meat, liquor, and concentrated humanity.

Against the wall opposite the bar, men armed with cue sticks circled a billiard table like hunters closing on prey. Ivory balls clacked above a hum of conversation.

Except for a rear staircase and a few rickety rocking chairs, baize-topped gaming tables piled with glittering coins and dusty pouches occupied the main portion of the room. A throng of intent players, hooraying wins and cursing losses, stopped to stare as Mr. Massett paraded us past.

"The hotel is laid out more with a view to profit than comfort," he said, shepherding us toward a door at the back of the room. "Roulette players, monte dealers, and chuck-a-luck men rent these tables. Pay a thousand dollars a month for the privilege."

"A thousand dollars! Surely, you jest, Mr. Massett."

"California prices, Mrs. Daniels. This hotel's annual lease is thirty thousand. A new hotel going up on the levee is already rented at thirty-five. Why, the erecting on J street alone cost half a million, at least. It's a wonder, this California. We're all going to get rich."

"Are you rich, Mr. Massett?" Janey asked.

"Janey!" I exclaimed. "Where are your manners?"

Mr. Massett laughed. "In California, dear child, a healthy, sensible, wide-awake man cannot fail to prosper. So says my friend Mr. Bayard Taylor." He turned to me. "Perhaps you've heard of him?"

"I don't believe so, Mr. Massett."

"No? A professional traveler, lecturer, writer for the New York papers. He's here, you know, collecting notes for a book on our El Dorado. Says Sacramento City is nothing behind San Francisco. Right as rain, he is. I'm in the auction business myself. Don't mind saying the profits are enormous. On our first venture — a thousand dollars' worth of pea jackets, shoes, boots, socks, blankets — my partner and I netted twice the cost."

He leaned against the wall next to the door, arms crossed, eyes squinching. I could see him winding up for a further reeling out of his assets, as young men are wont to do with new success.

"What have we here?" I asked, indicating the door.

Recalling his mission, Mr. Massett threw open the door. We followed him into an omnibus apartment festooned with printed calico. "Rather sleep in my salesroom," said Mr. Massett.

Bunks in tiers four deep lined a room large enough for a regiment. Despite the afternoon hour, snores issued from half a dozen. In the center of the room stood a large dressing table of unfinished wood topped by a spacious basin and surmounted by a looking glass. A hairbrush hung from a chain connected to the glass's frame. A toothbrush leaned against the basin.

"The order of the day," said Mr. Massett, nodding toward the dresser, "is 'one done, the other come on.' The rank of candidates with tucked-up sleeves and tucked-down collars stand their turns in file, the man next behind taking a rasp at the toothbrush, either to pass the time or have the job done."

"We cannot stay here, Mr. Massett," I said, collecting Hannah from her self-conducted tour.

"Thought not. Regular apartments are upstairs, I'll show you."

We climbed a rough staircase to the second floor, where Mr. Massett led us to a half-opened door. Its duplicates lined each side of a narrow corridor.

"Downstairs costs five dollars the night," he said, pushing the door open wide. "Rooms like this one are twenty-five."

"The night?"

"Yes, ma'am."

Alarmed at the prospect of such expenditure, I looked in to see what it bought. What met my eye was a pinched-up little cell furnished with a single mattress, a slim washstand, and a narrow chair. The remaining space would just permit one person to dress and undress. One person. We were four.

"This isn't possible," I said.

I meant the cost. Mr. Massett thought I meant the room.

"Top floor, then. Some half-dozen state sleeping rooms up there with more extensive dimensions," he said, "on which, of course, a correspondingly high tariff is exacted."

I rubbed my temples. My head ached from the smoke and smells, the journey, the worry. I didn't know what to do. Janey leaned against the wall, head down. Hannah plopped to the floor with her doll, about to cry, she was so tired.

Our guide turned solicitous. "Perhaps Captain Van Pelt will permit you aboard the *Senator* tonight. She goes tomorrow."

"I don't have our tickets yet. I don't even know their cost."

"Oh, all the steamers go the same. Thirty dollars deck passage, more for a cabin, of course."

"Thirty dollars! Each passenger?"

California prices. We couldn't afford to stay, and we couldn't afford to leave.

I proposed to the girls that we camp on the outskirts, in the cluster of emigrant tents. Mr. Massett wouldn't hear of it.

"Shouldn't do that if I were you, madam. All that land's been surveyed out by the original owners of the town, Captain Sutter foremost, and sold to others. The emigrants, supposing the land belongs by right to the United States and by extension to any citizen as wishes to settle on it, have laid claim to the lots against the threats of the rightful owners. Hostilities run high on both sides, but the squatters face constant danger of being run off."

Some months later there was a riot in Sacramento City between the squatters and landowners. I had left, but I read about it in the papers. Jesse and Martha Morgan, whom I came to know that winter from our days together in the American House hotel, were drawn into it. Jesse was one of eight killed. Another victim of the elephant.

As I leaned exhausted against that thin wall upstairs in the City Hotel, I must have looked blasted by despair. Mr. Massett, to whose generous intentions I remain indebted, offered to intercede on my behalf with the landlord of what he said was a recently vacated building on K street, next to the American House hotel. I accepted with gratitude.

Where a tent makes a hotel, a sign on a tree makes a corner, and some cobbled-up slats and canvas make a city, I should not have been surprised by the "building" on K street. Californians inflated everything, from prices to respectability. That the structure in question was a flea-infested canvas shanty in which a monte dealer had lived with his horse in no way diminished Mr. Massett's kindness.

That night, while my exhausted children slept unconscious of the fleas, I spent a wakeful night calculating our funds and our circumstances. Douglas had got a hundred dollars for the oxen, selling them cheap to a farmer he said would treat them kindly. But even with that and the money Zeb gave for the wagon, we hadn't enough to get home.

Dawn found me nothing short of furious and attacking the chief feature of the building on K street, a filthy stove. Douglas and Janey woke to the sound of clanging iron as I industriously dismantled it. Hannah slept on, oblivious to my noisy enterprise.

Douglas sat up, rubbing his eyes. "Ma . . ."

Janey snuggled down into her blanket and looked sad.

"This is how it is," I said, standing and brushing soot from my hands. "We are two thousand miles from Illinois, family decimated, charity canvas for a shelter, not five hundred dollars between us and starvation, one natty auctioneer for friend. That's it, that's everything."

"Ma," Douglas said, "I can — "

"Wait a minute. Listen to me. I know that excepting Mr. Massett this is not a cheerful inventory, and I can't bring back your father or your brother. But I can clean this dirty stove, and I can bake pies. However many it takes to go home, however long it takes, that's what it takes."

Douglas threw off the blanket, leapt from the monte dealer's cot he'd slept on in his clothes. "Ma, I can help."

"Good. You can start by finding me a bucket of water so I can finish cleaning this stove, then go over to Mr. Massett's and ask the cost of rent for this place. Janey, I want you to go next door to the hotel and see if you can borrow a broom."

Remembering myself that morning, sooty hands and rolled-up sleeves, spitting orders like a Mexican general, I wonder what my mother would have thought at the sight. Mine was not a *Godey's Lady's Book* image of the daughter she'd raised to wear sausage curls and satin slippers. And my father? Would he recognize the dutiful daughter he called Mouse? Ah, my dear dead father. He had for me such comfortably small expectation, I could rise to it without leaving my chair. And Caleb? I can't imagine what he would have thought, since I've concluded I never really knew him well enough to say. But surely the woman attacking that stove in the monte dealer's shanty, full of fury and purpose and resolve, was a stranger to the woman I had been in Illinois. And, without regret, so I remain.

You can't go back.

I don't mean to mock the picture I have of myself before California. But Illinois bound me to the purposes and expectations of others — parents, husband, the editors of *Godey's Lady's Book*, writers published in the *Mother's Assistant*. California required another contract, there being all the difference in the world between baking pies for a ribbon at the fair and baking pies to pay the rent.

The rent, it turned out, was three hundred dollars a month, payable to Orlando McKnight, proprietor of the hotel next door. I marched over, outraged, but Mr. McKnight, a canny Yankee from New England, stood firm by his price. I offered him half. We struck a bargain, half now, half at the end of the month. I intended to pay him and be gone on the first of December.

While Janey and Douglas finished cleaning the stove and Hannah played at sweeping, I collected Caleb's tools in a canvas sack and went to see Mr. Massett.

The salesroom on J street was a shanty with a canvas door. Above the door was nailed a frame tacked with a piece of red calico. Painted on the cloth in black letters was the announcement "Auction House."

Inside, with the exception of a countertop propped on a pair of boxes, the salesroom resembled my soon-to-be restaurant: dirt floor, slat walls, suspended lantern for light, canvas roof. I stood in the doorway and watched Mr. Massett conducting business before an audience of a dozen rapt observers. Seeing me, he waved me in without pause.

"Now then, gentlemen, we come on to the flour," he said. "I shall put it up in lots of five sacks, with the privilege, et cetera. You are all aware of the present scarcity of this article — the 'staff of life,' as the Psalmist, I believe, calls it. Gentlemen, it's a solemn fact that flour's rising. Yes, gentlemen, before thirty days are over our heads, loaves, even without fishes, will be selling at a dollar apiece. You can't eat your gold dust, gentlemen. You must have flour. So what's offered for the first sack of a hundred pounds? Give me a bid, if you please."

A shabby, unshaven man offered five dollars.

Mr. Massett's squinched-up eyes searched his audience. "Five, five, five, five — half, half, half. Gentlemen, this will never do. Give me six, six, six, six, six. I have seven, seven, seven, seven, seven. Gentlemen, I cannot throw it away at this figure. Say eight. Eight, I got."

And so it went until Mr. Massett elevated the shabby man's offer to eleven and a half.

"Once, twice, three times. Do I hear more? No? Then spizeratum bang!" he shouted, and slammed his fist on the countertop. "How many will you take, sir?"

"I'll take the lot."

The lot was three hundred sacks. And the buyer who looked like an escaped convict was Mr. Wolfe, owner of the City Bakery.

As it happened, I was still in Sacramento City when Mr. Wolfe left for his home in the East, having realized several thousand dollars on his investment in less than three months. How I envied him.

Mr. Massett predicted that success, and that of the man who the same day bought four hundred pairs of high boots, Russian leather they were, and knocked down to four dollars a pair. When the rains set in, the buyer retailed them first at an ounce, sixteen dollars a pair, and then at two, or thirty-two dollars a pair. He earned, Mr. Massett said, nearly ten thousand dollars by his speculation.

Which is why, in December, I bought the barley.

But that first day of my residency in Sacramento City, I only watched as Mr. Massett rattled through the sale of his goods. He had a showman's talent even then, inviting his audience to get stuck with molasses, filled with sausages, warmed with tea and coffee, sweetened with sugar, tight with gin and brandy. I was not surprised when he later made such a success in San Francisco, performing songs he wrote and composed.

Mr. Massett sold Caleb's tools for me, and with the proceeds I purchased my culinary supplies from Bailey, Morrison, & Co., the provisioners on Front street, opposite the steamboat landing. I needed dried apples, flour, sugar, pork fat. They had everything and more — wonderful spices and all manner of goods imported from China, too. The apples, from Chile, cost dearly. When I hesitated over the price, Mr. Morrison offered credit. I took it.

From a commission merchant on K street, near Second, I bought a plank table, two rough benches, and dishes, all on credit. As a woman, I think I could have bought the town on my word.

To announce my pie business, I hired the printing up of several dozen handbills. The office of the *Placer Times* was then on Front street. I went in to ask the cost of a notice placed in the paper. The printer was a harried man, "set his editorials from the case," he told me. Mr. Giles his name was, a newspaperman from New York.

The cost for a notice was three dollars for twelve lines, but Mr. Giles offered me handbills for the same money, which I thought better spent.

"Have it say, 'Cooked by a woman,' " I told him. I was learning.

The next day, I toured the town, delivering the sheets myself, up and down Front street, K street, J street, to the zinc store, hotels, saloons, gambling houses.

The things I saw. No one back in the States could appreciate the scene.

Most Sacramento City gambling and drinking houses offered something musical as an attraction. Establishments without musicians frequently placed a discordant yodeler by the door to hold forth a rousing "O Susanna." Simultaneously, a neighboring business might parry with another voice plaintively mourning "Old Virginny."

Add to this mixture the clamor of competing musical instruments. Anyone who once plagued a neighbor at home with his squeaking violin fancied himself a master musician in California. Some establishments set full bands in front of their open doors, others but a single rowdy trumpet or croaking violoncello. All being congregated in proximity, each outstrove the other in loudness and vigor.

Despite the indecipherable cacophony, I never saw any performer look the least embarrassed by this ear-splitting confusion, nor any onlooker or customer less than satisfied.

Someone told me that a Swiss organ-girl, in six months earned four thousand dollars by her playing. But I didn't see her.

Of the establishments I visited with my handbills, I most vividly remember two: The Plains, a drinking house frequented by overland emigrants, and the Round Tent.

An artist had decorated the interior board walls of The Plains with scenes well known to the customers, and to me. He had captured in dramatic depictions our memories of Independence Rock, Fort Laramie, the Sweetwater Valley, the Wind River Mountains. One illustration preserved the memory of terror: a wagon and team coming down the side of a hill nearly perpendicular. It looked like nothing could prevent the oxen and wagon from tumbling in a single fall from the summit to the valley below. Californians, and emigrants from the States and elsewhere who came by sea, dismissed the drawing as fanciful. Those who knew better recognized the route down Granite Mountain to Goose Creek.

I never set foot in that place again.

Nor did I repeat my visit to the Round Tent, though memory preserves the one occasion.

The Round Tent was on the north side of J street between Front street and Second, a circuslike place of mammoth proportions, perhaps fifty feet in diameter. Outside, flags and banners flew gaily, and inside all was aglitter. I remember a modest string band seated on an elevated bench opposite the bar, the music, especially that of the lead violinist, by no means of poor quality. The bar itself was the tent's most conspicuous feature.

Large and costly mirrors rose behind and above shelves sparkling with decanters, wine glasses, tumblers of cut glass. The proprietors, lavishing extravagance, tempted customers to the bar by adorning it with pyramids of bright yellow lemons, towers of Havana cigars, and crystal jars filled with peppermints for the taking.

The tent was jammed. By their costumes and speech I recognized emigrants from England, Germany, Ireland, South America, France. These newcomers, and men dusty from the mines, wagered at monte, roulette, chuck-a-luck, faro. I didn't know those games then, of course. I learned what they were later, at Nevada City, when Janey played the piano at Mr. Taylor's place.

At each Sacramento City establishment I visited, I asked permission to tack my handbill. No one denied me the small favor, seeing in my person, I suppose, need and purpose.

On this account, I was speaking to the barkeep of the Round Tent when I felt a hand on my shoulder.

"La, Mrs. Daniels!"

And then her hand was on mine, and her arms around me and mine around her. We hugged and stood back and looked at each other and hugged again. She wore the black brocade, altered, sleeves and skirt shortened, neck cut low and adorned at the bosom with the pink rosebuds I remembered from her coal-scuttle bonnet. More rosebuds decorated her hair, piled high on her head in a crown of curls.

I hardly recognized her.

Did Lucena and I talk then, or was it later, on the second floor of the American House hotel?

I think later, there was so much time for it then.

Winter 1849-1850

I've never eaten a lobster. I've never even seen one, except for a drawing in a book. But as a little girl I sat enthralled whenever Mother talked to me of her childhood in Boston, of long ago and faraway things I could only imagine — omnibuses and museums, a music hall, an ocean, lobsters.

We would have been in Ohio then, where my brother died, still on our inevitable way west to Illinois. Looking back, I see she was homesick.

"You boil them up live in a big pot of water," she said.

She didn't say the water boiled first, and the creature went to its death quick as hanging. And I didn't think to ask. To my youthful imagination, boiling a lobster sounded as awful and frightening as a tale from the storybook. I imagined a witch's cauldron with a monstrous, clawed thing in it swimming round and round. And then, gradually, so very gradually, the cool water got warmer and warmer. When did the creature notice? Too late. Death by indeterminate gradations. Seamless, accumulated. Like children wandering in the forest, accruing distance and trees, realizing late the fateful step, already taken, somewhere back on the trail.

That was my winter in Sacramento City, fateful as a lobster trap, seamless as a winding sheet.

It's all of a piece, looking back — Lucena, the quinces, Hannah, the flood, the barley.

I remember, too, the pumpkins, from Sutterville three miles down the river. There were squashes at Sutterville, too, and corn and potatoes. And ten thousand pounds of pumpkins. I don't know how many I bought. I made pies for a month. But that was in December, because I remember how much Zeb enjoyed those pies, and that was after the quinces.

I knew less of quinces than lobsters.

"Look, Ma," Douglas said, coming in one evening as I was serving supper. "I got it for Hannah."

He held out something the size of a pear, just as smooth-skinned, but orange-colored. I glanced at it as I served a slice of apple pie to Orlando McKnight. This, after three helpings of beef stew.

The owner of the hotel, and my canvas shanty, had struck an agreement with me. He kept a notice in the *Placer Times*, weekly on Saturdays, advising readers of the American House and Restaurant. I was the restaurant. My handbills for pies "Cooked by a woman" had come in with my first customers. All grins and surprise and eagerness, they handed them over like tickets, leaving vacancies in the hotels and saloons where I'd tacked them. In exchange for whatever custom — not inconsiderable — came my way by virtue of Mr. McKnight's weekly advertisement, he ate at my table.

"What is it?" I asked Douglas, wiping my hands on my apron and dropping to the bench opposite Mr. McKnight. I was bone tired every day then.

"Quince," said Mr. McKnight, elbows on my table, mouth full of my pie. "Fruit. Comes from the Orient."

Mr. McKnight, a New Englander, had been to sea as a youth, knew the world's geography and its resources. Despite being thin as a harpoon, he ate half a dozen times a day like a man starving. Our bargain was in his favor.

"This one comes from the Sandwich Islands," Douglas said, handing it to me. "That's what the lady told Mr. Bailey."

I sniffed its warm, lemony fragrance, imagined the Orient and oceans. "Did she give it to you?"

"I bought it, Ma. I know I shouldn't have, but I wanted one for Hannah."

Mr. McKnight brushed crumbs from his beard. "Asleep already, tuckered as a cabin boy from all that sweeping. No life for a child."

Janey wiped down the table, didn't look at him. "She likes helping Ma, so we can go home."

"Tart-tasting, puckery. Child won't like it."

"It only cost a dollar," Douglas said.

A dollar for a single piece of fruit. California prices.

Douglas, from the frequency of his errands for me to the provisioners on Front street, now worked there, stocking goods, delivering, hauling, sweeping the store, whatever was necessary. Mr. Bailey paid him twenty dollars a week, all of which Douglas had faithfully deposited, until now, to my keeping. I had first notice of fresh provisions, and their daily delivery. What was a dollar in California? Nothing.

"Brought crates of them from the Sandwich Islands," Douglas said. "Onions, too. Sold her jewelry there for twenty dollars to buy them. Said her husband wouldn't go it."

I gave Janey the fruit to look at, and cut a piece of pie for Douglas. "A woman did that?"

"She's from Boston. Husband's a sea captain. They sailed here on his ship. Tied up by the steamboat landing." Douglas forked pie between tellings. "Brought a China man to do for them, too."

Bostonians, quinces, China men, everything came to California. I wonder I never saw a lobster.

"She sold the quinces straight from the ship for two thousand dollars," Douglas added. "Good for scurvy, she says. Got eighteen hundred for the onions. Mr. Bailey bought some."

"Bring me a gunnybag of those onions home tomorrow, will you, Douglas? I'll make soup or something, maybe onion pies."

That's what I said, getting up and clearing the plates to rinse in a bucket of water kept for the purpose. But I was thinking on the woman's fortune. Nearly four thousand dollars! For a twenty-dollar investment. And she did it herself. Like the boot buyer at Mr. Massett's auction, and Mr. Wolfe with the flour. That was the way to make money, not this daily labor of cooking and more cooking.

I was making money — quite a lot of it — but the cost of provisions, wood for the stove, Mr. McKnight's rent, candles at five dollars a pound, it all depleted my steady accumulation. I needed to make money in a piece, one swoop, an investment, like the Boston lady.

Such an idea would not have attached itself in Illinois. In California, though, we all did things we didn't do at home. Lawyers opened bookstores, professors took to mining, and doctors did any number of things, they being so numerous two had to ride one horse. No one took notice of what anyone else had been at home. We were all of us, women too, free to do whatever necessity required and circumstance permitted. I heard of a woman who took in sewing and then loaned out the money she earned by it at five percent a month. Another, in San Francisco, made a fortune buying and selling property, and one lady established a soda works there so lucrative she wouldn't let her husband handle the profits but kept the task to herself. Over in Rough-and-Ready, not far from Nevada City, a woman, I believe her name was Mary Ann Dunleavy, opened a ten-pin bowling alley in 1850. When she divorced her husband, a Methodist minister, I heard she sued to keep the bowling alley, it being hers.

In the newspapers, I still see complaints opposing California's constitutional provision granting women separate property rights. Gets my dander up. A woman comes by property or money, it's rightly hers, I say.

Zeb is still surprised the delegates drawing up the document adopted such an advanced idea. "Men make the laws," he says in that thoughtful, gravelly way he has, "and they generally make them in their own interests."

We conjecture about things like that sometimes, when we sit together summer evenings, talking on the porch. That's my favorite time: supper done, crickets serenading, the cooling delta breeze rustling the ripening wheat.

It's a contrast to think, on those peaceful evenings, of the frantic time in Sacramento City when I determined to ask Mr. Massett's advice on investments.

Whether I actually did or not I don't remember. I know he came to eat at my table with Mr. Taylor before I bought the barley from Mr. Starr on J street.

Mr. Taylor was the newspaperman from New York who was touring California to write a book about it. We talked. That is, I talked. And talked. I don't know why. He was a good listener, that newspaperman. Like Mr. Massett, he came by sea, the Isthmus, knew inconvenience. I told him about the overland route, the suffering and hardships. No one who hadn't traveled overland conceived its ten thousand terrors, but Mr. Taylor got the sum of it into his book. He sent me a copy from New York last year.

Mr. Taylor and Mr. Massett took Douglas to the Eagle Theatre with them. That was in late November, and I remember it because Douglas came home drenched. The rains had begun.

I'd waited up, despite the price of candles. His trousers were soaked to the knees, but he'd had a wonderful time.

"There was an *actress*, Ma! Mrs. Ray. From New Zealand!"

I took his wet clothes, put them by the stove to dry. "New Zealand? Imagine that." I wondered what she'd brought to sell.

"Mr. Massett says he's going into the theater business, if he can do so well as her. She got a hundred and fifty dollars for the performance tonight, and we could hardly understand her. ''Is 'art is as 'ard as a stone!' That's what she said when asked if she would accept the hand of a bandit chief in marriage. That was the play, *The Bandit Chief.* Mostly she rushed onstage, threw her arms wide, and posed. Mr. Taylor said her main purpose in the play was to show the audience a woman."

"A hundred and fifty dollars!"

Douglas pulled his sleeping shirt on over his head. "Tickets cost five dollars for the boxes, three for the pit." He laughed. "Mr. Massett said those fortunate enough to get pit tickets got the price of a bath for free. It's raining so hard the water was on a level with the seats."

It rained the night Zeb first visited us, too. Pumpkin pies I had then, and too few customers to eat them because of the weather. That must have been the middle of December. Douglas and I stacked some of the barley sacks high for tables, others low, for seats. They were everywhere.

Zeb didn't speak at first, surprised perhaps by the shanty full of barley, or not expecting to see us still in Sacramento City, I don't know. We would have been gone had I the fare, but I didn't. The first week in December, after paying my creditors, I had six hundred dollars. Not enough to get home, but enough to invest. Mr. Starr on J street advertised in the *Placer Times* a shipment of barley recently received, two hundred bags. Winter meant scarcities of fresh provisions, no more pumpkins or corn. Barley was a keeper. If I could hold it a month or more, I concluded, its value must increase. Men from the mines were coming into the city for the winter, and they needed to eat. I got the barley cheap, took the entire consignment for four hundred dollars.

I wrote my mother about it on a pale blue letter sheet, thin as the skin of an onion, return address Sacramento City. I sent it express. In my mind I'd written her a thousand letters, telling all. But at the last I dissembled. There are truths too bitter to confide that serve nothing. I wrote "we" had arrived, and didn't enumerate. I wrote of our disappointment in the goldfields and didn't elaborate. I wrote that the emigrants were getting rich, some of them, from auctions and hotels, the buying and selling of commodities. I wrote about the quinces. And the barley. That "we" expected to sell at a substantial profit, that "we" expected to return home on the proceeds soon, sooner than "we" had anticipated. I expected the letter to cheer her. The truth would keep.

Why didn't I recognize Zeb? In part, because I hardly looked at my customers. They seemed so alike. And I was without expectation, inured to my wearisome daily routine. Every morning, I was up at four baking

pies and bread. I hardly had time to serve coffee to my breakfast customers before preparing soups and stews and more bread for dinner, and
again for supper.

So I barely glanced at the man who handed me a can of preserved
chicken — four dollars at Mr. Bailey's store, an expensive supper — and a
bag of potatoes and onions. Some of my regular customers did that —
came by provisions, brought them to me to cook.

"I'll make you a nice chicken stew with this," I said, examining the
food, not the man.

Janey called from the back corner, behind the calico partitioning
our "bedroom," where she was reading to Hannah from the book of fairy
tales. "Need help, Mama?"

"No, you read to your sister."

The weather had been so wet that I kept Hannah inside most of the
time. She preferred, when days were nice, being outside in the little yard
we shared with the hotel. Mr. McKnight had a cat she played with.

"Pumpkin?"

I should have registered that gravelly voice, but I didn't.

One of my regular customers, sitting on a barley sack by the door
with Mr. McKnight, said, "Best pumpkin pie in town."

"There's plenty," I said, paring potatoes, not looking up. I had several pies sitting out on a barley-sack table. "Dollar a slice." I sold nothing
for less than a dollar, not even a cup of coffee.

But Hannah knew him. "Punkin! Punkin!" she cried, racing from
behind the calico in her flannel sleeping gown, waving her red-kerchief
doll. She climbed right up on the table where Zeb sat and threw her arms
around his neck. And didn't he just hug her back like she was his own.

It was such a treat for her, seeing Zeb. At the time, my own surprise
eclipsed that awareness. I marked it, though. She was such a prattling
little thing, telling him all about the cat in the yard, showing him her
broom, fetching fork and plate for his pie — she liked to do the little
fixings for the table, my little helper.

What Zeb really meant to her, thinking on it now, and why she was
so excited, was that suddenly someone came back. For the better part of
a year no one had. That was a lot of lifetime to a child of four, no, five.
Five she was then.

Zeb came back. That must have meant the world to Hannah, to a
child confused by the absence of grandmother, brother, father. They were
gone. And the others in her life, too — Mrs. Hester and Sallie, Lucena
and Will, Celia, California Hat, Lord York — they were all gone, excepting Lucena, and I didn't say I'd seen her. To Hannah, it must have seemed

that everyone went away. No wonder there were days she clung to my skirts, or Janey's. To her, everyone eventually disappeared. Except for Zeb.

Did her tender perceptions take his return to mean she would see others again, too? Father, brother, grandmother, Celia? Or did her angel faculties intuit something I couldn't?

Hannah fell asleep on Zeb's lap long after Mr. McKnight and the other customers left, after Janey and Douglas had their fill of chicken stew and gone to sleep.

"I'd better put her to bed," I said, sitting across the table from Zeb with my cup of coffee. Overhead the wind and rain beat against the canvas roof.

Hannah's curly head lolled against Zeb's chest, the red-kerchief doll cradled in her lap as she was in his. Zeb looked at her, then at me, eyes the warm gray of dove's wings.

"You don't mind," he said softly, "I'll hold her a while longer."

The two of them, they looked like that, Hannah cradled to his chest, when he brought her to me after the flood. Except then Zeb's eyes were the gray of old scars.

Flood

Like Hannah, I was glad to see Zeb again. We all were. I suppose the fact that he had our wagon, Caleb's wagon, our home for so many months, attached us to him. Regardless the connection, in California few acquaintances renewed.

We were a transient population. If someone disappeared, he may have moved on, or died. In '49, no one knew or, to our shame, cared. It was everyone for himself, just to keep from starving. Business is what we concerned ourselves with. I suppose that's what Zeb and I talked about that first night, business. It's what everybody in California talked about.

I remember he said the carrying trade was good, that he outfitted with Bailey and Morrison. It was Mr. Bailey that sent him to my restaurant with his supper, not knowing our previous acquaintance.

"Rains will slow things some for trade, maybe a good deal," Zeb said. He pushed his plate away and crossed his arms on the table. The rolled red flannel sleeves of his shirt revealed muscled forearms. His hands were brown and strong-looking, a workingman's hands. He nodded an acknowledgment to the empty plate. "That was as fine a meal as I can remember. I thank you, missus."

"You're more than welcome, Zeb. And, please, my name is Sarah. Call me Sarah."

I don't know why I didn't say "Mrs. Daniels," why I suggested the familiar address. I suppose because the evening had felt so comfortable, like an old friend visiting, and for that brief time, I had felt desperation suspended.

"Sarah." He said my name so slow and gravelly I thought he wasn't sure of it.

"Yes," I said, "Sarah." Was he smiling at me from behind that brush of brown beard and mustache? I felt suddenly awkward and seized on conversation to hide it.

"Will you be returning to the Bear Valley?" I asked.

Zeb studied me and then said, as though he saw a map on my face, "Maybe Hangtown. That'd probably be the best bet for the season. Gets too wet, I expect I'll wait out the winter working at the livery."

"The livery," I said. "Yes." That was an awkward moment, mention of the livery.

"About your oxen — "

I was embarrassed, remembering my blunt departure, the rude scene. "I expect they're fine," I said, and to change the subject abruptly offered another piece of pumpkin pie and turned the conversation to commodities.

Zeb returned for supper several times that month, before and after his freighting trip to Hangtown. It was after Hangtown that he came in wearing a boiled shirt and no beard, and I didn't recognize him. His square, kind face is so familiar to me now that it's hard to remember being surprised at my first sight of it. I know I was surprised to see he wasn't young, more like forty than the thirty I'd taken him for. I suppose I'd thought him young because most men on their own were. And he never mentioned a wife. Most married men did. Seeing me in my apron and cap, bustling about my kitchen, I reminded them of home and loved ones far away.

Zeb came in clean-shaven and wearing that boiled shirt and sat me down at my table. He folded his hands like a congregant and said, "I'd be most grateful, Sarah, if you'd do me the honor of the Christmas Ball."

"Christmas Ball?" I said, as though the words were foreign and I had no clue to their meaning.

"At the City Hotel. There's to be a grand dinner and ball, the first in Sacramento City. I'd count it generous if you'd allow me the privilege."

I was so flustered I jumped up and mumbled something about biscuits on the stove needing checking. While I clattered the lid from my Dutch oven, I believe I said something inane about no suitable gown.

"Actually," I said, landing on the excuse of necessity like a graceless duck splashing into a pond, "I really must work. You understand, of course?" I hated to be rude, but I didn't know how to be polite. No one had ever asked me to a dance before.

Zeb nodded, rose. "I do understand, Sarah. It's too soon, I'm sorry."

Later, I don't recall when, probably at Nevada City, Zeb apologized again, explaining he'd hoped we might forget our individual destruction for that one evening. He was for putting the past behind, seeing no alternative. And he possessed ambition still, a good thing. It engages the future. I aimed for the brick house and confined my future to going back.

Which is why I blame myself for my neighbor's death.

I didn't know him, except to nod and say "Hello" when I hung clothes to dry on the line in the yard on sunny days. He occupied a tent next to my restaurant. Although he always smiled and said "Good morning" when chance occasioned, I knew him as just another nameless young man come to California.

For a few days early in December, I heard, through the thin canvas and slat boards that separated us, a moaning, and sometimes a pitiful cry for water. I never thought but that someone gave it.

I don't remember how I came to discover the body, except that Mr. Massett was with me. Janey may have mentioned the silence, our neighbor's long absence, and jarred me to my tardy investigation.

The tidy canvas dwelling suggested small comfort for the inhabitant who lay dead upon his cot, eyes fixed on the open tent flap. The poor soul had not, at the last, even a companion to close his sightless eyes.

"Scurvy," said Mr. Massett, turning away as I stroked shut the staring eyes with a hand too late for comfort. "I've seen it before. Dead like this one, drawn up into a ball by the contraction of his joints. Could have rolled him over and over like a bale of carpet. Most of the sick die in their beds. Why, just last week, over on H street, I saw a dead man in a lodging-house bunk, no one paying him any mind. Some of the boys were playing poker, and one was playing his harmonica, and there was this poor fellow staring out on the scene, dead in his bunk. No one knew him. The dead-cart came the next day, carried him off to the burying ground. I expect the new applicant for his bunk arranged it."

I drew my neighbor's blanket over his nameless face and stood staring through it, through the closed eyelids at the sightless eyes burned into my memory while Mr. Massett prattled about elections and hospitals. I think he was as undone by the sight as myself. I sensed him dancing from foot to foot behind me.

"Sutter's fort's been made a hospital, you know," he was saying. "Sutter, having lost the governor's election to Burnett — who trounced him in the Sacramento district returns, you know, some two thousand or more for Burnett and but eight hundred for Sutter — and Sutter having so much trouble with the squatters over his land titles and all, has removed himself and his goods to a farm up on the Feather River. The fort makes a good hospital, being away from town. Half the patients out there have the scurvy nearly as bad as this poor fellow. And they're the lucky ones, who can pay sixteen dollars a day for their care."

The shape beneath the blanket, those staring eyes, held me. Someone, somewhere, waited for this young man who would never come home. He had looked to be not much older than my Douglas. I turned to Mr. Massett. "This young man has a mother — "

"Dr. Morse and Dr. Stillman here in town charge twenty a day," he said, ignoring me. "Dr. Bryant, who offers private care on L street, has demanded a public hospital. There's scurvy, ague, and fever enough to get up the employment of fifty doctors. I hear the Odd Fellows and Freemasons are organizing an assistance to the sufferers."

Not much older than Douglas that young man was. For all that, maybe not so much younger than Caleb. Death distorts the visage, but he was someone's sweetheart, perhaps, and surely someone's son. But it fell to me, a stranger, to close his eyes in final rest. And I didn't even know his name.

I felt such a sadness then, for all the lost ones, and all the grieving hearts at home, waiting. And for all the lonely men, the sick especially, with no one to tend to their comfort, no one to bring even a drink of water. I vowed then to think of all those rough and solitary men of California not as nameless but as sons, and sweethearts, husbands, fathers, dear to someone faraway yearning for their return. So many would never go home. So many lay sick in lonely tents and hospitals.

I wondered what happened to all those sick men when the levee broke. I suppose they drowned in their beds.

Heavy storms hit hard three days before Christmas with a deluge of rain, gales of wind, and the most terrific claps of thunder. Several small craft broke from their moorings, but the Sacramento and American rivers remained within their banks. Some frame buildings blew down. The force of the wind extracted a large one on Second street from its foundations and set it down whole elsewhere.

Although delightful weather blessed the town with a benediction of blue sky and a warming sun between Christmas and the New Year, more rains arrived early in January. The merchants and those they drafted for the task, Douglas among them, hurriedly constructed levees from sand-bags and piled them along the riverfront near vulnerable I street. They held. And they continued to hold through several days of continuous rains that dissolved the broad, unpaved streets of Sacramento City into a muddy morass through which only the most determined slogged their way. My children and I could not have left Sacramento City then had we the means, which as yet we had not.

But hope propped my spirits. I expected that in February our barley must command a great price.

We endured the storms as best we could. Our roof of good, stout canvas, all but impervious to rain, protected us from the worst of the wet, but a steady damp invaded. Rain crept down the walls and pooled beneath the sills. We were never dry. Each morning we wrung out our blankets and heated them by the stove to a lesser dampness. Janey and I covered the floor with a sweet-smelling forest of fallen leaves and small branches harvested by the wind, and Douglas and I spread over this sheets of India rubber on which we piled the barley for safekeeping.

And then, on the evening of January 8, a violent storm assaulted from out of the south with a ferocious howling of winds and lashing rains. The already saturated ground rejected the additional downpour. Puddles formed, then pools, then streams that ran to the American and Sacramento rivers. And the rivers rose to meet them.

The town crier, a gaunt and bearded man on a thin, bobtailed Mexi-can pony, delivered the news. Usually he rang his bell to tell of a preach-ing, or the mail in, an auction, or a stray found. On the evening of January 8, hardy soul, he sloshed and slogged up K street on his floun-dering pony, furiously clanging his bell and shouting, "Levee's broke! Levee's broke!"

I was preparing supper for us, having served but two or three customers who sat, fork in hand, at my table. Douglas threw on his coat and rushed hatless out the door, yelling, "Gotta help, Ma!" My customers abandoned their meals and followed.

I stood in the doorway while they splashed through the rain and mud and disappeared toward the river. As I watched, I saw rivulets of water flowing up from it, and behind them a little wall of water three or four inches high. Almost before I realized it, the water rushed against my feet and over the door sill.

"Janey! Grab the blankets, clothes, whatever you can carry." I swooped Hannah into my arms, frightening her into tears. "Here's your dolly, sweetheart," I said. "Don't cry." I plucked the red-kerchief doll from her cot and ran with her and Janey for the hotel next door, it being raised above ground level on a stone foundation.

"Big room's upstairs," Mr. McKnight said, standing at his door. He pointed the way. "You and yours welcome up there, and not the first."

I tried to put Hannah into his arms. "Take her, please! I have to go back!"

"No, ma'am," he said, backing away. "Child's got the scareds enough. You stay. I'll go see what I can do."

Mr. McKnight commandeered one of his guests to my use. They returned in minutes with a trunk of clothing, our remaining blankets, some cooking utensils, and whatever food had come to hand. It wasn't much.

"Water's up two feet," Mr. McKnight said, breathing heavily as he stowed my rescued things in a back corner. He brushed water from his coat sleeves. "Found yer cots floatin'. Closed yer door 'fore they sailed fer San Francisco, though." He laughed.

At first, men made light of the flood and its inconvenience. They were accustomed to misfortune, most of them. And, too, it distracted from more permanent adversity.

The second-floor dormitory was spacious, perhaps twenty by forty feet, with a window centered in the front wall, overlooking K street. At the American House hotel, upstairs guests supplied their own bedding and slept on the floor. Consequently, the dormitory's only furnishing was a stove, near which each of us huddled on arrival. There was, fortunately, a good supply of firewood, later augmented with driftwood snagged through the window.

Before morning we were thirty in all, four of us women. Martha Morgan was one. The storm caught her and her husband Jesse, the man later murdered in the squatters' riots, on their way back from provisioning on Front street. Martha and I cordoned off a rear corner for privacy. My worry then was for Douglas, but he found us. He threw off his wet clothes as I bundled him into blankets I'd dried by the stove, his teeth chattering as he reported on the levee break. There was no possibility of repair, he said, until the water receded.

No one then realized how very long that would be.

I curled up with my daughters in a nest of clothes and blankets and fell into an exhausted sleep. I didn't hear Lucena and her friend come in. Janey woke me in the morning with the news.

"Ma, Mrs. Semple's here," she said in a whisper. "I hardly recognized her."

I wasn't surprised.

"La, don't I look dashy, though?" Lucena winked at me as I got up and sat on a trunk that partitioned our corner. She pirouetted in a water-spotted and bedraggled green satin frock short enough to reveal tiny feet and ankles encased in black silk stockings.

One man just rising whistled rudely. Lucena bobbed a mock curtsy as she retrieved a pair of fine calf boots with pointed toes sprawled in their tangled laces by the stove.

"Fannie," she called, "make yourself decent, girl, and come meet my friends."

I didn't know if she meant me and my children or the men ogling her from their blankets.

Adjoining the space Mrs. Morgan and I had settled was now an ingeniously suspended screen of damp and drying dresses hung through their sleeves on stockings tied to make a rope. The dresses looked like giant paper-doll cutouts. The screen stretched to the opposite corner from ours, securing, with our space, a private corridor six feet by twenty along the rear wall. Peeping out from between two fancy gowns were the laughing green eyes of a pretty young woman pinning up her mop of red hair.

"'Mornin', y'all!" She bestowed a grin on the staring men as merry as her greeting, then disappeared behind the screen of gowns. "Be out in a shake of a bunny's tail!"

We were, in all, nearly two weeks resident on the second floor of the American House hotel. In that time I came to know Fannie Seymour and even enjoy conversing with her. She was nineteen years old and had come from New Orleans to California via the Isthmus of Panama. She and Lucena shared a room in a boardinghouse on Second street. I knew the place. Everyone in town did. A woman named Annie Woods owned it and the saloon adjoining. Her "boarders" were often seen in their camisoles, leaning from windows and addressing passersby in much the same manner as Fannie that morning greeted the enforced society of Mr. McKnight's hotel.

I was sorry to see Lucena in Fannie Seymour's company, and when opportunity permitted I asked after Will.

"La, Mrs. Daniels," she said, "I didn't come all this way to be a miner's wife. Will left me a whole month in a little bitty one-room cabin with no window, worse than my uncle's buttery. One day Will was off to his claim — as he was every day, sunup to sundown, leaving me with nothing to do — so I went out walking in my best dress and bonnet, just to be civilized, and came on a stage road. The stage came by and I just hailed the driver, and here I am. When I seen that big Round Tent and all the nice things inside, soon as I laid eyes on the place, I knew it was for me. And Fannie says San Francisco's grandest of all. La, soon's this water's down, I'm going there."

"But you can't leave Will — "

"Oh, yes, ma'am, I can and I have. Went straightaway to find me a judge and I got me a divorce, just like that. Easy as pie it was. I just can't abide the idea of spending my days in gingham aprons and dimity wrappers. I like to wear pretty things."

She meant no affront to me, in my worn brown merino with the hem all frayed, Caleb's coat over my shoulders as much from habit as comfort. I suppose I should have felt some womanly protest against my sad state of dress, being my mother's daughter. Lacy Ridgeway always said that a woman out of fashion must be wanting either in spirit or purse. I was wanting in both.

The men at Mr. McKnight's hotel treated me, despite my attire, as they always did, with every respect due a lady. And they treated Lucena and Fannie the same. So did I. Mrs. Morgan disliked the association, but in our situation it was of no use to be particular.

And Fannie was entertaining, a storyteller with a voice sweet as magnolias and honey. She engaged us with a wink and a grin, finger-curling her coppery hair ornamented with a green ribbon. I instigated more than one of her ready discourses, interested as I was in her experiences on the Isthmus. I had accounts of the route from Mr. Taylor, the journalist, and others, but I wanted to know how a woman fared. That first day, while the rain continued to pour and floodwater to rise, I pressed her for information.

"Oh, dear," Fannie said, putting the back of her hand to her brow in feigned dismay, "such sights I saw, you would never believe. The steamer from New Orleans just left us at Chagres, just left us. There we were — I came over with my friend Annie Woods, you see — and she and I did not know the first thing about jungle travel. And we were just left by the captain at this terrible port, nothing more than a village of wild natives, to get across the Isthmus on our own as best we could."

We were all gathered around the stove, Martha Morgan and I preparing a stew from the miscellaneous provisions at hand. Lucena sat cross-legged among the men, elbows on knees, chin cupped in her hands, as mesmerized as the rest of us, despite her own world travels.

"La," Lucena said, "London to America was nothing to this."

I wondered what had happened to her memories of the desert, her treasures abandoned to it. Lucena possessed a great talent for forgetting. She seemed to have all but forgotten Will Semple.

Fannie Seymour rolled her eyes as if London were but a stage stop and the Atlantic a puddle.

"We were expected to engage a *bungo*, just a dugout tree trunk, and boatmen, which we did, to take us up the Chagres River. Well, my dear, such a sight you never did see. Those wild native boatmen were black as crows and just as naked!"

Probably half the men present had come to California via the Isthmus and knew firsthand every scene encountered there. But they hung on Fannie's telling as though she had traveled from Africa on the back of a crocodile. And, truth be told, so did I.

"We were two days coming up that river, with birds and monkeys screeching in the trees, and the boatmen grunting as they pushed along through the rapids. Why, every minute I expected we should be murdered, or worse!"

Lucena, who had heard the story before, said, "Tell about the hut and how you couldn't sleep, tell that!"

Fannie Seymour possessed a laugh like music, not the less charming for its being, I thought, rather practiced. She trilled through a bar of it, twirling a lock of red hair trailing over her shoulder.

"Oh, this hair has cost me, hasn't it just! Well, there was this little huddle of huts, not half a dozen, and our boatmen stopped us there for supper and accommodations. Gracious, what those people don't know about entertaining! A native woman fed us I'm not sure what, something like a stew, monkey probably, which we were expected to eat with our fingers! And dogs and chickens and children crowding around was not the worst of it. Why, Annie and I couldn't get a wink of sleep in that little hut. The natives for miles around kept coming to see my hair! Come right up and touched it, like to see if the color come off, I shouldn't wonder. Well, there was just no rest for the weary, so Annie and I took ourselves off and slept the night in the canoe. Oh, it was something to see — we who liked nothing better than fine featherbeds and snowy blankets, laid out like the dead in the bottom of this old hollowed-out tree trunk. Glad we were to see the sun come up, I can tell you."

Janey, sitting by the stove, peeling potatoes from Mrs. Morgan's stores, looked up, her nose wrinkling like she smelled something bad. "Monkey? You ate a monkey?"

"I expect so, dearie, that's what we were served most certainly in Gorgona. Gorgona is where the river ended and we hired mules to take us the rest of the way to Panama City. Such a place, that Gorgona! Annie and I, eager to see all the sights, you know, visited the church there. Hardly knew that's what it was — no better than a barn, no clapper for the bell, just some old Indian to pound it with a rock, and domestic animals wandering free as you please right through the place. Why, a skinny old mule just laid down and died, right there in the church, before our very eyes, and the natives took it as of no consequence! But to answer your question, Miss Janey, yes indeed, my dear, we were offered the chief dish of the place: baked monkey. My, it looked like a little child that had been burned to death!"

I shuddered at the comparison.

One of the men said, "Well, don't that beat the dutch!"

Another said, "Weren't all a lark, Miss Fannie, acknowledge the corn. Five of my companions come with me from Alabama died on the Isthmus from fever. And there was cholera, too, right bad. Regular cemetery there from Americans dyin' in that jungle. Buried at the American Burying Tree. You see that?"

"Why, sir, I just don't care to hear 'bout that, I don't. I don't care beans to hear about dyin' and cryin', not a single little old red-eyed bean, not a string bean!"

There was a part of me didn't care to hear it either. Perhaps that's why Fannie Seymour's amusements recur so clear to memory, and Mr. Massett's too, when he came to call in his little boat.

And perhaps, despite the gray fog in which I resided like a ghost, I thought I was done with dread.

American House Hotel

The storm struck on a Tuesday evening. By Wednesday afternoon we had reports of water rushing under the zinc building on J street, and rivers of water overflowing I street and surging down Second and Third. By Thursday morning the entire city lay underwater, except for the high parts of Tenth street. Houses and buildings that previously defied gale-force winds succumbed now to swift waters as currents swept them from their underpinnings. A new, two-story brick building at the corner of J and Second streets collapsed on Mr. Massett's auction house.

We had the news of it from him early on Friday afternoon, delivered personally through the second-floor window of the American House hotel. Although the rains had ceased, the water continued to rise. Mr. Massett arrived by boat, docked it below our window. I was sitting on the wide, low sill, with Hannah curled on my lap, taking a breath of fresh air.

We were a compact company. Some of the men smoked cigars or wanted for a bath. The smell of wet wool lingered, too. We all took turns, the women more especially, refreshing ourselves at the window. On that Friday afternoon, I remember seeing feathery white clouds patching the sky that had torn open to drench us. Their reflections floated on the vast watery expanse of inland sea that was Sacramento City. And so did the littering provisions and belongings of the dispossessed – trunks and cots and clothing, sticks of disassembled houses, bobbing pots from kitchens — drifting piecemeal to sea.

From my vantage I saw but a dozen rooftops above water. They resembled little islands. And the bare limbs of leafless trees reaching up through the water looked to me like the arms of drowning men.

"Ah, Mrs. Daniels! Thought you might be here, as I didn't discover you among the ladies taking refuge on the ships at the embarcadero."

Mr. Massett secured his boat to a porch post and clambered through the window. A duck dangled lifeless from his belt. Inside, he took Hannah from me and gave her a hug.

"Glad to see you, little miss!"

"Wet, all wet," she said, making a face and squirming from his grasp. She brushed at her dress with a finicky gesture I recognized as Fannie's.

"Mr. Massett, your clothes are soaked," Janey said. "Come sit by the stove and dry yourself."

"Don't mind if I do," he said, untying the duck and handing it to me. "This is for your supper, thought you might like something fresh. I was sailing down J street, and bump I went into the stump of a tree, then slap into another boat, and we both upset, and I got a duck in consequence." He laughed. "I suppose he was taking a stroll by the river when the storm caught him up."

Glad we were to have the duck, our few stores quickly diminishing. It wasn't much, but it made a nice soup. Later that day, Mr. Massett having spread word of our circumstance, others in boats brought us onions and potatoes from the store ships anchored in what was once a river and was now, from all reports, a lake. Zeb brought some beef already nicely cut up for a stew. And Mr. Massett returned with news, for which all of us hungered.

"The whole city's afloat, one mass of water, everyone and everything," he said as he docked his little boat against the porch post again and handed another bag of onions through the window to Douglas.

Mr. Massett joined our community at the stove, rubbing his hands together before it, dancing lightly from foot to foot. He nodded at a man whose shirt badly needed replacing. "I had," Mr. Massett said to him, "just this afternoon the felicity of seeing a trunk full of new shirts, recently arrived from New York, floating down the stream."

"Catch 'em, did you?" the man asked.

"Reeled in a few. They're in my boat. Help yourself."

The man — I think he was a mechanic of some sort, not much of a talker — disappeared out the window. Two or three others followed, and we heard their footsteps over our heads. That visit of Mr. Massett's marked the establishment, on the roof, of the men's dressing room, where from time to time the gentlemen of the house made their way and at their leisure rearranged their clothing, casting shirts and pants upon the waters as replacements presented themselves.

Mr. Massett said to Douglas, "Numberless other movables upon the water. Whole families passed me on rafts, one on the back of a cow. Although everybody agrees that a second edition of the Deluge has arrived, and Noah's ark's the thing to erect, everyone still seems jolly, as though it's a good joke."

Fannie Seymour, sitting on her trunk of beautifully embroidered silk shawls — from China, she had said when she showed them to us — laughed. Mr. Massett bowed and Fannie laughed again, coquettishly pinning up one of her ever escaping curls.

She and her flaming hair acted a constant pantomime of escape and capture, a performance that, like her laugh, suggested artful intent. All of us watched her like a play, so dramatic and colorful was she in costume and demeanor. Did Hannah notice the attraction? Vie for the attention to which she was accustomed by imitating the object of everyone's fascination? Or was she as captivated as the rest of us? It hardly matters. Everyone but I thought it coy of Hannah and encouraged the miniature caricature, especially Fannie.

Fannie gave Hannah pins for her hair and taught her their use in cunning gestures. The little burlesque made me uneasy, but it charmed everyone else. And Hannah was only five. I never thought to reprove her, nor could I have comfortably done so in the midst of company intent on enforced cheerfulness.

We were, as so many said with false gaiety, all in this boat together.

Sometimes at night, alone with my fears, mindful of the rising waters, I fancied I heard those waters lapping at the ceiling below. And when a wind came up and the house timbers shuddered and creaked, I thought I felt the currents. At any moment, I expected the makeshift carpentry to topple like a child's tree house. Even yet, the sound of heavy rain returns me to those frightful nights on the second floor of the American House hotel.

I filled the daylight hours with cooking, concocting soups and stews from salvaged provisions fished from the impromptu sea. No one else was inclined, and I didn't mind. Everyone found means to while away the long hours of waiting. The men talked of gold and home, wrote to loved ones on letter sheets found in a box caught like a carp and dried by the stove. Mostly they played cards, interminable games of draw poker and monte. Janey had rescued her sampler and spent hours embellishing its border. I looked over her shoulder one day, when she was sitting by the light of the window. I saw a second small tombstone against the miniature fence, the date and "C.D." stitched upon it in a single strand of silk. When had she memorialized her father? It took my breath, my daughter's brave grief.

Fannie and Lucena entertained themselves by costuming Hannah in gowns contrived from fringed silk shawls, powdering and painting her face like a China doll. It was an innocent amusement, I concluded, and it diverted Hannah from the restless boredom of captivity.

When not dressing my child like a doll or entertaining the company with stories of New Orleans and her travels on the Isthmus, Fannie sat at the window. To take the air, she said. But the provocative posture did not go unnoticed. I wondered if it was a habit from Annie Woods's house, the way she leaned back against the frame, left foot anchoring her inside, right leg draping the sill with the folds of a gown, a neat ankle exposed. Her hair, bright as a flame against the whitewashed casing, attracted boats of passersby like moths. She enjoyed waving to them. It was something to do.

I never suspected the danger in it.

We all found our routines. Martha Morgan read, a number of books having been salvaged by Mr. Massett from an abandoned house on Tenth street. He brought them one day, along with the latest news and some sheet music.

"A rescue from the residence of a friend, a doctor, gone now with his family to San Francisco," Mr. Massett said, handing the treasures through the window to grateful hands. "I went calling in my little boat to ascertain the safety of the ladies of the household. They, being entirely at the mercy of the elements, escaped their ocean-bound residence and have since removed westward, my friend just putting his affairs in order and intending to follow. I rowed right into their drawing room and came bump up against a piano. Found several of my songs floating about. One in particular I thought was now in its element: "When the Moon on the Lake is Beaming." Gathered them up, and some books off the higher shelves, thinking the prisoners of the American House receptive to the entertainment."

I was standing back with the women and noticed that Mr. Massett, although he handed in the books to Jesse Morgan, addressed Fannie.

She laughed. "I thought you might indeed be he, sir, the author of the songs I see published in the newspaper."

"And delighted to render the tune in person, should the company wish it."

Jesse Morgan handed a volume of Pope's essays to me to give to Martha and said, "If you're proposing to give a concert, Mr. Massett, you might consider Handel's *Water Music.*"

Mr. Massett visited daily, always bringing cheery news or something useful he'd rescued. I wondered whether the merry green eyes and laughter of Fannie Seymour drew his attentions, so frequently did she sit in the window, toying with her hair, hailing passersby. But as Zeb came nearly as often, and looked on Fannie with indifference, I concluded my suspicions a disservice to Mr. Massett's kindness, his visits so amused us.

"Those persons lucky enough to still own a house with a roof," Mr. Massett said one day, "are living on that roof. They are sleeping on that roof, cooking on that roof, writing letters on that roof, and making calls on that roof. Why, just this morning I witnessed a wedding on a roof. The people of Sacramento City are drinking on the roof, praying on the roof, singing on the roof, going to church on the roof, taking their baths on the roof, cursing the goldfields on the roof, and thinking they'll never get off the roof!"

Mr. Massett was born to entertain. The success of his subsequent theatrical career in San Francisco as Jeems Pipes of Pipesville didn't surprise me.

The first newspaper to publish after the storm was the *Placer Times,* which put out an extra edition. That was on January 15, a full week since we first fled to the hotel. And my last clear day of recollection.

Zeb brought us a copy. Fannie was sitting in the window when he arrived. She held Hannah on her lap, a squirming toy dressed in an elaborately embroidered apricot satin shawl with purple fringe.

I remember Zeb climbing through the window as Fannie moved aside, annoyed, flouncing off as he caught Hannah up in his arms. "How's my little Chinese pumpkin today?" he asked. I remember that. And Hannah giggling and throwing her arms around his neck.

The newspaper was full of the flood, and Zeb the center of attention. We all crowded around, passed off sheets of the paper, devoured it with our eyes. I know Hannah came to the stove with Zeb; she wasn't at the window by herself, there were rules about that. But he put her down to take the newspaper from his pocket. I remember seeing Fannie sitting on her trunk, looking petulant, so much attention being lavished and none of it on her. Someone read the account of poor Mr. Wilkinson, a passenger on the bark *Orb* who fell overboard during the storm and drowned. I recall thinking what a capricious fate was his, coming all this long way to die in a flood. And someone else related the news he'd heard on the rooftop earlier that day from a passerby in a boat, about how a man known as the Dutchman kept his gold in a belly bank, a money belt in more polite terms, and when his boat went down, he went with it because he would not part with his poke. Then someone else read an account of the horses and mules and cattle being carried away in great numbers. There was also an item about the brick building falling on Mr. Massett's auction house, as well as the good news that the water was receding at last, and quickly, too. The hope was that it would shortly be gone from Second street. The American House hotel sat closer to Third than Second, but our hopes rose in proportion to the reports of ebbing waters.

We all of us were taken with the news, crowding around the stove where I was cooking, Janey and Lucena helping. Martha was reading a book, and all the men handing around the newspaper. Onion soup, I was cooking onion soup, made in a beef broth from the bones of some poor cow that had drowned, I suppose. So many animals did, poor innocent creatures. When did someone miss her, and who was it? Zeb, I suppose. Or maybe I said to Janey, "Here's some soup for your sister." Though perhaps it was Douglas I said that to. Did I look for her myself, or was it Lucena?

I don't remember. I only remember the screaming, my screaming, and the sight of the red-kerchief doll on the floor by the window, then Zeb standing there, shaking, water running off his wet clothes like tears, his face white, his eyes the gray of old scars, and him holding her in his arms, her head lolling against his chest, and me standing there with the doll, saying, "Hannah, honey, Hannah, here's your doll, here's your doll," trying to put it in her lifeless hands, and then just the screaming and screaming and screaming.

Hannah

I have learned this from death: cherish the living. They are apt to die at any time. Cherish them daily.

These sound like church words, I know, like a prayer said by rote, no more registered than "Amen." Truths are like that, obvious. And consequently rarely regarded. Until.

Since that fateful flood, no day passes without thought of my dead daughter. Ten thousand times in memory I see her little face collapsed in surprise and bewilderment. And I see mud, red-brown gobbets of it caught in purple fringe and folds of apricot satin, and plastered in yellow hair.

Ten thousand times in imagination, events beyond reversal replay. I can neither stop her nor save her. I picture my daughter dashing to the window and hoisting herself up on its sill. I see a little leg too short for anchor. And I see her wave. The passerby, already diving for her when Zeb leapt from the window, said she waved to him in his boat. And fell from the window like a dropped doll.

It wasn't Fannie's fault, no one's really. I don't even blame myself anymore. Death just happens. Children fall from wagons and windows. Cholera strikes, and fever, thirst, starvation. Death takes ten thousand forms.

Cherish the living.

If I had been at home, I could have mourned her better than I did. And perhaps not be so haunted by the image of purple fringe and yellow hair forever toppling and plummeting. At home, in the brick house, I could have wept when I should.

Perhaps that's why my compass pointed toward Illinois with such urgency. I needed a place to grieve.

When my father died, I remember how Mother drifted from room to room, stroked his pipe, lay her head on his pillow, and mourned his absence from it. At home I might have had space for my grief, wandered from room to room and remembered my child's laughter instead of her imagined cry, remembered her happy tumbling from the stairs instead of imagining her fall from the sill. I could have caressed her things. And wept.

The rituals of dailiness salve our injuries. Deprived of them, our wounds heal, if at all, into gaping scars. Home is solace to a shattered heart, the familiar scenes of comfort and small events, life lived for years on end without large moments. But that lay behind us. Now ours was a life of stopgap, make-do, move on. And wounds.

Douglas, his old-looking young man's face ashy and tear-stained, fashioned another coffin. He built it from a few salvaged boards of deconstructed houses fished from the river. For a shroud, I wrapped my little girl in the embrace of her father's coat. And so buried Caleb with her, and the aching comfort of the lingered smell of him, that she might not be alone.

When the water was nearly off Second street, Zeb and Mr. Massett, Janey and Douglas and I slogged out to the cemetery on the low hill beyond town, where we dug a little grave in the wet, wet earth and placed a small marker. I know this more from Douglas than my own memory. I could not register my child's burial, there wasn't space in my grief for it. Douglas tells me Mr. Massett sang a sweet song, and Zeb, gray as granite, said the prayer. I picked the site, he said, a sheltered place beneath an ancient sycamore, for shade from the summer sun and the song of birds in spring. I don't recall. Janey collected stones, embroidering the edge of her sister's grave with them, and wept. She wept as though her heart should burst from such sorrow. I remember that because I wondered how she did it, and whether she could teach it to me. It was a strange thought, but I was half out of my mind.

I wept later, wept from a heart full of scars the first time I returned to that little stone-marked grave beneath the sycamore. In my wounded heart they are all there together: George, Hannah, Caleb. And I visit them all, so they won't be alone. And remember them. And remember to cherish the living.

But at first, when Hannah, my angel daughter, went to her rest in that mirey grave, shrouded in Caleb's coat, I could not weep. Instead I became half frantic for fear Janey should be next. I fixed on her the way my mother must have fixed on me when my brother died. *Don't take this one!* we mothers scream. *Leave me this one!*

Higher ground, I wanted higher ground, lest the rains should come again and some terrible accident take another from me.

Who didn't I accost for advice? "Where shall I go, where shall I go?" I must have screamed.

Deer Creek Diggings, someone said, one of my customers who called in hopes of a meal and found me frantically rescuing what little remained to us. Great piles of driftwood and the carcasses of dead animals had wedged between the supports of what had been my restaurant. The stove was rusted, the barley sprouted, and everything covered with slime and sediment.

We were destitute. The barley was ruined. And there were debts. I owed Mr. Bailey, and Mr. McKnight. Both offered to forgive my debts, strike the account from their books, but I refused. I had nothing left but my word. I would not part with my honor. Except that it was Douglas who would stand in my stead.

"You and Janey go, Ma," he said, the day I decided for Deer Creek Diggings.

Janey and I were standing in the middle of Mr. Bailey's store, surrounded by bags and boxes and barrels, new goods delivered from the ships arrived from San Francisco. At the counter behind us Mr. Bailey recorded numbers in a large gray journal as Douglas unpacked boxes and stocked shelves. Mr. Morrison, by his side, weighed the gold of customers purchasing goods as soon as they arrived.

"It'll be better if I stay here and work," Douglas said, stacking sardine tins on a shelf being dispossessed by eager buyers as fast as he furnished it.

"Stay here?" I said, dizzy with watching him climb up and down a ladder.

"I already asked Mr. Bailey, Ma," Douglas said, coming to me and taking my hand, "if I could stay here, sleep in the store. That way I can send money and provisions to you. It'd be best."

"But you're just a boy — "

"Ma, I'm fifteen next month. Lots of fellows not much older out here."

I thought of the dead boy in the tent next to my restaurant and covered my face. What would happen to my son without me? What would happen to me without him? Who else did I have?

And that thought stopped me. I didn't want to lean on anyone just because it was habit. And I was determined not to lean on my son's thin shoulders. It wasn't fair. To either of us. I may have felt hollow as a lightning-struck tree, but I was still standing. And I let my son convince me. It was the bravest thing I ever did, until I let Janey go to Australia.

For transport to higher ground, I haunted the livery stable and the stage stop on Front street, even confronted the happenstance freighter. I pleaded, "Are you going to Deer Creek Diggings? Or will you? The fare to Deer Creek Diggings, how much for two passengers and our goods?" They stared, each in turn, as I imagine they would at a madwoman.

Someone said he wouldn't do it for less than seven hundred dollars, but he wasn't going that direction. "On account of the mud, don't you see, ma'am? Nobody'd do it for less'n that. Take a week, for sure. Yep, you figure on seven hundred, if'n you can find the driver."

Seven hundred dollars? I didn't have seven hundred cents not owing to someone, but I barely blinked at the prospect of debt now. I could earn seven hundred dollars. And there was no shame in being destitute in California. Most of us arrived in that condition. My advantage was my sex. That was my line of credit, and having no other, I proposed to use it.

In the end, Zeb agreed to take us, me and Janey and the stove I bought from Orlando McKnight.

"All rusted up, Miz Daniels."

"I cleaned it once, Mr. McKnight, and I can do it again. How much for it, if you'll let me have it?"

"Reckon I'd take twenty-five dollars."

"Will you accept my word?"

He hesitated but a moment, being in the presence of Mr. Massett and Mr. Taylor, who had come to say goodbye. "Reckon so."

That accomplished, I slogged up to the livery at K and Sixth street again, where a half dozen freighters had congregated, Zeb among them. I announced I had need of transportation to Deer Creek Diggings, knew the price to be seven hundred dollars, and was prepared to pay it if I lived to earn it.

No one spoke.

I stared at them each in turn, and they all looked away except Zeb. He shook his head, started to speak. "Sarah — "

I could see he was against my going still. We had talked it at length. "Very well, I'll walk if I have to, my goods on my back and my stove in a handcart."

And that's how we came, for the last time, to load our things into the familiar old wagon Caleb had built for his dream.

On Front street, at Mr. Bailey's store, the day Janey and Zeb and I left Sacramento City, I hugged my son to me like life. And then I put my hands to Douglas's face and memorized it.

The river was all off the streets then, contained and quiet within its banks once more. It looked tame, like the trained bear I later saw chained to a tree in Grass Valley, but I no more trusted the appearance of innocence in a river than I did in that animal.

All of Sacramento City looked a ruin that day, but shipping from San Francisco crowded the riverfront, and auctioneers shouted from their decks the fresh arrival of goods and canvas. Pounding hammers and rasping saws advertised Sacramento City's imminent re-erection. The flood of 1850 was behind, a memory. The thing was to go ahead, keep one's eye on the prize, get the gold, make the pile.

I remember seeing, as I said goodbye to my son that bright February morning, a hundred men digging up and panning out Front street for its fresh-laid deposits of California promise.

Our road lay east, toward the foothills. Later I would travel the northern road to and from Sacramento by way of Marysville, it being flatter and more direct. But all that low-lying land then remained swampy from the rains, and Zeb headed for higher ground, despite the longer distance. It may have been a kindness on his part to allay my fear of the great floodplain that is the Sacramento Valley.

We traveled but a day before the land began to rise in the gentle undulation of the lower foothills. It was a well-trodden road, being the way to Sutter's mill at Coloma, the first route to the goldfields and still the most favored approach. Miners sought the spot of first discovery like religionists seek a shrine, just to lay eyes on it. Poor Mr. Marshall, who discovered the glittery metal in the millrace. I heard afterward he became a hounded man. Gold seekers followed him wherever he went, confident he possessed some secret means of detecting the metal. They pestered him with offers of payment if he would show them how to find it. And, possessing no more knowledge than they themselves, he was paid in resentment for the trouble he took in telling them so.

The higher the ground, the easier I breathed, as though elevation rendered a special treatment for my ailment of fear. The grandeur of the scenery open to our view as we headed east distracted my anxiety into admiration for that singular beauty. While the rains had pelted the valley, at the higher elevations snow had fallen. Against the far distance of blue sky rose the long, high crest of the mountains, draped in a magnificent mantle of white. My small knowledge of Spanish having been enlarged to include the translation of *Sierra Nevada* to "snowy range," I appreciated the appellation.

We lost the prospect as we entered the foothills, which obscured our view of farther reaches, and then our way was little more than a tedious toil north. We were a week at the journey, as more than one freighter had predicted, from the frequent necessity to dig out mired mules and sunken wheels. But despite this hardship, I felt calmer and more hopeful.

Until I saw the rose.

Deer Creek Diggings

Our travel took us past one mining camp after another: Fords Bar, Negro Bar, Sailor Bar, Texas Hill, Big Gulch, Forkville, Horseshoe Bar, Rattlesnake Bar, Newcastle, Forest Springs, Grass Valley. Every little collection of canvas store, saloon, and a dozen miners' tents cluttering a ravine or river bottom christened itself. As Zeb observed after we passed through one newly named community all but atop the one preceding, "California is a singular country. Hardly enough land to build all the towns required here."

Deer Creek Diggings differed in one respect: women were there.

As Zeb's mules headed up the hill toward the settlement, Janey and I saw, from beneath the wagon's rolled up canvas cover, crude cabins and shanties slung along the rutted, red dirt road hacked from the hillside. On one cabin a slip of climbing rose clung to a porch post, betraying a female presence.

That rose, how it stole my breath away. Some woman had found herself on the edge of wilderness, as my mother once had, and determined to tame it. The sight stabbed my heart with memories of home and all that I'd left behind. I felt so suddenly bereft I gripped the side of the wagon hard and looked away from the wispy reminder, found the hunched curve of Zeb's back through the oval of canvas, and stared hard at his worn coat and slouch hat. He hollered "Gee up, Dolly!" and urged his mules up the hill.

Janey had seen the rose, too. "Look, Mama," she said, pointing.

I forced a smile. "Yes, dear, I see it."

Together, as Zeb's mules hauled us past, we looked at the unpainted house with its unexpected display of tender, bronze-tipped buds. Suddenly, overwhelmingly, I wanted to beat the wagon's side until my fists bled. I wanted to shriek from the bursting ache in my throat.

And then the impulse passed, and I felt emptiness return, like a dead tree, all hollow inside, standing from habit and waiting to collapse. Fannie had her artifices, I remember thinking, and I had mine. Despite the impulse to scream, I realized I had, for Janey's sake, kept a fake smile pinned to my face. But I was not so practiced. She probably knew, but said nothing. Her mother's daughter.

"Deer Creek isn't much, Mama," Janey said, looking from the rose to the tent town stretched before us.

Seeing a pile of lumber in the road, a man busy erecting a house from it, I stemmed rising panic in the way I had learned to do. I would ask him to sell me two boards. On credit. Necessity buried dread and pride in the small space where I contained one and maintained the other.

More indebtedness, and I didn't even know what I owed Mr. Bailey for the provisions Douglas had packed for us in Zeb's wagon. But added to that and the seven hundred dollars I owed Zeb, a couple of planks couldn't matter.

"No, Janey, I suppose not." I offered the poor comfort of my arm around her shoulders as the wagon thumped to a halt. "I'm sorry."

Zeb turned, shifted the reins to one hand, lifted his hat with the other. "I guess this is as good as anywhere."

"Yes, I suppose it is." *Good as anywhere,* I thought, while he helped us from the wagon and I gazed past him at the rutted road behind us. I seemed always to be looking back, stunned, at the way I had come.

I heard Zeb talking to his mules, calming their impatience while he unroped the stove from our wagon — no, his wagon — again. I was impatient, too, impatient with myself. Indulging regret for what lay behind only sapped strength required for what lay ahead. I brushed road dust from Janey's cloak, a warm blue cassimere Fannie had pressed on her, and adjusted my bonnet, another gift. We watched Zeb unload the wagon and tried to ignore the gawking men gathered in a saloon doorway.

Janey tugged at my sleeve and nodded toward the log house next to the saloon, silently directing my attention to what had caught her eye. To my amazement, a young woman stood watching us from the steps, eyes wide with interest beneath a red kerchief covering her head. The long sleeves and high neck of her faded blue cotton dress and white pinafore contrasted sharply with her color: she was black as night.

I had but a small smile to offer this surprising apparition, my spirit being so blasted by sorrow, but she returned it a hundredfold. A smile wide as the sky brightened her aspect like sunshine.

Zeb finished unloading our things onto the boardwalk fronting the saloon. "That's everything, Sarah," he said, placing a valise on top of the stove, "if you're still determined on this. You know I'll take you back to Sacramento City, if you want. This place isn't much."

"This place is fine," I said. "You've done more than enough. And you shall have your seven hundred dollars if I live and earn the money."

"Mercy me!"

Zeb and I and Janey all looked up in surprise as the Negro woman on the steps added apologetically, "Y'all forgive me, I just never afore heard no white person say such a thing."

Just then a voice thundered from inside the house, "Who you talkin' to, girl? Get in here, Susan, and fix me somethin' to eat!"

The door flew open, and a portly, red-faced man of middle years dressed like a sea captain burst through it. Seeing us, he stopped, brushed at the sleeves of his rumpled coat, and adjusted his collar. "Name's Thorn," he said. "Captain Thorn. You folks new to the diggings?"

Zeb said, "The ladies are fixed on staying. Perhaps you can recommend a suitable lodging."

Thorn rubbed his chin, taking my measure. "Can you pay?"

"How much?" I asked.

"You can stay here for twenty-five a week, you don't mind sharing with this darky."

Susan grinned then, that sunshine smile lighting up her face. "I keeps a nice house, missus, and this be the best place in town for hearin' the piano, it bein' smack up against the wall, like."

"Piano!" Janey took my hand in both of hers and hugged it to her. "Oh, Mama, a piano!"

That settled it. And so we made the fateful acquaintance of Susan Jackson, Captain Thorn, and Mart Tyler, proud proprietor of the Empire Saloon and one out-of-tune, broken-keyed piano.

We suffered Captain Thorn's begrudged hospitality, in all, two months, the whole of it compensated only by my need and Susan's sunny disposition. Of Captain Thorn's character, I recall registering at once that it permitted vast opportunity for improvement. He was a vile-tempered, miserly man whose rudeness disinclined me to him long before our eventual dispute. I was not surprised to learn that his wife had left him.

"Oh, she disappear like the wind, that lady," Susan whispered that first evening, after the captain retired to his room with a bottle of brandy, a habit from which he deviated but rarely during our residence.

I had noticed evidences of a woman's presence — china dishes, velvet cushions — small comforts in a house rudely constructed but palatial by mining-camp standards. It boasted four rooms, two in the rear for sleeping and two forward for kitchen and parlor, divided by nicely papered walls.

"Captain, he build this place for his missus. Cost the moon, it did," Susan said when I remarked the luxury. "Reg'lar paper-hanger come out with us from San Francisco, mercy me." She laughed, deep and throaty. "Truth be told, these walls, they look reg'lar enough, but they not. Just stretched-up muslin is all, tacked up tight with paper pasted on. Whole inside of this house ain't nothin' but a fancy speakin' trumpet, sound carry so."

"Well," I said, "it does look nice."

"Oh, the missus she be promised high style," Susan said, her voice low. Susan and I were putting the kitchen to rights after a simple meal of stewed beef I'd helped prepare. "All the way 'cross to Panama City, the captain sayin' as how he be rich faster'n a lightnin' strike. He figurin' on rakin' in gold like leaves come winter, seein' as how he's got himself slaves for doin' the diggin'."

"Slaves? Here? In California?"

"Why, yes'm, Captain bring three of us he bought off a trader in Mobile, back in Alabama, where I comes from. Collected us up afore he got to New Orleans and married up Mrs. Thorn. Weren't but a short courtship, you know. Maybe a day." Susan laughed, then caught herself. She looked questioningly from me to Janey, visible to us through the doorway of the parlor. Oblivious to our conversation, Janey sat hunched up on a small sofa next to the wall nearest the saloon, listening to the barely muffled sound of a piano played badly.

"I regret my daughter's education in these parts includes the acquaintance of a woman named Fannie Seymour, also from New Orleans."

"Then you knows the class," Susan said, shaking her head. "Oh, my, that Missus Thorn, she see what the captain done brung her to — and this be the best in these parts, you know — she not happy no little bit.

Played the piano some next door when the captain was off to his mine, she did, and took up there with a gamblin' man. I don't say nothin', it bein' none o' my business, and she nothin' to me, not like my Miss Francine. Well, this gamblin' man, he won himself somethin' like twenty thousand dollars off a Mexican monte dealer one night, so Mr. Tyler say. He's proprietor to the Empire, you see. This gamblin' man come callin' next day, right up to the door, proud as a preacher, and Missus Thorn she just collect up her traps and off she goes with him. The captain, he come back from supervisin' his mine that night, he 'bout explode. Hired himself a sheriff to go find her, but she gone. I been bought to be her servant, but she left me behind along with all the other stuff he bought her, fancy furniture and dishes. Fancy for California, you understand. I know fancy when I see it, and this ain't it."

Through the wall separating the kitchen from the room behind we heard a thud, followed by a drunken snort.

"Dropped his bottle," Susan said. "Don't improve the captain's temper none, her goin' off."

"Why do you stay?" I asked.

Susan stared at me as though I were mad. "Why, I don't rightly got no choice in the matter, does I? Captain, he paid nine hundred dollars for me in Mobile."

I suppose it may one day surprise some that slavery existed in California, but it did. Any number of Southerners brought slaves here, intending to reap the golden harvest of their labor. But the miners wouldn't have it. Not from any abolitionist fervor, I regret to say. The overriding objection to slavery was economics: a white man digging gold for himself couldn't compete with a band of men digging for a Southerner. And it shamed them, the idea of digging next to slaves. Not from any ideal of freedom, but because they considered it demeaning to themselves.

That's how Zeb explained it to me the evening I became frantic over Susan's situation. Goodness, that was four years ago already, in 1852, after the state legislature's scandalous decision.

"Men make the laws, Sarah, and they make them in their own interest." It's what he said about women's property rights, but in this instance the rule held.

I still had my restaurant on Broad street then, and we would have been sitting to table late after my customers had left. Zeb always liked that time with me, drinking coffee and talking, the darkness outside surrounding us like a blanket. It's still our favorite time together.

"You shouldn't be shocked by the legislature's action, Sarah," Zeb had told me. "Barely a month after adoption of a free-state constitution, the first state assembly passed a bill outlawing the immigration of free Negroes to California. The state senate postponed the bill indefinitely, which effectively killed it, but you see the bent a lot of folks take."

I had seen, yes. Few people objected to the Captain Thorns of California.

For Susan, and all the slaves brought to California, the problem was that the law didn't tell slaveholders they had to free their slaves upon arrival. Nor did it say how long they could continue keeping them in bondage.

And, truth be told, Susan didn't object.

That surprised me, at first, until I realized it was all she knew. I had lived a life in Illinois, "tolerable-like," as Susan was fond of saying about Alabama, and it was all I knew. Until forced to, I couldn't have imagined living differently. The familiar, if not unpleasant, is comfortable. And until Captain Thorn, Susan's life had been comfortable.

And there was this: the dependency of slavery was as much ingrained in her as was the concept of freedom in me. A great many slaves came to California and remained slaves from habit. Some returned to the South with their owners, others were sold here. I saw, not infrequently, notices of slave auctions in the papers. And offers of reward for runaways. Yes, there was slavery in California in those early days, and it's hardly eradicated even now, despite Union sentiment and the trouble everyone says is coming.

"Oh, I lived in a fine, big house, I did," Susan said one evening when Janey asked about Alabama. Dinner was done, Captain Thorn had retired with his brandy, and the three of us, Janey, Susan, and I, were sitting in the parlor listening to the saloon piano through the wall. Exhausted from my day's work, I curled into the sofa next to my daughter while Susan's velvety Alabama voice wrapped around me.

"Oh, yes, mercy me, such a big house," Susan repeated, leaning back in her chair and gazing at the stretched-muslin ceiling. "I lived in it, not outside with those field people, same as if it was my own. Always did, can't remember nothin' else."

"And your mother lived there, too?" Janey asked.

Susan shook her head, slow, thinking. "No, not so's I remember. Don't remember no mama. 'Course, Miss Francine, she didn't have no mama neither. Poor woman died when that child borned. Oh, but she a sweet child, Francine, and her and me be like sisters. I was give to her for to keep her comp'ny, you see, she bein' weakly. And neither of us knowin' different, we be friends. She play the piano like a angel, that girl did, teacher comin' ever' week, and me sitting 'neath the big ol' thing, quiet like a mouse. And she teached me to read some, too, and I can do my letters. 'Don't tell Papa,' she'd say to me. Readin' and writin' 'gainst the law in Alabama for Nigras. But she learned me some anyway. I didn't have no teachers like she did, and weren't allowed to stay for her lessons from the governess, but Miss Francine, she liked to play school and be the teacher when no one lookin' in on us."

I could see a homesickness in Susan's expression, her eyes misty and sad-looking. "What happened?" I asked, knowing the answer a sorrowful one. Captain Thorn was not an improvement on the life she described.

"Oh, Miss Francine, she died of the consumption. And Master, he don't know what to do with me. I put in the kitchen, and it was tolerable-like. Mayleen — she the cook — she teach me some, but that don't work out. Every time Master see me, he sad. Reckon because I alive and his daughter dead. But I miss her, too. She the only person ever cared for me, only friend I ever had."

I began then to mourn my own loss with less despair and feel fortunate with the privilege of love and family and freedom. And, crushed as I was by circumstance, I still had a home waiting for me. Susan Jackson had only California. I thought it then, as did she, but a poor advance on the South.

Pies, $3

What a respite were those calm evenings with Susan and Janey in Captain Thorn's log parlor, thin strains of badly played piano surrounding low conversation, ginger tea sipped slowly. By contrast my days resembled rifle shots, full of sound and fury, to borrow from Mr. Shakespeare, but signifying, for me, hope and home.

I bought my two boards on credit and set them up on stumps for a counter in a vacant spot on Deer Creek Diggings' principal thoroughfare, a road rough and rutted and not yet officially named Main street. My stove I installed in the shelter of a towering pine, to which I nailed a sign: "Pies, $3." A bargain price certain to ensure custom.

From the provisions carried from Sacramento City I had a goodly portion of flour and dried apples and proceeded to the task at hand, baking from sunup till sundown every day of the week. I did a brisk business from the first. The mining population of that vicinity was then some two thousand, all hungry for a pie baked by a woman, despite my being less of a curiosity here than at You Bet and Dutch Flat.

As the wispy rose attested, Deer Creek Diggings boasted at least one woman besides Susan Jackson. There were, in fact, several. Mrs. Stamps, who had come from Tennessee the year before with her husband and children, owned the rose. She had pear trees, too, a delicacy of such rarity and high regard that, come spring, she sold the fruit in blossom, tying name tags to the branches for two-dollar reservations.

There was Harriet Turner, as well, and Martha Womack, and Phoebe Ann Kidd. They had all gone to keeping hotels. Martha Womack and her husband, Peyton, had the Miner's Hotel, a canvas affair like the Missouri owned by Phoebe and her husband. In May, Harriet and Nick Turner opened the first frame-built hotel, of sumptuous proportions, being a story and a half, and nearly forty feet by fifty.

We were all of us wonderfully successful, for the gold-rich ravines of Deer Creek, at first, yielded what the miners called "pound diggings" — twelve troy ounces per man per day. The word spread fast as gunshot, and throughout that spring the little mining camp increased in magnitude marvelously. In March the townspeople elected Mr. Stamps alcalde and selected a new name for the town. Nevada, they called it, and later, Nevada City.

By summer, with the population no less than six thousand, Janey and I were comfortably established in my restaurant on Broad street, just below Main, where town lots of seventy by ninety feet had been offered free to anyone willing to put them to immediate use.

I knew from my experience in Sacramento City that a restaurant promised more substantial profits than pies. And with the land free for the asking, I had my restaurant from but a morning's work with canvas and nails and the convenience of pine trees for uprights. The removal of my stove from Main street to Broad was the accomplishment of a customer happy to enjoy his dinner at the Daniels Restaurant that evening in exchange. A small investment in a tent, cots, bedding, some rough-made benches and tables and other necessaries — which I expected to recoup upon their sale when we departed — and I was again as well situated as my limited expectations required. I will say this from having lived in the mines, it is a wonder how little it takes to make one comfortable.

From the first I made money fast, an immense satisfaction, as anyone who has enjoyed the accomplishment will attest, and with the arrival of pleasant weather, kept open late into the evening. For assistance, I had Janey, of course, but success and circumstance soon freed her to other pursuits. And I hired of Captain Thorn, for evenings, the services of Susan Jackson in her stead.

I arrived at the log house unannounced one warm June night and, interrupting the captain at his supper table, said, "I understand you have hired out your man Robert."

Captain Thorn regarded me with a flat gaze of silent disfavor. We were not on friendly terms for more reasons than that he wore his cap to table. He tossed off a glass of warm beer, wiped his mouth with his hand, and folded his arms across his ample front. "And how is it come to be your business, eh, Mrs. Daniels?"

Were I not affronted by his habits, I should have been amused by his dictatorial manner, it being so undermined by the flood of napkin tucked at his fleshy throat. "The whole town well knows your business, Captain Thorn, and dislikes it. We have before spoken of this matter and your slaves — "

"Ha! So you say." He turned his brick-colored face to regard Susan's black one. She stood at his elbow, looking puzzled, holding suspended a plate of fried chops she had been in the act of delivering. "Still," he said, returning his gaze to me, "it is very handy to have one to clean one's boots and prepare one's supper. It's my luxury. I paid for it."

"I've not come to argue but to present a proposal. I wish to hire the services of Susan, four hours each evening — "

"She has her work here," Captain Thorn said, interrupting more for show than objection. I'd seen his eyebrows lift when I'd said the word *hire.*

Susan stared at me. I had not consulted her on the matter.

Confident in the acceptability of my proposal, I plunged home my sword. "Your habits, Captain, are as well known as your business. I'd like to hire Susan evenings, when you have no need of your 'luxury.' "

In my two months under his roof, I saw him deviate but once from the routine of early retirement with his brandy. On that occasion a fellow Southerner had sought him out, and rather than entertain the man himself, the captain took him next door to the Empire. Susan and I had laughed, confident the captain intended letting his visitor buy. Except for his lavishness with the departed Mrs. Thorn, the captain was pinchfisted as Mr. Dickens' Scrooge. I knew he wouldn't say no to my offer.

"Twenty-five dollars a week," I said, and had him. He'd been disgruntled at losing from me that exact sum when I built and furnished my restaurant on Broad street and moved into the back of it. The captain had resented my having subtracted it from his purse, no amount being trivial to a man whose predilections did not favor personal labor. Now I was offering it back.

"In gold?"

"Of course. With one proviso."

He scowled. "Being?"

"Ten percent shall go to Susan."

"To Susan!"

"As her own."

"Her own what?"

"Wages, Captain Thorn, her own wages."

Susan, eyes wide, dropped the plate of chops to the table. "Wages?" she said, her dignified silence undone by surprise. "Mercy me."

I had not spoken of my intent to her, as it was, after all, the captain who would decide. But it was Susan I took the idea from, she having related to me that Robert, one of two slaves the captain brought to dig gold for him, had been hired out. Susan delivered lunch each noon to the captain's claim on Deer Creek, where Robert and Wilson labored under his supervision six days a week. Robert, being strong and determined on freedom, received Captain Thorn's permission to hire out to anyone wishing to employ him on the seventh, in return for half his wages. "He ask the cap'n," Susan had confided. "He say, 'I be a free man someday, if I live and earn the money?' And the cap'n, he say, 'that's right.' "

I suspect Captain Thorn feared his man might otherwise run, and he be put to the expense of rewarding the capture.

By her telling, I saw that Susan had not educed from Robert's circumstance any application to her own, being so completely without expectation. This habit prevented the running away of any number of slaves in California. And, truth be told, to what might they run? In absence of any clear law, the likely consequence was return to captivity. It was a rare judge, even in California, who, lacking legal specifics, said no to the irate property holders of the South.

But I thought Susan's chance ought to be equal to the rest and told her so that very evening, having secured, as I expected, agreement for her employment.

"You need not depend on the vagaries of others," I said, showing her how I liked my table set with little cruets and butter cups arranged down the middle.

"Yes, ma'am," Susan said without conviction.

"I mean this, Susan," I said. "You might just as well hire out as cook or housekeeper like any number of less able women and profit by it. And before I leave for Illinois, I'll speak to one of the hotel women about another position for you."

"With wages?"

"Of course. And eventually you'll have the whole of them, as you should."

"How much be this ten percent, you don't mind my askin'?"

"It's not much, but I feared the captain would balk at more. We'll get it higher as he gets used to the idea. For now it's two dollars and fifty cents a week."

Susan slid her black hands over the oilcloth covering my table, smoothing it by the light of the lantern suspended from the pine-branch crossbeam supporting my canvas ceiling. She looked puzzled.

"Can you do figures, Susan?"

"No, ma'am. Miss Francine, she don't like no 'rithmetic, and she don't teach me nothin' but letters."

"Then Janey will teach you. It will be good practice for her, now that she's studying with Mr. Tyler."

Mart Tyler, proprietor of the Empire Saloon, had been a professor of economics at Yale University. I made this surprising discovery one Sunday morning shortly after our arrival in town.

A Methodist minister — I've forgotten his name, I believe I last heard he has gone to the business of selling monte cards — in preparation for launching a street sermon was singing up a crowd in front of the saloon. This was when I still had my pie business on Main street, hard by that establishment. Janey and I heard the singing from there.

"Mama," Janey said, dishing up a slice of apple pie for a customer, "remember that old hymn? It's one of the first Gran taught me to play."

" 'Rock of Ages,' " said the customer, a tall, confident-looking man with a hawkish face framed by a trim beard. He put one foot up on a stump, leaned an elbow on his knee, and stared at the crowd. He wore a good broadcloth coat over a matching waistcoat, evidence enough, without his uncallused hands, that he was not a miner. He turned when Janey handed him his pie, and ate it standing, in small, neat bites.

"Another, I believe," he said, extracting three silver coins from a waistcoat pocket.

I examined one.

"Ecuadorian," he said. "Equal to one dollar. Good as gold. Or you may have that metal in dust, if you prefer."

I took the coins. We saw everything in the manner of currency in those days.

"May as well indulge myself," he said. "The preacher preventing my business, as it were."

"Pardon?"

"Blocking the door. Such as it is." He laughed, and I had to smile with him, since little that resembled a door had yet established itself on Main street. Canvas curtains generally filled the part.

"You are the proprietor of the Empire?"

"At your service. Professor Martin Tyler. Economics. Yale University."

"Indeed." I was not inclined to believe him, knowing the California propensity for self-advancement.

He stared, brow knitted, at the crowd fronting his saloon, then at Janey as she handed him a second pie. He took a bite and turned his gaze on me. "Your girl here — "

"My daughter. Janey."

"Yes, Janey. Well, I've a proposition for you. For her. Whichever." He studied her. "You can play it on the piano, that hymn, girl?"

"Yes," Janey said, "I can."

"I propose you do it. On my instrument. Move that crowd inside."

"Getting those men into your saloon to buy a drink, that's a Sabbath observance?" I said.

"Commerce is commerce, madam, as you know." He swallowed the last of his pie and dusted the crumbs from his fingers. "Let us not quibble."

He was right, of course. Sunday was when the miners came to town, and my most profitable day of the week. The business of that one day alone would, in time, have seen us home. Had I not been devoted to larger purpose, I would have been shamed by my failure to observe the Sabbath. And with that thought it occurred to me that Sabbath observance might be imminent.

"If my daughter plays the hymn and you invite the crowd, must you not invite the preacher as well?"

"I suppose the logic follows."

"Then we might suppose the sermon shall also?"

The man grinned. "You are proposing I host Sunday services, are you, madam?"

"I suppose I am."

And so it was, that, lacking better, our little community commenced Sabbath services in a saloon, and Janey played the hymns.

It was a poor instrument, as I saw on inspection that first Sunday morning. Two books — Thackeray and Macaulay, as I recall — did duty for a missing leg. Several texts on economics and mathematics ornamented the top.

To my surprise and undisguised delight, the Empire looked as much library as saloon. Books were piled everywhere. They lined the back bar in a neat row. They served, in small, square towers, for shelf supports. They balanced in weighty stacks on boards that substituted for a counter.

Nailed to a support, I saw a black-framed diploma. Inspecting it, I discovered the proprietor of the Empire Saloon was indeed what he claimed to be: a professor. The diploma caught my attention as the congregation dissolved following that first impromptu Sunday service. The minister had enjoined his listeners to leave off imbibing spirits, to Professor Tyler's amusement. Most of them had departed on the minister's coattails, milled in the street briefly, then ducked back in through the canvas door in ones and twos, looking sheepish.

"I have abandoned the university, you see, in hopes of 'greater prospects,' " the professor said, noting my examination of his premises.

"I should say you have not so much abandoned the university as carted it with you, Professor, from the looks of your library."

"Mart, please. Call me Mart. It's more suited to my new profession. As for the books," he shrugged, "a habit, a hobby. A few I brought. Some I found by the roadside in my travels. Most came to me, carried by men grown weary of the weight. Word gets around. It's believed I'll exchange drink for a book."

"And will you?"

His eyes twinkled. "Madam, are you proposing a trade?"

I smiled. "No, just getting the measure of your devotion to your new calling."

"Ah, you have found me out. I am but a dilettante, a dabbler, a neophyte. That is my calling. California dizzies me with possibilities. Anything is likely here. Even that I be a pianist, having acquired the instrument."

"Yes," I said, looking at Janey, who remained at its broken keys, coaxing from them another hymn. She had continued to play, oblivious of the congregation's departure.

"I fear it is not such an instrument as to be envied," Mart said, watching with me. "Nor is my talent."

"Is it you, then, plays evenings?" I asked.

"Commonly. Take that as you wish. It is no astonishment, I suppose, that I have but recently made my debut as a pianist. I envy your daughter's accomplishments."

"Yes," I said.

She looked up at me then and smiled.

Janey's expression on sitting down to the piano, poor instrument though it was, lightened my heart. And when, in short time, Mart Tyler proposed Janey play an hour each evening for his customers, I could not say no. It was a small thing to give my dear daughter who had lost so much.

Janey was thirteen now, and more a young woman than a girl. Until then, I had not permitted myself to think how her education had been neglected since leaving Illinois. I had such larger regrets. But here was opportunity to amend the deficiency.

I elicited from Professor Tyler a ready commitment to instruct Janey in suitable studies in exchange for her playing. After a survey of his library, we agreed on mathematics, Latin, rhetoric, and history. And it was in support of this arrangement that I obtained the services of Susan Jackson to help me evenings in my restaurant while Janey, after her hour at the Empire's piano, studied. It was a solution of such elegance all around that I took untoward pride in the achieving of it.

Zeb tells me that's when I first began to "puff up," as he calls it, from being so taken by success. And that it became me. I don't recollect his saying so. But I believe him. He's a praising kind of man.

Statehood

Traders and teamsters followed news of a strike the way carnival wagons trail a circus parade, so I was not surprised to see Zeb every six weeks or so. For me, his arrival meant fresh provisions and news of Douglas, whose good health and well-being Zeb announced at once, knowing my ears yearned to hear it.

Just this morning Zeb asked how my narrative progressed and laughed when I told him that's all I remember of his visits until November of that year. "Sarah, Sarah," he said, "you thought I brought you so little? You never noticed my heart on my sleeve?"

"Even then?" I said.

"Even then."

Half the men in town might have declared themselves, for all I knew, so intent was I on my business. I wrote Mother of it, brief letters she never saw, announcing we would be home soon, and little more. I could not say what was in my heart, and little enough of how we lived. She would have been appalled to know Janey performed in a saloon. I never mentioned it. Few back home would have believed how things were in California, they were that different.

My daughter's audience of dusty-booted miners might have been Boston Brahmins and the Empire Saloon a concert hall, there was that much respect in it. After Janey agreed to play, Mart laid out rough-hewn planks for a stage, on which he placed the piano, surrounding it with footlights he manufactured from candles stuck in whiskey bottles. She played at six each weekday evening, familiar ballads mostly, requested by her homesick audience circled up close on unmated chairs, hands on their knees, tears in their eyes.

Townspeople came, too, including me. As often as possible. It gave me such joy to see my daughter happy. I would sit in the back with my eyes closed, imagining her at the old piano at home, pink roses perfuming the parlor, Mother humming the tune as she rocked with her knitting in her lap. So long ago.

As a consequence of the townspeople gathering so often to hear Janey play, the Empire Saloon evolved into a town hall of sorts. It was where we met to exchange news and announcements, to plan fund-raising events, and it served as the foremost locus of the town's state-hood observance.

For months the whole town had been all on tiptoe to hear of California's admission to the Union. We had the good news in October. I confess I caught the excitement, it was that contagious. Zeb delivered the flags and bunting and banners Mart had ordered, and Janey and I helped decorate the Empire for celebration of the great event. I baked, with Susan's help, great numbers of apple pies, warmly fragrant with the cinnamon Douglas sent. Susan made her sweet-potato pies, too. I recognized competition when I tasted it, and congratulated her with the prediction that the miners' Sunday footraces would one day be run for her pies and not mine.

All the women brought heaps of food, stews and baked beans and put-up pickles they spread out on the Empire's bar top skirted with swooped bunting. At the appointed hour, Mr. Stamps, the town alcalde, awkward with responsibility, mounted the stage, leaned an elbow on the banner-draped piano, and delivered a notably nasal speech appreciated principally for its brevity.

One of the Stamps children, a girl, recited a poem, and Janey played all the favorites the miners loved, giving two recitations of "O Susanna." Mart banged out his edition of a patriotic march. Everyone ate heartily, littering the street with pie crumbs and dropped pickles as they trooped to the square at Broad and Main streets. Mrs. Stamps had stitched a flag, and with suitable ceremony it was raised on a pine tree trimmed and rigged for a flagpole. The flag's likeness of a grizzly bear was at best implied, some critics observing the resemblance more favored a pig.

The women and children retired amid shouts and cries when the miners, lacking ball and cannon, lighted a barrel of black powder for the purpose of launching an anvil skyward. The planners were well satisfied, their objective being met when the anvil flew a not inconsiderable distance before thudding into the street. As anticipated, the miners, imbibing immoderately, discharged their pistols and rifles skyward throughout the night and well into the morning, fortunately without untoward consequence.

My enthusiasm for this event, I suppose, was buoyed by the imminent prospect of returning home. By October I had paid all my debts, including the seven hundred dollars owed Zeb. He objected when I delivered the first payment, one hundred dollars in gold, into his hands in April, but he never objected again. "And risk your lavish condemnation twice?" he laughed, when I reminded him this morning. "No, thank you."

I did light into him, I fear, so great was my affront. I had worked myself to exhaustion, baking from dawn to dusk and serving up countless pies from my little counter on Main street, each evening weighing out the dust and coins collected in a tin bowl, putting a little aside toward my debt, and proud of the accomplishment.

When I had saved one hundred dollars and Zeb arrived the end of April, he said something foolish about it having been his pleasure to deliver me to such success. And I replied, polite enough, "Please allow me the dignity of paying my debts without argument, Zeb." But persisting in his objection, he then said he never expected payment.

"I am not come so far to accept charity, Mr. Zebulon Tillman!" I exploded, and thrust the bag of dust and coins at him.

No more was said on the matter. I had the debt paid in full, as all others, by the end of September. And I set my sights on home.

"I think we can be home for Christmas, Janey," I said late that evening of the statehood celebration, offering the news like a present. In the dark beyond our tent, we heard gunshots and shouts intended for California. My imagination borrowed their exuberance for Illinois.

Janey was reading by the light of a lantern some treatise on democracy that Mart had set her to for the occasion. She looked up from her book and said, "That soon?"

In my enthusiasm I assumed hers. And failed to note its absence in her voice.

"With what we have now, plus the sale of the restaurant things for whatever they'll bring, we'll have close to fifteen hundred dollars by the time Zeb comes again," I said, columning with my pencil on a scrap of paper a tower of encouraging numbers. "We'll go back with him to Sacramento City and collect up your brother, and — "

I stopped there, unable to continue. I had been about to say "board the steamer," when remembrance overwhelmed me. Sacramento City. Last repose of my laughing, curly-headed Hannah. In memory I saw her again, playing with the kitten behind my shanty restaurant on K street; running to Zeb at sound of his voice, squealing "Punkin!" and cradling her red-kerchief doll; preening in Fannie's Chinese shawls. And buried beneath the sycamores. Like Caleb beneath the desert sands, and George in the wilderness. Remembrance collapsed my heart when I thought how half my family had been lost to me.

More than half, as it happened.

Zeb returned to Nevada City the first week in November, bringing Douglas with him. And Douglas brought the letter.

November in the Sierra foothills is beautiful, with hillsides carpeted in crisping, rust-colored leaves drifted from oak and madrone, a prediction of winter on the wind whispering the pines, the air clear and brilliant as new glass. It was just such an afternoon, that one, when Zeb and Douglas stepped through the canvas doorway of my restaurant. I rushed to Douglas at the welcome and unexpected sight of him, crying my thanks to Zeb. I thought he had brought Douglas to me as a gift, that I might have his company for the journey home the sooner.

I threw my mothering arms about my son, a boy of fifteen grown to manhood. He was so tall, so much taller than I remembered. I stood back, my hands clutching his elbows, my eyes drinking in his face. His mien, always sober, looked too solemn. Behind me, the stove spit and crackled.

"What is it?" I asked, knowing there was something, seeing it in his eyes, feeling breath depart, tasting ashes in my mouth. I could not think, from having endured the worst, what injury might now be ours.

"There's a letter, Ma."

"A letter?" I stepped back, knowing in my marrow, I suppose, I didn't want this letter.

Douglas took from his pocket a thin blue envelope, orderly black script on its face, and held it out to me. "Came addressed to us," he said, "the family, general delivery, Sacramento City." And he put it in my hand.

I stared at the words on the front — "Daniels Family," neat and tidy in black — then turned it to the Illinois address on the reverse and saw the open flap. I looked up at my son. "You've read it?" I asked, knowing he had.

The letter from the church sexton's wife said my mother had died in June of 1849, nearly eighteen months ago, of cholera contracted from an emigrant family returning east from Independence with a change of heart. My mother had invited them to stay with her.

The black script crept on: "We buried her in her Sunday best," it said, "the lavender silk with lace at the sleeves. She was as beautiful in death as in life. We put her to rest next to Harlan and covered their graves with the pink roses she loved so. The ceremony was a simple one, but fitting. All Lacy's music students still about were there, and each played on the church piano a hymn she loved. We did all we could for her that we thought you might wish."

Across the bottom of the sheet, in another hand, which I took for the sexton's, was the message that the men of the village had boarded up the house and that we might expect on our return to find it as we left it.

In my mind's eye I saw the brick house with its windows boarded. It looked like a dead person with the eyes stroked shut. That image seemed more credible than my mother's death, which, by reason of its remoteness in time and distance, refused belief. Not having beheld her death, nor touched its insult upon her countenance, not having laid her out, nor seen the earth embrace her, this death had no substance. It was but words, black ink on blue paper. I knew death, and this was not it. Death I had held in all its stillness, felt absence against my heart. Death by missive was no death at all. My mother dead? I couldn't fathom it.

"I just wrote her to say we'd be home for Christmas," I said, staring at the letter. I folded the sheet and replaced it in its thin blue envelope.

"Janey," I said through a tightened throat, looking up into my son's sympathetic eyes. Having absorbed the news before, he was less possessed by it than I. "She's gone to the book and stationery store."

"I'll tell her, if you want me to, Ma."

"No, it's my place, but come. She'll want to see you."

Zeb took my shawl from its piney hook. "It's cold out," he said, placing it around my shoulders. It was a tender gesture.

"She'll want to see you, too, Zeb."

Such a long walk it seemed, that short distance down Broad street to where it formed an elbow and returned back up the hill as Main. Our boots on the plank walkways sounded loud but remote, removed. In a stiff voice I introduced Douglas to smiling neighbors and customers encountered en route. I identified to him, as we passed, the Bella Union gambling hall, the Empire Saloon, and the Dawson, and the new wood buildings that were Billy Williams' tin shop, Mr. Gates' ten-pin bowling alley, the Nevada Hotel, and the Yuba, too. I named them like a sightseer's guide. It was something to do. Zeb followed behind, as though to catch me should I lose my starch and crumple.

For his part, Douglas remarked our cosmopolitan populace as a dozen placid-faced Chinese men trudged past toward the creek in their costume of gowns and wide trousers. "This town looks a miniature of Sacramento City."

My sightseer's-guide voice replied, "The China men keep to themselves mostly, like the Kanakas. Eat their own food. I've fed most of the others, though. Chileans and French, Irish and Dutch, Germans and Turks."

And then we were at Truex and Blackman's, the general merchandise store at the bend where Coyote street forked right from Main. "Here," I said, stopping on the boardwalk in front.

Inside, we found Janey perched on a nail keg in the corner Charles Mulford claimed for his book and stationery store. His "store" consisted mostly of a plank board displaying letter paper and envelopes, sealing wax and wafers, indelible inks and steel pens. He also kept a nice selection of periodicals and newspapers, books of fiction, poetry, and religion. He allowed Janey the privilege of reading whatever volumes of fiction came his way, she having exhausted Mart's. She held in her hands a new volume, closed it when she saw us, started to smile and then didn't. A flourish of embossed gold proclaimed the title in her hands, *Dombey and Son.* Janey was at an age to favor Dickens.

"Afternoon, Mrs. Daniels," said Charley Mulford with a nod of recognition to Zeb.

Charley and his friend Niles Searles, a young lawyer also from New York, had, like so many young men who expected to mine California's gold, gone to less laborious avenues for it. From their rented corner in the store of Truex and Blackman, young men like themselves, they dispensed books or legal advice, as the community required. Unfortunately, they were destined to lose everything in the fire.

I introduced Douglas to Charley in a wooden voice not lost on Janey. She stared at her brother and he at her. I saw between them a private exchange, a secret and silent language grown from suffering shared and endured. Janey came and leaned against her brother, and he took her in like a wanderer. "It's Gran," Douglas whispered, and held her as she began to weep.

I turned away, unable to bear the sight of my children grieving again, still. And I dry-eyed yet. Where did I store all those tears?

"They'll comfort one another more than you can," Zeb said. "I want you to come with me."

I didn't protest as he led me out, boots thumping on the wooden floor, and down the wooden steps.

"This way," he said, turning up Coyote street.

Coyote street ended in a path to Buckeye Ravine, and we followed that toward the stiff green fringe of trees surrounding the scarified bowl that was Nevada City and its diggings. Zeb was speaking, uttering sympathetic words I barely attended. I said nothing, felt hollow, didn't know or care where he was leading me as we climbed. But at last he stopped and turned to gaze at the town below us.

"Look at it, Sarah. That town, it's the beginning of things. You need to favor new beginnings now."

I remember thinking, as he sat me down on a tree stump and we caught our breath from the climb, how harsh and ugly and denuded the ramshackle town appeared. It didn't look like the beginning of anything. It looked like a sore, the hillsides rising from it scabbed by the stumps of trees sacrificed to planks for saloons and hotels. And gouged, too, by a thousand stabbing shovels. The men called this hill the Coyote Diggings, from its resemblance to the burrows of wild animals. The entrances to shaft mines gaped across the hillside like wounded mouths, the heaped pay dirt at their edges an earthy regurgitation. The place was all but deserted now, late in the day, digging done. Sounds from town rose distant and unidentifiable. A blue jay squawked from the branch of a wind-whispering pine atop the ridge.

I shook my head at the plank-and-canvas town cobbled together in the bottom of the red-brown bowl with the dirty dribbling ribbon that was Deer Creek. It did not look like a place one could love. "I leave it with small regret," I said.

I watched miners, miniatured by distance, laboring slowly at the creek, dots of red shirts, and blue. November's brittle light, bright as splintered glass, hurt my eyes. I covered them with my hands and buried my face in my lap.

Zeb hunkered down beside me and after a time began speaking to the hard sky, and I at length began to attend him. I heard him talking about Missouri, and a farm, and someone named Elizabeth. His familiar gravelly voice sounded different, not his, more the monotone of a child put to recitation.

"Elizabeth was from Massachusetts, too, like my ma and pa," he said, "and like them not fit enough for Missouri's hardships. Something about New England must put ideas in motion. All those unrealistic expectations of land. They learned land from books and visionaries and romantic societies. They were just a headmaster and a teacher, misled by expectation to love the land. It did not love them back. The land's not that easy. Not for people who know it just from books. But I was their only child, born to them late, and they thought to give me the great gift of land. And set out for it and found it in Missouri, a hardscrabble place that ruined their health. But they instilled in me, true enough, a love for soil, taught it to me the way a mother bird teaches flight, without alternative. And they succeeded. I loved as much as anything in the world the sight of green creeping from the earth to meet the sun.

"Elizabeth was a neighbor's cousin, came out to teach school. Forsook it for us, for my mother and father, to care for them when I could not. They had grown so old and frail. The ague finally took them. And then there was just me, and Elizabeth. And she stayed on. Me, a farmer with no prospect but hardship. She had a kind heart, but a weak one. It failed her when the girl was born. Buried two before that, both boys, born still and blue. The girl lived, for a time, not much, maybe a week. She was too little. I didn't name her, knew she wouldn't survive. Didn't name any of them. Elizabeth died the day after the girl. I buried them together, our daughter in Elizabeth's arms. She always said she wanted just to hold one of her babies."

Zeb's arm was around my shoulders, and shaking. But it wasn't him. It was me, wracked with sobbing. I don't know when I began to weep, when my hands over my eyes became slick with tears, when the taste of ash in my mouth turned salt, nor when my breath and shoulders failed to contain my weeping. Sometime in the telling, from that voice, that sorrowful voice. I wept. And then sobbed. And cried some more, and couldn't stop. I wept for Zeb's sorrow, and for mine, for all of us. I wept for my mother, and poor Elizabeth who departed life never knowing a child's love, and for all the children. I wept for Caleb, for Hannah, for George. I wept from an overwhelming grief for lives not lived, and lives too brief. And from the terrible unbearable anguish of loss.

When I could speak, I raised my head, stared at the ugly little town below, and said, "I want to go home. I just want to go home."

"You won't find them there, Sarah," Zeb said, looking at me, shaking his head. "It's lonely, the company of ghosts. I know."

I stared into his sad gray eyes. "How do you abide it?"

He had one knee on the ground, in the crisp November leaves, an elbow on the other. He regarded my tear-stained face as though gauging my ability to understand, then said, "This is how it is, Sarah. We just continue. We go on, life goes on." He took my hand, stroked it with his own. "Joy survives. You'll see. In the small things, like the sight of green in spring. I'm still moved by that miracle."

I reclaimed my hand, pulled my shawl close against the chill. "I just want to go home," I said, shaking my head.

Zeb stood. "You can't."

Nevada City

Being neither philosopher nor religionist, I cannot position to my mind's satisfaction a slaughtering disease like cholera. It will not cipher. Were it the work of a wrathful God, as some insist, why should the innocent suffer? Some, claiming God chastised the nation for greed, laid the blame to gold. I think perhaps we lend explanation to the inexplicable from need of the comfort, that we might provide reason where reason is defied. I do not know.

I do know that the cholera epidemic of 1849, which gathered in my mother, defied every conception previously respected. We thousands heading west on the road to California knew not of the devastation behind us and learned it late. More than five thousand perished in New York City alone. St. Louis lost ten percent of its populace. Scores succumbed in villages and towns in every state. And the respectable householder fell with the vice-ridden and slothful. What retribution of a vengeful God should be thus visited upon innocent and guilty alike? What cried the pastors from the pulpits when the very president of the United States fell to it? Poor man, he did not live to see the day of national fast and prayer he had called for against the disease.

To a rational mind, the conclusion was clear: cholera held no favorites. No one was exempt. A sensible man was right to fear it.

And so, when the pestilence revisited in 1850, touching down in Sacramento City like a tornado, Zeb plucked my son from its path. I shall be forever grateful. That city's newspapers reported the cemetery looked like a newly ploughed field, so numerous were the graves. In a brief three weeks, nearly a thousand victims fallen to cholera joined my Hannah on the hillside.

And Zeb was right. I could not go home.

In that November of hard light and soft breezes, cholera stayed the steamers. Half Sacramento City's population fled, by horse, mule, wagon, afoot, and aboard such ships as could sail. The remaining vessels lay at anchor in the river, unmanned or quarantined.

By the time circumstances permitted travel, I had lost fervor for the journey, though not intention. The brick house would keep. No one waited for us there. I had begun the slow weaning from its illusion of safety. Though I had not witnessed it, death had invaded there, and the loss of my mother sucked wind from my sails, subtracted urgency from my plans. So it seemed a small thing to indulge my son, beguiled by gold.

"Ma," he said one day, after a morning's staring at the pockmarked hillside, "I could maybe try my hand at coyoting for a time. What do you think?"

"We'll be leaving soon, you know."

"We're not gone yet."

I heard reluctance in his deepened voice. What was there for him in Illinois? But I suppose I believed that I owned him, the way Captain Thorn owned Susan, although I never entertained the thought in that light. Whither I goest.

I thought a few months of toilsome labor must arrest ambitions of a mineral nature. "I expect we might go home in the spring instead of now," I said, "and you might occupy yourself with mining in the meanwhile."

The rains came late that winter. Half the miners had moved on, discouraged. A third of the town was for sale, and claims readily available.

"You give your boy most your goin'-home money, didn't you?" Susan said one evening as she set out the little cruets and fixings for our diminished trade.

I shrugged. "I'll earn more, or maybe he'll make a strike."

"You gots the better chance, and you know it. But not by much measure. Mercy me, if'n the rains don't come, won't be a miner left to feed."

The truth of it was that business about town had all but collapsed with the departing miners. And the wonder was the town didn't. But there were women there — I should think at least thirty, perhaps forty, and not anxious to move on. More than a dozen took boarders or ran hotels with their husbands. Others worked in the taverns. Three were married to prominent merchants and kept servants themselves. The women of Nevada City possessed the makings of a permanent community.

It began to emerge after Christmas.

Most of the town's nearly three thousand residents celebrated the holiday in a particularly secular, California fashion. Men on their own readily discard the conventional and decorous ceremonies women advocate. No church services or hymn singing disturbed the miners of Nevada City from their irreverent Christmas observance of immoderate drinking, shouting, and shooting. I expect the drink and din drowned their longing for loved ones at home.

They organized two balls, tickets ten dollars, patronized almost exclusively by themselves. Mary Mahaffey attended both, but most of the "lady" dancers could be identified only by strategically placed patches upon their pants. Or so Douglas reported from a curiosity not to be denied. He slipped away a time or two from our gathering on Broad street.

Ours was a secular observance, too. Circumstance inclined me from religion, to which I had never been greatly attracted. I liked the fact of church and sermons but lacked devotion. It might have comforted me in the bad times, but I was too late for adoption.

Still I was not without my list of things to be grateful for. I had my first-born son, tall and brown and strong, and my beautiful Janey. We had our health and good friends in the town. Douglas brought in a small and beautifully shaped fir tree, which we decorated with ornaments fashioned from bits of colored paper, and a garland of bright red berries Janey collected from bushes along the creek.

We had gifts for each other on Christmas Eve, too, as we sat warm by the stove, amid the fragrance of our tree and the fir boughs Janey fastened everywhere with strips of red calico. I gave Douglas a brass scale to weigh out the gold from his claim, and he presented me with a brandy bottle containing an inch of the golden metal he'd dug, tied with a bit of ribbon, and to his sister, its junior likeness in a syrup jar. I'd bought sheet music and two Dickens novels for Janey, handsome editions Charley Mulford obtained for me, and a length of dress cloth in soft merino woolen of a blue that matched her eyes. In return she gave us a concert of songs she'd written herself, singing in a voice so sweet I could not fault Miss Montez for wanting to confiscate it to her own use when that time came.

I invited Susan and proudly put into her hands a set of primers all her own, with paper and pencils for practicing her figures. And she brought a wonderfully worked gingerbread house fragrant with spices, its rooftop rimmed in a candy confection of imagined icicles.

Christmas Day dawned clear and gentle as any day in May. The California climate is a wonder in winter, with unexpected gifts of spring-time. Zeb was early at the door, having come to town the night before on a freighting trip from Marysville. He surprised us with a fat goose, preserved cranberries, walnuts, raisins, all the fixings for a fine Christmas dinner, the procurement of which made a generous gift. He cracked and shelled the walnuts and told the children stories of his travels, while outside, miners thronged the streets and shot the sky, and auctioneers hollered a brisk Christmas business. I cooked through the morning, and we had such bounty I sent Douglas to invite Mart Tyler to our table, he'd been so good to Janey, and Susan, if she could come. Mart returned with Douglas, bringing books for all of us, two on geology for my son, his passion undiminished, plus wine for the table. I added some to a sauce I concocted from cranberries and raisins, and it was roundly acknowledged delicious.

It was a Christmas joy, our table. Despite the tears I brushed away throughout the day, thinking of those forever lost, I had still this family, these friends, and Christmas never seemed so precious. Zeb's presence and the knowledge of his loss lent me grateful awareness; some had no family at all, and I counted my blessings.

How memory recalls the fragrance of that roasting goose with its dried-apple-and-walnut stuffing, the crackling and spitting from the stove. It transports me back. That was my first day in California not wracked by heartache and regret. We all of us sang carols and shared happy remembrances of Christmases past, toasting our unknown future with Mart's wine. Susan joined us, reporting that Captain Thorn retired early to his especially "spirited" observance. She brought a Christmas cake warm from the oven and fragrant with rum.

Laughing, she said, "Captain, he don't miss a little rum, and if he do, I figure he don't want no cake around it." She handed it to me with a bright smile. "'Bout got shot by those crazy miners, I did, bringin' it over here. Never seen no Christmas like this one."

Nor had any of us. We all joined in the old, dear carols and Susan sang us songs from the South in her round Alabama voice, and I blessed freedom. I can still wrap that Christmas around me like a shawl just thinking on its warmth. We never keep Christmas now without roast goose. Zeb sees to that. And Susan never fails to send a rum cake.

It was from Susan we had first news of Mary Mahaffey's proposal.

"That Miss Mary, she traipse over to the captain's this morning, bold as brass," Susan said, cutting Douglas a second piece of cake. "She still in her dancin' dress! Tells the captain she want to hire me for a servant at her weddin' party."

Mart Tyler nearly choked on his wine. "Wedding! Who's the lucky man? And I say 'lucky' advisedly."

Susan clucked agreement. "Can't be from around here, I don't suppose. But I 'spect you be gettin' your invitation. 'All the important people' to be invited, that what she said. Captain won't be goin', nor me. Told her, he did, I weren't for rent to the likes of her. Reminds him of his wife, I 'spect."

Because Mary Mahaffey's hoax provoked the respectable women of Nevada City into the church fund-raising, I include the telling in this account. It was, as Mart Tyler observed, "as superb a take-in as was ever got up to guzzle the gullible."

Mary Mahaffey was a passing-through kind of woman who stayed a time in Nevada City. Young, pretty, and wild, she was a favorite with a certain class — the loafers, gamblers, cheats, and blacklegs. Thinking it a great joke, some of them persuaded a young rancher visiting from Bear Valley to ask Mary for her hand. Green as grass, and smitten, he did. She joined in the mischief, confessed she loved him above everything and needed three hundred dollars for wedding clothes. He gave it, and fifty more to the "minister" who married them, a gambler by name of Jack White, and an ounce to a masquerading county clerk, Tom Marsh, proprietor of Dawson's Saloon, where the "wedding" was got up on New Year's Eve with dinner and drinks for all the guests. Only when the greenhorn attempted to take his "wife" off to his ranch did Mary announce the joke by flourishing a pistol and calling him a fool. That he was, and something near a thousand dollars poorer for it.

Everyone in town had the story. Most of the single men, I suppose, thought California "against the world for fun and adventure," as they were fond of saying. But the ladies of Nevada City were not amused by this mockery of matrimony. And when Mary Mahaffey's "committee of organizers" let out they expected to try the performance over again, the ladies leaned on their men to put a stop to it. And they did.

I believe that was the beginning of civilized expectations for the little town. Soon after, Miss Bowers, sister of the Bowers brothers, came calling with her proposal.

The Bowers brothers had an express office on the road to Sacramento, just south of Deer Creek. Before the post office was established, they took letters to San Francisco and brought back mail addressed to Nevada City. They did a respectable business in that trade, charging two dollars and a half for whichever direction they carried letters. It may have been their collection of undeliverable mail from the States that prompted Miss Bowers' idea.

"A fund-raising bazaar is what I'm thinking," she said, sipping tea proper as a queen from the cracked cup I offered. She was a long-faced woman with pinched manners, a spinster of advancing years, dependent on her brothers. I expect they may have thought her chances better in California than the East, and I believe I did hear recently of her marriage to a lapsed Episcopalian with plans for a ten-pin bowling alley in Trinity County.

"A fund-raising?" I said, offering the sugar bowl.

She spooned a large helping. "Indeed, you are agreed, I am sure, that society here is in need of improvement," she said, vigorously stirring her tea. The spoon made a noisy clicking.

"Indeed."

"Godforsaken, that's what these miners are, Mrs. Daniels, godforsaken. Of women like Mary Mahaffey, I need say nothing." She frowned over her cup as she took a delicate sip.

"And you propose to – ?"

"Build a church and hire a pastor. In support of which I take upon myself the task of a ladies' bazaar for the purpose of obtaining the money. I expect you shall wish to participate."

"If I can assist your cause, Miss Bowers – "

"*Our* cause, Mrs. Daniels, *our* cause. We shall improve society. And you may assist most admirably, I am sure, by the selling of your pies."

Miss Bowers, proving indefatigable to her purpose, soon enough organized Nevada City's first fund-raising ladies' bazaar. She secured the use of a building at the head of Broad street, erected by the owner, Dr. Weaver, for trade. With the decline in population, it stood empty. Miss Bowers enlisted Janey for the decorating committee, and Janey prevailed upon Mart Tyler to lend his bunting and banners from the statehood celebration. These she mounted on the walls, along with sweet-smelling fir boughs.

We all got caught up in the preparations, it being a worthy cause and a change from routine. Douglas induced some carpenters who made a living shoring tunnels to erect a booth inside for my pie and coffee stand. Janey agreed to sing songs for a dollar a minute, and Phoebe Kidd to sell taffy, and I can't recall what all Miss Bowers devised for the dozen or more women she pressed to partake. I do remember that Mrs. Scott, who worked in one of the taverns, persuaded its owner to lend a large scale. It reminded me of the one the Pioneers had used to weigh baggage.

"To guess weights," Miss Bowers said with triumphant satisfaction on seeing it installed.

Almost before we knew it, Miss Bowers had her bazaar. The novelty drew nearly everyone respectable, including any miner with a nugget to spend.

First off, there was a two-dollar admission charge. As I recall, Mrs. Stamps collected that. Then, just inside the door, Miss Bowers had set up a kind of post office with herself as postmistress.

"I believe I have a letter for you," she announced to each visitor.

As her brothers' express service was well known to the town, nearly everyone fell to her game. I had my pie and coffee booth opposite and watched with admiration as she drew in visitors as guilelessly as a practiced monte dealer. I remember a young friend of Douglas's, a boy of seventeen from Ohio named Charley Ferguson, getting caught out twice.

"Two dollars and a half," she announced when he asked for the promised letter.

Young Ferguson eagerly handed over the amount, not suspecting the game. Seeing me, he waved and came over for a pie, the letter in his hand. He looked at it curiously, opened it, turned it this way and that.

"What's the problem?" I asked, all innocence.

"This looks to be written in Dutch or Indian or something," he said, showing it to me. "I can't make out a word of it."

"There's been some mistake, and you've got the wrong letter," I said, smiling past him at Miss Bowers. She was biting her lip to keep from laughing.

"Yes, that's it, I suppose," Charley said.

He returned the letter to her, and she took it with a smile, saying, "Dear me, how stupid I was." She fumbled through her pile of mail again, procured a second letter, and held it aloft like a prize. "Ah, here's yours."

Charley held out his hand, but Miss Bowers shook her head. "Two dollars and a half."

Poor Charley, on opening a second indecipherable letter, caught on, and then fell in with Mrs. Scott.

"Why, Charles Ferguson," she exclaimed, "dear me, is that you? I hardly knew you. Have you been sick?"

"Why, no, ma'am, I haven't."

"Oh, you do look fallen away though!"

"I don't think so."

"I'm sure you have. Just step up on these scales and we'll see."

He dropped to her game, innocent as a lamb, and when he weighed five pounds more than usual, Mrs. Scott shook her head and said, "Well, well, I was mistaken. People are liable to be deceived. That will be two dollars, please."

Douglas laughingly reported that Charley wasn't in the house an hour before he reckoned the experience cost him thirty dollars.

I don't remember how much money was raised, but it was considerable.

And no one blamed the ladies' bazaar for the rowdy celebration got up later that night by Mary Mahaffey and her friends in sham imitation. They held their event at the bowling alley on Main street, which they decorated with bouquets of newspapers. No one present could recall who, dancing a jig for a dollar whiskey in the wee hours, kicked over the lantern that ignited the decorations.

And burned down half the town.

Fire

Clanging bells and shouts of "Fire! Fire!" jolted us from sleep. Janey and
I leapt from our beds, threw shawls over our nightclothes, and rushed
into the street. Douglas, whose tent formed a lean-to against the restaurant, joined us in an instant.

All was pandemonium, people running, screaming, shouting, avail-
ing nothing. A tower of fire lighted the night sky, casting dancing
shadows among the people scurrying about in its eerie illumination.
There was nothing to do but flee. Building after building of tinder-dry
planks and canvas caught fire, flaring like pine-needle torches. Flames
spread from the bowling alley at Main and Coyote streets, consumed
one side of Main, then the other. They passed to Broad via Pine street,
burned all of Pine and the lower portion of Broad.

Nevada City's great fire of March 1851 raged from one-thirty in the
morning until seven, when it extinguished itself in the pink light of
dawn for want of anything left to destroy. More than a hundred buildings had turned to ash. Losses were staggering. The Turners' hotel,
valued at ten thousand dollars, was entirely consumed. Mart lost the
Empire, lost everything, his books and the piano, for all of which
Janey wept. Charley Mulford and Niles Searles found their slate wiped
clean, everything they owned gone, to the estimated value of four

thousand dollars. The tin shop went, as did stores, homes, taverns, Captain Thorn's log house, the Masonic lodge, the blacksmith's shop. The catalog of loss is too lengthy to list.

Among the buildings that survived, most of them farther up Broad street or away from town, I number my own.

I set down these particulars with little feeling now, despite the sense of devastation I shared with those who lost all. I suppose that is because the greater sensation resides with the memory of nearly missing happiness. For it was at the time of the fire I told Zeb I would not marry. The thought that I might have missed this happiness — and you! — sucks breath from me like a fireball.

I remember how the scene of ruin drove me. I was a woman possessed. Disaster had bypassed me this time, albeit within a hair's breadth, and I felt I must feed everyone, rebuild their homes, restore the place I had gripped with my fingertips for a year. Was it because I had been spared? Or because I could do something? Did I recall the desert, when I could barely help my own? I don't remember and have not the wisdom to know.

By noon that first day, I had exhausted my provisions. Whatever I had, I pressed on those who had not. So many lost everything and could not buy the meanest necessaries. I dispensed what remained of my going-home money, bought provisions from those who had them, then spent on credit for more. I baked and cooked and put an eager Janey to the task of pressing food on the hungry. Douglas was a whirlwind, too, carting away the debris of blackened ruins, removing from sight and smell their acrid stench. Afterward, he carried down the mountain fresh-cut pine planks pungent with forest fragrance, helped erect new walls.

It was wonderful to see how quickly the town bandaged its wounds with new buildings. I number among my satisfactions my participation in that achievement. When there was nothing else I could do, I took up a hammer or saw, laid a sill on earth still warm from ashes, nailed shakes, stretched new muslin. It is a fine feeling to admire one's own useful handiwork, though it be but a patch on the quilt.

"You were learning to love beginnings, Sarah," Zeb said, when I recounted the memory at breakfast this morning.

Some of the people ruined moved on, left devastation and took its memory. But there was a sense of town here for many, among them my friends, for whom this was home. I was the more fortunate, not just because my Broad street building had been spared, but because a home, a real home, awaited me in Illinois. *When there is nothing else,* I thought, *there must at least be the hope of home.* And so I helped however I could to secure for others what I held so dear in memory.

Zeb arrived a few days after the fire, news of it having found him in Marysville.

I was at my table, its oilcloth strewn with flour, kneading dough for bread. I looked up from my work to see his kind gray eyes as he stood in my open doorway.

At sight of him, the tears I had but lately learned to shed again leapt into my own. "Oh, Zeb, it was terrible! Mart lost all his books. Everything was so black and ugly." I wiped my floury hands on my apron, dabbed by eyes. "Oh, forgive me. Come in, sit down. You must be hungry. Let me get you something to eat."

"Sarah, I've seen Mart, talked to Douglas there, and Janey. You need to get away from this for a while."

"Get away? Why would I want to get away? I've got this bread to finish, and – "

"No argument, Sarah. Come take a ride with me, it'll do you good. Besides, I want you to see a piece of California that – "

"California!" I was raw with indignation over the town's devastation, dazed still by the memory of women weeping for treasures hauled half a continent and turned to ash. "I've seen all I want of California!"

"You haven't seen all *I* want of California, Sarah, and I'm asking you to come with me now. For my sake, if not your own. From what I hear, you could do with a rest. It's not much I'm asking."

I couldn't argue with that, and truth be told I was too tired to try.

Zeb had borrowed a horse and buggy, and before I knew it we were out of town and on the road toward Marysville. It was new to me then, that road, but I know it well now. Sun-dappled and fringed with oak and pine and madrone, it meanders down a gentle lessening of hills until it finally surprises with a broad and sudden vista of the great Sacramento Valley.

At that lowest of elevations, spring comes first and carpets the valley with lupine, butter yellow and creamy white, but mostly a blue so extensive it counterfeits a lake. Into this vast springtime exuberance, nature, for good measure, spills great golden tides of bright orange poppies like melted sun.

That first spring of my opened eyes, how those poppies dazzled. I had never beheld such a sea of color, never imagined such a wilderness garden. Flitting white butterflies danced among the flowers, bees buzzed their industry, the sun warmed my back, and the earth smelled rich and new.

I must have looked like a child at Christmas, Zeb grinned so as he helped me from the buggy. He unhitched the horse, and it nosed into a drift of pink-flowering clover as we strolled the edge of the garden carpet. Zeb plucked a poppy, handed me the vibrant color. Awed, I stroked the golden petals. They felt like velvet.

"I'm fixing to buy it, Sarah, a few hundred acres. And fixing to make it say "wheat." It's what I came to do, I suppose, although I didn't know it when I left Missouri. I was just going west then for want of better direction. But now I know my purpose. And it's come to this."

I found my voice. "I'm happy for you," I said, and meant it.

"It's a new beginning, California is. For lots of us. Even for some who never sought it, Sarah." He looked at me. "It's all new here, and new again, like Nevada City. Life, that's what counts. That's how things are, Sarah. We just keep going."

And then, as though he had rehearsed it, he took the kerchief from his neck and a penknife from his pocket. I watched as he dug up a clump of lupine and wrapped its roots in the kerchief.

"I was thinking you might plant this by your door, see if it takes," he said, handing it to me like a bouquet.

I smiled and took the flowers, but shook my head. "I can't tend them," I said, "as I expect to be going home soon. But thank you."

"Don't go, Sarah." Zeb put his hands on my shoulders and shook his head. "Don't go back. There's no one there. Stay here." And then, gentle as a child, he kissed me.

The unexpected gesture stunned me. I didn't know what to think. I started to say something, I can't imagine what, but Zeb put a finger to my lips.

"Hush, Sarah. Listen to me. Flowers can transplant. So can you. You start these lupine a new home. And I'll start you one. Stay."

Such a prospect defied my comprehension. It was an unconsidered possibility, as foreign to my thinking as Greek. We can so embrace an idea that it crowds all else from regard. The brick house was my sentinel, attaining it my engulfing objective. My compass possessed but one direction, and I was a blindered horse to everything else.

Zeb saw bewilderment and took it for indecision. "Marry me, Sarah. Think on it at least."

"Oh, Zeb, I'm as honored as I am surprised, but I can't stay here. I want to go home, I must go home. California frightens me. I'm such a mouse, you know."

"A mouse! You don't know yourself at all. Why, Sarah Daniels, you're the bravest woman I've ever known!"

That was such a nonsensical statement, I lay it at the feet of judgment besotted by spring. And I did not yet know one cannot go back. Or perhaps I did not recognize happiness, its being so long absent. I remained beyond the edge of wisdom then, blindered still, and unswayable.

Not that Zeb chanced further refusal. "As you wish, Sarah, as you wish." And never again, either by word or deed, did he revisit the subject. I might have thought the day imagined, so profound was his subsequent silence on it, were it not for the languishing lupine planted by my door.

As I had exhausted my funds for the present, I set my sights on Christmas for going home and put myself once again to accumulating the cost.

I did not think it would be difficult. Nevada City seemed a phoenix, it arose so quickly from its ashes. How the little town grew and prospered amazed us all. Several merchants built more substantially the second time, raised their buildings two stories and added false fronts. A meat market opened, as did a bakery. And a circus came to town. Janey studied Spanish lessons at the new reading room. A newspaper, the first, began publishing in mid-April. The *Nevada Journal* announced in its inaugural issue the election of the town's first mayor and ten aldermen, miners every one. Enthusiasts for a "real" town chose, in addition, a recorder, a constable, and a postmaster for the new post office.

In its September issue, the *Journal* published its first business directory. We had thirteen hotels, fifteen stores, eight saloons, two theaters, two churches, and any number of restaurants, boardinghouses, and taverns.

Douglas lent his newly learned carpentering skills to enlarging my restaurant and our home. By Christmas, we had a sizable and comfortably furnished house, with two bedrooms and a parlor adjoining the restaurant. It was a small expense, and I imagined that when the time came to leave, we could realize a good profit on the investment. I had pushed our departure date forward to spring, my funds accumulating steadily enough, although more slowly than in the past.

It seemed impossible that Christmas had come again so soon. Janey redoubled her efforts over the previous year, mounting boughs of fragrant fir everywhere. Douglas installed a perfectly shaped spruce tree in the parlor, and good friends helped us decorate, Mart Tyler, Susan, and Zeb among them. For dinner we enjoyed roast goose.

And Janey played the new piano.

Zeb drove his wagon into our yard late on Christmas Eve day, a huge crate aboard. While Janey and I stood mystified, Zeb signaled Douglas, who grinned in return, and the two of them walked off down the street. "Need to collect some hands," Zeb called over his shoulder.

It seemed but moments before they returned with a dozen beaming townsmen, and Susan Jackson, too. She stood by me in the falling dusk, approving the proceedings and shushing my questions. "You all just wait," she said.

With great huffing and puffing, and a "Heave to, boys!" shouted out, the crate came off the wagon and into my parlor, along with the crowd. My questions and Janey's went ignored.

"Got something to pry these boards off, Doug?" Zeb asked.

"Sure do."

And then to my utter amazement, the crate peeled away to reveal a piano, the most beautiful instrument I'd ever laid eyes on. Janey just stared, speechless, as someone knowledgeable began the task of tuning.

I turned on Zeb, a thousand thoughts tangling in my mind, convinced his long silence on the subject of my staying had come to this. Some vanity — or unconscious wish — concluded the piano a bribe. "You have spent your land money, your wheat money," I accused.

He shook his head and laughed. "You mistake the deliveryman for the giver, madam." He looked to Mart Tyler, who nodded back. There was a general puffing of importance among the assembled townsmen as Mart found a chair and pushed it into position before the instrument.

After looking around and receiving nods of approval from those gathered, he gestured to the seat and said to Janey, "Will you play? No one wants to hear me."

Janey stared at Mart, the chair, the piano. And remained rooted where she stood. Then suddenly everyone was laughing and talking as Mart took Janey's hand and led her to the piano. She touched a silky ivory key with one finger, the single note silencing the room. She looked at me, tears in her eyes, and the image of her standing there, caressing that one key, swam in my own wet vision.

Mart said, "Play, dear, we've all been waiting to hear you since the fire took your music from us." He turned to me. "You gave the town all you had and then some, Mrs. Daniels, you and yours. We wanted to show our gratitude."

My voice cracked, I was so moved. "But how — ? Who — ?"

Mart laughed. "Oh, a dozen or so readily raised the subscription. Even that old tightwad Thorn chipped in, though I think it was Susan threatening to run off may have done it." He winked at Susan, who shrugged and grinned back.

"Zeb passed the order through a steamer captain at Sacramento City," Mart said, "who took it to a consignment merchant in San Francisco. He pressed it on the first supercargo returning to New York City, and the whole process in reverse returned the instrument you see before you. Simplicity itself, madam. And tendered herewith, accompanied by our compliments and gratitude."

I whisked tears from my cheeks. "I don't know what to say, how to thank you, but — "

Mart came and took my hands in his. "We all know you're bent on leaving us. We want you to know we wish you wouldn't, that's all. And if you do, well, until then we'll have the pleasure of Janey's playing again." He kissed my hand.

Zeb had gone to Janey and was whispering in her ear. She smiled at him, dried her eyes with her apron hem, and sat to the instrument. She placed her fingers on the keys as delicately as a butterfly alights on a flower and began to play a piece she had learned the year before, a German song Mart translated as "Silent Night." The beautiful melody filled the room, and our hearts. My daughter played lovingly, sweetly, taking my thoughts to Christmases past, to a remembrance of my mother playing and teaching Janey, a child on her lap. It felt like home.

They still talk, those who were there, of the Christmas the piano came to Nevada City. Janey played for hours — all the carols, all the favorite ballads, all the songs that took hearts to thoughts of home. It was Douglas, stepping out late for more firewood, who discovered the listeners. He came for me, took my hand, said, "Come look, Ma, just come look."

Outside the house, miners had gathered in the hundreds, drawn from their drinking and cards by the sweet sound of Janey playing the piano. They stood everywhere — by the house, in the yard, in the street — silent as sentinels. They were listening to Christmas, to home. Tears on their faces glistened in the moonlight.

Freedom

So began my surcease from sorrow. For the gladness of present fortune I remain daily grateful. It was the other, all the death and suffering, I feared I could not tell. Now, from having told it upon these pages, I feel released. My lost loved ones, revisited in painful memory, have blessed me, permitted me the joy of new beginnings. These people, loved and gone, I want you to know them, and so understand the tears I may sometimes shed. One day you will ask about the sampler framed upon the parlor wall, the four tiny embroidered gravestones, the little house worked in red floss. And you will have the explanation in these pages.

This account goes too long, and the hard part told. People will share with you the happy stories, remember the good times, so I will but limn them here.

I did not, of course, go home to Illinois in that spring of 1852. California kept me, I might say by law. For in April of that year, the state legislature condemned Susan to slavery.

On an evening but three weeks before my own anticipated departure, she flew into my restaurant distraught.

"The captain say he going back to Georgia, where he come from," she cried, banging cruets and butter cups. "He say I gots to go, too!"

"That's nonsense, Susan. California's a free state. He can't — "

"Oh, he say he can, yes ma'am. I his, that's what he say, and he say the law says so."

"What law? There's no law — "

"Oh, there is now, yes ma'am. He read it out to me, that's the fact of it. And I talk to Mister Tyler, he being such a book and reading kind of man, and he say it true."

And it was true, and a sham on justice. In 1852, three years after a unanimously adopted constitution prohibited slavery, the California legislature, influenced by Southerners and pro-slavery forces, passed its own Fugitive Slave Bill. All slaves who had escaped into California, it stated, or who had been brought here before its admission to the Union as a free state were fugitives. And any person harboring them from return to their owners was subject to a thousand-dollar fine and six months' imprisonment.

Susan had come with Thorn in '49 in bondage, as his property. And now California law, in respect of property rights, determined she must remain so.

Her earnings from me she kept in a box buried beneath her cot. She brought them and we counted twice. Two hundred and twelve dollars.

The next day, as Susan's emissary, bristling with outrage, I took the box to Thorn at his dinner table. His rebuilt house was not so fine as the log one. He had not replaced the cushions and fine things after the fire. He sat then upon a rough bench before an equally rude table, eating his meal of chops. Susan, fear and hope in her eyes, stood at my side as I shoved the box of money at him.

"For the love of mercy," I cried, "you cannot return this woman to slavery. She knows the feel of freedom now and can earn her way. Take this and let her stay."

Thorn glanced at the box and then at me. "You got nine hundred dollars, she's yours," he said, sawing at his meat. "That's what I told your friend Tyler, that's what I'm telling you."

Did I hesitate? I don't recall. I remember only staring at him and turning on my heel. And then the finest satisfaction. I feel privileged it was mine.

It was but an hour's work. Our town was the seat of the newly created Nevada County. I knew everyone I needed — a lawyer, the justice of the peace, the county recorder. At one time or another, all had eaten at my table. I flew through the town, rousting them from their dinners, the lawyer first.

"Can you draw up some paper to say Susan Jackson is a free woman and Captain Josiah Thorn has no hold over her?"

"In respect for what?"

"What do you charge? I'll pay you."

"Nonsense. That's not what I mean. A deed of manumission requires a consideration, an exchange, a sum of money."

"Have it say nine hundred dollars."

I dragged the justice of the peace from his meal, and the recorder from his, collected the attorney's paper, and sent Douglas to tell Thorn and Susan to meet me at the courthouse.

For safekeeping, I had my funds on deposit with Wells Fargo, a new express agency on Main street. The agent lived above his office. He was Charley Mulford.

"I need a draft," I announced when he opened the door. I stood there as he prepared it and told him why.

At the courthouse there was a good deal of witnessing and sealing and signing. And smiling. And weeping. Susan and I hugged and cried, and I'll never forget her bright-shining eyes and awestruck countenance, the very face of freedom, when I laid the document across her pink palm.

She stared at it the longest while, repeating, "This my freedom paper, my freedom paper."

Charley Mulford was there, and Janey, and Douglas, and Mart Tyler, too. Was the happiness Janey and Douglas expressed entirely for Susan? Sometimes, in memory, I think back and believe I see reprieve on their countenances, a reprieve as much for themselves as Susan. They wouldn't be going home after all, not then, and they were glad. There was nothing in Illinois for them but my sorrow. California offered all possibilities. They saw it when I did not.

I later wished I'd contained my impulse until Zeb joined us, for it was a moment I wish I'd shared with him. Ah, if wishes were horses . . . I had not believed it possible, but new feelings, then too infant to identify, were quickening in my heart, were creeping from their long hiding. "Like green in spring," as Zeb says.

I first felt that quickening in the courthouse the day Susan Jackson held freedom in her palm. My heart swelled for her and missed another. Zeb had entwined his life with mine, but I was too blindered to see.

Charley Mulford said, "You want me to read it to you?"

Janey bristled. "She can read."

And Susan, with great dignity, read out in her round Alabama voice: "Know all men by these presents that I, Josiah Thorn, lately a citizen of the State of Georgia, and owner of slaves, do here by this instrument, under my hand and seal, and in consideration of the sum of nine hundred dollars to me in hand paid, have this day liberated, set free, and fully and effectually manumitted Susan Jackson, heretofore a slave for life, the lawful property of said Josiah Thorn."

Susan turned her soulful eyes on me and said, "You done give that man your goin'-home money, didn't you?" She shook her head. "I'll pay you back, Sarah Daniels, every penny, if I live and earn it."

That memory always conjures another, of crossing the Missouri on the St. Joseph ferry and meeting the colored man going to California for gold to redeem his wife and children. I pray he succeeded and so knew joy exceeding even my own. I never put gold to such good purpose as the day I bought freedom with it. I bless California for that incomparable privilege.

I refused Susan's two hundred and twelve dollars, advised her to start a pie shop with it. She did, and it prospers. She visits regularly with news and a pie and a ten-dollar gold piece.

The happy times everyone will talk about and long remember. Like the wedding, and the building of this house. And Janey — but lately surprising and gladdening us with her return, and you surprising her, in turn — will tell you her adventures in Australia. In fact, she has already begun, despite your infant comprehension.

When I began this long account, it was April. I have whiled away these many hours, watched summer come and go, the wheat grow tall and golden, and autumn come. Geese, flying south, stopped and fed from Zeb's second mowing. It's a joy to see them. And now it is late November, with its hard light and crisp nights, and Christmas coming. I had thought to invite Miss Montez for dinner, having forgiven her, but I read in the papers she sailed for New York on the twentieth. I hope she finds there some of the small happiness she enjoyed in Grass Valley.

When Lola Montez arrived in California in the summer of 1853, I was still bent on Illinois, although why, from my present perspective, I cannot say. My aim on the brick house had become habit, and departure, although less urgent, not the less inevitable. To that end I continued my business, accumulating funds more slowly. The town had grown, and so had my competition. Janey's days then were filled with her studies and hours at the beautiful piano in preparation for frequent concerts for the townspeople. Douglas continued mining and studying geology, but his claim was not so productive that he said no when Zeb offered employment in plowing and planting his wheat fields.

Into this scene, Lola Montez, all black curls and blue eyes and ivory complexion, burst like lightning. We all knew of her reputed beauty, her affairs in Europe, her politics, her outrageous spider dance. California newspapers reported she was known on occasion to wear men's clothes, to smoke, to challenge editors to duels for affronting her. Not a soul in the county but didn't know who she was and want to see her. She did not fail expectations.

Following theatrical engagements in San Francisco, she had toured the interior, first Sacramento, then Marysville. There she disbanded her troupe of musicians, and in passing through Grass Valley in a stage-coach, word has it she liked the little town so much she decided to stay. This is true. She told me so when, hearing of Janey's concerts, she came to see my daughter play. For a time, I rued that day.

In Grass Valley, a town much like Nevada City and but three miles distant, Miss Montez lived alone in a nice little cottage she painted white. On it she installed an enormous colonial door. I know this from observation, having visited by invitation several times on gardening days.

You will hear many things of her, for she is one whom history will recall. But I hope the record tells how she loved Grass Valley, and her little home, and her garden. I spent hours with her there, while she joyously dug and weeded her front yard and tended, really, a very nice garden.

We had that in common. And I will say that to me she was as proper and polite as any gentlewoman. Except for her performances, which I know only from reports, she dressed soberly in black, sometimes white. She and I spoke mostly of plants and flowers.

She had noted, when she first came to hear Janey play, my lupine, which had succeeded. She asked my advice on cactus. She often went riding in the foothills, she said, and collected specimens there.

She collected everything. Husbands and lovers, everyone knew about. But she was also particularly fond of pets and numbered among her Grass Valley menagerie a bear, which she kept chained to a tree in her yard. Her other pets included a monkey, a parrot — and my children.

New Beginnings

Miss Montez held Wednesday salons every week, to which she invited any number of people — men, mostly — for conversation and music and wine. Anyone of note passing through the county received an invitation. There was a famous Swedish violinist, I heard, and two nephews of Victor Hugo. Not to mention, as the *San Francisco Herald* did, "a quartet of cashiered German barons, and a couple of shady French counts." I heard everybody smoked, drank wine and champagne, ate fruit and cake from expensive hampers delivered from the city. Janey was often called upon to entertain, a carriage sent for her. And Douglas invited to accompany his sister.

How many times I stood in my doorway and watched them go I cannot say, nor how often I felt old wounds burn and blamed the bright flame toward which my children flew like moths.

Hard enough it was, this seeming loss. Until threat of greater.

Late one Wednesday evening, upon her return from the house at Grass Valley, Janey said, "Miss Montez is thinking of a tour."

Something in my daughter's voice suggested more than a casual announcement. I had waited up for her in the parlor, busied myself with making a traveling cloak for eventual departure. Janey pulled a chair next to mine, as if to assist my stitching.

"Is she?" I said, smoothing the seams of the soft, cinnamon-colored merino in my lap. "I hear a great many are going. Men will go anywhere for gold. Women, too, it seems."

The recent discovery of gold in Australia had spurred any number of miners to set sail for that distant land. I believe should some fool announce the discovery of gold on the moon, another would put himself to devising a way to get it. And the grass always seeming greener, where the men went mining, so went the women who mined the men.

"She's talking of forming up a troupe for an engagement."

"When does she propose leaving?" I asked, folding up my work. I would not be sorry to see Miss Montez go.

"Not until next summer, but — "

I looked at my daughter. "But what?"

"She says I might go with her — "

"She says what!"

" — if you have no objection, and — "

"No! You can just put that thought right out of your pretty head!"

"Mother, please just think about it. I'll never have another chance to do something like this. I'll — "

I recall nothing more of the argument, but memory of the scene stayed with me. One can throw "No!" at dreams, but they don't shatter as a consequence.

Miss Montez wanted Lotta, too. The red-haired little elf, with her enchanting laughter, was Lola's neighbor and constant visitor. I think it was Lola taught the child to dance. Mrs. Crabtree said no to Australia, as she was right to do, Lotta being but eight years old. And when Lola left, Mary Ann Crabtree took Lotta off to tour the mining camps herself. I hear that the homesick miners, enchanted to see a child, especially one so charming and talented, showered the stage with gold. Mrs. Crabtree shall make a fortune.

Child actors have been all the rage here since 1853, when eight-year-old Sue Robinson first danced on the stage of the American Theatre in San Francisco. The next year the Bateman sisters, Kate and Ellen, just ten and twelve, were performing Shakespeare there, and even briefly toured the interior.

So I was not greatly surprised that Miss Montez, having failed to gain Lotta for her Australian tour, should turn her attentions on Janey. My daughter was not so young she couldn't be cajoled directly. She was after all, nearly eighteen. How strange to think it, but she was then the age I was when her father stopped in the road before the brick house. Ah, so long ago.

And when did the letter come about the house? I forget, it gets all mixed up together, letting the house go, letting Janey go.

They offered twenty-five hundred dollars. The woman wrote she loved the house, thought it beautiful, would never leave it if I let her have it. And her husband remarked its convenience, it being on the newly completed National Road.

The National Road complete? How remarkable. It seemed another lifetime now, that road and the brick house. The truth of it is that it was another lifetime, but I hadn't let it go yet.

I know now we can never go back. And we must ever let go.

When the letter came, I went to Zeb. I thought I was going to Douglas, but it was Zeb.

Zeb's land adjoined the stage road to Marysville, and we were such a go-ahead town by then the stage ran every day. It was early October, the weather already crisping the leaves, when I bought that ticket — and California.

I can see myself still, sitting in that bouncing coach, a food basket in my lap. I had made pumpkin pies. I wore my new cinnamon-colored merino cloak, done up in my persistent preparations for travel that never transpired. I had a new bonnet, too, silk-covered in a shade the milliner called "London brown" and trimmed with silk flowers in chrome yellow, what she called "California gold," or *"bouton d'or."* I had seen it at the new shop in town, and it reminded me of Lucena.

What did I think, staring out the stage's tiny window at the red dust raised by the spinning wheels and trotting horses? I can tell you, as I remember it clearly. I thought I was in need of advice, a man's advice — my son's, or perhaps Zeb's. I thought one of them, maybe both, would tell me what I must do about this offer on the red brick house. As is common in such anticipations, I imagined the scene, rehearsed my speech. I saw myself asking advice, holding out my letter like an invitation for assistance.

But it wouldn't set, that scene. It refused to serve. Rather, my intent called up scraps and remnants of other scenes, the diffident hours perusing domestic guides for advice, for how to do this or that, Father smiling indulgently and calling me "Mouse," all the instructions of youth, of the past. And I realized I hadn't needed instruction for years. And I didn't need it now. I had kept my own counsel too long to bow before another's.

The stage driver let me out at the clearing Zeb had cut to a huge oak, two hundred yards off the stage road. Beneath its shade was the old wagon, a tent, a scatter of provisions. Beyond it, in the middle

distance, I saw dust raised by mules put to plow, Zeb's figure following. Farther out, my son wrestled a tree stump from the midst of
tawny wild oats, clearing land to say "wheat." I heard geese honking
overhead and looked up into a canopy of blue, saw their winging vee
headed south.

And when I looked back at that speading oak, I saw a house. As
clear as if it were there. It was white, with a broad verandah on three
sides for the view. And I saw the wheat fields, how they would
look in spring, creeping green from the earth, and in autumn, like
spilled sunshine.

And I heard my mother saying, "Oh, Sarah Jane, it will be the
most beautiful house. You'll never want to leave it."

I came to it late, Lacy Ridgeway's gift, the seeing of what could be
from what was.

Zeb saw me before Douglas did, turned his mules and came in, all
dust and smiles, like he'd been expecting me.

"Brought pie," I said, handing him the basket.

He sniffed it. "Pumpkin."

"Looks like a nooning, your place," I said, as Zeb set the basket on
a packing-box table, pushing aside two unwashed tin dishes.

"Serves me."

"I believe you're in need of a house."

Zeb grinned. "Am I?"

"That's not all."

He began to laugh then, gravelly and warm, and he came to me,
smelling of sun and earth. He put his arms around me and held me to
him. "What more might I be in need of?" he whispered.

"Are you going to make me say it?"

He laughed and looked at me. "I am indeed, Sarah Daniels. We're
on equal footing here. And I believe it's your turn."

I laughed, too, pushed my bonnet back, kissed him, and said,
"Zeb Tillman, I believe you're in need of a wife."

"Ah, Sarah, I thought you'd never ask."

"I'm asking," I said, and took his face in my hands and photo-
graphed it with my eyes. It was a face I know my mother would have
loved.

"I said it three years ago, Sarah. I'll say it again if you want."

"What's that?"

"I said, 'As you wish.' "

"My mother always said if wishes were horses — "

"I know, 'beggars would ride.' "

"Do you know what it means?"

"I don't know what anything means, Sarah. Except I love you, I know what that means."

"Do you?"

"Do I love you, or do I know what it means?"

"Both," I said, kissing him again.

He stroked my face then and said, "You know I love you, have for years."

"Yes, I know."

"I know you know. I wouldn't say I'm a secret-keeping man. I'd say I was a lucky man, who had springtime once and thought winter had come forever. And now springtime's come again. New beginnings, Sarah, new beginnings."

And so I sold the red brick house. But I keep it always in my heart, filled with memories of another lifetime.

With the proceeds, Zeb and Douglas and a dozen good friends built my white one, this house, the one I'll someday tell you is the most beautiful house in the world. I'll tell you you'll always love it, but you'll leave it. I want you to. I want you to go out in the world, be strong and brave and fearless. If someday you remember that in your childhood your father and I called you "Tiger," you'll know why.

You'll have your sister's footsteps for a guide. I let her go, finally, as Zeb said I must. She left with Miss Montez for Australia in June last year, saw the house built first and Zeb and me married in Nevada City. And for a gift planted pink roses all along the verandah, dear thing.

Zeb and I wed in April, springtime, with a hundred friends, old and new. Douglas gave his mother away. Susan Jackson cooked our wedding dinner, Mart Tyler brought the wine. And the whole town, it seemed, chivareed us with bell gongs and banged pots.

And the next day we drove out here, Zeb and I, and my wedding present was waiting, a gift beyond imagining. As we drove up to the house, I saw them in the pasture, grazing on wildflowers. The scene looked to my mind like a watercolor, so softened was it by my instant tears.

You'll grow up loving the gentle creatures, and you'll know a laughing little boy named the one called Buck, and the sister we visit beneath the sycamores in Sacramento City named Cherry.

And you've your sister Janey, restored to me in my double happiness. She'll tell you of the great adventure that was her debut upon the stage of Sydney's Royal Victoria Theatre. And of how cunning I was, in her absence, to debut you, surprise of my second springtime, on California's stage.

One day you'll read these words. The moment that is now for me will be a mysterious past for you. The future, I've learned, is too uncertain. And so I want you to have as much of the past as I can share. I want you to know that once your father and I were new to this land, and the house in which you were born. Your sister Janey is new to her future, teaching music now at the Benicia Female Seminary. Your brother Douglas, through the influence of Miss Montez, has secured a happy competence at Grass Valley's Empire Mine, apprenticed to the mining engineer. I cannot predict what they will be when you come of age, there is such possibility in this country.

Nor can I say what California will be. Already there is anticipation of the "talking wire," the telegraph, and of railroads. I cannot imagine it, the California that awaits you, the transformation of these seven years past being so profound as to defy comprehension.

But I will not forget the California that was, the hard land and the difficult times, the suffering and the great sacrifice. People will not talk of it, from the pain and sorrow it resurrects. But when California hums with the talking wires, and the trains clack over the mountains, and the buildings all rise tall on streets paved and tree-shaded, you will know. You will know, and remember and tell, who carved the road and crept across the mountains in wagons so steam trains could one day follow.

You, my most precious of new beginnings, I want you to know who we were, those who lived and those who died, for the new beginnings of your California.

Acknowledgments

In 1991, actress Rue McClanahan, expressing interest in acquiring film rights to my first book, *They Saw the Elephant: Women in the California Gold Rush*, requested a 'treatment' based on that book's several stories. In the spring of 1993, I began adding flesh to the skeleton of that failed hope — and discovered Sarah's voice waiting to speak. I'm grateful to Ms. McClanahan for the impetus.

My thanks also to more witting contributors: Lygia Ionnitiu cheerfully read early drafts and responded with encouragement. Jim Miller kindly shared his extensive knowledge of pioneer clothing and fabrics. David King offered invaluable editorial advice. Unable to interest a New York publisher, I hopefully sent the manuscript to the University Press of Colorado. There, Sybil Downing, tireless champion of the women's west and historical fiction, had persuaded the editorial board and director Luther Wilson to undertake a fledgling fiction program. My gratitude to Ms. Downing, who relayed the welcome news of the board's unanimous approval, remains unbounded.

J.S. Holliday, the eminent gold rush historian, generously read the story for historical accuracy. The memory of him sitting on my porch with me on a summer day, going through the manuscript page by page, alternately praising and critiquing, is cherished. On the last page, he scrawled, "This is good!" underlined *four* times, and thus paid me for all my hardship. For this and other kindnesses I am forever in his debt.

I'm grateful to the editorial staff at University Press of Colorado for making the production process a pleasure. Particular thanks go to gifted copyeditor Debbie Korte whose talented attentions rescued many a sentence from infelicitous expression.

Finally, my immeasurable gratitude to my personal patron of the arts, Dan Levy, without whose constant support and unwavering belief I would not have come to much. After twenty-five years of marriage, he still thinks I hung the moon. My cup runneth over.